CONTENTS

Chapter One
How Mark Strong wanted to go 9

Chapter Two
How Billy Widgeon brought a Letter 13

Chapter Three
How First-Mate Gregory did not like Dogs 20

Chapter Four
How there was an unwelcome Passenger 24

Chapter Five
How Bruff showed he had a Nose 30

Chapter Six
How Mark Strong made Friends 41

Chapter Seven
How Mark had a Surprise 46

Chapter Eight
How Captain Jack came on Deck 50

Chapter Nine
How the Stowaway stowed himself 56

Chapter Ten
How Bruff sounded the Alarm 66

Chapter Eleven
How Jack proved to be an Impostor 76

Chapter Twelve
How Mark first tasted Jungle 82

Chapter Thirteen
How there was a startling Surprise 93

Chapter Fourteen
How the Major showed himself to be a Man o'
War 101

Chapter Fifteen
How the Crew of the "Black Petrel" were in
sore Straits 108

Chapter Sixteen
How Mark passed a bad Night 119

Chapter Seventeen
How Men fight for Life 124

Chapter Eighteen
How the Major gave his Advice 133

Chapter Nineteen
How there was another Enemy to Fight 136

Chapter Twenty
How they fell in with greater Peril 141

Chapter Twenty One
How Help came in Time of Need 147

Chapter Twenty Two
How the Watch heard a Noise 155

Chapter Twenty Three
How Billy Widgeon was damped 161

Chapter Twenty Four
How Mark Strong passed a bad night 169

Chapter Twenty Five
How the awful Roar was canvassed 173

Chapter Twenty Six
How Mark and the Major saw Signs 181

Chapter Twenty Seven
How Mark encountered a Savage 191

Chapter Twenty Eight
How Mark found something that was
not Game 198

Chapter Twenty Nine
How Jack did not appreciate a Storm.....................................207

Chapter Thirty
How Mark saw the Sea-Serpent..213

Chapter Thirty One
How they entered Crater Bay..220

Chapter Thirty Two
How that Fish meant Mischief, and
became Meat 227

Chapter Thirty Three
How the Circumnavigators rested and
heard News 238

Chapter Thirty Four
How Billy Widgeon went somewhere 244

Chapter Thirty Five
How the Sulphur Cavern was found 251

Chapter Thirty Six
How Mark and Billy Widgeon went wrong..........................257

Chapter Thirty Seven
How Mark sought the Clue 264

Chapter Thirty Eight
How Mark and Billy found a strange Bed.............................271

Chapter Thirty Nine
How the roaring Spot was found..276

Chapter Forty
How the Roar proved to be—a Roar 282

Chapter Forty One
How there was no Peace on the beautiful Isle 286

Chapter Forty Two
How they struggled to Crater Bay..293

Chapter Forty Three
How Hope revived like a Sunshine Gleam 299

Chapter Forty Four
   How Matters got to the Worst 303

Chapter Forty Five
   How Nature seemed a Foe 309

Chapter Forty Six
   How Safety was won 315

Chapter Forty Seven
   How they sought Mother Carey's Chicken,
   and she was gone 320

ABOUT THE AUTHOR

George Manville Fenn was a very productive author of novels, a writer, an editor, and an educator from England. He was born on January 3, 1831, in Pimlico, London. He mostly learned on his own; he taught himself Italian, French, and German. During the years 1851–1854, he went to Battersea Training College for Teachers and then became the head of a state school in Alford, Lincolnshire. In the early 1850s, Fenn started to write short stories and pieces for newspapers and magazines. The Old Forest Ranger, his first book, came out in 1856. Afterward, he wrote more than 100 books, many of them for teenagers and young adults. He was one of the most famous writers of his time, and his books were well-liked and read by many people. He also worked as a reporter and writer for Fenn. Among the newspapers and magazines, he worked for was The Boy's Own Paper, which he ran from 1866 to 1874. He worked hard to make children's books better and was a strong supporter of education and reading. The Englishman Fenn passed away on August 26, 1909, in Isleworth.

Chapter One
How Mark Strong wanted to go

"Go with me, Mark? What for? To live hard, work hard, and run the risk every day of having to die hard. Get out! You're as bad as your mother."

"Not very bad, is it, James, to wish to share my husband's life and cares?"

Captain Strong put down his pipe, got up from his easy-chair, crossed to the other side of the fire, and laid his hand upon Mrs Strong's shoulder, while she turned her pleasant sweet womanly face upward and smiled in that of the fine, manly, handsome merchant captain, tanned and reddened by many a fight with the sea.

"No, my dear," he said softly; "but it's a man's duty to face danger, a woman's to keep the nest snug for him and the bairns. Why, Mary, you don't know what the perils of the sea are."

Mrs Strong shook her head slowly, and that shake, as interpreted by her eyes, meant a great deal.

"Ah! you may look," the captain said, "but you do not; and as for this cub—come here, you great, strong, impudent young ruffian!" he added; and as his son rose from his chair he took him by the shoulders, gave him a hearty shake, followed it up with a back-handed blow in the chest, and ended by gripping his right hand in a firm, manly clasp, his voice turning slightly husky as he continued:

"Mark, my lad, Heaven knows how often, when I'm far away at sea, I feel as if I'd give anything for a sight of your mother's face, ay, and a good look at yours, you ugly young imitation! How dare you try and grow up like me!"

Mrs Strong smiled.

"But it won't do, my lad. I'm earning the pennies in my ship, and you must go on with your studies, take care of your mother, and when I come back after my next voyage we'll have a talk about what you're to be. Let's see; how old are you?"

"Sixteen, father."

"Sixteen, and discontented! Why, Mark, do you know that you possess what hundreds of thousands of men most envy?"

"I do, father?"

"To be sure, sir; health, strength, all your faculties, and all the world before you."

"But I never see any of the world like you do," said Mark dolefully.

"Ha—ha—ha—ha!"

It was a broad, honest, hearty laugh, such as a sturdy Englishman who is in the habit of using his lungs indulges in; and as Mark Strong's brow wrinkled, and he felt irritated at being laughed at, his father thrust him back into his chair.

"I'm not laughing at you, my boy," he said; "but at your notion—the common one, that a sailor who goes all round the world is always seeing wonderful sights."

"Well, my dear," said Mrs Strong, taking her son's part, "you know you have seen strange things."

As she spoke her eyes ran over the decorations of their handsomely-furnished room in the old-fashioned house in old-fashioned Hackney, where there were traces of the captain's wanderings in the shape of stuffed birds of gorgeous plumage, shells of iridescent tints, masses of well-bleached corals, spears and carven clubs from New Zealand, feather ornaments from Polynesia, boomerangs and nulla-nullas from Australia, ostrich eggs from the Cape, ivory carvings from China, a hideous suit of black iron armour from Japan, and carpets and rugs from India and Persia to make snug the floor.

"Strange things, wife! Well, of course I have a few. A man can't be at sea thirty years without seeing something; but, generally speaking, a sailor's life is one of terrible monotony. He is a seaman, and he sees the sea day after day—day after day; rough seas and smooth seas, stormy seas and sunny seas; and enough to do to keep his ship afloat and away from rocks and lee shores. Here, what are you opening your eyes and mouth for in that way, Mark? Do you expect I'm going to tell you about the sea-serpent?"

"No, father," said the lad laughing. "It was because what you said was so interesting."

"Interesting! Nonsense! A sailor's is a wearisome life, full of dangers."

"But you see strange countries, father, and all their wonders."

"No, I do not, boy," said the captain half angrily, "A sailor sees nothing but his ship, and she's all anxiety to him from the time he goes aboard till he comes back. We see strange ports, and precious little in them. Why, Mark, if you were in some places on the other side of the world, you'd find everything so English that you would hardly believe you had left home. No, no, my lad. You be content to get on well with your studies, and some day we'll make a doctor or a lawyer of you. Soldier, if you like, but not a sailor."

"It's my turn to speak now," said Mrs Strong, smiling lovingly at her frank, manly-looking son. "No soldiering."

"I don't want to be a soldier, mother," said Mark gloomily. "I want to travel; and as I have kept to my books as father wished during his last two voyages, and won my certificates, he might give me the prize I worked for."

"Why, you ungrateful young dog," cried the captain, "haven't I given you a first-class watch?"

"Yes, father; but that isn't the prize I want. I say: do take me with you."

"Take you with me!" cried the captain with an impatient snort such as a sea-horse might give. "Here, mother, what have you been doing with this boy?"

"Doing everything I could to set him against the sea, my dear," said Mrs Strong sadly.

"And a nice mess you have made of it," growled the captain. "Pass my tobacco. Well, Mark, my lad; I want my spell ashore to be happy and restful, and when there's a rock ahead I must steer clear of it at once; so here goes, my lad, I may as well say it and have done with it. I know so much of the sea that I shall never consent to your being a sailor. Your mother is with me there. Eh, my dear?"

"Yes, James, thoroughly," said Mrs Strong.

"Now, my lad, you've got to make the best of it."

"But if you would take me for one voyage only, father, I wouldn't ask you to take me again."

"Won't trust you," said the captain. "Hallo, Bruff!" he continued, patting the rough head of a great retriever dog which had just come slouching into the room, carrying the said rough head hanging down as if it were too heavy for its body, an idea endorsed by its act of laying it upon the captain's knee. "Is it you who teaches your young master to be so obstinate?"

The dog uttered a low growl as if of protest.

"Perhaps you'd like me to take you for a voyage, old chap," continued the captain, pausing in his smoking to wipe the corners of the dog's eyes with its ears. "You'd look well sea-sick in a corner of the deck, or swung in a hammock."

Bruff showed the whites of his expressive eyes and uttered a dismal howl.

"Don't be afraid, old fellow," said the captain. "I sha'n't take you, nor your master neither, so you may both make the best of it."

"Don't say that, father," said Mark earnestly. "Take me this once. I do so want to see China!"

"Here, mother," said the captain laughing; "take Mark up stairs and show him your best tea-service, the one I brought home last year. Like to see Japan, too, my lad?"

Mark frowned and bent his head over his book, while Mrs Strong shook her head at her husband.

The captain rose once more, and laid his hand upon his son's shoulder.

"Come, come, my lad, don't fret over it," he said; "you have done well, and I should like to give you a treat, but I can't take you to Hong-Kong for many reasons. Your mother would not like it, I shouldn't like it, and it would do you no good."

"But, father—" began Mark.

"Hear me out, my lad," said the captain gravely. "I say I want to give you a treat, so I tell you what I will do. You and your mother shall come aboard as we're warping out of the dock, or at Gravesend if you like, and I'll take you down Channel with me. I've got to put in at Plymouth, and I'll drop you there, or at Penzance, whichever you like, and then you can come back to London by rail. Hallo, who's that?"

There was a ring at the old iron gate, and Mark rose and walked to the window.

"A sailor, father."

"Sailor!" said the captain, rising. "Oh, it's Billy Widgeon! Tell the girl to show him in."

Mark went out to speak to the servant, and the next minute the big front door-mat was having a hard time as the sailor stood rubbing away at his perfectly clean boots, and breathing hard with the exertion, staring furtively at Mark Strong the while.

Chapter Two
How Billy Widgeon brought a Letter

The man who was working so hard at the mat was a sailor of apparently about five-and-thirty, carefully dressed in his shore-going suit of navy blue, and carrying a very tightly-done-up dandified umbrella, which looked as out of place in his hands as a parasol would daintily poised by a grenadier guard.

He was a strong squarely-built fellow, with crisp black hair and close beard, and if he had gone under a standard the height he would have reached would probably have been five feet, the result of this being that he had to look up at Mark Strong, who was about five feet six, and at the maid, who was only a couple of inches less.

"Want to see my father?" said Mark, as the man continued to stare and wipe his shoes.

"Ware sharks! Heave off, you ugly lubber! I say: will he bite?"

This was consequent upon a pattering of toe-nails upon the oil-cloth and the appearance of Bruff, the dog, who began to walk round the visitor and smell him.

"No, he won't bite friends," said Mark.

"Tip us your fin, then, messm't," said the sailor, holding out his hand.

"Give him your paw, Bruff," cried Mark; but the dog paid no heed, only continued to smell the visitor.

"Wheer's the skipper?" said the sailor then, hoarsely. "You his boy?"

"Yes," said Mark, gazing enviously at a man who was probably one of those about to sail with Captain Strong on his voyage to Singapore and China. "I say, don't wear out the door-mat."

"Eh? No, m'lad, I won't wear out the mat. You see we don't have no mats afloat. I say! my!"

The man bent down, as if seized with a cramping internal pain, and gave his right leg a slap with his horny paw, whose back was as hairy as that of a monkey.

"What's the matter?" said Mark.

"Matter! I was only larfin. My! you are like the skipper! Wheer is he?"

"This way," said Mark, leading him to the comfortable room, where, as soon as he entered and saw Mrs Strong, the man began ducking his head and kicking out one leg.

Mrs Strong nodded and smiled at the man, feeling a kindly leaning toward one of those who would be under her husband's orders for the next six months, and perhaps his guardians in some storm.

"I'll leave you now, dear," she said.

"Oh, you need not go!" said the captain; but Mrs Strong left the room.

"Shall I go, father?" asked Mark.

"No, my boy, no. Sit down. Well, Billy, what news?"

"None at all, sir, only we shall soon be full up; they've bent on a new mains'l and fores'l; we've been a-painting of her streak to-day, and she do look lovely, and no mistake. But here's a letter I was to give you, sir."

The man evidently had a letter somewhere, from the confident way in which he began to search for it, looking in his cap, then feeling about in his loose blue jumper, and ending with his trousers' pockets.

"Well," said Captain Strong sharply, "where's the letter?"

"Ah! wheer is it?" muttered the man, stroking himself down the sleeves, the chest, and the back. "I had that theer letter somewheres, but it seems to be gone."

"Did you leave it aboard?"

"No, sir, I didn't leave it aboard; I'm sure of that. It's somewheres about me."

"Hang it, man! have you felt in all your pockets?"

"Ain't got but two, sir, and I feeled in both o' them. Think o' that, now, arter Mr Gregory saying as I was to be werry careful o' that letter!"

"So careful that you've lost it," cried Captain Strong. "Bill Widgeon, you're about the biggest blockhead in the crew."

"Well, I dunno about that, sir; I may be a blockhead, but I arn't lost the letter."

"Where is it, then?" cried the captain angrily.

"That's just what I want to know, sir."

"Bah! it's lost."

"No, sir, it arn't lost; I were too careful for that, and—theer, I telled you so. I remember now. Mr Gregory says, says he, 'you, Billy Widgeon,' he says, 'you've got to take great care of that letter,' he says; and 'all right, sir,' I says, 'I just will,' and I put it wheer I thought it would be safest, and here it is."

As he spoke, grinning broadly the while, he slipped off one of his shoes, stooped and picked it up, and drew out the letter all warm and crinkled up with the pressure.

"It's all right, sir," he said, smoothing and patting the letter, and handing it to his captain, before balancing himself on one leg to replace his shoe.

"Why didn't you carry it in your pocket, man?" said the captain angrily, and he tore open the letter and began to read.

"I say, youngster," whispered the sailor, whom the dog was still slowly going round and smelling suspiciously, "will that there chap bite?"

"Bite! No," replied Mark. "Here, lie down, Bruff!"

The dog obeyed, laying his head upon his forepaws and blinking at the visitor, whom he watched intently as if he were in doubt about his character.

"Looks a nipper, he do, squire," said the sailor. "He could take hold pretty tight, eh?"

"Take hold and keep hold," said Mark, who could not help a feeling of envy creeping into his breast—envy of the easy-looking, active little man who was to be his father's companion over the seas to wonderland.

"He looks as if he would," said the sailor after a few moments' pause. "I say, youngster, I'd rayther be ins with him than outs."

"What! rather be friends than enemies?"

"That's it, youngster. I say, what are you going to be—first-mate, and skipper arter?"

"No," said Mark, speaking in the same low tone as his questioner; "I'm not going to be a sailor."

"Lor!"

"It is not decided what I'm to be yet."

"Arn't it now? Why, if you'd come to sea along o' us what a lot I could ha' taught you surety. Why, I could ha' most made a man of you."

"Here, Widgeon," said the captain sharply, "take that back to Mr Gregory, and tell him I shall be aboard to-morrow."

"Right, sir," said the sailor, giving his head a duck and his right leg another kick out—courtesies called forth by the well-furnished room and the soft carpet, for on the bare deck of the ship he put off his manners with his shore-going clothes. "Day, sir. Day, youngster. Day, shipmet."

This last was intended for the dog; but, a few moments before, Bruff had slowly risen, crossed the room, and drawn the door open by inserting one paw in the crack, and then passed through.

"Why, he arn't there!" said Billy Widgeon after a glance round. "My sarvice to him all the same," he added, and went out.

The door had hardly closed when there was the sound of a rush, a roar, the fall of a chair, a crash of china, and a stentorian "Ahoy!"

"I shall have to kill that dog," cried the captain, as he and Mark rushed into the hall, where Bruff was barking and growling savagely.

"Down, Bruff!" shouted Mark, seizing the dog by the collar and enforcing his order by pressing his head down upon the oil-cloth, and setting one knee upon his side. "Why, where's—"

Mark did not finish, but burst into a roar of laughter, in which his father joined, as they both gazed up at the little sailor.

Explanation of the state of affairs was not needed, for matters spoke for themselves.

It was evident that Bruff had, for some reason, made a rush at Billy Widgeon, who had leaped upon a hall chair, from thence upon the table, upsetting the chair in his spring. From the table he had leaped to the top of a great cabinet, knocking down a handsome Indian jar, which was shattered to fragments on the oil-cloth; and from the cabinet springing to the balusters of the first-floor landing of the staircase.

There he hung, swinging by first one hand, then by the other, so as to get a good look down at his assailant, who was barking at him furiously as Mark rushed out; but Bruff had not the brains to see that if he rushed up stairs he could renew his attack.

"Got him safe?" said Billy Widgeon, as he swung by one hand as easily as would a monkey, and unconsciously imitating one of these active little creatures in the pose of his head.

"Yes; he sha'n't hurt you now," cried Mark.

"'Cause dogs' bites don't come in one's pay, eh, cap'n?"

"The dog's all right now, Widgeon," said the captain. "Here, Mark, shut him in the parlour."

"All right, father! but he won't stir now."

"Come down, my lad," said the captain. "You can climb over the balustrade."

"Bee-low!" cried the sailor in a gruff, sing-song tone, and loosening his hold he dropped lightly on to the oil-cloth within a couple of yards of the dog.

Bruff's head was pressed close down to the floor, but he showed his teeth and uttered a growl like a lilliputian peal of thunder.

"Quiet!" cried Mark, as Billy Widgeon struck an attitude with his fists doubled, ready for attack or defence.

"Lor', if you was aboard our ship, wouldn't I heave you overboard fust chance!" cried the sailor.

"What did you do to the dog?" said the captain angrily.

"I never did nothing at all, sir. I only wanted my umbrella as I stood up in the corner. Soon as I went to take it he come at me, and if I hadn't done Jacko and nipped up there he'd have had a piece out of my leg."

As he spoke he went to take the umbrella from the corner, when, looking upon the movement as an attempt to carry out a robbery, Bruff uttered another savage growl aid struggled to get free.

"All, would yer!" cried Billy Widgeon, snatching up his umbrella and holding it by the toe in cudgel-fashion. "Now, then, youngster, lot him go. Come on, you ugly big-headed lubber. I'm ready for you now."

As he spoke Billy Widgeon did Jacko, as he termed it, again, hopping about, flourishing his weapon, and giving it a bang down upon the floor after the fashion of a wild Irishman with his shillelagh.

It was a risky proceeding, for it infuriated the dog, who began to struggle fiercely, while Mark laughed so heartily that he could hardly retain his hold.

"That will do, Widgeon," said the captain, wiping his eyes. "Here, Mark, make that dog friends with him."

"Here, give me the umbrella," said the lad.

"Nay, if I do you'll let him go at me," said the sailor doubtingly.

"Nonsense, man! Give him the umbrella," cried the captain.

The sailor obeyed; and as Mark took it he held it down before the dog, and then returned it to its owner.

Bruff did not say "All right!" but he gave three pats on the oil-cloth with his long bushy tail, a sign that he accepted the position, and then he was allowed to get up.

"Who's afeard!" cried Billy Widgeon, looking from one to the other. "I say, I was too many for him, sir."

"Yes," said the captain; "and what about my Indian jar?"

"Ah! that was the dog's fault, cap'n," said the man earnestly.

"Dog's fault!" said Captain Strong. "You knocked it down and broke it, and I shall stop the cost out of your pay."

Billy Widgeon stood for a moment looking solemn. Then, as if he had suddenly been engaged as a dentist's specimen, he bared all his fine white teeth in the broadest of broad grins.

"Nay, skipper," he said, "you wouldn't do that. Me and my shipmets wouldn't want to make another v'yge with you if you was that sort o' capt'n. I'll buy you another one when we gets to Chany. Here's off!"

He nodded to all in turn, went out of the door, rattled his umbrella on the iron railings in front, making Bruff utter a low discontented growl, and then, as the door was closed, the growl became a deeply-drawn breath like a sigh, while putting his nose to the crack at the bottom, he stood with his ears twitching, giving forth a faint whine now and then, apparently not quite satisfied as to whether he had done his duty, and uneasy in his mind about that umbrella. "You will have to be careful with that dog, Mark," said the captain. "He must be tamed down, or we shall have worse mischief than a broken jar."

"He thought the man was stealing the umbrella," pleaded Mark on behalf of his favourite.

"Then he must be taught to think sensibly, my lad. Billy Widgeon's one of my best fore-mast men, and I can't afford to have my sailors used to feed your dog."

"You're joking, father."

"Ah! but that would be no joke," said the captain. "I should not approve of his devouring the lowest and most worthless class of tramp, or a savage; but when it comes to sailors—"

"What nonsense, father!" cried Mark.

"Why, Mark, my boy, what a good idea! I think I'll borrow that dog and take him to sea."

"Take him to sea, father?"

"Yes: he would be a treasure at clearing the deck of unwelcome visitors—Chinamen or Malays."

"What, pirates?"

"Well, men who would be pirates if they dared: the low-class scoundrels who haunt some of the ports."

"All right, father! you shall have him," said Mark.

"Then I will, my boy," said the captain, looking at his son curiously, for he could not understand his willingness to part with his ugly favourite. "He shall be well treated so long as he behaves himself."

"But you can't take the dog without his master," said Mark, smiling.

"Oh, that's it! is it?" said the captain. "I thought there was something behind. Well, that was news for you," he continued.

"News?"

"Yes, that Billy Widgeon brought. I was afraid that we should be crowded in the cabin and I was beginning to regret my promise to take you; but Mr Gregory writes me word that a gentleman and his wife and daughter who were coming with us as far as Singapore have backed out, to go by one of the fast mail-boats, so we shall have plenty of room."

"That's capital!" cried Mark. "Mr Gregory is the second-mate, isn't he?"

"First-mate now, my boy. He was second-mate, but my first-mate is now in command of another vessel, and I was afraid he would take all my old crew."

"But he does not, father, because that sailor said—"

"Yes; the crew stay with me to a man."

Chapter Three
How First-Mate Gregory did not like Dogs

"Hullo! whose dog's that?"

It was a hoarse gruff voice, which made Mark Strong turn sharply round just as he had crossed the gangway and stepped from the quay at the East India Dock on board the *Black Petrel,* or Mother Carey's Chicken, as the sailors often called her, a large ship conspicuous among the forest of masts rising from the basin.

The speaker was a tall angular-looking man with a pimply face and a red nose, at the top of which he seemed to be frowning angrily as if annoyed with the colour which he could not help. He had turned sharply round from where he was giving orders to some sailors who were busily lowering great bales and packages into the hold; and as Mark faced the tall thin man, whose hands were tucked deep down in the pockets of his pea-jacket, the lad thought he had never seen a more sour-looking personage in his life.

"Hullo, I say!" he cried again, "whose dog's that?"

"Mine, sir."

"Then just take him ashore. I don't allow dogs on my deck. Here, I say, you sir," he roared, turning to where the men were making fast the hooks of a kind of derrick to a great package, protected by an open-work lattice of deal, "hadn't you better take that crate of pottery first, and put at the bottom, and then stow that portable steam-engine on the top."

The man addressed—a red-faced, good-humoured-looking sailor, whose bare arms formed a sort of picture-gallery of subjects tattooed in blue—rubbed his ear and stared.

"Why, the ironwork's heavy and might break the pottery," he said at last.

"Well, won't it break that light carriage, you double-distilled, round-headed wise man of the west, you! Put the heavy goods at the bottom and the light at the top."

"Ay, ay, sir!" shouted the man. "Bear a hand, lads. Now, then."

He unhooked the tackle and attached another great package, while the tall man turned again upon Mark.

"Did you hear what I said about that dog?"

"Yes, I heard," said Mark; "but he's coming part of the way."

"That he is not, my lad, so off you go!"

"Hullo, youngster!" said a cheery voice; and Mark turned sharply, to find the little squatty sailor before him, in tarry trousers and flannel shirt, bare-headed and heated with work.

"Hullo, Widgeon!" cried Mark.

"Hullo, shipmet!" cried the little sailor. "Now, then, just you mind, or—"

He did not finish, but made a peculiar gesture as if he were about to pitch the dog over the side.

"Here, show this young gentleman the way ashore," said the tall man. "Take the dog first."

"No, thankye," said the sailor grinning, "me and him's friends now, aren't we, shipmet? We won't begin by falling out again."

He stooped down and patted Bruff, who blinked up at him, and gave his bushy tail two wags, after which he walked slowly to the tall officer and began to smell his legs.

"Stop: don't do that!" cried Mark, as he saw the officer draw back as if to deliver a kick.

"Nay, don't you kick him, Mr Gregory, sir," said Widgeon. "If you do, he'll take hold; and I know this here sort, you can't get them off again without a knife."

"Are you Mr Gregory?" said Mark.

"Yes, sir, I am; and what then?" cried the mate angrily.

"My name is Strong, and I'm going with my father as far as Penzance."

"You may go with your father as far as Shanghai if you like, young man," said the mate angrily; "but I'm not going to have my deck turned into a kennel, so you'd better take your dog ashore."

Mark stood staring as the mate walked away to give some orders in an angry tone to another gang of sailors working aft. Then he shouted a command to some men busy in the rigging; while, when Mark turned his head, it was to find Billy Widgeon patting the dog, and smiling up at him.

"He's a bit waxy to-day. Just going outer dock into the river, and there's a lot o' work to be done."

"But I thought my father was captain of this ship?" said Mark.

"So he is, youngster, but old Greg does what he likes when the skipper aren't aboard. Oh, here is the skipper!"

"Ah! Mark, my lad, here you are then. So you've brought the dog?"

"Yes, father, and—"

"Where's Mr Gregory?"

"Over yonder, sir," said Billy Widgeon. "Pst!" he whispered to Mark, "say somewhat about the dog."

"Do you want him to stay then?" said Mark.

"Stop! Sartin I do. Why, theer'll be him and old Jack, and they'll have no end of a game aboard when theer's a calm. There, the skipper's gone to old Greg, and you aren't said a word."

"But I will," said Mark. "Who is Jack?"

"Who is Jack! Why, I thought every one knowed who Jack is. Our big monkey. He's tucked up somewhere 'cause it's cold. You wait till the sun's out."

"Well, Captain Strong, I object to dogs and cats on board ship."

"They are no worse than monkeys."

"A deal, sir, and I object to them."

"Nonsense, Gregory!" said Captain Strong persuasively. "The boy's only going as far as Penzance, and he loves his dog."

"Can't help that, sir. Dogs are no addition to a crew."

"Not a bit, Gregory. Neither are monkeys; but, to oblige me—"

"Oh very well, captain, if it's to oblige you, I have no more to say, and the dog can stop."

"Hear that, youngster?" said Billy.

It was plainly audible to half the deck; and as Mark nodded his head he fell a-wondering how it was that his father, who was captain, could allow his inferior officer to be so dictatorial and to bully every one about him.

"It's all right," said Billy Widgeon, with a confidential wink and a smile; "he's going to let him stop."

This was another puzzle for Mark, but he kept his thoughts to himself.

"Look here—where are you going to stow him?" continued the little sailor, speaking of the dog as if he were a box or bale.

"Keep him with me," replied the lad.

"But you'll want a place for him somewheres. You come along o' me and I'll find you one in the forksle."

After a momentary hesitation Mark accepted the offer, and the sailor pointed out a suitable corner, according to his ideas.

"He'll be pretty close to my berth, and I can give an eye to him."

The offer was friendly, and Bruff seemed disposed to accept the sailor's advances to some extent, suffering himself to be patted and his ears pulled; but when the friendliness took the form of a pull at his tail he began to make thunder somewhere in his chest, and turned so sharply round that by an involuntary action Billy. Widgeon popped his hands in his pockets.

All the same when Bruff was told to lie down in there he flatly refused, and followed his master aft once more, the little sailor having run before them in answer to the mate's shout; and Mark saw him directly afterward hauling away at a rope with some more so as to raise the main-yard, which was not quite to the mate's satisfaction.

"What a disagreeable brute!" thought Mark as the mate seemed to spend his time in shouting here, finding fault there, and everywhere making himself disagreeable, while the captain looked on once or twice and then got out of the way as fast as he could, and appeared to be generally of no account whatever.

Chapter Four
How there was an unwelcome Passenger

"Here, Mark, my boy," said the captain; "come here and I'll show you your cabin."

The lad was standing watching half a dozen men who were reefing a square sail high up on the mainmast, and the process gave him a peculiar sensation of moisture in the hands and chill in the back, for the men were standing upon a rope looped beneath the yard, and apparently holding on by resting the top button of their trousers upon this horizontal spar, their hands being fully occupied with hauling in and folding up the new stiff canvas of the sail.

"I say, father," he said, "isn't that dangerous?"

"What, my lad?"

"The work those men are doing."

"What, up aloft? H'm, yes, no! They're so used to it that it has ceased to be dangerous, my boy. Use is second nature. It would be dangerous for you or me."

Mark followed, and the captain showed him his cabin.

"You're a lucky one," he said. "There's a place all to yourself. Are you going to stay aboard?"

"Yes, father. I've sent my bag, and mother is going to meet me here this evening."

"That's right. Now I must be off to see the owners. Keep out of the way as well as you can. I suppose you will find plenty to amuse yourself."

Mark said, "Oh, yes!" but he felt as if there was going to be very little that was amusing; and as he saw his father go toward the gangway and speak to the first-mate, who seemed to reply with a surly nod, the office of captain seemed of less account than ever.

The scene was not inspiring. It was a dull, cold, cheerless afternoon in May; the deck was one chaos of bales, packages, and boxes. Ropes were lying about as if there was no such thing as order on board a ship. Forward there was a pile of rusty chain, and if the new-comer stirred a step he was sure to be in somebody's way; and when, in response to a hoarse "by yer leave," he moved somewhere else, it was to find himself in a worse position still.

Bruff quite shared his feelings, and showed it by shivering from time to time, and, after getting behind Mark, trying to drive his head between his master's legs, an attempt that was always met by a rebuff, for Mark had not yet gained his sea-legs and taken to walking with his feet very wide apart.

But all the same there was a deal to notice, and by degrees the lad grew interested as he wondered how it was possible for the yawning hatch in the middle of the deck to swallow up such an endless number of crates and boxes, bales and packages, of all kinds. While what seemed more astonishing was the fact, that as fast as the cargo disappeared more was brought aboard from the quay, where it was unloaded from vans and carts.

"Here, hi! young Strong!" cried the mate suddenly. "Come here."

Mark walked up to him hastily as he stood near the gangway, talking to a custom-house officer.

"Oh, there you are! Look here, which is it—wasp or bee!"

"Wasp or bee, sir—which?"

The customs-officer laughed, and Mark coloured up, but Mr Gregory stood with his red nose shining and his pimply face as hard and cold as a statue's.

"Which? Why, you—come aboard to idle or work?"

"I don't know, sir. Can I do anything?"

"How should I know? I should say not, by the look of you. Will you try?"

"Yes, sir. I should be glad to," cried Mark.

"Come, that's better. Take that piece of chalk, and tally."

"I—I don't know how."

"Bah! what do they teach boys at schools nowadays? Do you mean to tell me you can't make a mark and keep count of those barrels of beer they're going to bring on board?"

"Why, of course I can, sir."

"Then why did you say you couldn't?"

"You told me to tallow something, sir."

"I didn't! Here, catch hold of the chalk and make a mark there against every one that's rolled on board. Hallo, ugly! you're there then!" continued the mate, suppressing a smile and addressing Bruff, who gave him a sour look and went behind his master.

Mark took the chalk, and for the next half-hour he was busy checking the barrels. This done there was a succession of boxes to be accounted for in the same way, and after them a hundred sacks, the arrival of the latter putting the mate in a furious passion.

"For two straws I wouldn't have them aboard," he roared. "They were to have been delivered a week ago, and here are we kept waiting like this."

And still the vessel kept on swallowing up cargo, the riggers gave the finishing touches to the vessel's ropes and sails, and the confusion appeared to grow worse instead of better; but in spite of a low-spirited sensation, Mark was fain to confess to himself that he had been interested if not amused, when the least sailor-like man he had seen on board came from the cabin-door and spoke to the mate, who gave a slight nod, and the man went back.

The former individual then went to the big opening in the deck:

"Below! Morgan!" he shouted.

"Ahoy!" came from somewhere in the interior of the great vessel, and directly after a pleasant, manly, brown face appeared above the steps.

"Take charge; I'm going to have some tea."

"All right! Who's this?"

"Skipper's cub," said the first-mate shortly. "Here, boy, come along."

The new arrival gave him a friendly nod, and Mark's first sensation was that he would have preferred to stay with him, but the first-mate looked back, and he followed quickly into the cabin, where the sight of a comfortable meal, with clean cloth, and an appetising odour, changed the current of his thoughts.

"Engines that work want coal and water," said the mate gruffly. "We've been at work; let's coal. Sit down."

Mark obeyed, and Bruff crept under his seat.

"You've brought that dog with you, then?"

"He came, sir."

"Same thing. I hate dogs. Take off that cover."

Mark obeyed, and there was a steaming dish of fried steak and onions, looking tempting in the extreme.

"Now, then, will you carve or be old woman?"

"I—I'll carve," said Mark, for though he had a suspicion that to be old woman meant pouring out the tea, he was not sure.

"Go ahead, then, my lad. Plates hot?"

"Yes, sir."

"That's your style. Don't be afraid of the onions. No ladies aboard."

Mark helped the steak, and the mate poured out the tea and hewed a couple of lumps off a cottage-loaf.

"There you are," he said; "and make much of it. No steaks and new bread at sea."

"But you've plenty of other things, sir."

"Humph, yes! We manage to live. More sugar?"

"No, sir, thanks."

"Help yourself, my lad. Rum un, aren't I?"

"You don't expect me to say what I think, do you?" said Mark smiling.

"One to you, boy," said the mate, nodding; and this time there was a vestige of a smile on his plain face. "Here, ugly, try that."

This was the outside of a big piece of gristly steak which the mate cut off, and held toward the dog, who approached slowly and as if in doubt, but ended by taking it.

"Yah! What are you sniffing at? Think there was mustard on it? Big friends, I suppose, you and him?"

"Yes, sir, we're capital friends."

"Humph! Better make friends with a good lad of your age. I hate dogs. What are you laughing at?"

"You, sir."

"Eh? Oh! I see!" paid the mate grimly. "I do, though, all the same. Don't you believe it?"

"No," replied Mark smiling; "and Bruff does not believe it either."

For after the mate had given the dog a couple of pieces of steak, Bruff had stopped by him and laid the heavy head upon his knee to patiently wait for further consignments of cargo, which, however, did not come, for the chief officer was thoughtfully stirring his tea with his left hand, while his right, as he said he hated dogs, was involuntarily rubbing the rough jowl, the process being so satisfactory that Bruff half-closed his eyes.

"Humph! This seems a better dog than some," said the mate. "No business on board ship, though. I don't even like chickens; but we're obliged to put up with them. I'm always glad, though, when they're eaten. I once went a voyage with a cow on deck. They wanted the milk for an officer's lady and her children. That cow used to make me melancholy."

"Why, sir? Was she such a bad sailor?"

"No; she was always stretching out her neck to try and lick some green paint off one of the boats. Thought it was grass. Cows have no brains. Hallo! What is it, Billy?"

"Mr Morgan wants you, sir."

"What is it?"

"One on 'em, sir, right below."

"Bah!" ejaculated the mate. "Coming directly. Let him wait till I've finished my tea."

The sailor gave Mark a knowing look, and made a sign which the lad did not comprehend, as he disappeared through the door.

Mark would have given something to ask who "one on 'em" was, for the news seemed to have ruffled the mate terribly. A few minutes before he had been growing quite friendly; now he was as gruff as ever, finishing his steak viciously, and drinking his tea far hotter than was good for him.

"I'd like to trice them all up and give them the cat," he exclaimed suddenly, and with so much emphasis that at the last magic word Bruff suddenly sprang into action, cocked his ears and tail, uttered a fierce growling bark, and then looked excitedly from one to the other, his eyes plainly enough asking the question "Where?"

"Get out with you, ugly!" cried the mate. "I meant the cat with nine tails, not the cat with nine lives. Here, young Strong, whatever you do, never take to being mate in the merchant service."

He went out on deck, and Mark followed him, eager to see what was the matter; and as he passed out, it was to hear the second-mate say:

"I was coming after you; the poor wretch's groans are awful."

"Serve him right, the scoundrel! Government ought to interfere and put a stop to it."

"But, my dear Gregory, hadn't we better get the poor wretch out, and settle the government interference afterwards?"

"These men make me half mad," cried the first-mate. "Where do you suppose he is?"

"A long way down, I'm afraid."

"And we are behind with our lading. How can a man be such an idiot as to expose himself to such risks?" cried the first-mate.

"Sheer ignorance. If they thought they were likely to be crushed to death or suffocated, they would not do it."

"What is the matter?" asked Mark anxiously.

"Stowaway, my lad," said the second-mate. "Man hidden himself in the hold, and is frightened now the cargo has been packed over him."

A peculiar chill ran through Mark as he realised the horror of the man's position, perhaps below the huge bales and cases which he had seen lowered down into the hold, and so inclosed that it would be impossible to get to him before life was extinct.

Chapter Five
How Bruff showed he had a Nose

As Mark reached the great opening in the deck it was to find that the men who had been at work below were all clustered together listening and waiting for instructions from their officers.

"Hush! Don't speak!" cried the first-mate, bending over the opening. "Are you sure it isn't a cat?"

A low deep moaning sound that was smothered and strange came from below, and the mate gave a stamp with his foot on the deck.

"No mistake, Gregory," said the second-mate.

"Mistake! No. It's a man or a boy. He deserves to be left; he does, upon my honour."

"Yes, we all deserve more than we get," said the second-mate patiently. "Here, what do you make of it? The sound puzzles me, and I don't know where to begin."

The mate descended, the second-mate followed, and a big dark fellow with a silver whistle hanging from his neck was about to step down next, but he made way for Mark, who slipped down the steps, to the great dismay of Bruff, who sat on the top looking over the coamings, and whining in a low tone.

Mark found himself upon a lower deck, with a hole in it of similar dimensions to that through which he had passed. Mr Gregory was lowering himself down upon the cargo, the second-mate followed, and then gave orders for silence.

This stopped the buzzing conversation of the men, who all seemed to be scared, and now the moaning sound came from somewhere—a faint, dismal, despairing "Oh! Oh! Oh!" of some one in sore distress.

"Humph!" ejaculated the mate, "I suppose we must behave like Christians and get him out. But when I do! Here! Below there: where are you?"

No response; only the continuous moaning.

"Do you hear there? Answer—where are you?" shouted the second-mate with his mouth down to an opening in the great packages beneath their feet.

Still no reply but this dismal moaning "Oh!" a piteous appeal in its way, which made Mark shudder.

"I'll try again," said the first-mate. "Here, hi! Where are you?"

He paused, and they all listened. He shouted again and again, but with no result, and turning to the second-mate he said:

"The poor wretch is insensible, I'm afraid."

"Yes, he seems beyond answering. Where do you make him out to be?"

"That's what I can't make out," said the first-mate. "It's just as if he were practising ventriloquism. Sometimes it sounds to the right and sometimes to the left."

"Yes, that's how it strikes me," said the second-mate. "Listen, youngster. Here: silence there on deck!"

A pin fall might have been heard the next moment, and the silence was broken by the low piteous moan.

"It seems down here at one time, and then more forward there," said Mark.

"Yes, it does now," said the first-mate. "Here, Billy Widgeon, Small, you come and try."

The boatswain and the little sailor both lay down in different places on the cases and bales and listened, but only to rise up and declare that the sound came from quite a different direction.

"Hang it all!" cried the first-mate; "it isn't a question of amount of cargo to unstow, but of time before we get at the miserable wretch. Now, what right has a man to come and hide down here, and upset the whole cargo and crew!"

"My dear Gregory," cried the second-mate, "do let's begin somewhere."

"Yes, but where, my lad—where? Listen again. There, it's further in—ever so much."

"Sounds like it," assented the second-mate. "Here, stop your noise!"

This last was consequent upon a dismal howl uttered by Bruff, who felt himself aggrieved at being left alone.

"Here, here!" cried Mark excitedly, and, raising his hands, he took the dog as he was passed down by the sailors. "Stop a minute, Mr Gregory, my dog will smell him out."

"Bravo, boy!" cried the first-mate, as Bruff was set down, no light-weight, on the stowed-in cargo. "Good dog, then!"

"Hush!" cried Mark, whose heart was beating painfully.

"Silence there!" cried Mr Small.

"Now, Bruff, old boy, listen."

There was utter silence for quite a minute, and then, as the chill of dread deepened, and it seemed as if the hidden man had fainted, the moaning arose once more, but certainly more feebly.

Mark was kneeling and holding Bruff with a hand on each side of the collar, and as the piteous moan arose the dog uttered a sharp bark.

"Good dog, then! Find him, boy!" cried Mark; and as the moaning continued, the dog went scuffling and scratching over the cargo, snuffing here and there, and uttering a bark from time to time.

"No, no, not there," cried the second-mate.

"Let the dog be," said the first; and the result was that Bruff suddenly stopped a dozen yards away from them toward the forecastle, and began scratching and barking loudly.

"It can't be there," said Small, creeping over the packages till he was beside the dog, and then quieting him as he listened. "Yes; it is!" he cried. "You can hear him as plain as plain."

The first-mate came to his side, and confirmed the assertion; the second-mate endorsed his brother officer's opinion; and now began the terrible task of dragging out the closely fitted-in lading of the ship, so as to work right down to where the poor wretch had concealed himself. It seemed to Mark's uninitiated eyes to be a task which would take days, but the men set-to with willing hands under the first-mate's guidance, and package after package was hauled out by main force, and sent on to the deck above, till quite a cutting was formed through the cargo.

Every now and then the work was stopped for one of the officers to listen, and make sure that they were working in the right direction, and this precaution was not without its results in the saving of labour, for the faint moanings, more plainly heard now that a portion of the cargo was removed, seemed to be a little more to their right.

Mark Strong's first sensation, after the dog had thoroughly localised the place of the man's imprisonment, was a desire to go right away, to get off the ship and go ashore, where he could be beyond hearing of those terrible moans; but directly after he found himself thinking that it would be very cowardly, worse still that the chief mate and this Mr Morgan would look upon him as being girlish. The result was that he crept along over the top of the cargo on his hands and knees to just beyond the place where the men were working, and seating himself there, with Bruff between his legs, he watched the progress of the search.

It was a curious experience to a lad fresh from school, and the aspect of the place added to the horror of knowing that a fellow-creature was perhaps dying by inches beneath the sailors' feet. Where he sat the beams and planks of the lower deck were only about four feet above his head, and to right, left, and behind him all was thick darkness, faintly illumined by the yellow light of a couple of swinging lanthorns, which shed a curious ghastly halo all around; sixty feet away was the great hatch, down which came the light of day; and between this and where Mark sat, the dark figures of the busy sailors were constantly on the move in a way that looked weird in the extreme. Now, half of them were out of sight fastening the hooks and loops of the tackle to some bale; then there was a loud "yoho-ing," and, with creaking and rasping, the great package was dragged away into the patch of daylight, which it darkened for a few moments, and then disappeared to the deck.

For the first few minutes Mr Gregory—"Old Greg," as the sailors called him—stormed and raved about the labour and waste of time; but soon after he was at work as energetically as any man in the crew, and in the intervals of a great package being secured he kept coming to where Mark sat with his dog.

"Rough work this, my lad, isn't it?" he said every time, and as he spoke his hand went unconsciously to Bruff's head to rub and pat it.

Then he was off again, giving orders which package to take next, and securing the loops of the rope-tackle himself.

"Now, all together my lads," he shouted, and away went the load.

It was dreary work, and yet full of excitement, for the men toiled on with terrible energy, for there was the knowledge that though a great deal of cargo had been removed, the moans of the poor wretch were being heard less plainly.

It was Mr Morgan who now came to where Mark was seated, and he too began to pat and rub Bruff's head.

"No, my lad," he said, in answer to a question, "we can do no more than we are doing. If we got more hands at work they would be in each other's way."

He was panting with exertion as he spoke, and began to wipe his brow.

"It's a horrible set out. The man must have been mad to hide himself there."

"But you'll get him out?"

"Yes, we shall get him out," said the young officer; "but I'm growing sadly afraid that he'll die from sheer fright before we reach him."

"But you will keep on?"

"Keep on, my lad! Yes, if we have to empty the hold. Why, what sort of savages do you think us?"

He hurried away, and after a lapse Mr Gregory came.

"Help? no, my boy—poor old doggie then! Good old man!—no, you can't help. If I set you to hold a lanthorn, you'd be in somebody's way. We can't half of us work as it is, for want of room. It's a sad job."

As he spoke he kept on caressing Bruff, who rolled his stupid great head from side to side with evident enjoyment, while, in spite of the horror of what was going on, Mark could not help a feeling of satisfaction at the way in which his dog was growing in favour.

One hour—two hours—three hours must have gone by, and still the men toiled on at their fearfully difficult task, one which seemed to grow more solemn as they went on.

"Can't hear a sound, my lad," said the first-mate; "and I think we'll try the dog again. Come along, old chap."

Mark loosened his hold on the dog, and he followed the mate and was lifted down into the great cavernous hole the men had made, while a lanthorn was held so that they could watch his proceedings.

Bruff did not leave them long in doubt, but began snuffing at one side, close to the end, following it up by scratching and whining.

"That'll do," shouted the first-mate hoarsely. "Come, my lad. That's it. Good old dog, then!"

He lifted Bruff out and passed him up to Mark, who leaned over and listened as in the midst of a deep silence Mr Gregory slapped the side of a case.

"Now, then, where are you?" he shouted.

There was no reply; and he shouted again and again, but without effect.

"At it you go, my lads," he said, drawing in his breath with a hiss. "He must be in here; the dog says so."

"Ay, ay, sir!" rose in chorus, and the task was resumed with fresh energy, and but for the careful management of the two officers there must have been a fresh mishap, the sailors being rather reckless and ready to loosen packages whose removal would have caused the sides of the heaps to come crumbling down in a cargo avalanche, to cause disaster as well as delay.

Another hour had passed and Bruff had been had down four more times, always after his fashion to show where the man they sought must be, but still there was no result to their task, and Mark felt a blank sensation of despair troubling him, for he could see that the first-mate was beginning to lose faith in the dog's instinct, though there had for long enough past been nothing to prove that he was wrong, not so much as a sigh being heard.

"I think we'd better have the dog down again," said Mr Gregory at last, his voice sounding strange from deep among the cargo. "Stop a moment, my lads. Silence, and pass me a lanthorn."

At the sound of his voice Bruff uttered a whine, and Mark had to hold tight by his collar to keep him back.

Directly after, as the lad looked down he could see the mate tap once more upon a case in the curious-looking hollow.

"Now, then," he shouted, "where are you?"

There was a silence that was painful in its intensity, and then plainly heard came a faint groan.

"Hooray, my lads! he's here, and alive yet," cried the mate, and the men set up a hearty cheer. "Steady, steady! He's close here. Let's have out this case next."

"No, no," cried the second-mate; "I see."

"See what?" said Mr Gregory gruffly.

"Ease off that bale a little, and we can draw him out."

"Draw him out! How? Well, of all! Of course!"

A lanthorn was being held to the side beneath Mark, and, staring over, he, too, grasped the position, which was plain enough now to all.

The case which the mate proposed to remove was one of the great deal chests with the top angle cut right off and used to pack pianos, and in the triangular space nearly six feet long between the case and the chests around the unfortunate man had crept, taking it for granted that he would be able to creep out again forward or backward after the ship had sailed.

The easing away of one package was enough now, and as the light was held, the legs of the prisoner were seen, and he was carefully drawn out. A rope was placed round his chest, and he was hauled out of the great chasm and hoisted carefully on deck, followed by the whole crew of workers, who formed a circle about him, as the first-mate went down on one knee and trickled a little brandy between his teeth.

"Shall I send one of the lads for a doctor?" said Mr Morgan.

"Wait a minute," was the first-mate's answer. "He was not suffocating, as you can see. It was sheer fright, I think. He'll come round in a few minutes out here in the fresh air."

The second-mate held down the light, and as Mark, for whom room had been made, gazed down in the ghastly face of the shabby-looking man, Bruff pushed his head forward and sniffed at him.

"Yes, that's him, old fellow," said the mate patting his head. "You are a good dog, then."

Bruff whined, and just then the prostrate stowaway moved slightly.

"There, he's coming to; give him a little more brandy, Gregory," said the second-mate.

"Not a drop," cried the other fiercely. "Yes, he's coming round now. I think I'll finish off with the rope's end—a scoundrel!"

A minute before, in spite of his rough ways, Mark had begun to feel somewhat of a liking for the first-mate, especially as he had taken to the dog; but now all this was swept away.

"Oh, yes, he's coming to," said Mr Gregory, as the man's eyelids were seen to tremble in the light of the lanthorn, and then open widely in a vacant stare.

"Where—where am I?" he said in a hoarse whisper; and then he uttered a wild cry and started up in a sitting position, for Bruff had touched his cheek with his cold nose.

"Where are you! On the deck of the *Black Petrel*, my lad, and you're just going to have that dirty shirt stripped off your back, ready for a good rope's-ending."

"No, no! no, no!" cried the poor wretch, grovelling at the first-mate's feet, and looking up at him appealingly.

This was too much for Bruff, who set up a fierce bark, and seeing his new friend apparently attacked he would have seized the crouching man had not Mark dropped down and seized his collar.

"Not do it, eh! You scoundrel! what do you mean by this hiding down in that hold and giving us hours of work to get out your wretched carcass, eh?"

"Please, sir—forgive me, sir. Let me off this time, sir."

"Kick the poor wretch out of the ship and let him go," said the second-mate in a low voice.

"Let him go! Not I. I'm going to flog him and then hand him over to the police."

"Ay, ay," rose in chorus from the men, who, now that they had with all respect to humanity saved the interloper's life, were quite ready to see him punished for his wrong-doing, and the trouble and extra labour he had caused.

"There, you idle vagabond, you hear what the jury of your own countrymen say."

"Let me off this time, sir. I was nearly killed down there."

"Nearly killed, you scoundrel! Serve you right; trying to steal a passage and food from the owner of this ship. How dare you do it?"

"I—I wanted to go abroad so badly, sir," said the shivering wretch. "I'd no money, and no friends."

"I should think not indeed. Who'd make a friend, do you think, of you?"

"Nobody, sir. I did try lots of captains to take me as a sailor, but no one would."

"Why, of course they wouldn't, you scoundrel!" stormed the first-mate. "Can you reef and splice and take your turn at the wheel?"

"No, sir," whimpered the man.

"Can you go aloft without tumbling down and breaking somebody's head instead of your own idle neck? Could you lay out on the foretop yard?"

"No, sir, but—but I'd try, sir, I would indeed, if you'd let me."

"Let the poor wretch go, Gregory," whispered the second-mate.

"Sha'n't!" snapped the first-mate; and as he raged and stormed Mark felt more than ever that this was the real captain of the ship, and that his father must occupy a very secondary position.

"I would work so hard," said the poor fellow piteously. "I only want to get into another country and try again."

"At our owner's expense, eh? Do you think the crew here want you?"

"No, no," rose in chorus; and Mark's heart gave a leap of sympathy, and anger against the men.

"There, you hear, you idle, cheating vagabond. Where did you want to go?"

"Anywhere, sir, anywhere. Do let me go!"

"Yes, to the police station. You'll have to answer for all this."

Mark looked at the poor, wretched, piteous face, and then up at the mate, whose countenance was like cast-iron with the tip of his nose red-hot. He glanced at Mr Morgan, who was frowning and looked annoyed, but who smiled at Mark as their eyes met.

"Here, Billy Widgeon, fetch one of the dock police," cried the first-mate.

"Ay, ay, sir," cried the little sailor with alacrity; and he was in the act of starting, while the stowaway was once more appealing piteously and Mark was about to take his part, when a quiet firm voice said aloud:

"What's the matter?"

Mark's heart gave a bound, and for the moment he thought everything would be set right in a humane way. Then, as he heard the chief mate speak, he felt that it would be all wrong.

"What's the matter, Captain Strong!" thundered the officer. "Everything's the matter. Here we've to sail first tide to-morrow, and look at us. My cargo, that was all stowed, hauled all over the ship. We've been ever since four o'clock getting him out, and now it's nearly ten. And look at him—all hands unstowing cargo to get out a thing like that!"

"Where was he?" said the captain sternly.

"Where was he!" roared the mate, who looked as if one of his legs was quivering to kick the grovelling stowaway; "where wasn't he? Groaning all over the ship; and if it hadn't been for that dog—"

"Ah! the dog helped, did he?"

"Yes, sir; smelt him out buried down below a thousand tons—"

"More or less," said Mr Morgan laughing.

"Well, I didn't weigh or measure the cargo, did I, sir?" roared the first-mate. "Look at it, sir—look at it, captain. We shall be at work all night re-stowing it, and then sha'n't be done."

"He was right down there?"

"Yes, sir; and if we hadn't got to him he'd have been a dead man in a few hours; and a good job too, only see what a nuisance he would have been."

"How came you to do this, sir?" cried Captain Strong, turning to the man, who still crouched upon the deck.

"I wanted to get abroad, sir. Pray forgive me this time."

"You must have been mad," cried the captain. "Did you want to be buried alive?"

"No, sir. I didn't think you'd fill up above me, and I thought I could creep out by and by; but—but they stopped up both ends of the hole, and then—then they piled up the boxes over my head, and it got so hot, sir, that—that—I could hardly breathe, and—and—and, sir, I couldn't bear it, I was obliged to cry for help; but I wish I'd died in my hole."

"Poor wretch!" muttered the captain; but his son heard him and pressed nearer to his side, as he gazed at the stowaway, a man grown, but who was sobbing hysterically, and crying like a woman.

"Here, Widgeon, I told you to fetch one of the dock police," said the first-mate fiercely.

"Ay, ay, sir!" cried Billy Widgeon, and Mark's heart sank as he felt that his father was only secondary in power to the fierce red-nosed mate. But the next instant a thrill of satisfaction shot through him, for his father said in a calm, firm way:

"Stop!"

"Ah, we'll soon set him right," said the mate; "a miserable, snivelling cur!"

There was a laugh among the crew, and at a word from the mate they would have been ready to pitch the miserable object overboard.

"What is your name?" said the captain.

"Jimpny, sir. David Jimpny."

"Pretty name for a Christian man," said the mate; and the crew all laughed.

"What have you been?" said the captain.

"Anything, sir. No trade. Been out o' work, sir, and half starved and faint."

"Out of work!" roared the mate. "Why, you wouldn't work if you had it."

"Wouldn't I! You give me the chance, sir."

"Chance!" retorted the mate scornfully.

"Perhaps the poor wretch has not had one," said the captain. "Look here, my man."

"I haven't, sir; I haven't had a chance. Pray, pray, give me one, sir. I'll—I'll do anything, sir. I'll be like a slave if you'll only let me try."

"We don't want slaves," said the captain sternly; "we want honest true men who will work. Small."

"Ay, ay, sir," said the boatswain.

"This man has been half starved; take him below and see to him, and see that he is well treated."

"Ay, ay, sir," cried the boatswain. "Now, my swab."

"God—bless—"

"That will do," said the captain coldly. "No words. Let's have deeds, my man."

The abject-looking wretch shrank away, and the first-mate gave an angry stamp upon the deck.

"Look here, Captain Strong," he began furiously.

"That will do, my dear Gregory," said the captain, clapping him on the shoulder. "I wish the man to stay."

Mark Strong felt his heart at rest, for, as he saw the effect of his father's words upon the chief mate, he knew once and for all who was the real captain of the ship.

Chapter Six
How Mark Strong made Friends

"Of course we shall not be able to sail at the time down," said the first-mate rather huffily.

"Of course we shall, Gregory," said the captain quietly. "Morgan, I'm sorry you've had such a job as this. Divide the men into two watches. I'll take the first with some extra hands. Gregory and I will get on as far as we can till you and your watch are roused up. You'll go at it fresher. Pick out the most tired men for turning-in."

"They're all tired alike," said the first-mate gruffly. The captain did not answer, but went aft with his son.

"Rather a queer experience for you, Mark," he said as they entered the cabin, to find that Mrs Strong was there, waiting eagerly to know what was wrong on board.

Her anxieties were soon set at rest, and after a little examination of the place, the steward pointing out which were the cabins of the passengers expected to come on board the next day, Mrs Strong settled herself calmly down beneath the lamp and took out her work.

"Why, mother," said Mark, "anyone would think you were at home."

"Well," she replied smiling, "is it not home where your father is."

The reply was unanswerable, and being too restless to stay below when all was so novel on deck, Mark soon after went to where, by the light of many lanterns, about a third of the crew, supplemented by a gang of men from the dock, were hard at work trying to restore order in the hold.

"Hallo, youngster!" said a sharp voice; "don't get in the way. Here, hallo, old what's-your-name! Come here."

Bruff gave his tail a wag, and butted the first-mate's leg, submitting afterwards to being patted in the most friendly manner.

"Good dog that, young Strong."

The mate did not wait to hear what was said in reply, but dived down into the hold, while Mark joined his father.

"This is trying to bring order out of chaos, Mark," he said good-humouredly; and then turned sharply to look at a strange, gaunt sailor who came up and touched his hat.

"Hallo! Who are you? Oh, I see; our stowaway friend!"

"Yes, sir. Can I help, sir?"

"Well, yes—no—you had better not try at present, my man. Get used to the deck first, and try and put some strength in your arms."

"Please, sir, I—"

"That will do," said the captain coldly. "Obey orders, and prove that you are worthy of what I have done, and what I am going to do. I don't like professions."

The captain walked away, and the stowaway stood looking after him, while Bruff walked up and smelled him suspiciously.

"Nobody don't seem to believe in me," said the man in a discontented tone of voice.

"Try and make them, then," said Mark, who felt repelled by the man's servile manner.

"That's just what I'm agoin' to do, sir," said the man, speaking with the most villainous of low London accents.

"What did you say was your name?"

"David, sir; David Jimpny. He won't bite, will he, sir?"

"No. Here, Bruff, leave that alone and come here."

Mark's declaration that the dog would not bite seemed to give the man very little confidence, and no wonder, for Bruff kept eyeing the stowaway suspiciously in a way which seemed to indicate that he was looking out for a fleshy place to seize, but to his disappointment found none, only good opportunities for a grip at a bone.

Just then Small the boatswain came up from the hold, nodded at Mark, and gave one of his thumbs a jerk.

"I showed you your berth, my lad, go and turn in."

The man went forward and disappeared below, while the big rough boatswain gave the captain's son another friendly nod.

"Got to be drilled," he said. "Rough stuff to work up into a sailor. Rather have you, squire."

"Oh! I should not make a good sailor," said Mark lingering.

"Not if I took you in hand, my lad? Why, I'd make a man of you in no time. Is the skipper going to hand you over to me?"

"No; I'm only going as far as Plymouth or Penzance for a trip."

"More's the pity, my lad. Think twiced of it, and don't you go wasting your time ashore when there's such a profession as the sea opening of its arms to you and a arstin of you to come. Look at your father: there's a man!"

"Is he a very fine sailor?"

"Is he a fine sailor!" said the boatswain staring. "What a question to ask! why, there aren't a better one nowhere. Think twiced on it, my lad, and come all the way."

"I wish I could," said the boy to himself as he went back to the cabin, to find his father already there; and half an hour later, after a little joking about trying to sleep on a shelf in a cupboard, Mark clumsily turned in, far too much excited by the events of the day to go to sleep, and gradually getting so uneasy in the cramped space in which he had to lie, that he came to the conclusion that it was of no use to try; and as he lay thinking that he might as well get up and go and watch the re-stowing of the cargo, he found himself down low in the darkness, occupying the long triangular place from which the stowaway had been dragged.

How hot and stifling it seemed, and yet how little he felt surprised at being there, even when a strange dread came over him and he struggled to escape, with the knowledge all the time that the sailors and dock labourers were piling and ramming in cases and barrels, bales and boxes, wedging him in so closely that he knew he should never get out. Every minute his position grew more hopeless and the desire to struggle less. Once or twice he did try, but his efforts were vain; and at last he lay panting and exhausted and staring at the black darkness which suddenly seemed to have grown grey.

Was he awake? Had he been to sleep? Where was he?

He realised it all like a flash. He was in that cramped berth in the little cabin; and though he had not felt the approach of sleep, he must have been fast for some hours and had an attack of nightmare, from which he had awakened flat upon his back.

Mark uttered a sigh of relief, changed his position, lay looking at the grey light of morning and listening to some faintly-heard sounds, and then made up his mind to get up and dress.

Almost as a matter of course the result was that he dropped off fast asleep, and lay till a pleasant familiar voice cried to him that breakfast was nearly ready.

Getting off the shelf was nearly as difficult as getting upon it, but Mark took his first lesson in a determined way, and entered the cabin well rested and hungry just as the captain made his appearance.

"Oh, father, I feel so ashamed!" cried Mark.

"Why, my lad?"

"Sleeping comfortably there while you've been up at work all night."

"Nothing of the kind, my boy. Mr Morgan relieved us at three, and I've had five hours' sleep since then. Here they come."

Mr Gregory and Mr Morgan entered the cabin directly, both looking as calm and comfortable as if nothing had disturbed them. After the first greetings the first-mate began to look round the cabin.

"What's wrong, Gregory?" said the captain.

"Wrong!" said the first-mate. "Nothing. I was only looking after that dog."

"Why, surely you don't want to send him ashore?"

"Ashore, nonsense! Very fine dog, sir. I should like to have him. Ah, there you are!"

For just then Bruff came slowly and sedately into the cabin from a walk round the deck, and going straight up to the mate, blinked at him, and gave his tail two wags before going under the table to lay his head in his master's lap.

"Well, Morgan, how are you getting on?" asked the captain.

"Splendidly, sir. Quite like home to have a lady pouring out the coffee."

"No, no; I mean with the cargo."

"Oh! I beg pardon, sir. All right. We're about where we were before the accident."

"Ah, I thought we should be able to sail to-day, Gregory!"

"Humph!" said the first-mate. "I'll trouble you for a little more of that fried ham, Captain Strong. Good ham, young Strong. I recommend it."

Mark was already paying attention to it, and, well rested as he was, thoroughly enjoyed his novel meal, and was soon after as eagerly feasting upon the various sights and sounds of the deck.

For the next four hours all was busy turmoil. Passengers were arriving with their luggage marked "For use in cabin," last packages of cargo were being received, a couple of van-loads of fresh vegetables were shot down upon the deck as if some one was about to start a green-grocer's shop on the other side of the world, and the state of confusion increased to such a degree that it seemed to Mark that order could never by any possibility reign again. Wheels squeaked as ropes ran through tackle, iron chains clanged; there was a continuous roaring of orders, here, there, and everywhere; and at last, when the time for going out of dock arrived, the deck was piled up in all directions with cargo and luggage, and every vacant place was occupied by passengers, their friends, dock people, and crew.

It seemed impossible for the tall three-masted ship to get out of that dock through the narrow gates ahead and into the crowded river; but, just about one o'clock, a man in blue came on board and took charge, began shouting orders to men on the quay, ropes were made fast here and there and hauled upon, and the great ship was in motion.

Before many minutes had elapsed she had glided majestically into a narrow canal with stone walls, and from the high stern deck Mark saw that a pair of great gates were closed behind them, as if the ship had been taken in a trap. But no sooner was this achieved than another pair of gates was opened before her bows, and the slow gliding motion was continued till, almost before he knew it, the *Black Petrel* East Indiaman, Captain Strong, outward-bound for Colombo, Singapore, and Hong-Kong, was out in the river without having crushed any other craft.

As she swung out there in the tide, a large unwieldy object which threatened to come in contact with one or other of the many ships and long black screws lying in the river, all of a sudden a little, panting, puffing steamer came alongside and, amidst more shouting, ropes were thrown and she was made fast, while another appeared off the *Black Petrel's* bows, where the same throwing of ropes took place, but this time for a stout hawser to be fastened to the rope which had come through the air in rings. Then the rope was hauled back, the stout hawser dragged aboard, a great loop at its end placed over a hook on the tug-boat, which went slowly ahead, the hawser tightened, slackened, and splashed in the water, tightened and slackened again and again, till the great steamer's inertia was overcome without the hawser being parted, and kept by the tug at the side from swinging here and there, the great ship went grandly down the Thames.

Chapter Seven
How Mark had a Surprise

Blackwall and Woolwich, Gravesend, and the vessel moored for the night. There a few preliminaries were adjusted, and the next morning, with the deck not quite in such a state of confusion, the vessel began to drop down with the tide.

And now Mark woke to the fact that the captain was once more only a secondary personage on board, the pilot taking command, under whose guidance sails dropped down and the great ship gradually made her way in and out of the dangerous shoals and sand-banks, till, well out to sea on a fine calm day, the pilot-boat came alongside, and Captain Strong, as the pilot wished him a lucky voyage, again took command.

There had been so much going on in lashing spars in their places, getting down the last of the cargo, and securing the ship's boats, along with a hundred other matters connected with clearing the decks and making things ship-shape, that Mark saw little of his father and the officers, except at mealtimes; and hence he was thrown almost entirely in the company of his mother. There were the passengers, but they, for the most part, were somewhat distant and strange at first; but now, as the great ship began to go steadily down channel, before a pleasant south-easterly breeze, the decks were clear, ropes coiled down, hatches battened over, and there was a disposition among the strangers on board to become friendly.

They were not a very striking party whom Captain Strong had gathered round his table, but, as he told Mrs Strong, he had to make the best of them. There was a curiously dry-looking Scotch merchant on his way back to Hong-Kong. An Irish major, with his wife and daughter, bound for the same place. A quiet stout gentleman, supposed to be a doctor, and three young German agricultural students on their way to Singapore, from which place, after a short stay, they were going to Northern Queensland to introduce some new way of growing sugar.

But just as the passengers were growing social, and the panorama of Southern England was growing more and more beautiful, the weather began to change.

Its first vagary was in the shape of a fog while they were off the Dorsetshire coast, and with the fog there was its companion, a calm.

"One of a sailor's greatest troubles," Mr Morgan said to Mark as they were leaning over the taffrail watching the gulls, which seemed to come in and out of the mist.

"But capital for a passenger who only wants to make his trip as long as he can," said Mark laughingly.

"Ah! I forgot that you leave us at Plymouth," said the second-mate.

"Penzance," cried Mark.

"That depends on the weather, young man. If that happens to be bad you will be dropped at Plymouth, and I'm afraid we are going to have a change."

The second-mate was right, for before many hours had passed, and when Start and Prawle points had been pointed out as they loomed up out of the haze upon their right, the sea began to rise. That night the wind was increasing to a gale, and Mark was oblivious, like several of the passengers, of the grandeur of the waves; neither did he hear the shrieking of the wind through the rigging. What he did hear was the creaking and groaning of the timbers of the large ship as she rose and fell, and the heavy thud of some wave which smote her bows and came down like a cataract upon her deck.

"Come, Mark, Mark, my lad," the captain said, "you must hold up. You're as bad as your mother."

"Are we going to the bottom, father?" was all Mark could gasp out.

"No, my boy," said the captain, laughing, "I hope not. This is only what we sailors call a capful of wind."

Mrs Strong was too ill to leave her cabin, but the first-mate came to give the sea-sick lad a friendly grip of the hand, and pat poor Bruff's head as he sat looking extremely doleful, and seeming to wonder what it all meant Mr Morgan, too, made his appearance from time to time.

Then all seemed to be rising up and plunging down with the shrieking of wind, the beating of the waves, and darkness, and sickness, and misery.

Was it day or was it night? How long had he been ill? How long was all this going to last?

Once or twice Mark tried to crawl out of his berth, but he was too weak and ill to stir; besides which, the ship was tossing frightfully, and once when the captain came in it seemed to the lad that he looked careworn and anxious. But Mark was too ill to trouble himself about the storm or the ship, or what was to become of them, and he lay there perfectly prostrate.

The steward came from time to time anxious looking and pale, but Mark did not notice it. He for the most part refused the food that was brought to him, and lay back in a sort of stupor, till at last it seemed to him that the ship was not rocking about so violently.

Then came a time when the cabin seemed to grow light, and the steps of men sounded overhead as they were removing some kind of shutter.

Lastly he woke one morning with the sun shining, and his father, looking very haggard, sitting by his berth.

"Well, my lad," he said, "this has been a sorry holiday for you. Come, can't you hold up a bit? The steward's going to bring you some tea."

"I—can't touch anything, father; but has the storm gone?"

"Thank Heaven! yes, my lad. I never was in a worse!"

"But you said it was a capful of wind," said Mark faintly.

"Capful, my lad! it was a hurricane, and I'm afraid many a good ship has fared badly."

"But the *Petrel's* all right, father?"

"Behaved splendidly."

"Are we—nearly at Plymouth?" was Mark's next question.

"Nearly where?"

"At Plymouth. I think, as I'm so ill, I'd better not go any farther. How is mother?"

"Going to get up, my lad, and that's what you've got to do."

"I'll try, father. When shall I go ashore?"

"If you like, at Malta, for a few hours," said the captain drily; "not before."

"At Malta!" said Mark, raising himself upon one arm.

"Yes, at Malta. Do you know where we are?"

"Somewhere off the Devon coast, I suppose."

"You were, a week ago, my boy. There, get up and dress yourself; the sun shines and the sea's calm, and in a few hours I can show you the coast of Spain."

"But, father," cried Mark, upon whom this news seemed to have a magical effect, "aren't we going ashore at Penzance."

"Penzance, my boy! We had one of the narrowest of shaves of going on the Lizard Rocks, and were only too glad to get plenty of sea-room. Do you know we've been running for a week under storm topsails, and in as dangerous a storm as a ship could face?"

"I knew it had been very bad, father, but not like that. What are you going to do?"

"Make the best of things, sir. Look here, Mark, you wanted to come for a voyage with me."

"Yes, father."

"Well, I said I wouldn't take you."

"Yes, father."

"And now I'm obliged to: for I can't put back."

"Going to take me to China?" cried Mark.

"Yes, unless I put in at Lisbon, and send you home from there, and that's not worth while."

"Father!"

"What! are you so much better as that? Here, what are you going to do?"

"Get up directly, father, and see the coast of Spain."

Chapter Eight
How Captain Jack came on Deck

"Yes, my lad, you've had a narrow squeak for it," said the first-mate, shaking hands. "You're in for it now."

He patted Mark's shoulder as he stood gazing over the port bulwark at a dim blue line.

"I couldn't get to you more, Mark, my lad," said the second-mate, "but you'll be all right now. We've had a rough time."

"And to think of you coming all the way with us after all!" said the boatswain in a pleasant growl. "Here, I'm going to make a sailor o' you."

Mark was alone soon after, when Billy Widgeon came up smiling to say a few friendly words, and directly after a thin pale sailor came edging along the bulwarks to say feebly:

"I see you've been very bad too, sir. I thought once we should have been all drowned."

Mark had an instinctive dislike to this man, he could not tell why, and as he felt this he was at the same time angry with himself, for it seemed unjust.

The man noted it, and sighed as he went away, and even this sigh troubled its hearer, for he could not make out whether it was genuine or uttered to excite sympathy.

There was some excuse, for Mr David Jimpny's personal appearance was not much improved by the composite sailor suit he wore. His trousers were an old pair of the captain's, and his jacket had been routed out by the boatswain, both officers being about as opposite in physique to the stowaway as could well be imagined. In fact, as Mark Strong saw him going forward he could not help thinking that the poor fellow looked better in his shore-going rags.

Then his manner of coming on board had not been of a kind to produce a favourable impression.

"I can't help it," said Mark aloud. "I don't want to jump upon the poor fellow, but how can we take to him when even one's dog looks at him suspiciously."

"I shouldn't set up my dog as a model to go by if I were you," said a voice at his elbow; and turning suddenly, with his face flushing, Mark found that the second-mate was at his elbow.

"I didn't know that I was thinking aloud," said Mark.

"But you were, and very loudly. I don't wonder at your not liking that man: I don't. Perhaps he'll improve though. We will not judge him yet. So you're coming all the way with us?"

"Yes."

"I'm glad of it. Be a change for you, and for us too. This is rather different to what we've been having, eh?"

"Why, it's lovely!" cried Mark. "I didn't think the weather could be so beautiful at sea."

"Nor so stormy, eh?"

"I didn't notice much of the storm," said Mark. "I was too ill."

"Ah! it is bad that first attack of 'waves in motion,' as I call it. But that's all past, and we shall have fine weather, I daresay, all the rest of the voyage. One never gets much worse weather than we have near home."

"Was much damage done," asked Mark, "in the storm?"

"Nothing serious. We were just starting after all our faulty rigging had been replaced. If we had been coming home after a voyage it might have been different. One or two sails were blown to shreds, but the old ship behaved nobly."

"I wish I had not been so ill," said Mark thoughtfully.

"So do I, my lad; but why do you speak so?"

"Because I should have liked to be on deck."

"Ah! well, you need not regret your sickness, for you would not have been on deck. It was as much as we could do to hold our own and not get washed overboard. That's worth looking at."

He pointed, as he spoke, to a blue line of hills away to the east bathed in the brilliant sunshine, while the water between them and the shore seemed to be as blue, but of another shade.

"Spain!" said Mark. "How lovely!"

"Portugal, my lad. Yes, it's pretty enough, but I've often seen bits of the Welsh coast look far more lovely. Don't you run away with the idea that you are going to see more beautiful countries than your own."

"Oh, but, Mr Morgan, Spain, and Italy, and Egypt, and Ceylon, and Singapore, they are all more beautiful than England."

"They're different, my lad," said Morgan, laughing, "and they look new to you and fresh; but when the weather's fine, take my word for it there's no place like home."

"Oh, but I thought—"

"You were going to see Arabian Night's wonders, eh? Well, you will not, my lad. Of course there are parts of foreign countries that are glorious. I thought Sydney harbour a paradise when I first saw it; but then I had been four months at sea, and the weather horrible. Hallo! here's an old friend. He always disappears when the weather's bad, and buries himself somewhere. I think he gets down among the stores. Mind your dog!"

Mark caught Bruff by the collar, for he was moving slowly off to meet Billy Widgeon, who was coming along the deck in company with a large monkey of a dingy brownish-black. The sailor was holding it by one hand, and the animal was making a pretence of walking erect, but in a very awkward shuffling manner, while its quick eyes were watching the dog.

"I've brought the captain to see you, Mr Mark, sir," said Billy grinning. "He hasn't been well, and only come out of his berth this morning. Here, Jack, shake hands with the gent."

"Chick, chicker—chack, chack," cried the monkey; and turning sharply, he gave Billy's detaining hand a nip with his teeth, sharply enough to make the man utter an exclamation and let go, when the monkey leaped on to the bulwark, seized a rope, and went up it hand over hand in a quadrumanous manner to a height that he considered safe, and there held on and hung, looking down at the dog, chattering volubly the while.

"He don't like the looks on him, sir," said Billy grinning. "I told him he was a nipper. I say, look at 'em. Haw! haw!"

The scene was curious, for as soon as Bruff was set at liberty he stared up at the monkey and began walking round and round, while after carefully lifting its tail with one hand, as if in dread that it might be seized, an act which would have required a ten-feet jump, the monkey went on chattering loudly as if scolding the dog for being there.

"What would be the consequences if we fetched the monkey down?" said the second-mate, laughing and watching the two animals.

"Bruff would kill him," said Mark decidedly.

"He would have to catch him first, and the monkey is wonderfully strong. But we must have no fighting. Let's see if we can't make them friends. Can you manage your dog?"

"Oh, yes!" said Mark laughing. "I can make him do what I like. Here, Bruff."

The dog came to him sidewise, keeping an eye on the monkey; and as soon as Morgan saw that Bruff was held by the collar he turned to the monkey.

"Here, Jack, come down!"

The monkey paid no heed, but swung himself to and fro, straining out his neck to peep round the mate and get a look at the dog.

"Do you hear, sir! come down!" cried the mate.

He was now so near that he could reach within a yard of where the active animal hung, and it looked down in his face with a comical look, and began to chatter, as if remonstrating and calling his attention to the dog, which uttered a low growl.

"Quiet, Bruff!" cried Mark.

"If you don't come down, Jack, I'll heave you overboard."

There was another voluble burst of chattering, but the monkey did not stir.

"Shall I fetch him down, sir?" said Billy grinning.

"Yes, but don't scare him."

"I won't scare him, sir. Here, Jack, old man, come down."

The monkey turned sharply at the sound of his voice, and chattered at him.

"All right! I hears what you says," replied Billy solemnly; "but the young gent's got tight hold of the dog, and he won't hurt you. Down you comes!"

The situation was ludicrous in the extreme, for, as if the monkey understood every word, and was angrily protesting and pointing out the danger, he kept on chattering, and bobbed his head from side to side.

"Yes, that's all right enough," continued Billy, "but you're a coward, that's what you are. Down you come!"

Another fierce burst of chattering, and the rope shaken angrily.

"Well, I've asked you twice," cried Billy. "Here goes once more. Down you comes!"

If ever monkey said, "I won't," Jack did at that moment; but he changed his tone directly, for Billy ran to the bulwarks and began to unfasten the rope from the belaying-pin about which it was twisted, when, probably from a vivid recollection of having once been shaken off a rope, and apparently ignorant of the ease with which he could have escaped up into the rigging, the monkey began to slide down, uttering a low whining sound, and allowed the sailor to take him in his arms, but only to cling tightly to his neck.

"Ah, it's all werry fine for you to come a-cuddling up like that! You bit me just now."

The monkey moaned and whined piteously, and kept its eyes fixed upon the dog, who was watching him all the time.

"Ah, well: I forgives you!" said Billy. "Now, then, sir, what next?"

"Bring him to the dog."

"But he thinks the dog's going to eat him, sir."

"Then let's teach him better," said Mark. "Here, Bruff, make friends here."

Bruff looked up at his master and gave his tail a couple of wags. Then turning to the monkey again he seemed lost in thought.

"He won't bite now, will he, sir?" said Billy.

"No, he's all right; but will the monkey bite?"

"Not he, sir. I should like to catch him at it. Now, Jack," he continued, with one arm round his companion, "shake hands."

He held the animal forward toward Bruff, who was watching him stolidly, and gave his head a shake.

This act produced a frightened start on the monkey's part, and another burst of chattering.

"Better let him go," said Morgan. "I daresay they'll get used to one another by and by."

"He'll do it, sir; give him time," said Billy. "Now, Jack, give us your hand. You just pat his head. Sure he won't bite, sir?"

"Certain," cried Mark.

"It's all right: do you hear, stoopid? Ah! would you bite? You do, and I'll chuck yer overboard. Now, then."

In spite of the monkey's struggles he forced one hand to within reach of the dog's head, and pressed it down till he could pat it with the thin black fingers.

Bruff whined, but he was held by the collar, and suffered the touch without other protest, while, as if relieved by finding that his hand was neither burned nor bitten off, the monkey made no resistance the second time, ending by touching the dog himself, and, as if overcome by curiosity, struggling to be free, and squatting down and examining the interior of his new acquaintance's ears.

Bruff half-closed his eyes and made no resistance, and, cautiously loosening his hold upon the collar but kneeling ready to seize him at the least inimical display, Mark watched the little comedy which went on.

For after a rigid examination of one ear, and a loud chattering, probably a lecture upon its structure, Jack pulled the head over and proceeded to examine the other ear, after which he made several pokes at the dog's eyes, and held his head while he looked into them as if they were something entirely new, all of which Bruff submitted to in the calmest manner.

"They will not fight now," said the second-mate laughing.

It was evident they would not, for the dog suddenly leaped up and ran away with the monkey in chase, the one big-headed and clumsy, the other all activity and life; and for the next ten minutes they were careering about the deck, chasing each other and in the best of companionship, the game ending by Jack making a rush and clambering into one of the boats, where he lay panting and gazing over the side at the dog, who crouched, blinking up at him with his tongue out, waiting for him to come down.

Chapter Nine
How the Stowaway stowed himself

Glorious weather with the coasts of Africa and Europe visible together as they passed the straits. Then lovely summer days with pleasant winds as they sailed along the Mediterranean. The passengers were nearly always on deck, basking in the morning sunshine or taking refuge under the awning. The Scotch merchant took snuff; the three German students, who all wore spectacles and seemed exactly alike, leaned over the side in a row, smoked big meerschaum pipes, looked round-faced and bibulous, and very often uttered the word *Zo*. The stout doctor read books all day long; and the Irish major followed he captain everywhere, to declaim against the injustices practised in the army. "Injustices, sor, which have kept me down to meejor when I ought to have been a gineral;" and as he talked Mrs Major worked with Mrs Strong, and watched her daughter, a pretty bright girl of twelve, who passed her time between her books and watching the three German students as she tried to recollect which was which.

"Ah, captain," said the major to him one day, as they were all gazing at a large steamer that was passing them easily, "you won't understand me. You're a backward man, or you'd be in command of a fast steamer instead of a slow sailing ship."

"Sailing ships are quite dangerous enough, major, without having hundreds of tons of coal aboard, and a large fire roaring night and day. Fires are risky things aboard ship."

"Not if there's a properly disciplined crew on board, sor," said the major. "Bah!"

He cocked his cap on one side, and leaned forward to watch the passing steamer.

"I hope we should do our duty if we did have a fire, discipline or no discipline," said the captain gruffly, and the subject dropped.

It was a trifling incident, but it set several people on board thinking. It was, however, soon forgotten, and with the sea, as Billy Widgeon said, as smooth as a mill-pond, and all sail set, the great East Indiaman continued her course, the journey now being thoroughly enjoyable.

There were plenty of little incidents occurring to keep the trip from being monotonous. About every twenty-four hours Mr Gregory was finding fault with David Jimpny, who seemed to be one of those unfortunates who never succeed. From scraps of his history, which he insisted upon retailing to Mark when he could find him alone, it seemed that his life had been so many scenes of trouble.

"I'm a-trying hard, sir, as hard as I can, to be a sailor, but I don't get on. My hands never seem to manage ropes, and it's no use for Mr Gregory to bully me. I daren't go up these rope ladders; if I did I know I should be drowned."

In spite of this Mr Gregory one day ordered him aloft, and the poor fellow managed to get up as high as the mainmast head, when he seemed entirely to lose his nerve, and, letting his legs slip in between the shrouds, he clung there with his hands clutching the ratlines, and holding on for life.

"Go on up, sir; go on up," shouted the first-mate, and his hoarse orders attracted the attention of the passengers. But the poor fellow did not move, and growing tired at last, the mate ordered him to come down.

This order was of as much effect as those which preceded it, the man remaining motionless.

"If this was only the royal navy," cried the mate, "I'd have you spread-eagled up there and lashed to the rigging till you got used to it. Here, where are you going, youngster?"

"Up to see what's the matter," said Mark coolly; and swinging himself up he began to climb the rigging.

It was his first attempt, and as his feet began to make acquaintance with the ratlines he awoke for the first time to the fact that though they looked just like a ladder to climb it was a very different matter. They gave and the shrouds felt loose and seemed to sway; the height above looked terrific, and the distance below to the deck quite startling. That clean-boarded deck, too, appeared as if it would be horribly hard to fall upon; but a doubt arose in his mind as to what would be the consequences if he slipped — would he fall with a crash upon the deck, or slip part of the way down the shrouds, and be shot off into that extremely soft place, the sea?

The idea was so startling that he glanced down at it, to see that it looked gloriously clear and sunlit — transparent to a degree; but the great ship was gliding through it swiftly, and he knew that he would go down and down with the impetus of his fall, and come up somewhere in the current to be carried far astern in the troubled water in the wake of the ship.

How long would it take them to get down a boat? and what would become of him while he was waiting? He could swim as boys do swim in an ordinary way, who learn in some river or pool at school; but that was very different to being left astern in the sea with the ship going eight or nine knots an hour; and he felt that he would be drowned before help could come.

Then there were the sharks!

He did not know that there were any sharks, but his brain suggested to him that there would certainly be at least one big fellow whose back fin would be seen cutting the water as he glided towards his victim, his cross-cut mouth with its cruel, triangular saw-edged teeth ready; and then there would be the water stained with blood, and as he rose to the surface without, say, a leg, he would hear his mother's despairing shriek, and then—

He had got up about a dozen ratlines while his imagination had painted all that picture for him, and the result was that he set his teeth hard and went on climbing, but thoroughly realising the while how it was David Jimpny, the miserable stowaway, had lost his nerve, and was now clinging above him in that absurd attitude, with his legs stuck through between the shrouds.

Another minute and he was as high, holding on with both hands, and listening to the buzz of voices on deck, but particularly careful not to look down again.

"I'll think about what I'm doing," he said to himself, "and then I sha'n't be afraid."

"Hullo! Jimpny," he said aloud, "what's the matter?" and, setting one hand at liberty, he gave the man a slap on the shoulder.

"Don't, don't! Pray, don't touch me, or I shall fall," groaned the wretched man.

"Nonsense! you won't fall. Get up through that hole on to the woodwork."

"What, is it you, Mr Strong, sir?"

"Me? yes. I've come up to see what's the matter."

"Oh, take care, sir, or you'll tumble overboard."

"Nonsense! you've only got to hold tight," cried Mark to his own astonishment, for he could not understand how the man's cowardice should make him brave.

"I—I did hold tight. I am holding tight, sir, but I daren't move. Oh, I do feel so giddy. What shall I do?"

"Try and be a man," said Mark. "The mate's horribly cross with you. Here, hold tight with your hands and draw your legs out."

"I—I daren't stir," groaned the wretched man, "I should fall if I did. My head's all of a swim."

"Yes, because you frighten yourself," said Mark.

"Now then, Strong," cried the mate, "is that fellow asleep?"

"No, sir, he's coming down directly."

"Coming down!" growled the mate. "There, take care of him and mind he don't fall."

"You hear what he says," whispered Mark. "Come on up here. I'll go first and show you the way."

Truth to tell Mark did not want to go any higher, but under the circumstances he felt bound, terrible as it looked, and the remainder of the climb over the man's head was not made any the pleasanter by the poor wretch moaning out—

"Oh, don't! oh, don't! You'll push me off! You'll fall! I know you'll fall."

But Mark did not fall, and though he chose the easier way up he did display some courage, and lay flat down to extend a hand to his miserable companion.

"There, take hold of my hand. I'll help you," he said.

The man shook his head—wisely, perhaps, for Mark's help would not have been great as far as sustaining him went.

"I can't—I daren't move," he said. "It's as bad as being shut up in the hold. Please call for help."

"Ahoy, there!" shouted a familiar voice. "What are you doing, Mark?"

"Trying to help this man, father."

"Here, Jimpny," shouted the captain, "get up, sir. Don't hang in the rigging there like that."

The man moaned, and only clung the closer.

"Do you hear, sir?" cried the captain; but the man was livid, and as he gazed wildly up at Mark, the lad lowered himself down, thrust an arm round one of the ropes, and took a firm grasp of his collar.

"What's the matter, Mark?" cried the captain.

"He's going to faint, I think."

"Here, Small, up aloft with a rope there," cried the captain, "and make it fast round him."

The boatswain seized a coil of line and trotted to the other side of the deck. Mark saw him cross, but was astonished to see how soon he appeared at the mast-head.

"Hold tight, youngster," he said, "I'll soon give him his physic."

"What are you going to do?" cried Mark.

"Hang him. You'll see," said the boatswain with a chuckle.

Jimpny groaned and seemed to cling spasmodically to the shrouds as the great seaman slipped the end of the rope round him and made it fast. After which he passed the other end of the rope over a stay and lowered it down to the deck.

"Ready below?" he shouted.

"All right!" came up.

"You get a bit higher, youngster. That's your sort. Now, my London prime, let go with them hands."

"No, no," groaned the unfortunate man. "I dare not."

"Then I shall have to make you," roared the boatswain. "Heave ahead there!"

The rope tightened and there was a tremendous strain upon the man's chest, while, by a dexterous snatch, Small jerked one of the clinging hands free and thrust Jimpny off the shroud, making him swing round in the air, and this helped to jerk the other hand from its grip.

"Now you have him. Down he goes."

It was all so rapidly done that it took Mark's breath away. One minute the miserable man was clinging there half fainting, the next he was swinging in the air and being slowly lowered down to the deck.

"You don't want sarving that way, my lad," said the boatswain laughing. "Catch hold o' that rope and slide down. I'll go this way."

Mark shrank for a moment but seized the rope the next, and slid down so quickly that his hands felt uncomfortably warm, and he reached the deck as Billy Widgeon was unfastening the rope from round Jimpny's chest.

"Nice sorter sailor that, Captain Strong," said Mr Gregory sourly.

"Yes," said the captain quietly. "Don't send him aloft again. Let him help the cook."

"Help the cook! Do you want to poison us, sir?"

"No. The man has no nerve, but he may prove himself useful some other way."

"You are a brave boy," said a pleasant silvery voice behind Mark, and turning sharply round, it was to see the major's little daughter hurrying toward the cabin, in which she disappeared.

"There, go below," said the mate angrily, "and don't show yourself to me again for a week."

The stowaway rose and crept away, looking sideways at the sea, and somehow Mark could not help feeling sorry for his pitiful case.

Mark did not feel as if he had been brave, and as they sat at tea that evening and he looked across at where Mary O'Halloran was seated with her mother, he said to himself that if she knew all he had thought up aloft and what his sensations were she would have looked upon him as an impostor.

He felt so uncomfortable all that evening, and worried, that he longed to get away by himself, for the conversation seemed to be all about him.

"I should make a soldier of him," said the major to Captain Strong. "The only career for a brave boy, sir, in spite of the disgraceful management at the War Office."

Mark winced, and glanced towards those peaceful young gentlemen, the German agricultural students; but they were all three beaming upon him with their spectacles, looking about as round in the face and as inexpressive as so many enlarged buns.

He glanced at the little Scottish merchant, but he took snuff and nodded at him.

The stout doctor was looking at him and making notes in a memorandum book, as if he were writing down an account of the affair.

Mr Morgan was on deck; but Mr Gregory, as soon as their eyes met, deliberately winked at him.

He turned his gaze upon his father, to find that he was thoughtfully watching him; while, after receiving a friendly shake of the head from Mrs Major and a merry look from Mary, who seemed to be enjoying his confusion, as a last resource the lad looked at his mother, to find she had ready for him a tender smile.

"And she put three extra lumps of sugar in my tea," said Mark to himself. "I never felt so ashamed of anything in my life."

To make matters worse, the major began in a loud voice to talk about the heroic deeds of boys as found in history, and though the saloon cabin was hot enough before, it seemed now to Mark that it was tropical, and he was only too glad to go out on deck and wipe his streaming face in the company of Bruff and Jack the monkey, who, from becoming the companion of the dog, was willing enough to transfer some of his friendliness to the dog's master.

But even here he was not left in peace, for Billy Widgeon came up to compliment him on his climbing.

"Look ye here, Mr Strong, sir, you'll do it. You come up with me and we'll go right up to the main-topgallant cross-trees to-morrow. I'll see as you don't fall."

"Oh, bother the climbing!" cried Mark. "I wish there wasn't a bit of rigging in the ship."

"But we couldn't get on without rigging, Mr Mark, sir," said the little sailor taking the impatient words literally. "See how them sails is spread. Rigging's a fine thing, sir; so's a ship. You be a sailor, sir, and when you're a skipper you have me for your bosun. I aren't so big as old Small, but I'd put a deal o' heart into it, and keep the men up to the mark."

"Oh, I shall never be a captain," said Mark impatiently.

"I don't know so much about that, sir. All the lads says as it was wonderful the way you went up after the rat."

"After the what!"

"Rat, sir. The lads calls that stowaway chap the rat because he made hisself a hole down in the cargo. Lor' a me, think of a thing like that calling hisself a man!"

"But he has been half starved, Billy, and kicked about in the world. Perhaps if you'd been brought down as low you would have been as great a coward."

"Hah! I never thought o' that," said Billy scratching his head. "I say, Mr Mark, sir, how you do put things. But no, sir, you aren't right—leastwise not quite, you see; because if I'd been brought down like that, and felt as scared as he did, I wouldn't have let anyone know, fear o' being laughed at."

"You don't know and I don't know, so we can't discuss it," said Mark. "Here, what are you going to do?"

"Ketch Master Jack and take him to his snuggery. He's a-getting into bad habits since your dog's come aboard, sir. Monkeys is a sooperior sort o' animal, and the men's been talking it over."

"Talking it over?"

"Yes, sir. They says as a monkey's next door to a man. Not as I thinks so."

"Then what do you think, Billy?"

"Oh, I think he lives several streets off, sir; but the men thinks tother, and they says as though it's all werry well for a monkey to play with a dog and be friends, just as a man might; it's going down hill like for him to make a habit o' sleeping in a dog-kennel."

"Nonsense! the monkey's happy enough with the dog."

"So was a mate o' mine with the Noo Zeeling savages, after cutting away from his ship; but our old skipper said he ought to be ashamed of hisself for going and living that way, and them beginning to tattoo him in a pattern. He said he was a-degrading of hisself, and fetched him aboard, saying as if he wanted tattooing some of his messmates should mark his back with a rope's end. No, sir, we thinks a deal o' that monkey—our crew does—and we don't want to see him go wrong."

"What stuff! My Bruff is quite as intelligent an animal as your monkey. Suppose I said he should not associate with the ugly brute?"

"No, no, sir: Jack aren't ugly," said Billy Widgeon in protest. "He aren't handsome, but no one can't say as he's ugly; while that dog—"

"Oh, he isn't handsome either, but it's absurd to draw the line between the two animals like that."

"Well, sir, I tell you what the men says; and they thinks a deal o' Jacko, and looks after his morals wonderful. We do let him chew tobacco, though it don't agree with him, 'cause he will swaller it; but as to a drop o' rum, why, Old Greg nearly chucked a man overboard once for giving him a tot, and Small the boatswain stopped one chap's grog for a week for teaching Jack to drink. We thinks a deal of that monkey, sir."

"And I think a deal of my dog, and keep him a deal cleaner than Jack. But I don't want them to be together. Take Jack away."

"Werry sorry, Mr Mark, sir. Mean no offence," said Billy apologetically; "but it's the men, sir. They think a deal o' that monkey."

Billy went forward with a chain and a strap to where a kennel had been made for Bruff, by turning a flour barrel on its side and wedging it between two hencoops, and here, greatly to the vexation of the chickens, who lived in dread of Jack's long hairy arm and clever fingers, which were always stretching through the bars to pull their feathers, the monkey had—to use Billy's words—"just turned in." The barrel held the two animals tightly, and there they were cuddled up together in the most friendly manner, Jack with his head right in towards the end, Bruff with his long black muzzle to the front, and Jacko's tail moving up and down in regular motion as he breathed.

"Here! you've got to come home," cried Billy, making a dash at the monkey's legs, but he started back as quickly as he went forward, for Bruff sprang up, and, twitching his ears, burst into a furious fit of barking, while Jack got behind him and chattered his defiance.

"Well, that's a rum game," said Billy, rubbing his nose with a rusty link of the chain he held; "think o' them two sticking up for one another like that."

"Now, then, which is the more intelligent animal?" said Mark, laughing.

"Well, sir, I dunno, but if so be as you'd take your dog away—"

"No," said Mark quietly, "I sha'n't interfere. The monkey's happier there than down in your stuffy forecastle."

"Which I won't deny as it is stuffy, sir, far from it," said Billy; "but when you get used to the smell you don't mind, and I'm sure Jack likes it. So call away your dog."

"No," said Mark, "you may get him away if you like."

"Well, if so be as I must, I must," said the little sailor. "The men says they wants Jacko, and—Lor' a me!"

As he spoke he had gone down on one knee to reach into the barrel and get hold of Jack's leg, but at the angry remonstrative cry of the monkey as he felt it seized, Bruff made so furious an attack upon the sailor that he started back and rolled over, to find Bruff spring upon his chest.

"Hold hard, mate; don't bite. I gives up," said Billy quietly. "Call him off, Mr Mark, sir."

But the lad had already caught the dog by the collar, and dragged him away growling.

Just then Jack sprang out of the barrel chattering loudly, and bounded toward the main hatchway. Bruff followed as if understanding the call, and as the monkey sprang down the dog leaped after him, but did not descend the steps so cleverly as his quadrumanous friend, the fact being made plain to those on deck by a loud scratching and scuffling noise, followed by a heavy bump.

"That there's the dog," said Billy sitting up and scratching his ear. "His head's too heavy for going down them steps nose fust. Think we can catch Jack now?"

"No, that you will not," said Mark, laughing at his companion's troubled face. "Did Bruff frighten you?"

"S'pose he did, sir. He made me feel mortal queer for a minute. But I s'pose he wouldn't bite. Here, they may fetch the monkey theirselves," he continued, rising slowly; "I shan't try no more; and if his manners is spylte by 'sociating with dogs it aren't my fault."

Billy Widgeon went forward toward the forecastle in his calm even-tempered way, and Mr Morgan, who had been looking on from the poop-deck, came and joined Mark, to stand talking with him as they leaned over the side gazing up at the transparent starry sky, or down at the clear dark sea, while they listened to the rushing water as the great ship glided on under quite a cloud of canvas. The night was now dark, with the ship's sailing lanterns and the glow from the cabin-windows showing faintly and casting reflections upon the unruffled sea.

"Suppose we were to run on to another ship, Mr Morgan," said Mark at last, breaking a long silence. "What then?"

"If we kept such a bad look-out, and they did the same, most likely we should go to the bottom, perhaps both of us; but you turn in and leave all that to the watch."

Chapter Ten
How Bruff sounded the Alarm

It was turning-in time, and after a couple of sleepy yawns Mark went to the cabin to find that nearly everyone had retired for the night.

As soon as he had climbed upon his shelf he found that it was going to be one of those hot uncomfortable nights when pillow and sheet get ticklish and make the skin feel itchy. The air he breathed was stifling, and for a long time he lay awake listening to the rippling of the water against the sides of the ship. But at last he slept deeply and dreamlessly, to be awakened by a hand laid upon his shoulder.

"Mark, my lad. Hist! don't make a noise."

"What's the matter, Mr Gregory?"

"Nothing much, my lad; only that dog of yours is somewhere below howling dreadfully. I want you to come and quiet him."

"Won't he lie down when you speak, sir?" said Mark drowsily.

"No. Come: wake up my lad!"

"All right, sir!"

"Nonsense, boy! you're going to sleep again. Come, now, rouse up!"

"All—yes, sir, I'm awake," said Mark, springing out of his berth. "I'll slip on something and come."

"I'll wait for you," said the mate dryly.

It was a wise decision, for Mark was so confused with drowsiness that he dressed mechanically, and suffered himself to be led out on to the deck where the comparative coolness made him a little more aware of what was going on.

"Now, are you awake?"

"Yes, sir. Quite awake now, sir," said Mark wonderingly. "What do you want? Is the ship going down?"

"Nonsense, boy!" said the mate laughing. "Why, you sleepy-headed fellow, didn't you understand what I said?"

"That I was to get up?" said Mark.

"Yes, and quiet your dog. There, do you hear that?"

A long piteous howl now fell upon Mark's ears, and recalling how the dog had gone below, he concluded that the animal was eager to escape on deck, but after his experience in falling down the steps he did not care to attack them again.

"What a noise!" cried Mark, as the long persistent howl came up. "Has he got stuck somewhere in the cargo?"

"No; he could not be, I think. Hark, there's the monkey too."

An angry chattering sound came up, followed by another howl and an angry bark.

"There, go down and quiet him. The men in the forecastle can't sleep."

Mark, now thoroughly awake, went sharply to the hatchway and descended, wondering why one of the sailors had not been sent down to quiet Bruff, and of course ignorant of the fact that they had one and all declined to go and face him, for certain reasons associated with the sharpness of his teeth and strength of his jaws, while the mate felt that it would be an easier way of solving the difficulty to send down the dog's master than to go himself.

It was very dark below, and the dog's howl came once more as Mark took a lantern from where it was swinging.

"Why, where can he be? Here, Bruff, Bruff!"

Mark dropped the lantern with a crash, and the candle within it flickered for a moment and went out, as a horrible thought struck him, and turning back to the ladder he sprang up, and was about to shout, but his better sense prevailed, and he ran to where the first-mate stood by the bulwarks talking to one of the men.

"Well, have you quieted him?"

"Mr Gregory! Here! I want to speak to you," said Mark huskily.

"What, has he bitten you?"

Mark dragged at his arm, and as soon as they were on the other side, panted out in a low whisper:

"There's something on fire down below."

"What!" shouted the mate in his surprise and horror. Then recovering himself, and knowing the risks attending a scare, "Poor boy!" he cried aloud. "Well, we shall be obliged to have that dog shot."

This quieted the men, who were advancing, and they went back to their places, while Mr Gregory walked Mark slowly by him to the cabin-door.

"Are you sure you smelt fire?" he whispered.

"Yes, sir, and there is smoke coming out from between those lower hatches."

"If I go down to make sure the men will take alarm and there may be a rush," said the mate coolly. "Here, go and rouse up Morgan quietly. Don't say what's wrong. I want him."

"And my father?" panted Mark.

"Be cool, boy; everything depends on coolness now. I'm going there."

In two minutes the captain and second-mate were out on deck, and Mark caught a glimpse of a pistol in his father's breast, and saw him slip two into the officers' hands.

"Gregory, Morgan," he said, "you stop with the men. You, Gregory, with the watch; you, Morgan, keep guard over the forecastle hatch."

"Ay, ay, sir."

The next minute the captain was below, Mark following him, and he heard him utter a deep sigh, almost a groan.

"Is it fire, father?" whispered Mark.

"Yes, my lad, somewhere down in the hold. Heaven help us! we are in a sore strait now. Who first noticed the fire?"

"It was Bruff, father; he is howling now."

"Poor dog! he must not be burned to death. Go and try and find him; but if you find there is any smoke or strange smelling vapour, come back at once."

"Yes, father."

"No, stop; I'll go with you. Where is the dog?"

"Somewhere below."

"Then he must wait. I have the ship and people to try and save."

"Then let me go, father."

"Well, go, my boy, and Heaven be with you."

The necessity for risking his life was put aside, for there was a scuffling of feet over the deck, and the dog came up whining and then tried to go back. Mark called to him, but it was of no use, and he rushed back a little way, barking now fiercely.

"I can't let him go," said Mark hoarsely, and he dashed after the dog; but before he had gone a dozen yards he kicked against something soft, and fell down, but only to scramble up again, for the mystery of the dog's behaviour was explained. His companion the monkey was half overcome by the vapour arising from the fire in the hold, and had crawled, it seemed, part of the way toward the hatch and then sank down, the dog refusing to leave him till he heard voices.

Mark dragged the poor, half inanimate animal to the hatch and carried him on deck, Bruff barking loudly till they were on deck, where a scene of excitement was rapidly growing.

"Silence!" the captain roared as Mark reached his side. "No man is to go near a boat save those who are picked out. Listen, my lads, and you gentlemen as well. I will have discipline observed. And mind this: I'm going to extinguish this fire and save the ship if possible. If it proves to be impossible we'll take to the boats."

"When it's too late," shouted one of the crew.

"No; when it is necessary. Mr Morgan, take three men and the passengers, and put provisions and water in the boats with compasses, and lower them down ready. As soon as each boat is ready place one of the gentlemen armed by her, and he is to shoot down any man who turns coward and rushes for the boats before orders are given. Now, sir, you have your orders. Go on."

"Ay, ay, sir," cried the second-mate. "Widgeon, Small, Smith, this way. Now, gentlemen, quick!"

There was a rush to follow the mate, while the rest of the men on deck stood in a knot whispering and excited, for the smell of burning now grew plainer and plainer, and a dense fume rose from the hatch.

"Now, Gregory, have up the men from the forecastle. Did they hear what was said?"

"Ay, ay, sir," came in a chorus as the men came scrambling up.

"But, captain—the ladies," cried Major O'Halloran excitedly.

"Well, sir, they will behave like English ladies should," said the captain loudly. "My wife will have charge of them, and they will be ready to go down to the boats slowly and in order. Mark, my boy, go to your mother's side and help her in every way you can."

Mark ran to where his mother was standing with Mrs O'Halloran and Mary, all half-dressed and trembling.

"I heard what your father said, Mark, my boy, and we are going to be calm. You can go back and help."

Mark ran back, to find his father giving orders sharply, but in as cool and matter-of-fact a manner as if there was no danger on the way. The pump handiest was rigged with the fire hose attached, and another was being got ready for supplying the buckets with which the men were preparing to deluge the flame.

"Now, Gregory, I must stay on deck. Go down and haul off the hatches. Find as near as you can where the fire seems to be before you begin to work. Remember one gallon well placed is worth five hundred thrown at random."

"You may trust me, Captain Strong," said the mate quietly. "Now then, two men—volunteers. Go down on your hands and knees as soon as we are below, and you will not feel the smoke."

The mate disappeared down the main hatch, and the men stood panting to begin, buckets filled, the hose distended, and one of the sailors holding his thumb tightly over the hole in the branch.

As the men went down the captain drew a long breath, for he realised how difficult it would be to apply the water effectively. The lower deck was growing more dense with smoke moment by moment, and the men who were to direct the water upon the flames would be compelled to stand below in that stifling heat.

It was an awful time, and every soul there realised the horror of the position—a hundred miles from the nearest land, the vessel all of wood and laden with a fairly inflammable cargo, which must be well alight by now to judge from the tremendous fume.

The captain's manner and his orders, however, gave some confidence to the men, who, as they waited, saw one boat lowered and heard it kiss the water, while directly after preparations were being made for the lowering of another.

"That's right," said the captain cheerily. "We have plenty of boats, so there is nothing to fear. Now, Mr Gregory, how is it below?"

There was a faint reply, evidently from a distance, and then a rush was heard, and the two men came up blinded, choking, and coughing violently.

"Where's Mr Gregory?" cried the captain.

"Here!" was the reply, and the first-mate's head appeared above the coamings of the hatchway.

"Well?"

"I can make out nothing, sir," said the mate, setting down his lantern, "only that the smoke is rising all over."

"Can't you localise the place?"

"No."

"Up with the hatches, then, and let's have the water in," cried the captain. "You take the deck now, and I'll go down. Three fresh men here."

Half a dozen stepped forward and part were selected, for the discipline of the ship told, and not a man so much as glanced at the boats now.

"Axes," said the captain, "and as soon as we haul off some hatches pass down that hose, Gregory, and begin handing down the buckets."

"Are you going to stay below, sir?"

"Yes, for a spell," said the captain; and Mark felt a swelling sensation at his breast as he saw his father go down into that suffocating fume to risk his life.

At that moment a hand was laid upon his shoulder, and turning sharply it was to see that the major was just passing him, laden with provisions for the next boat.

"What a soldier he would have made, my lad!" said the major, and passed on.

"He could not have done anything more brave," said Mark to himself, "if he had been a soldier;" and he ran close to the hatchway as the buckets of water were being handed steadily down, while the pumps clanked heavily with the labour given by willing hands.

"Bravo, my lads!" cried Mr Gregory excitedly. "Cheerily ho! Now then."

The men uttered a tremendous cheer, and another and another, and for the next half-hour there was the clanking of the pumps, and the loud slushing noise of the water being thrown below, and the hiss and rush of the constant stream from the hose.

The next hatches were thrown open, risky as the proceeding was; but without a current of air through the ship it would have been impossible for those below to have kept on with their suffocating task.

For the first quarter of an hour the captain and those with him worked like giants, and then came up, to be relieved by the mate and others, those who had been below now passing the water.

But it was blind and helpless work, and when this had been going on for about three-quarters of an hour, and the toilers were getting exhausted by the heat and smoke, Mr Morgan came up and announced that the boats were all ready, and this set four strong men at liberty to help with the water.

The second-mate went down at once, and in a quarter of an hour was relieved by the captain, who came up in turn, looking more stern than Mark had ever seen before.

"I can't help feeling that we are wasting our energy," he said to Mr Morgan. "We are not making the slightest impression."

"I'm afraid not," said the officer addressed. "The fire is increasing."

"Yes; and at any moment it may burst forth with a roar, Morgan," whispered the captain; "but for heaven's sake don't show that we think so."

Another anxious quarter of an hour passed, and matters were evidently growing worse. The water was passed down into the hold with unabated vigour, the men working desperately, but the pillar of smoke which rose from the hold grew thicker and thicker and half hid some of the flapping sails, for now it had fallen quite a calm. From time to time Mark had been to his mother, who was trying, with the major's wife, to whisper hope and encouragement to Mary, the poor girl being horrified at the idea of having to leave the ship in an open boat. But at last there seemed to be no hope to whisper from one to the other. Men grew more stern as they worked with savage energy; and in spite of the time which had elapsed since the first alarm there had not been a murmur nor a whisper of going to the boats, which floated on either side and astern.

But the captain and the two mates knew that before long there must be a rush of fire up through the great hatch, that the sails would immediately catch, and then the masts and rigging would rapidly be a blaze from stem to stern.

Mark had just returned from one of his visits to the front of the cabin, where the helpless women stood gazing at the dimly-seen crowd about the hatch, going and coming, and blotting out the dim light of the lanterns placed here and there. He was close to his father as once Mr Gregory came up, blinded with the smoke, and half suffocated.

"I can't hit upon the place," he said angrily. "We're wasting time, Captain Strong, for the smoke comes up all over, and we have never yet touched its source."

"No," said the captain gloomily; "but we must persevere."

"Oh, yes, sir, we'll persevere; never fear for that."

"If I could only think of what would be likely to light by spontaneous combustion, it might help us."

"I can help you to that," said the mate.

"The fire's gaining fast, sir," said Small, the boatswain, coming up; "Mr Morgan says we must have more hands below."

A thrill ran through the men, and one of them threw down his bucket.

"It's labour in vain, captain," he said. "Better keep our strength for the oars."

"Take up that bucket, sir," roared the captain furiously, "or—"

He did not finish his sentence but took a couple of strides forward, and the man resumed his work.

"I give orders here," said the captain in a loud deep voice. "Now, Mr Gregory, what is it?"

"Matches. A chest or two must have been sent by some scoundrel described as something else, and the pressure or crushing in of the case has ignited them."

"That does not help us, sir," said the captain bitterly. "I want to know where they are."

"Matches—did you say matches?" cried a highly-pitched voice; and Jimpny dropped his bucket and started forward.

"Back to your work!" cried one of the men, but the captain stopped him.

"Yes, matches, my man," he said, for there was a faint hope that Jimpny might know something.

"There were chests of 'em down below where I lay," said Jimpny eagerly. "I could smell 'em strong all the time."

"Smell them?" cried Mr Gregory.

"Yes, sir, onion phosphory smell, you know."

"Hurrah!" cried the first-mate excitedly. "Axes, my lad, and lanterns. We know now."

Three men started forward, but the captain caught the axe from one and a lantern from another, and was about to follow the first-mate when an uneasy movement among the crew arrested him, and he handed the axe and light to Mr Morgan.

"You go down," he said. "I may be wanted here."

It was a wise resolve, for it stayed a rush to the boats just at the moment when a chance was left of saving the vessel.

The captain's stern presence was, however, sufficient to keep the men back; and as the pumping and carrying of water ceased, all stood irresolute, listening to the blows of hatchets and the breaking of wood below.

All doubt as to the right place being found was ended the next minute, for a lurid light shot up from the hatch, and a shout arose from the men, who would have rushed away in panic but for the captain's words.

"Pump! pump!" he roared; "now then, pass on that water."

The hiss and splash of water arose directly from below, showing that the well-directed stream was now striking the fire.

There was a cheer from below, too, which sent a thrill through them; and for the next half-hour the water was sent down with the energy of despair. Then despair began to give way to hope, for the glare from below was fainter; then it grew paler still, and at last nothing but a dense white blinding smoke came up; and directly after the two mates, Small, and a couple of men came staggering up, to fall on the deck exhausted.

"Major O'Halloran!" shouted the captain, handing him his revolver, "take charge here, sir, till these men recover. Now, my lads, we've nearly won. Two men to go with me below."

The captain sprang down, followed by Billy Widgeon and Jimpny, while, as the men cheered and went on pumping, Mark ran to the cabin to return with spirits to revive the exhausted men.

It was a good idea, followed out by Mrs Strong and the major's wife, who handed refreshments to all the men in turn.

Mr Morgan was the first to rise to his feet and try to go down again, but he was too weak, and staggered away from the hatchway.

One of the men started forward, but Mark was before him.

"If my father can live down there, I can," he thought; and he dropped down to crawl through the smoke beside the leather hose of the fire pump, and this led him directly to where his father was directing the nozzle of the branch down through the broken deck, a dim lantern beside showing that a pillar of smoke was slowly rising up and away from the captain.

"That you, Mark? Go and tell them to stop sending down buckets; the hose will do now. The fire is mastered, and—"

He did not finish his sentence, for his voice was choking and husky as Mark ran to the other hatch and climbed up with his message.

It was received with a tremendous burst of cheering, the men who had been handing the buckets dashing them down and seizing each other's hands, while others indulged in a hearty hug.

For the danger was indeed past, and at the end of an hour the men, who had been working in relays, were able to leave off pumping just as the dawn was beginning to appear in the east, while an hour later, when it was broad daylight, the sun rose upon a thin blue thread of steam rising from the hold, and disclosed a group of haggard-looking, smoke-blackened, red-eyed men, utterly worn out by their efforts.

But the ship was saved, and the captain said, "Thank God!"

Chapter Eleven
How Jack proved to be an Impostor

The damage could not be thoroughly ascertained, for a vast deal of mischief must have been done by the water poured into the hold, water which exercised the men's patience a good, deal before it was all cleared out; but the amount destroyed by fire when they worked down to the seat of the mishap was comparatively small, for the smouldering had produced a vast amount of smoke.

One little matter which took place toward the next evening, when order was once more restored, the boats in their places, and everyone assured that there was no chance of a fresh outbreak, deserves recording.

It was close upon dusk when, as Jimpny came slouching along the deck, he encountered the first-mate, and was about to turn aside; but Mr Gregory, who had been chatting with Mark, and patting Bruff, who had won the distinction of giving first warning of the fire, stopped him.

"I'm rather rough sometimes with the men, Jimpny, and I have been particularly hard on you. I can't say a good word for you as a sailor, but you have saved this ship by coming aboard, and if Captain Strong—"

"What about him?" said the captain. "Oh, I see; you were talking to Jimpny here. Ah! he has his strong points, you see, Gregory. I shall not forget what took place last night."

"Don't talk about it, sir," said the stowaway in a shamefaced fashion. "Only too glad to have recollected about the matches."

"Ah," said the mate; "and if you could only recollect the scoundrel who sent them, he should pay for the damage, eh, Captain Strong?"

"Yes," said the captain; "it was a cruel trick, for the sake of saving a few pounds. But, as I said before, Jimpny, I shall not forget last night's work."

"I thank you kindly, sir," said the man, "but I don't want nothing, only a chance to get on a bit."

"And that," said the captain, "you have found."

The damaged cargo was thrown overboard, the hold pumped dry, and exposed to the air as much as possible, and the risk they had all run began to be looked upon as a thing of the past. But there was one personage, if he could be so styled, who did not recover quite so quickly from the troubles of that night, and that was Jacko, who suffered so severely from the overpowering nature of the smoke in the hold that he became quite an invalid, and had to be brought up on deck by Billy Widgeon, and laid upon a wool mat in the sun.

The poor animal was very ill, but his ludicrous aspect and caricature-like imitation of sick humanity excited laughter among passengers and men. He used to lie perfectly still, with his face contracted into comical wrinkles; but his eyes were bright and always on the move, while, if Bruff were away from his side for five minutes, he would begin to chatter uneasily, and then howl till the dog returned, to take hold of his arm, and pretend to bite him, ending by lying down and watching him with half-closed eyes.

After a while Bruff would utter a remonstrant growl, for Jack would set to work trying to solve the problem why the dog's curly coat would not lie down smooth and straight; and in his efforts to produce that smoothness that he was accustomed to see upon his own skin, he sometimes tugged vigorously enough to cause pain.

Mark was watching the pair one day, when Billy Widgeon came up.

"Why don't he get better?" said Mark. "He ought to be all right by now."

Billy Widgeon looked at the monkey, which seemed to be watching them both intently, and mysteriously drew Mark aside.

"That there settles it, Mr Mark, sir," he said.

"Settles what?"

"'Bout his being so ill, sir. I see it all just then in his wicked old eyes."

"I don't understand you, Billy."

"Don't you? He's a-gammoning on us, sir."

"Gammoning us?"

"Yes, sir. That's his artfulness. He likes to be carried down to his snug warm bed, and carried up again, and set here in the sun, and being fed with figs and sweet biscuits and lumps of sugar. It's my 'pinion that he's as well as you and me."

"No, no," said Mark. "I believe the poor thing is very ill."

"I don't, sir, and if you'll let me, I'll cure him in a minute."

"But you'd hurt him."

"Well, sir, I might hurt his feelings, but I wouldn't hurt him nowheres else."

"What will you do, then?"

"Here, hold hard," said Billy in a whisper. "Don't talk so loud; he's a-watching of us."

Mark glanced in the direction of the monkey, and sure enough the animal had drawn himself up a little, and was peering at them over the dog's back, as the latter lay down at full length in the sunshine.

"That's his artfulness, Mr Mark, sir," whispered Billy. "I've had the keer of that there monkey ever since he come aboard, and have stood by him many's the time when the men was up to their larks, and wanted to make him pick up red-hot ha'pennies, and to give him pepper pills to eat. Why, there was one chap used to spend hours setting traps for him. What d'yer think he used to do?"

"I don't know," replied Mark.

"Well, I'll just tell you, sir: he used to shove a little thin old file through a cotton reel, and make a drill of it. You know what a drill is, sir?"

"Yes, I've seen it used," said Mark; "worked to and fro with a steel bow and catgut."

"That's him, sir; only my messmate hadn't no steel bow and no catgut, but he made hisself a sort of bow out of a bit o' cane and some string, and then he used to get a few nuts and stick 'em one at a time in a crack, and drill holes in the sides. When he'd done this, he used to sit o' nights and pick all the kernels out, a bit at a time, with a pin, just the same as you used to do with the periwinkles, sir."

"That I never did," said Mark, laughing, as he seated himself outside the bulwark, and gazed down in the clear water while he listened.

"Well, I used to, sir, and werry nice they is."

"I daresay, but go on."

"Well, sir, he used to pick all the kernels out, and when they was empty, fill 'em up with snuff, and plug the holes with a bit o' tar."

"What for?"

"That's just what I'm a-coming to, sir, only you keeps a-interrupting so. Then he used to put these here nuts full o' snuff in one pocket, and some good uns in the other, and wait till he see Jack. Fust time he did it, I didn't know there was any game on, and I see him give Jack a nut. He cracked it, and ate the kernel, and then my mate give him another, and he cracked and ate that, and held out his hand for more. This time he give him one full o' snuff, but Jack tasted the tar as stopped up the hole, and was too many for him. He wouldn't crack it, but chucked it away. I thought it was only a bad one, for I never smelt the snuff; but what does my mate do but begs a bit o' wheeling sacks o' the steward."

"A bit of what?" said Mark.

"Wheeling sacks, sir; what they fastens up letters with."

"Oh, sealing wax," cried Mark.

"Yes, sir, I said so—sealing wax, and stops up the holes with that. Jack didn't taste that, and first time he cracks one o' them bad uns he gets his mouth full o' snuff, and there he was a-coughing and sneezing for 'bout half an hour, while as soon as he see as it was a trick, he jumps on my back and bites me in the neck, and runs away to get up in the rigging and swear—oh my eye, but he did swear!"

"Nonsense, Billy! a monkey can't swear."

"But he did, sir. He went on calling us all the names he could lay his tongue to in monkey, and whenever my mate give him nuts again, he used to crack 'em on the deck with a marline-spike. Then my mate used to try it on with other tricks, but I wouldn't have it, and I've had no end o' rows with my messmates on account o' that little chap, for I've got to love him like a brother a'most—ah, more than you do your dog; but he's that howdacious artful that I get ashamed on him. He aren't got no more morals than a lobster, as would pinch his best friend's finger off as soon as look at him."

"And Jack bites you, then, same as he would anyone else?"

"More, sir; ever so much more. Why, I'm all over his bites."

"And so you think he's shamming?" said Mark.

"I'm sure of it, and I'm a-going to cure him."

"What will you do?"

"Well, I shall try him easy-like at first, sir, and if that don't do I shall try rope's end."

"No, no, do it by kindness, Billy," said Mark.

"Well, that would be kindness, sir. Monkey's only a monkey, but even a monkey ought to be taught to have some morals. You come along o' me."

Mark leaped down, and followed the little sailor back to where Jack was lying watching them; and as soon as they reached the spot, Billy bent down, placed his hands upon his knees, and poured forth a stream of the most voluble vituperation ever invented by man. He called the monkey all the lazy, idle, good-for-nothing swabs, lubbers, and humbugs possible, while the effect was droll in the extreme.

At first the little animal chattered at him, then he shook his head, then he grew angry, and at last curled himself up, covering his head with his long arms, and howled piteously.

"That's a-touching of him up, sir," said Billy. "He knows it, you see. Why, you miserable little black-faced, bandy-legged sneak," he continued, addressing the monkey, "what's in my mind is to—"

Woof!

Billy Widgeon made a bound, and caught a rope, by whose help he swung himself up into the rigging.

"Lay hold o' that dog, Mr Mark, sir," he cried.

For Bruff, who had been lying down when this tirade began, slowly raised his head, then placed himself in a sitting posture, and ended by staring at Billy, till Jack gave a more piteous howl than any he had before uttered, when the dog gave vent to one low growling bark, and sprang at the sailor.

"Ah!" said Billy, as soon as Bruff was quieted down, "you see he takes his part. Being a dog he don't know no better, sir. I must try another way."

Billy slowly swung himself down, displaying wonderful muscular strength of arm as he did so, and beckoning Mark aside he continued:

"I'm going to show you now, sir. Can you make your dog howl?"

"Oh, yes, Billy, easily."

"How will you do it?"

"Shut him up somewhere, or chain him, and then call him. As soon as he finds he can't get to me, he'll make noise enough."

"That's your sort," said Billy. "You bring him along, then."

Mark called the dog, who leaped up and bounded to him, and five minutes later he was chained up under the main hatch and left, while Billy led the way back to the deck, and helped Mark up to a place of vantage, where they could see the monkey without being seen, and at the same time make the dog hear.

"Now then, Mr Mark, sir. You call old Bruff."

Mark obeyed, and there was a sharp bark in reply, then a volley of barks, a rattling of the chain, and, on the call being repeated, quite a howl.

At the first bark Jack turned his head and listened, then, as the barking continued more angrily, he raised his head and looked in the direction from whence the sounds came. At the first howl he went upon his hands and knees, and uttered an uneasy kind of noise, but threw himself down again, and laid his head close to the deck, shuffling about uneasily.

Then there was peace for a few moments.

"Call him again, Mr Mark, sir," whispered Billy.

Mark obeyed, and, leaning down, uttered the dog's name in a suppressed way, which sounded as if it came from a great distance.

The result was a burst of barking, followed by a series of the most piteous howls, wild and prolonged, such as an animal might utter who was suffering from some terrible torture.

"That'll fetch him," whispered Billy; and he seemed to be right, for, as the howling continued, Jack grew restless. He sat up, listened, threw himself down, turned over, then on the other side, and ended by bursting out into a fit of chattering, and going at full speed along the deck to the hatchway, down which he disappeared at a bound, old practice teaching him that he would drop upon the steps, and his experience being right.

"Come along," said Billy chuckling. "I told you so, Mr Mark, sir; I told you so. I thought it was his games."

Billy Widgeon took up the sheepskin rug, and carried it down below in the forecastle, while, when Bruff was let loose, and the two animals returned on deck, Jack walked slowly to his sunny corner, and stood staring about him as if unable to make out what it all meant, ending by lying down on the bare deck.

But this did not seem to afford any satisfaction, and as if realising that his companion was quite well once more, Bruff charged at him, and rolled him over. Jack retaliated by getting hold of his curly coat with both hands, and making a playful bite at his neck, when the game went on, and for the next half-hour they were frisking and bounding about the deck till they were tired, and Bruff found a sunny spot for a nap, as Jack had sought refuge among the sails.

Chapter Twelve
How Mark first tasted Jungle

A hot but uneventful voyage succeeded, during which the passengers were well roasted in the Suez Canal, and saturated with the steamy moisture of Ceylon, where Mark stared with wonder at the grandees, whose costume strongly resembled that of some gorgeously-decked little girl of fifty years ago dressed up for a party.

Then there was a glimpse of Sumatra, and a stay at busy bazaar-like Singapore, with its shipping of all nations from great steamers down to Malay praus, with their bamboo sides and decks, and copper-coloured wide-nostrilled Malays in little flat military caps, and each wearing the national check sarong, so much after the fashion of a Highlander's tartan, baju jacket, and deadly-looking kris.

"Yes, these are Malays, Mark," said Mr Morgan as they stood gazing over the side at the hundreds of vessels of all sizes. "Clever sailors they are too."

"And pirates?" said Mark.

"Yes, whenever they can get the chance with some one weaker than themselves, but our cruisers have made their trade less profitable than it used to be."

"Should you think these are pirates?" said Mark, pointing towards one particularly swift-looking prau just gliding out of the harbour.

"Very likely," said the second-mate. "They are traders and fishermen, and sometimes all's fish that comes to their net. Not very formidable looking enemies, though."

"They've no guns," said Mark, looking rather contemptuously at the quaint craft.

"Not visible," said the second-mate, "but I daresay they may have two or three down below ready for mounting as soon as they get to sea."

"Very large guns?"

"No; small brass pieces which they call lelahs, and which send a ball weighing perhaps a pound."

"But pirates would not dare to attack a great ship like this," said Mark.

"Oh, yes, they would, for these Malays are fighting men, who always go armed, while they know that our merchantmen, as a rule, are not. But there is not much to fear. They generally attack weak or helpless vessels, and most of their strongholds have been rooted out."

Mark watched the departing prau with no little eagerness as he recalled accounts which he had read of attacks by pirates, poisoned krises, and goodly vessels plundered by the bloodthirsty men of Moslem creed, who looked upon the slaying of a Christian as a meritorious act.

As he gazed after the retiring prau, with its dusky crew, a vessel, similar in shape and size, and which had been lying close alongside of the *Petrel*, heaved up her anchor and set sail.

"Where are they likely to be going?" Mark asked.

"Trading among the islands. They are rare fellows for pushing their way in a slow fashion, but are not such business people as the Chinese."

"One might have thought that this was China," said Mark, as he gazed ashore at the celestial quarter, and noted the great junks manned by Chinamen lying anchored here and there.

The stay at Singapore was not long. The three German students bade the passengers good-bye politely, and took their departure, beaming upon everyone through their spectacles, making quite a gap at the saloon table, though they were not much missed, for they had all been remarkably quiet, only talking to each other in a subdued manner, and always being busy with a book a piece, whose contents were tremendous dissertations on agricultural chemistry, all of which they were going to apply out in Queensland as soon as they got there.

Then one bright morning, well supplied with fresh provisions, and, to Mark's great delight, with an ample store of fruit—from bananas, of three or four kinds, to pine-apples, the delicious mangosteen, and the ill-odoured durian, with its wooden husk, delicate custard, and large seeds—the ship continued her course.

The sea was like crystal, and with the sun hot, but not to discomfort, and a soft breeze blowing, the great vessel glided gently eastward. It was a trifle monotonous, but this troubled Mark in only small degree, for there was always something fresh to take his attention. Sea-birds were seen; then some fish or another reared itself out of the limpid sea, and fell back with a splash. Then a shoal of some smaller kind rippled the surface as they played about, silvering the blue water with their armoured sides.

Small the boatswain and Billy Widgeon rigged up tackle for the lad to fish; and he fished, but caught nothing.

"But then, you know, you might have ketched real big fish," said the little sailor encouragingly, "because, you see, you know they are there."

It was a consolation, but not much, to one who has tried for days to capture something or another worthy of being placed by the cook upon the captain's table.

And so three days of slow progress passed on, after which the progress grew more slow, and ended in a complete calm, just as they were a few miles north of a verdant-looking island, whose waving palms, seen above and beyond a broad belt of dingy mangroves, looked particularly tempting to those who had been cooped up so long on shipboard, where, now that the breeze had sunk, it seemed insufferably hot.

"I suppose it can't be hotter than this, Mr Gregory, can it?" asked Mark, soon after noontide on the second day of the calm.

"Hotter than this?" said the first-mate with an assumed look of astonishment. "Do you hear him, Morgan? He calls it hot!"

"I say, captain," said the major, "how long's this calm going to last?"

"Impossible to say," said the captain. "I am hoping for a fresh breeze at sundown, but I dare not prophesy."

"Well, then, let's have the boat out and manned, and two or three of us go ashore with our guns, to see if we can't shoot something."

The captain hesitated, looked at the sky, at the offing, studied his glass, and then said that there was no prospect of wind before night, and if the major liked, they would make up a little party and go.

"We can get some handsome birds for specimens if we get none for food," said the major, "and perhaps we may get hold of a snake, or a big lizard, to make into a stew."

"Stewed lizard! Ugh!" ejaculated Mark.

"And why not, young fellow?" cried the major. "Once upon a time, as the geologists tell us, the lizard and the fowl were very much alike, only they divided, and while one went on growing more like a bird, the other lost his wings and the feathers in his tail, and ran more upon the ground. Now, I'll be bound to say, sir, that if I shot a lizard, an iguana, or something of that kind, and made it into a curry, you would not be able to tell the difference. Come, captain."

"Oh, I'm not coming," said the captain. "I shall stay aboard and look after my two wives—Mark's mother and the ship. You youngsters can go and enjoy yourselves. You'll go with them, Gregory."

"No, no, I'll stop with the ship," said the first-mate.

"Then it will be to keep me company," said the captain, "for I shall not stir."

"Oh, well then, sir, I will take a run," said Mr Gregory.

"You'll go too, Morgan?"

"I should enjoy it much, sir," said the second-mate.

"All right, then. I'll have the gig lowered and manned. The sooner you are off the better."

"We shall want a man or two to carry the bags," said Mr Gregory. "I'll have Small."

"And I'll have Widgeon," said Mr Morgan, "in case we find ducks."

"I'll have Bruff," said Mark to himself.

"Look here," said the captain; "this island seems to be uninhabited, and it may be a foolish precaution, but I should take it. The crew will have pistols, and I should advise you all to take your revolvers."

"Hot enough carrying our guns," said the first-mate.

"Never mind, sir," said the major. "I remember once in the neighbourhood of Malacca, how a party of us officers landed to get a shot at the snipe, and we were surprised by a party of copper-coloured scoundrels. By George, sir, there we were with nothing better than snipe-shot, sir, to defend ourselves against as murderous-looking a set of haythens as ever stepped."

"What did you do, Major O'Halloran?" said Mark.

"Bolted, sir—I mean we retreated through the bog. Murder! that was a retreat. Take your weapons, gentlemen, and young Strong here shall carry my revolver."

"No," said the captain, "carry your own, major. I'm going to lend him mine."

The preparations did not take long, and soon after the little party were being rowed over the deep dark blue water toward the lonely island, whose shores were right and left of a rocky nature, save in the direction they had chosen, where a slight indentation that could hardly be called a bay offered a splendid landing-place, being a curved stretch of soft white sand.

All at once the water seemed to change colour from dark blue to pale green, and on looking over the side the little party found that, instead of gazing down into the black depths, they were gliding over rocky shallows illumined by the sun, which showed them sea gardens full of growths of the most wondrous shapes, among which startled shoals of fish glided, while others, unmoved by the coming of the boat, played about, showing their armoured sides dazzling with orange and scarlet, blue and gold.

Mark could have stopped for hours, content to gaze down into the lovely transparent waters, but the boat glided on and soon afterwards touched the shore.

"There, my lads," said the first-mate, taking out a big india-rubber pouch of tobacco and pitching it to one of the men, "there is not a great deal of tide, but take care to keep the boat afloat. You can smoke and sleep, but take it in turns, so as to have some one on the watch."

The party sprang out, and the men left in the boat looked rather glum till the major supplemented the first-mate's gift by handing his cigar-case to another of the men.

"One minute," he said. "I think there are eight cigars in there, and I should like one for myself. I'll have that, and then you four men will have a cigar and three-quarters apiece, and you must divide them according to taste."

As this was going on, Mark stood gazing toward the ship, and as he looked he saw a white handkerchief waved.

It was too far off to be sure who waved that handkerchief, but it was either Mrs Strong, the major's wife, or Mary O'Halloran.

"It doesn't matter which," thought Mark, and taking off his cap he waved it in return.

"Now, gentlemen," said the first-mate, "load away, and then we had better decide where to go."

"Not necessary," said the major, closing the breech of his piece and giving the stock an affectionate slap.

"Not necessary?" said Morgan.

"No, sir. This is an uninhabited island, where there are no roads and nature has it all her own way. We shall have to go which way we can."

They struck inland, and the major's words, the result of old experience, proved to be true, for as they reached the belt of jungle, which came within some fifty yards of the shore, it was to find their course stayed by a dense wall of verdure that was literally impassable, the great trees being woven together with creepers, notable among which there was the rattan cane, which wound in and out and climbed up and down in a way that was almost marvellous.

"This is pleasant," said the major.

"Oh, we can get through, sir," said Mark. "Let me go first."

"Do," said the major, with a smile at Gregory, and as the lad pressed forward, "*Experientia docet*," he whispered. "I've been in a jungle before now."

"You can't get through here without an axe to cut your way," said Mark at the end of five minutes, as he stood perspiring and panting, gazing half angrily at the dense thicket.

"Thank you for the information, my lad," said the major smiling; "we knew that before."

"But the island can't be all like this?" said Gregory.

"Oh, yes, it can, my dear sir," said the major. "Islands can be anything out here in the tropics, especially near the Ayquator. Now look here: if we want to get inland—as we do, we must find the mouth of the first river and follow the sides of the stream."

"Sure, sor," said Billy Widgeon, "we passed that same about a hundred yards back, and the bosun and I knelt down and had a dhrink."

The major turned upon little Billy, who had spoken with a broad Irish accent, and stared at him, sticking his glass in one eye so as to have a better look.

"Look here, sir," he said; "you're not an Irishman, and that's a bad imitation of the brogue. Do you hear? You are not an Irishman, I say?"

"Sorra a bit, sor."

"Then is it making fun of me you are?" cried the major, suddenly growing broad in turn.

"No, sir, not I," said Billy, looking as serious as a judge and scratching his head the while.

"Then why did you talk like that?"

"I dunno, sor."

"You don't know, you scoundrel?"

"No, sir. I once lived in Ireland for a whole year, and we used to talk like that; and I suppose it was hearing you say Ayquator, sir, turned on the tap."

Gregory turned away so as to ask the second-mate a question just then, and they both looked very red in the face as the major coughed, blew out his cheeks, and ended by clearing his throat and speaking as a drill-sergeant does.

"You'd better be careful, sir. Now, gentlemen," he added, "suppose we go on."

"I say, bosun," said Billy, rubbing one ear until it was quite red, "what have I been a-doing of?"

"Getting your tongue in a knot, my lad. Come on."

He led the way and Billy Widgeon followed, talking to himself and evidently thoroughly puzzled as to the meaning of the major's attack.

But now the attention of all was attracted by the little trickling stream which made its way from beneath some low growth, and lost itself directly in the sand; but though the way was blocked up it was evident that here was a road into the island, for the dense wall of verdure took somewhat the form of an arch; and as soon as a way had been forced through, Bruff dashed on ahead, splashing about and barking excitedly.

"That's not the way to get sport, is it?" said Morgan. "Hadn't we better call the dog back?"

"Yes, call him," said the major.

Mark called, but the dog had evidently gone beyond hearing, so they followed, finding themselves in an opening about sixty feet wide as soon as they had passed the arch, and with the sky above them, while they were walking in the gravelly zigzagging and winding bed of a little river, with a wall of mighty trees to right and left.

It was evident that at times there was a tremendous current here, and that the whole place was flooded after the heavy rains, for the first-mate pointed out, some five feet from the ground, a patch of dry grass and broken twigs, matted together just as they had been washed down the river and left there from the last flood, while now the stream was reduced to a trickling rivulet, with a pool here and a pool there, some of which were deep and, from the swirling motion of the water, evidently contained big fish.

There was plenty of room for walking at the sides of the gravelly stream, and after progressing some little distance inland, at the bottom of what was like a channel, whose walls were huge tree-trunks towering to a great height, the party began to look out for birds.

"Phew! it's hot work," said Morgan, wiping his face, for the heat in that airless chasm was terrific. "I don't think we shall get many birds."

"I'm not going to try," said Gregory, "for it's neck-breaking work staring up in the tops of these trees."

"We'll find some ducks soon," said the major, "or some ground pigeons. You leave it to me. But where's that dog?"

There was no answer, for evidently no one knew. One thing was certain, however, Bruff had ceased barking, and therefore was not likely to disturb any game that might be on the way.

But though they progressed nearly a mile inland not a bird was visible. There was the loud whizzing whirr of innumerable cicadas, and once or twice they heard a piping cry, after that all was stifling heat and silence.

Their progress was very slow, for after finding there was not much chance of getting a shot the various members of the party began to inspect the objects around them. The major lit his cigar, Mr Gregory examined the sand to see if it contained gold, Mr Morgan tried to find crystals among the pebbles, Mark gazed up at the patches of ferns and orchids among the branches of the trees, and Small and Billy Widgeon took a great deal of interest in the various pools they passed, but found no fish, for at their coming the occupants of the pools took fright and stirred up the sand and mud so that the water became discoloured.

"And I lays as they're eels," said Billy Widgeon, as he carried on a discussion with Small.

"And I says they're big jacks or pikes," replied the boatswain; "but I want to know wheer they're going to feed the beasts."

"Feed what beasts?" said Mark, who was listening to their dispute and gazing down into a good-sized pool where the water was still in motion.

"These here beasts, sir," said Small with a grin. "All on us. These canvas bags is heavy, and I want to see the weight o' the wittles distributed. Much easier to carry that way, and the bottles pitched overboard."

"Hist!" whispered Billy Widgeon, who was peering through some bushes where the little river made a curve.

"Whatch yer found, Billy?"

"Don't make a row, and come and look here, Mr Mark, sir. Here's such a whacking great effet, same as used to be in our pond at home."

Mark hurried to his side, followed by Small.

"Why, it's a 'gator," the latter said as he reached the spot where there was an extensive pool, quite undisturbed, for the screen of bushes had hidden it from the passers-by.

"A crocodile!" said Mark as he gazed excitedly into the clear water at the plainly defined shape of the little saurian, for it was not above four feet long.

"Wait a minute," whispered Billy; "I'll give him such a wonner in the skull," and picking up a heavy piece of stone from the many lying in the half-dry river-bed he pitched it with fairly good aim just above the basking reptile.

There was a dull plunge; the water seemed to be all alive for a few minutes, swirling and eddying, and sending rings to the edge, and then it began to subside, but it was discoloured now, and evident that the one crocodile they had seen was not without companions.

"Now, it's my 'pinion," said Billy, "that if you'd come fishing instead o' shooting, and rigged up rods and lines and tried for these here things in these ponds, you'd have had some sport."

"But what would you have baited with?" said Mark, laughing.

"I d'know," said Billy Widgeon. "Yes, I do," he continued, "dog. They say as 'gators and crockydiles is rare and fond o' dog."

At that moment, by an odd coincidence, there was a piteous howling heard, followed directly after by a shot and then by another.

"Major's shot your dog, Mr Mark," said the boatswain, with a comical look at the captain's son, as they hurried on.

"Bruff wouldn't have howled before he was hurt," said Mark excitedly. "They've shot some wild beast. Why didn't we keep up with them?"

"Hope it ar'n't lions or tigers," said Billy, as he panted on under the load of a bag which contained certain bottles of beer.

"No lions or tigers in an island like this," said Small oracularly. "Oh, there they are."

A turn in the river-bed had brought Mark and his companions in sight of the major and the two mates about a hundred and fifty yards away. Mr Morgan was kneeling down by a pool doing something to the dog, while the major and Gregory looked on.

"I was right," said Small; "they have shot your dog, Mr Mark."

At that moment Bruff caught sight of his master, and uttering a loud bark, he started off from where he stood and came limping on three legs towards Mark, holding his right fore-paw in the air and whimpering piteously.

"Why, Bruff, old chap, what is it?" cried Mark, as the dog came up holding out his leg as if for sympathy; "have they shot you? Why, no; he has been in a trap."

"No," said the boatswain, examining the dog's leg, "he's been fighting and something has bitten him. Wild pig, for a penny."

"Here, Mark, my lad," cried the major, "you nearly lost your dog."

"What's been the matter?" cried Mark.

"A crocodile got hold of him by this pool."

"How, how!" cried Bruff, throwing up his head and giving vent to a most dismal yell, as if overpowered by the recollection.

"Ah, I said as they likes dog," said Billy Widgeon sententiously.

Bang, bang!

Then, as the smoke rose up slowly after the discharge of both barrels of his piece, Morgan exclaimed:

"See that?"

"See it! I nearly felt it," cried the major, drawing back from the edge of the disturbed pool, from which a good-sized crocodile, evidently pressed by hunger, had charged out at his legs. "Did you hit him?"

"Yes, I must have hit him both times, for he swerved at the first shot, and turned back at the second; but small-shot can't do much harm to one of these scaly-hided ruffians."

"Well, I should like to kill that brute," said the major, looking ruffled, and speaking as if he thought that a great insult had been offered to an officer in Her Majesty's service. "Think it was the one which laid hold of the dog?"

"How, how!" cried Bruff piteously, and then, trotting on three legs to the water's edge, he began to bark furiously.

"Call him away," cried Morgan excitedly, cocking his gun and following the dog; "that pool swarms with the beasts."

"Here, Bruff, Bruff, Bruff!" cried Mark.

But his cry would have been too late, even if the dog had obeyed, for at that moment the water was parted and a hideous head with dull gleaming eyes appeared, as one of the monsters made a rush at Bruff.

Morgan was ready for him, though, and quick as thought, from a distance of not more than four yards, he poured the contents of his gun right in the reptile's face, following it up with the second barrel.

To the delight of all, the monster gave a bound and made a clumsy leap out on to the dry ground, where it lay beating the water with its tail, giving it resounding blows, and only lying still to begin again.

"Shall I give him another shot?" said Gregory.

"No; half his skull is blown away," said the major. "Let him die."

"Put the game in the bag, sir?" said Billy respectfully.

"Ask Mr Morgan," said the major haughtily. "I did not fire the shot."

Small took out his great pocket-knife, and cut a rattan to a length of about twenty feet, and after trimming off the leaves readily contrived a running noose at the end, then cleverly contrived to noose one leg as well. A sharp snatch drew the noose tight, and at the boatswain's suggestion everyone took hold of the cane and the struggling reptile was hauled right away from the water to die, proving a goodly weight though it was not above nine feet long.

"There, Bruff, old man," said the boatswain, "suppose you give one of his paws a nip to serve him out. It would be only fair. Shall I give him the knife, sir?"

"No," said Mr Gregory, "the brute is dying. Good heavens! what's that?"

It was unmistakably a shot, and not fired with a fowling-piece, but evidently from some good-sized gun.

Chapter Thirteen
How there was a startling Surprise

"What in the world is that?" cried Gregory.

"That sir?" said the major importantly. "That was the report of a gun."

"Good gracious, man, I know that," said the mate.

"There again," cried Morgan.

"Ship firing signals for recall," said the major. "We are wanted aboard."

"Nonsense, sir!" said Gregory tartly. "We have no guns that would make such a report as that. What?"

This last was to Morgan, who whispered something to him excitedly.

"Pooh! nonsense, man!" cried Gregory again. Just then there was another shot, and another, and the first-mate's face turned of a muddy hue.

"It's fighting, as sure as I'm a soldier," said the major nodding his head.

"You're right, Morgan," said the first-mate hoarsely.

"Come along, quick! There's something wrong aboard the ship."

"Aboard our ship—the *Petrel*?" cried Mark, with a curious choking sensation coming upon him, and his heart beating rapidly.

"There, don't turn like that, my lad," said Morgan kindly, as he clapped the lad on the shoulder. "We only fancy there may be something wrong, and I hope we have been deceived."

"Do you think there will be a fight, Gregory?" said the major excitedly.

"Heaven forbid, sir!" said the first-mate solemnly.

"What are you talking about, sir? and you all the time with a double gun in your fist. Why, it warms the very blood in my veins."

"You see I'm not a fighting man, sir," said Gregory sternly. "Yes," he continued, as he saw the major give him a peculiar look, and reading his meaning, "you're quite right, sir, I am white, and I feel afraid—horribly afraid, as I think of what may be happening to those poor women left on board, and my poor captain and our men."

"And I forgot all about my wife and child," cried the major, increasing his pace, as he wiped the perspiration from his brow. "Come on, gentlemen, for heaven's sake!"

They were already going along at a double, where the rough river-bed would allow, but the progress was very slow, while, though they had come along leisurely, it was astounding how great a distance they had placed between them and the boat.

"For heaven's sake, come on, gentlemen!" said the major again, and at another time his remark would have seemed very Irish and droll, for he was last but one in the little party, and hard pressed to keep up in the intense heat of the inclosed and stifling place.

"Ahoy!" came from ahead just then.

"Ahoy!" answered the mate, who was leading, with Mark next; and the next minute they were face to face with the four men who had been left with the boat. "What is it, my lads?" he panted.

"Pirates, sir, praus!"

"Nonsense!" cried the mate fiercely.

"'Strue as true, sir. We was all half dozing in the boat when we heared a shot, and saw a prau alongside of the old Chicken, and another running up fast, and then there were more firing went on."

"And we ashore!" muttered the mate. "Keep on, my men. What next?"

"Don't know, sir," panted the spokesman; "we come on after you, sir."

"And left the boat?"

"She's got the grapnel out, sir, on the sands."

"But the men in the prau—they could see her."

"Oh, yes, sir; they could see her, sir."

"Man, man! what have you done? They will fetch her off and we shall be unable to follow."

"Don't blame the man, Gregory, but keep on. We may be in time to save her. Let me go first, I can run."

Mr Morgan sprang to the front, and with his gun at the trail ran on ahead at a pace that seemed marvellous; but Mark followed as rapidly as he could, Mr Gregory next, then the major, and the men in single file.

Mark ran on with a horrible feeling of despair growing upon him as he thought of those on board; his heart beat; there was the hot suffocating sensation growing more painful at his throat, and to his misery, in spite of his efforts, the ground was so rough and stone-strewn that he was being left behind, while Mr Morgan had disappeared from his view round one of the sharp turns of the river-bed.

All at once he remembered what he had before forgotten, namely, that he was wearing a belt and pouch, and that in the soft leather holster attached there was the revolver his father had lent him.

He had never fired such a weapon in his life, but he had seen this one handled and loaded, and taking it out, he hardly knew why in his excitement, he cocked it, and ran on with the piece in his hand.

Directly after he found himself close to the low growth through which the little river trickled to lose itself in the sand, and through the opening now broken larger by the passage of so many of his companions he forced his way out and stood upon the sands.

The sight which met his eye took from him the power of action for the moment, and he stood there panting, gazing straight away.

Out at sea lay the great *Petrel* with a couple of praus alongside, and as far as he could see, in his quick glance, the deck was covered with swarthy figures. But there was a scene being enacted close at hand which made him turn giddy, and the blood seemed to run to his eyes.

Mr Morgan had always been a pleasant friend to him from the time of his joining the ship; and now as Mark gazed it was to see him in a peril that promised instant death.

Out there in the bright sunshine on the glancing sea lay the gig in which they had come ashore, and every detail in those brief moments seemed to be photographed on the lad's active brain. The gig was anchored as the men had said, but it was at some distance from the shore to which the men must have waded; and he recollected now how wet they had been. There before him was a small boat of Malay build coming from one of the praus, full of men, some rowing, some standing up with spears in their hands. They were swarthy-looking savages, in plaid sarongs of bright colours, these being twisted tightly about their waists, and in the band thus formed each had a kris stuck, above which the man's dark naked body glistened in the sun.

They were so near that the sun gleamed on their rolling eyes as well as flashed from their spears, two of which were now poised and held by their owners as if about to be hurled.

Mark shuddered as he saw all this, and the rest of the picture before him has yet to be described.

The boat was evidently coming to secure the gig, and to save this, and to prevent their being left alone and helpless upon this island without the means of communicating with the ship, Mr Morgan was straining every nerve. As Mark came out through the bushes, it was to see the second-mate reach the edge of the water, the sea having gone down some distance, and then he had a hundred yards to wade.

How it all happened Mark only knew afterwards from what he was told, but as he grasped the position he stood, as has been said, paralysed, and then in his agony of mind his power of action returned. Running down over the hard sand as quickly as he could, he watched the progress of events, and saw that the second-mate was still some distance from the gig, while the Malays were nearing fast. He was evidently so exhausted that he would not be able to reach the gig first, and as he realised this he paused for a moment, raised his gun and fired at the men.

This drew from them a savage yell, which seemed to be echoed from the praus; when as if to intimidate enemies and encourage the men a small gun was fired on board one of the vessels, and a little ball came skipping over the sea, to go crashing into the jungle.

Morgan went on a few steps farther and fired again; but though his shots evidently told, the men wincing and one falling, but only to spring up again, the fire did not check their progress, and they were fast nearing the gig.

Morgan made another desperate effort to reach it, when first one and then another of the Malays hurled his spear, which went through the air in a low curve.

Mark was now at the edge of the shallow water, with a blind feeling of despairing rage urging him on, boy as he was. What he was about to do he did not know himself. All he realised was that he must try and help Mr Morgan, who, as the spears were hurled, fell headlong into the deeper water, which splashed up around him glistening in the sun.

At this Mark uttered a groan and once more stopped short, as if paralysed, while, with a yell of triumph at the apparent success of their aim, the Malay boat came on and had nearly reached the gig.

But at that moment, as if moved by some other power, Mark raised the revolver and fired point-blank at the advancing boat.

Again and then again he fired—three shots—each, as the little weapon uttered its sharp ringing crack, sending a rifled bullet whizzing at the Malays. One ball struck the water before them, and went over their heads;

the second passed before them, and the third struck one of the rowers, who leaped up with a yell and fell overboard.

This checked the progress of the on-coming boat. But as they dragged their wounded companion back into the boat they uttered another defiant yell, and, in spite of the two remaining shots sent pinging at them without effect, they reached the gig, and one man sprang in to cut the grapnel line.

At that moment there was quite a little volley fired from the edge of the jungle, the major and Gregory discharging four barrels at the Malays, and then with a shout they and the six sailors came running down the sands.

The man in the gig leaped back into the boat, and as the shots from the fowling-pieces were supplemented by bullets from the men's pistols the Malays rapidly paddled away, while Mark thrust back his revolver, and waded out to where Mr Morgan was trying to raise himself in the water and kept falling back.

"No, no, not much hurt, my lad," he gasped. "Got the gig ashore? Hah! That's saved."

He had just caught sight of Gregory's excited face as he came splashing towards him to pant hoarsely:

"That's right! Hold him a moment and I'll be back."

He was back directly with the gig, and by that time the men were about him, and the injured man was carried ashore, two of the sailors dragging the gig right up to the sands, upon which Mr Morgan was laid.

"Let me look," said the major, taking out his knife and ripping up the mate's shirt. "Ah! I see. I've had some experience of these things. A nasty cut, my dear boy, but it isn't wide enough to let out your spirit. You let me put a bandage on it, and I warrant it will soon heal."

"Poisoned, major?" whispered the injured man.

"Poisoned, bedad! Nonsense, man. It's a clean cut in your shoulder, and thank your stars it was there, and not in your chest."

"Look out!" shouted one of the men.

His reason was apparent, for one of the praus, seeing that the Malays were going back discomfited, began firing from her brass gun, sending a ball skipping over the water, and it finally dashed high up among the trees.

"Bah! let him fire," said the major scornfully; "they couldn't hit the Hill o' Howth, and the safest place to be in is the one they aim at. There, my dear boy, that's a business-like job, and it's in your left shoulder. Now, Gregory, what's to be done?"

"We must go off at once in the gig and retake the ship," said Gregory sternly.

"No," said the major, shaking his head, as he gazed out to where the *Petrel* lay.

"Not go, sir, and you've got a wife and child on board."

"And I a father and mother," groaned Mark to himself.

"Yes, sir; and I've got a wife and child on board," said the major sadly; "and I want to help them. But I'm a soldier, Mr Gregory, and I've learned a little of the art of war, and it isn't the way to save people in a beleaguered fort to go blindly and throw away your life and that of your men."

"But those on board, sir," groaned Morgan. "Hadn't we better share their fate?"

"We don't know their peril yet," said the major; "but I know this, if anything has happened to my poor wife—and child," he added softly, "my sword and pistol were in the cabin, and some one or two black scoundrels have gone to the other world to announce what has been done."

"For heaven's sake, sir, don't talk," cried Gregory, who was half frantic with excitement; "what shall we do that is better?"

"There's another shot," said the major coolly. "Go on, my fine fellows, waste all the powder you can."

This shot was wider than the last, and it was followed by one from the other prau which went farther away still.

"What shall we do?" said the major—"by the way, those shot were meant to sink that gig, and they went fifty yards away—Do? Wait and see what the scoundrels go about next."

"But the *Petrel*?"

"Well, they can't sail that away, sir, in this calm."

"But we must retake her," said Gregory.

"Well, we'll try," said the major, "but it must be by cunning, not force. Now, it's my belief that the captain has intrenched himself in the cabin, and that he will keep the scoundrels at bay till we get to him."

"It's my belief, sir, that they are all murdered by those cut-throats. They're Sulu men. I saw two of their praus leave Singapore, and they've been on the watch for us. Idiot that I was to come away. Ah, Mark, my lad, I didn't mean you to hear that," he added, as he saw the lad's ashy face.

"And he's all wrong. Erin-go-bragh!" cried the major; "there, what did I say: that's the captain speaking, I'll swear."

For just then a series of shots were heard from the *Petrel*, and a faint film of smoke was seen to rise.

There was the distant sound of yelling for a time, every shot being followed by a fierce shout, and as the party on the sands tried to realise the conflict going on their feelings were of the most poignant kind.

"He's all right so far," said the major confidently.

"Or beaten," said the mate.

"Beaten, sir? No," cried the major. "If he had been beaten there would have been yelling to a different tune;" and he whispered in the mate's ear: "We should have seen the water splash up about the vessel's stern."

Another shot followed, and then another; but the brass lelahs carried very wildly at that distance, and no harm was done.

"Hadn't we better go off at once, major? There: it is our duty. Come, my lads, in with you."

"Stop!" shouted the major fiercely. "Mr Gregory, we can only succeed in doing good by being sensible. What you propose is rash folly. Counter-order that command, sir, and as soon as it is night we'll see what can be done."

The mate hesitated between an eager desire to afford help and the feeling that the major's science-taught ideas were right.

"Stop, my lads," he said sadly; "the major's right, but I ask you to bear witness, Morgan, that I do this unwillingly."

"The major is quite right," said Morgan, sitting up, his brow knit with pain. "Mark, my lad, we have you to thank for saving the gig."

"Oh, nonsense, Mr Morgan," said the lad.

"It's quite right," he said; "and I believe you saved my life too. At all events, you gave the others time to get up and stop them. Without a boat we should have been helpless."

"Hah! he'd make a capital soldier," said the major, as he shaded his eyes with his hand. "Now, then, Mr Gregory, can your lads get the gig right up the sands and into the river-bed yonder?"

"Yes, sir."

"Do it, then, for one of the praus is coming on so as to be within reach of the shore, and either land men, or try and shatter the gig. Now, I tell you what: we'll intrench ourselves a bit, and then when they're near enough, and I've got the barrel resting in a fork of one of these trees, if I can't pick off a few men with a revolver, my name's not O'Halloran. Now, then, to work."

The order was given; and as the men ran up the gig, one of the two praus was seen to swing slowly round, and then began to move toward them, with her long sweeps dipping regularly in the calm blue sunlit sea, while at that moment, forgotten till then, Bruff, the dog, came limping over the sand, after a laborious journey on three legs, to lie down uttering a low whine at his master's feet.

Chapter Fourteen
How the Major showed himself to be a Man o' War

Poor Bruff had to be contented with a pat on the head, and then creep after his master back through the bushes to where the major was doing his best to bring his military knowledge to bear.

"It's a hard job," he said, "but it must be done. As they come nearer they'll keep on firing at that boat, and in it lie all our hopes. Mr Gregory, that boat must be got through those bushes and hidden."

"All hands," said the mate, in answer; and setting the example, he helped to drag the boat round, so that her bows pointed at the narrow opening in the bushes up to which she was run, and then, with the prau continuing her fire, the gig was with great labour forced through to the open ground beyond, and placed behind some rocks in the river-bed.

The next task was to help Morgan through, and Small and Billy Widgeon went to where he was lying on the sand, with Bruff beside him, sharing the wounded couch.

"No, my lads, I can walk," said the second-mate. "Sorry I am so helpless."

"Not more sorry than we, sir," said Billy Widgeon respectfully. "I wish we'd brought Jacko with us instead of the dog."

"Why?" asked Morgan, as he walked slowly and painfully toward the opening.

"Might have climbed a tree, sir, and got us a cocoa-nut."

"I'll be content with some water, my lad," said Morgan; and then he turned so faint that he gladly took Mark's arm as he came up to help Bruff, who was limping along in a very pitiful way.

"There," said the major, as soon as all were through the gap; "now, I think if we bend down, and lace together some of these boughs across, we shall have a natural palisade which we are going to defend. That's right; fire away; I don't think we have much to fear from their gun. Now, Mr Gregory, if you will examine that side, I'll look over this, and see if we have any weak points on our flanks, and then we'll prepare for our friends."

A hasty look round right and left showed that, save after a long task of cutting down trees and creepers, no attack could be made on the flanks, while, on gathering together in the front, a strong low hedge of thorny bushes separated them from the coming foes—a breastwork of sufficient width to guard them from spear thrusts, while the defenders would find it sufficiently open to fire through.

Points of vantage were selected, and a careful division of the arms made, two of the men, in addition to their pistols, being furnished with the spears which had been thrown at Morgan, and were found sticking in the sand, with their shafts above water.

Small took possession of these, and handed one to Billy Widgeon.

"I'm the biggest, Billy, and you're the littlest," he said, "so we'll have 'em. I don't know much about using 'em, but I should say the way's to handle 'em as you would a toasting-fork on a slice o' bread, these here savage chaps being the bread."

"Or," said Billy, making a thrust through a bush, "like a skewer in a chicken. Well, I'm a peaceable man, Mr Mark, sir, and if they let me alone and us, why it's all I ask; but if they won't, all I hopes is, as two on 'em'll be together, one behind the other, when I makes my first job at 'em with this here long-handled spike."

"Now, my lads," said the major, who seemed to be enjoying his task, "just two words before we begin. I'm going to tell you what's the fault of the British soldier: it's firing away his ammunition too fast. Now, in this case, I want you to make every shot tell. Don't be flurried into shooting without you have a chance, and don't give the enemy opportunities by exposing yourselves. Lastly, I need not tell you to stick together. You'll do that."

"Ay, ay, sir."

"That's good, and now recollect you are Englishmen fighting for women as well as yourselves."

"Ay, ay, sir."

"Mr Gregory lets me command, because I'm used to this sort of thing, so don't mind me taking the lead."

"No, sir, we won't," chorused the men.

"Very well, then: don't be bloodthirsty, but kill every scoundrel you can."

There was a hearty laugh at this, for, even in times of peril, your genuine British seaman has a strong appreciation of fun, and in spite of their position the major's ways and words had a spice of the droll in them.

Just at that moment Morgan came up, pistol in hand, his gun having been given to one of the men.

"Why, my dear Mr Morgan," said the major, "this is not right. You are in hospital, sir."

"No," said Morgan grimly; "I am better now, and I'm not a bad shot with a revolver."

"You had better leave it to us, Morgan," said the first-mate. "You and Mark Strong go and lie down in shelter."

"Oh, Mr Gregory," cried Mark.

"Why, you miserable young cockerel," said the major, "you don't want to fight?"

"No, sir; but it seems so cowardly to go and hide away when the men are fighting."

"So it does, my lad, so you shall stop with me, and load for me while I'm firing. Come along. Now, my lads, steady, and not a Malay pirate shall get through that bush."

Every man uttered a low cheer, and settled in his place, well hidden from the occupants of the coming prau, and ready to deliver his fire when the enemy came near.

It was coming steadily in, the sweeps being worked by the motley crew of scoundrels on board with a regularity which drew rough compliments from the men, and made Mr Gregory utter a remark.

"Oh, yes," said the major, "they row well enough, but so did the old galley-slaves in the convict boats. Now, I won't use my revolver yet, but I've got four cartridges of BB shot that were meant for cassowaries or wild swans. Now, Mark, I think I'll give our friends their first peppering with them."

"They will not kill, will they, sir?" said Mark anxiously.

"No, not at the distance I shall fire from. Ah, that was better aimed," he said, as the brass lelah on board the prau was fired, to strike the sand in front of the natural stockade, and then fly right over the sailors' heads. "I'll lay a wager, Gregory, that our friends don't make such another shot as that to-day."

Then followed a few minutes of painful inaction, which seemed drawn out to hours. While the prau swept slowly in, the sun beat down with terrible force, and there was not a breath of wind to cool the burning air. Fortunately, though, the little stream gurgled among the stones, and was so handy that the men had but to scoop out holes in the sand, or to form them by turning over some huge stone, to have in a few minutes tiny pools of clear cool water with which to slake their thirst.

On came the prau, with her swarthy crew crowding her bamboo decks, and their dark skins shining in the sun. Their spears bristled, and as they leaned over the side and peered eagerly among the bushes, the party ashore felt to a man that once they were in the power of so savage-looking a crew no mercy must be expected.

The men lay close, and to the enemy there was nothing to indicate that there would be any defence.

This seemed to make the Malays more careless, for they came on excitedly, and, as it was about low water, made no difficulty in that calm sea of running their vessel's prow right ashore.

Then there was a few minutes' pause, which the defending party did not understand.

"I see," said Mr Gregory, at last; "they're getting the lelah in a better place, so as to have another shot at us before the men charge."

The first-mate was right, for all at once there was a loud roar, and a charge of stones, it seemed, came hurtling over their heads, and flew up, to break down twigs and huge leaves from the trees, while, as the smoke rose, the Malays leaped overboard on either side, yelling excitedly, splashing in the water, and then began to wade ashore.

"Eighty yards is a long shot," said the major just then, "but I may as well give them a taste of our quality."

"No; wait a few moments," said Gregory, for the men were collecting in a cluster, and directly after began to rush up the sands toward the opening, yelling furiously and shaking their spears, ready to hurl. "Now," said the mate.

By this time the Malays were little over fifty yards away, and taking careful aim low down the major drew both triggers so quickly, one after the other, that the report was almost simultaneous.

The smoke as it cleared away unveiled a strange scene of men running here and there evidently in pain, others were spluttering about and leaping in the water, others were returning hurriedly toward the prau, while about a dozen still came on yelling with rage and brandishing their spears.

"Now," said the major, "fire steadily—gunners only. Pistols quiet."

Two shots followed, then two more, and the effect was an instantaneous retreat. One man dropped, but he sprang to his feet again and followed his companions, the whole party regaining the prau and climbing aboard, while the firing was resumed from the lelah.

"Now I call that pleasant practice, gentlemen," said the major. "Plenty of wounded, and no one killed. It has done some good work besides, for it has let the captain know we are all right, and ready to help. By Saint George—and it's being a bad Irishman to take such an oath—see that!"

"See what?" cried the mate.

"The flag, Mr Gregory. Look!" cried Mark.

For plainly enough now a signal was being made from one of the stern windows of the ship, and as far as they could make out it was a white cloth being waved to and fro.

"Now if we could only answer that," said the major, "it would encourage them."

"I could answer it, sir," cried Mark.

"How, my lad?"

"Give me a big handkerchief, and I'll climb up that tree and tie it to one of those branches."

"Capital, my lad," said the major. "But, no; risky."

"They could not hit me, sir," cried Mark; "and it's like taking no notice of my father's signals to do nothing."

"I think he might risk it, major," said Gregory.

"All right, then, my lad. Go on."

Mark started, and after a struggle reached an enormous pandanus, one of the many-branched screw-pines. It was not a very suitable tree for a signal staff, and there were cocoa palms and others of a far more appropriate kind, but these were unclimbable without notches being prepared for the feet, whereas the pandanus offered better facility.

Still it was no easy task, and it was made the more difficult by the fact that the Malays began firing at him with their brass gun, a fact enough to startle the strongest nerves.

But Mark recalled for his own encouragement the fact that the major had laughingly announced the spot at which the enemy aimed as being the safest, and so he climbed on till about thirty feet above the ground he managed to attach the major's great yellow handkerchief, so that it hung out broadly, and then came down.

Four shots were fired at him as he performed this feat, and on rejoining the major and Mr Gregory, the former laughingly said that not a shot had gone within fifty yards of him.

"But I tell you what," he continued, "that's a bad signal—the yellow flag; they'll think we have got fever."

"So we have, sir," said Morgan grimly—"war fever."

"Look!" cried Mr Gregory; "they see the flag signal, and are answering it. Do you see?"

It was plain enough; two flags were held out of the cabin-window, and after being waved withdrawn.

"Yes," said the major, "it's mighty pretty, but there's one drawback—one don't know what it means."

The firing from the lelah was kept up at intervals, but every shot went over them, whether fired point-blank or made to ricochet from the sands. There was tremendous bustle and excitement on board the prau, but no fresh attempts were made to land, and as the long, hot, weary hours crept on the question rose as to what would be the enemy's next move.

"They'll wait till dusk and attack us then," said Mr Gregory.

"No," said the major, "I think not. These people never seem to me to be fond of night work. I think they'll wait till the tide rises and then go back."

"Without destroying our boat?" said Morgan.

"Yes, my lad. It's bad warfare to leave an enemy behind; but you'll see that is what they'll do."

The major proved to be right, for after a time the prau began to move slowly round, and they saw it go back leisurely, the great sweeps dipping in the calm blue sea and an ever-widening line left behind.

"That's one to us, my lads," said the major, "and next time it's our play."

The men gave a cheer, and Small rose and came forward.

"Lads says, sir," he began respectfully, "that if it were all the same to you they'd like me to pipe down to dinner."

"Of course," said Gregory. "Where are the provisions?"

"Well, you see, sir, when we all come running down, the bags o' wittles was chucked away in the jungo—in the wood, sir."

"Then a couple of men must go after it—those who threw it away."

"Well, sir, seeing as it were me and Billy Widgeon, we'll go arter it, if you like."

The necessary permission was given, the two men departed, and at the end of an hour returned to find their companions still watching the praus, which were both made fast to the ship.

"Thought as the crockydiles had been at it, sir," said Small grimly; "but we found it at last. I've brought Billy Widgeon back safe."

"Of course," said the mate quietly. "Why not?"

"Well, you see, sir, there was one crock took a fancy to him, and we see another lying on the edge of the pool, smiling at him with his mouth wide open; but Billy wouldn't stop, and here's the prog."

Chapter Fifteen
How the Crew of the "Black Petrel" were in sore Straits

The supply of food, supplemented by the bottles of beer, which were equitably distributed so as to give all the men a tiny cup or two, had a wonderful effect upon their spirits, so that the rest of the afternoon was passed waiting patiently for the night, the sailors expressing themselves as willing to do whatever their leaders bade.

Billy Widgeon was the spokesman, Small occupying a sort of middle position between officers and men.

"We says, sir," he began, addressing the major—"I mean they says as we—I mean they ain't fighting men, never having 'llsted or gone in the ryle navy; but in a case like this they will—no, we will, for of course I ar'n't going to stand back—have no objection to a bit of a set-to so as to lick the niggers. For if ever niggers wanted licking it's niggers as'll take advantage of a ship being in a calm, and part of her officers and crew away, and—and—here: what was I to say next, lads?"

Billy Widgeon had come to a stand-still, and had to appeal to his companions.

"That's about all," said one of the men. "I'd stow it now."

"Right, mate; I will," said Billy, who had recovered himself a little and was beginning to think of a great many more things he would like to say. "So we're ready, sir, whether it's fisties or pistols, and if Mr Gregory yonder and Mr Morgan—as we're werry sorry he's wounded—don't give no orders another way, we'll do as you wants us to, so what's it to be? Theer, that's all."

"Thank you, my lads, thank you," said the major quietly.

"Not much of a speech, were it?" said Billy to one of his forecastle mates.

"What, yourn?" said the man.

"Tchah! No! The major's."

"Didn't think much o' yourn anyhow," said the man.

"Why didn't you make one, then?" growled Billy fiercely.

"There, don't get up a quarrel, mate," said the man. "P'r'aps we shall all be trussed up like larks 'fore to-morrow morning; so let's be friends."

"Eight," said Billy, slapping his great palm into his companion's; and Mark smiled to himself as he thought how much these big men were like school-boys in spite of their years.

The evening drew near after what seemed to be an interminable space of time, and to the great delight of Mr Gregory there was no change in the weather. There had been every probability of a breeze springing up at sundown, but the great orange globe had slowly rolled down and disappeared in the golden west, amidst the loud barking of the hornbills and the strident shrieks of flocks of parrots, and not a breath of wind was astir. Then came down the night, a purply black darkness spangled with stars overhead and reflected in the water, and with that darkness a hot intense silence.

"Finish your pipes, my lads," said the major, "and then we're going afloat once more."

The men replied with a cheery "Ay, ay, sir," and at once extinguished their pipes in token of their readiness; and soon after, in accordance with plans made by the three officers, Small assisting at their council, the boat was safely run down through the bushes, over the sand, and away into the calmly placid sea, which wavered from her touch in golden spangles, and then in silence all embarked, the rowlocks being muffled with handkerchiefs and jacket sleeves.

It was not a long journey, but had to be taken with the greatest of caution, for the slightest sound would have betrayed their whereabouts, and, in view of this, Mr Gregory had whispered to Mark:

"I don't want to oppose your dog coming again, Mark, but can you depend upon his being quiet?"

"Oh, yes, Mr Gregory."

"I mean when we near the praus. Will he bark?"

"No," said Mark confidently.

"Good. Pull easy, my lads; we've plenty of time. If the wind holds off,"—he added to himself, for he knew that with ever so light a breeze the *Petrel* would be soon taken far beyond their reach.

As the boat left the shore Mark strained his eyes to make out the ship and its attendants; but all was dark, save the spangling of the stars, till they were about a hundred yards from the shore, when a beautiful phenomenon caught the lad's eye, for wherever the oars disturbed the water it seemed as if fiery snakes darted away in an undulating line which seemed to run through the transparent black water in every direction.

Mark only checked himself in time, for his lips began to form ejaculations of delight as he found that he was about to call upon those about him to share his pleasure.

At times the sea appeared to be literally on fire with the undulating ribbons of light, and as Mr Gregory realised this he had to reduce their speed and caution the rowers to dip their oars with greater care.

They glided on through the darkness, looking vainly for the ship, and from Mr Gregory's manner it soon became evident that he was doubtful as to whether they were going in a straight line towards it, for after a few minutes he made the men cease rowing, and bent down to take counsel with Morgan, who sat in the bottom of the boat resting his back against one of the thwarts.

"You ought to be able to see her now," whispered Morgan, "but I fear that the current has carried her more east."

"That's what I was afraid of," said Gregory softly, "and I'm afraid of missing her. If she would only show a light!"

Just then there was a low, ominous-sounding growl which made Mark hug the dog's head to his breast and hold it tightly, while he ordered it to be silent.

There was occasion for the growl; and it was their temporary saving that the men had ceased rowing, for the fiery look of the water would have betrayed their whereabouts as it did that of a vessel coming toward them, and they were not long in realising that it was one of the praus being rowed cautiously toward the shore.

The prau came on with the golden snakes undulating away at every dip of the sweeps, and right and left of the keel as she softly divided the water. All was silent on board, and nothing visible but what seemed like a darkening of the horizon; but, as he held Bruff tightly to keep him silent and stared excitedly at the passing vessel, Mark pictured in his mind the deck crowded with fierce-looking opal-eyed savage men, spear and kris armed, and ready to slay if they had the chance.

Those were perilous moments; for as the prau drew near it seemed impossible for its occupants to pass without seeing the gig lying little more than a few yards away. And as the English party sat there hardly daring to breathe, and knowing that a growl from the dog would result in a shower of spears, it seemed as if the vessel would never pass.

But pass it did, with the wonderful display of golden coruscations undulating from the spots where the long oars softly dipped still going on, but gradually growing more faint, and at last invisible.

"Bless that dog!" said Mr Gregory, drawing a long breath. "Now, my lads, pull softly. We're in the right track. Give way."

The men rowed, and a whispered conversation went on between the three heads of the little party.

"Couldn't be better, gentlemen," said the major. "Here we have half the enemy's forces gone ashore, and the other half not expecting us; that's clear, or else they wouldn't have sent that expedition to surprise us. What do you mane to do?"

"Get close up under the cabin-window," said Mr Gregory, "if we can find the ship. If we can lay the boat right under the stern we shall be safer from those on deck, for they could not see us."

"Yes," said the major gazing over the sea; "but, my dear sir, we must find the ship first before we can get to her stern."

"Is there no light?" said Morgan at last, after they had been rowing softly about for quite a quarter of an hour.

"No, not a spark," whispered Mr Gregory. "I've tried to keep in the course by which the prau came when it passed us, but the darkness is so deceptive that we might as well be blind."

Another ten minutes or so were passed and still they could not make out the tall spars and huge hull of the ship, while a feeling of despair began to come over Mark as he asked himself whether he should ever look upon those he loved again. He had never before realised the vastness of the ocean and how easy it was to go astray and be lost, for as minute by minute glided away, the search for the great ship became more hopeless, and the darkness that was over the sea began to settle down upon the young adventurer's heart.

"I'm about done, major," whispered Mr Gregory. "We're just as likely to be going right away from her as to her."

"A current must be setting strongly now at the change of tide," said Morgan. "We shall have to wait for day."

"And throw away our chance of doing some good!" said Mr Gregory pettishly. "Here you, Mark Strong, this dog of yours seems as if he could do anything. Do you think if we put him in the water he'd swim toward the ship?"

"If I let him go into the water he would begin to bark loudly," whispered Mark.

"Ah! and do more harm than good," said the major. "Now, look here, gentlemen: my wife and daughter are on board that ship, and we've got to find her, so let's have no talk of giving up, if you please."

"Give up, major!" said the first-mate with an angry growl; "don't you run away with that idea. I'm not going to give up."

There was so much decision in Mr Gregory's tone and words that Mark's heart grew light again, and the horrible picture his fancy painted of his father and mother being left at the mercy of the Malays once more grew dim.

"What shall we do, then, next?—go west?"

"No, sir, I think north," replied Gregory. "There isn't a breath of air, so we cannot have gone far. What say, Morgan?"

"The tide may have taken her many miles," said the second-mate, speaking painfully; "but try north."

The first-mate was about to whisper to the men to easy on the port side when all at once there was a flash at a distance, followed by a sharp report.

"From the ship," said Gregory. "A signal."

"No, no," said Morgan peevishly. "That is from the shore."

"Oh, impossible!" said the major. "That shot was fired from the ship."

Another flash, evidently from half-a-mile away in quite a different direction.

"That is from the ship," whispered Morgan as the report of the gun went vibrating through the dark night air.

"No, no, man; from the shore," said the major pettishly.

"I stake my life, sir, it is from the ship," said Morgan, straining his eyes in the direction from which the last signal had been made.

"Morgan's right, major," said Gregory firmly.

"Yes; that there last shot was from seaward," whispered the boatswain. "I haven't not no doubt about that."

"Steady, my lads, and give way now," whispered Gregory; and the boat was turned and rowed steadily for quite a quarter of an hour as nearly as they could tell in the direction from which the last shot had come.

At the end of that time, though, they were as badly off, it seemed, as ever, for they ceased rowing, to find that the darkness was more dense, for a soft mist was gathering overhead and blotting out the stars.

"If we only dared hail," muttered Gregory. "Major, this is horrible. Pst!"

This was consequent upon a faint flash of light appearing not twenty yards away; then it seemed as if there was a tiny flame burning, and directly after complete darkness.

"The *Petrel* or a prau," said Mr Gregory in a low voice, and with his lips to the major's ear.

"The ship," said Mark excitedly, striking in.

"How do you know, lad?"

"By the height up."

"You're right, boy; so it is."

"And there," said Mark softly, "it was someone lighting a cigar."

"Yes; I can smell it. But hist!"

"It was my father," said Mark excitedly. "I know what he's doing: smoking at the cabin-window."

"May be," whispered back the mate cautiously. "Here, pull that starboard oar, Small."

The boatswain obeyed, and the one impulse seemed to send them all into a greater darkness, while the odour of tobacco pervaded the air quite strongly and a little point of light shone above their heads.

"Father!" whispered Mark, for he could not control himself, and the word slipped from his tongue.

"Mark? Hush!" came back to set all doubts at rest.

"Here, hook on, Small, keep the boat as she is," said Mr Gregory; and this was done in silence; but it was some few minutes before they were in their former position, all being done with the most extreme caution.

"Have you a rope, Strong?" said Gregory in a low voice.

There was no reply, but the glowing end of the cigar disappeared from where it shone some fifteen feet above their heads, and at the end of a few minutes something was lowered down, which proved to be so many sheets tightly rolled up and knotted together.

The first-mate seized the extemporised cord and drew hard upon it to see if it would bear. It proved to be made quite fast, so he turned to Mark:

"Now, young un," he said, "you can climb that rope. Go up and hear from your father how matters stand."

Mark said nothing, but seized the soft cord, and, with the mate's help, was soon half-way up, but the rest, as he quitted the support of the mate's shoulders, was more difficult. Still, the knots helped him, the distance was short, and, after a little exertion, he felt a couple of strong hands passed under his arms, when, after a bit of scuffling and plenty of hoist, he felt himself half-lifted in at the cabin-window, and the next instant clasped in a pair of softly-clinging arms.

"My poor boy!" whispered Mrs Strong.

"Hist! don't speak! Don't make a sound!" said the captain sternly. "There may be a sentry at the door."

"But, father, are you hurt?"

"A little, my boy; not much," said the captain.

"Terribly, Mark," whispered Mrs Strong; and the lad felt a shudder run through him.

"No, no! Don't alarm the boy," said the captain; and just then Mark felt a little hand steal into his, and heard a faint sob, while another hand was laid upon his shoulder.

"Miss O'Halloran! Mary!" whispered Mark.

"Yes: the major?"

"Papa?"

Two voices whispered those questions at the same moment.

"He's quite right, and down there in the boat," said Mark.

"Now, my boy, quick!" said the captain, catching Mark by the shoulder; "who's below in the boat?"

"All of them, father."

"Unhurt?"

"Mr Morgan has got a nasty spear wound."

"Ah!" ejaculated the captain. "Very bad?"

"Through his shoulder, father."

"Did you meet one of the praus?"

"Yes, as we came across."

"Gone to destroy your boat," said the captain. "I heard the orders given. Now go down to the boat and tell Mr Gregory that we are partly prisoners here. I say partly, because I have barricaded the cabin-door. Tell him that one of the praus came alongside to beg for water. The crew said they were dying for want of it, and the scoundrels had hidden their arms. I can hardly tell now how it was done, my lad, but one moment I was giving orders for the water to be passed over the side, the next I was lying on the deck struck down, and when I came to, the men were secured below and the deck was in possession of the Malays, a second prau having come up and helped the men of the first."

"But we heard firing, father?"

"Yes, my boy, so did I, as if it was in a dream, and I found afterwards that my poor lads had made a brave fight of it, and driven the first party out, but the crew were without a leader, and the Malays fired into them till they came close alongside and boarded together."

"Was—was anyone killed?"

"Don't ask now, my lad. Tell Gregory we were driven in here, and the ladies are all right. Ask him to climb up and talk the matter over with me, as to what we shall do."

"Pst!" came from the cabin-window, and directly after Mr Gregory climbed in.

"I could not wait," he said, "and I found the rope would bear me. Now, Strong, how do matters stand?"

The captain explained the position.

"And the men—down below deck?"

"No," said the captain bitterly; "half the poor fellows died like men—no, like sheep," he cried excitedly, "for they had no weapons but the capstan bars. The other half were sent afloat in one of the boats, I suppose, and one of the praus kept firing at them till they got beyond reach."

"Ha!" ejaculated the mate.

"Now go down and talk with the major. Poor Morgan is helpless?"

"Yes, quite."

"Well, ask the major if he will stand by me. There are only two courses open. We must either try and retake the ship or escape at once before morning."

"Which do you think is best, Strong?" said Mr Gregory huskily.

"I'm pulled two ways, Gregory. I want to save my ship; but, on the other hand, there is the thought of these helpless women and our position if we should fail."

"Well," said Gregory slowly, "I'm for the fight. We've got some weapons now, and hang me if I'm going to strike to a set of treacherous pirates like this."

The captain grasped his hand and began smoking.

"Quiets the pain a bit," he whispered. "An ugly wound; but I don't think the kris was poisoned."

"Why, Strong," said the first-mate sympathetically, "we ought to give up and escape."

"My dear Gregory, I'm quite a cripple; but if you and the others will stand by me, we'll stick to the ship till she sinks, if we have such bad luck as that; and if she doesn't sink, we'll save her."

"I'll answer for it they will stand by you," said the mate, and going to the window he lowered himself down, and told those below how matters stood.

"Now, major," he said, "what do you say?"

"Say, sor!" whispered the major; "why, there isn't anything to say. I've paid for my passage and the passages of the wife and daughter to Hong-Kong, and does Captain Strong think I'm going to let them finish the voyage in a scrap of an open boat. No, sor; fight, sor, fight, of course."

"Will you stand by us, my lads?" said Mr Gregory.

"Will we stand by you, sir!" growled Small. "Why, of course we will. I want to make J Small, his mark, on some of their brown carkidges. Don't you, boys?"

A low whispered growl came in reply, a sound that was as full of fight as if it had been uttered by some fierce beast.

"That will do then," said the first-mate. "You slip up there first, Billy Widgeon, and you others go next. Stop: Billy, send down a table-cloth."

"Table-cloth, sir?"

"Yes, to tie the dog in; we mustn't leave him."

Widgeon went up, his mates followed one by one, for the cotton rope stood the strain, and then a big white table-cloth was dropped into the boat.

"Now, Bruff, my lad, you've got to go up like a bundle. Will you go quietly, or are you going to betray us?"

The dog made no resistance, but allowed himself to be stowed in the middle of the cloth, which was tied up bundle-wise, the end of the sheet-rope was attached, a signal made, and the animal drawn up and in at the cabin-window without his uttering a sound.

A minute more and the rope came down.

"Can you bear it round you, my lad?" whispered Gregory to Morgan.

"I'll bear anything," was the calm reply; and he did not wince as the rope was secured about his chest. Then a signal was given, and he was drawn up, to be dragged in at the cabin-window with his wound bleeding again and he insensible.

"Can you climb up, major?" said Gregory as the rope came down again.

"No, sir," said the major stoutly. "I shall have to be hauled up like a passenger, I suppose. I am no climber. But won't they hear us on deck?"

"I wonder they have not already," said the mate, though all was perfectly still, and the stern stood out so much that they were in some degree protected.

"This is confoundedly undignified, sir, confoundedly," said the major, as the cotton rope was secured about his waist. "Hang it, Gregory, I don't like it, sir. Can't I climb?"

"You said you could not. Will you try?"

"No; it's of no use. But really I do object to be swinging there at the end of a string like a confounded leg of mutton under a bottle-jack. Not too tight."

"No; that knot will not slip. There, shall I give the signal?"

"Yes—no—yes; and let me get it over as soon as I can. Good gracious! if the men of my regiment were to see me now!"

The signal was given, the rope tightened, and the major uttered a low cry as he was sharply lifted off his feet, and before he could check himself surely enough he began to turn slowly round and round as if he were being roasted.

Left alone now, Mr Gregory waited patiently till the rope came down again, when he caught it and secured it round his waist, after which he went to the bows of the gig, took the painter, and by pressing the stern of the ship managed to draw the prow close up to the hull, and then after a little search he discovered a ring-bolt upon the rudder-post, to which he drew the boat, running the painter right through and making it fast, so that the little vessel was well out of sight, unless seen by the crews of one of the praus.

This done he went to the stern, tightened the rope, and found that if he swung off he would go into the sea with a splash, an act sufficiently noisy to arouse the watch presumably set on deck.

This was out of the question, and he was about to lower himself into the water when the thought occurred to him to feel about the boat as to whether anything had been left; and it proved to be as well that he did, for beneath one of the thwarts his hand came in contact with a bag which proved to contain the ammunition and one of the revolvers.

Gregory secured the bag to his neck, hoping and believing that he would be able to keep it dry; and now, taking well hold of the rope, he let himself glide down over the side of the boat into the deep water, hanging suspended till the men above began to haul and without leaving him to climb, he was drawn up to the window and helped in, to stand dripping on the floor, and far more concerned about the contents of the bag than his own state.

Chapter Sixteen
How Mark passed a bad Night

The prisoners had been gathered together in the cabins, of which the whole were in their possession, and were still discussing various plans for proceeding when the splash of oars was heard through the open cabin-window, and as Mark was one of the first to run and look out he could plainly see that the prau they had passed was returning, her course being marked by the undulating streams of light which flashed away at each dip of the long sweeps.

In a few minutes the vessel had passed, going right up to the bows of the *Petrel*, and now a loud burst of talking was heard on the night air. It rose and fell and rose again, quite a discussion full of commands and protests, so they seemed from the tones of the voices, lasting for a full quarter of an hour, and then all was still, not so much as the tramp of a foot being heard upon the deck of the ship.

The ladies had retired into one of the cabins, the sailors seated themselves quietly in one corner, sipping the cold grog the captain gave them, and Mark sat near his father listening to the discussion going on.

The major was for a bold attack upon the pirates and driving them overboard.

Morgan, who was wounded, proposed that the ladies should be lowered down into the boat at once, and that they should escape and take refuge upon the island.

Gregory said scarcely anything, and when pressed he cried in a harsh tone:

"I'm ready for what my captain settles to do. Then I'll do my best, but I'll not take any responsibility."

"But you'll fight, Gregory, if called on, eh?" said the major.

"Try me," replied the first-mate gruffly.

"Well, Captain Strong, what's it to be?" said the major; "a bold attack upon the scoundrelly set of jail-sweepings and a lesson for them in British valour?"

"No attack, Major O'Halloran, but a bold defence, sir. Weak as we are it is the better policy."

"Then you mean to hold the ship, Strong?"

"To the last," said the captain sternly.

"Good!" said Gregory. "Then let's get to work before it's daylight."

"What are you going to do?"

"First thing, sir, is to get out a few tools I have in my cabin and take down two or three doors."

"What for?"

"To screw up over the skylights, for that is our weak point. The scoundrels could stand up there and shoot us down or spear us as they pleased."

"Right!" said Captain Strong shortly. "And while you do that we'll strengthen the barricade across the door."

"Serve that the same," said the first-mate. "A couple of doors can be screwed across silently. Then up against them you can plant your chests and cases and the place will be as firm again."

"Ah, Gregory, you were meant for a soldier!" said the major sadly. "My word, sir, what a sapper you would have made!"

"And what should I have done for a first-mate?" said the captain pleasantly.

"Well, we won't stop passing compliments," said the major. "Let's get to work. You're hurt, captain, so you sit down and give orders to your boy to lay out the fighting tools. Get 'em all ready, ammunition and all. Bedad, sir, I haven't had a fight since I was up in the hill country having a turn at the niggers, and this promises to be a rare treat."

"I'll have everything ready for your feast, major," said the captain sadly.

"Hold up, man, and don't talk as if you had lost a half-sovereign, or, worse still, your ship. Keep a good heart, as I do. Sure, captain, haven't I got my two darlings on board—and do you think I don't love them?" he added in a whisper.

The captain's answer was a firm grip of the hand extended to him in the dark.

"That's it, my boy," whispered the major. "Now, next time you speak try and forget you are wounded, if you can, and say things cheerily. It puts heart in your men and yourself too. That's the beauty of being a soldier, sir. He isn't often called upon to fight; but when he does he has to take his wounds pleasantly, and set an example to his men by dying with a smile on his lip and a laugh in his eye."

Meanwhile Mr Gregory had got out the tool-drawer from his chest, and was busily attacking the lath which kept in place the sliding-door of his cabin.

It was a toughish task, but with Small and Widgeon for his helpmates he soon had it off, and before long the two sailors were holding it crosswise over the saloon sky-light, while Mr Gregory rapidly secured it in its place with screws.

Another and another was fitted up in a similar way, and all so silently that very little was heard beyond the heavy breathing of the first-mate as he drove the screws home.

"There, major!" he whispered; "those doors are not very strong, but wherever they drive through a hole we can put a gun to that place as easily as they can."

"And better, too," said the major. "Now, then, as soon as you get a couple more cabin-doors off, we'll move away these boxes and things the captain has clapped here, and you shall screw up your barricade."

"I'll soon be ready," said the mate; and he kept his word; while, as soon as he had let his two men lift out the second door, the major brought up the reserve, as he called it, the chests piled against the door by the captain, Mrs Strong, and the major's wife, were lifted over, and in an incredibly short time the opening, with the door bolted, was covered breast-high with the other doors, which were securely fastened, and the chests were once more piled up in their places.

Meanwhile, in spite of his injury, the captain had been busily engaged placing the weapons in order in his own cabin, off the saloon—the door not being required; and this he carried out by the help of a lamp, Mark eagerly obeying his slightest wishes, with the result that at last there was an ample supply of charged weapons ready, with ammunition so placed as to be at hand.

"If it comes to fighting, my boy—which Heaven forbid!" said the captain—"you will take your place here, and as rapidly as you can you will recharge the pieces brought back to you. Now, try that revolver."

Mark caught up the weapon.

"Unload it."

He was sufficiently versed to understand the process, and rapidly drove out each cartridge.

"Now reload," said the captain.

Mark's fingers were just as active in replacing the cartridges; and this done, the guns were tried in the same way.

"I don't see what more we can do," said the captain. "So lie down and have a sleep, my boy. I'll keep watch. To-morrow may be a very weary day for us all."

"Don't ask me, father," said the boy in tones of remonstrance. "I feel as if I couldn't sleep to-night. Let me go and talk to mother."

"They may be asleep," said the captain. "No; it is not likely. Yes; go if you like."

Mark went softly to the cabin-door and tapped.

The door was opened softly by Mrs Strong, who held up her hand and then pointed to where Mary O'Halloran lay fast asleep, while her mother was seated by the berth, her head fallen sidewise and resting against her child. Soldier's wife and daughter, they were so inured to peril and anxiety that these did not hinder them from taking necessary rest, and being ready for the troubles of the day to come.

There was a tender embrace, a kiss, and Mark stole away once more to return to his father, whom he found seated on a locker faint and exhausted from his injury.

"It's a hard fight, Mark," he whispered hoarsely; "and I feel as weak as man can feel. Don't let me go to sleep."

"Why not, father? I'll watch and call you if there is anything wrong."

"No, my boy," said the captain sadly. "I could not sleep, I believe, after all, even if I tried. It was a momentary weakness."

"The captain awake?" said a deep harsh voice.

"Yes, Gregory, I'm awake," was the reply.

"Well, sir, I think we've done all we can. The lads are asleep; so is Morgan. The major is on guard, and the men understand what to do if they are roused. Now, sir, why don't you turn in?"

"No, Gregory; I'll keep watch too."

"Well, sir, we mustn't waste strength. If you and the major are going to watch I'll turn in, for I'm dead beat. Hullo! what's that?"

There was a low whining sigh, and a faint bark answered the first-mate's question.

"Oh, it's that dog again, eh? Well, sir, shall I turn in?"

"Yes, Gregory. We'll rouse you if there's anything wrong."

"All right!" said the mate; "but it's my opinion that we shall have no fighting at present. They'll wait for wind and get us ashore in some creek hidden among the mangroves, and there plunder the ship."

The mate went out, whispered a few words to the major, and then turned in—a process which consisted in lying down on the cabin-floor, with a revolver in his hand; while to the major, who was seated on a chest by the barricaded door, with an unlighted cigar in his lips, it seemed as if Gregory sighed softly and was then fast asleep.

Mark got up once or twice and went into the saloon, where all was still. Then he walked to the window and looked out, to find that not a breath of air had arisen, and that the mist was gathering more thickly over the sea.

Going back to where his father was seated he too sat down; and then it seemed to him that a dull oval sun rose out of the sea—a sun so dull that its flattened oval shape suggested that it must have been squeezed so as to get nearly all the light out of it. And there that sun stared at him blankly, as if wondering to see him there; while he was as much surprised to see the sun—and more surprised as his brain cleared and he realised that he had been asleep and was staring at the plate-glass cabin-window, and that it was broad day!

Chapter Seventeen
How Men fight for Life

Mark started up in terror as he saw his father's face, pale, haggard, and smeared with blood; but as soon as he encountered his son's eye he smiled pleasantly.

"Have I been asleep, father?"

"Capitally, my boy," said the captain kindly. "A good four hours, I should say."

"And you've been watching?"

"No—only resting and thinking, my boy. I'm better now. Go out and see how things are."

Mark stepped softly into the saloon, which was now full of light from the stern windows, and a dull sense of horror and misery came over him as he noted the desolate aspect of the place, with the screwed-up doors, the barricade, the look of the men asleep, and above all the pallid aspect of Mr Morgan, who seemed to have grown old since the previous day, so seriously had his wound affected him.

This was all seen at a glance; and he was going toward the door when he stopped short, startled, for there stood the major with a double gun at his shoulder taking so straight an aim at him that Mark seemed to see nothing of the gun but the muzzle, looking like a pair of spectacles without glasses, and through which frames he was trying to peer.

Not a pleasant prospect for him if he could have looked, for it would have been right down the barrels at the wads of a couple of cartridges; but as he stared the piece was lowered and the major said in a low voice:

"I could have brought you down like a bird. Why, you looked just like a Malay. Mark, what have you been doing, sir? rubbing your powdery hands all over your face?"

"I suppose so, major. What time is it?"

"Time the ship was cleared, my lad, but I suppose we must wait. Let me see," he continued, referring to his watch. "I didn't like to look before;

it makes a man impatient for his breakfast, I'm seven o'clock. That's three bells, isn't it?"

"I think so," said Mark.

"Think, and you the son of a captain in the merchant service! Why, I should have thought you would have been born a sailor."

"Have you heard the Malays, sir?"

"Heard them! Yes, my lad, going about the ship with their bare feet on the planks; but they haven't tried the door. There, rouse up the men while I wake Gregory."

He touched the first-mate, who sprang up, revolver in hand, wide-awake, and ready for instant action.

He glanced sharply round, realised that all was right, and stuck the revolver in his belt.

"How's the skipper?" he asked.

"My father seems worn out and ill," said Mark sadly.

"Make him lie down," muttered the mate; and he strode across to the captain's cabin, but came back shaking his head, and went to the cabin-window, where he leaned out and was trying to see whether the boat was all right when a faint noise overhead made him instinctively draw in his head.

It was a narrow escape, for as the mate drew back there was a dark line seen to dart across the cabin-window and return.

"Well, I'm not a spiteful man," said the mate, rubbing his ear, "but I should certainly like to give that fellow a pill that would lay him up for six months. Now, what pleasure would it have afforded him, Mark, my lad, if he had run that spear through my neck?"

"It's his nature, sir," said the major shortly. "Those fellows value a life at about a rupee, and sometimes not at that."

The men had risen, stretched, and were looking round in a discontented way; but they began to beam shortly after when a fair supply of biscuits and sardines from the captain's private supply was handed round, and followed by some bottled beer, the opening of which seemed to cause a commotion on deck, and an excited talking as if the Malays thought some kind of weapon was being fired.

The breakfast worked wonders in the gaunt, untidy-looking throng, and when the captain said a few words to them asking their help, and that they would stand by him to the last, there was a hearty cheer, one which caused a rush of feet upon the deck, and then a hurried buzzing sound was heard as if the Malays were gathering for an attack.

In view of this the men were placed well armed by the barricaded door, and the major stood ready at their side, while Small was stationed beneath the sky-light armed with a gun, and with orders to fire through the first hole driven down in the panels of the door Mr Gregory had placed for protection.

"So far so good," said the captain cheerily, and the excitement seemed to remove the haggard look in his pale face. "But look here, gentlemen, we must leave a way open for retreat."

"Of course," said the major, "never lose touch of that."

"My plan is to defend the ship to the last, and then take to the boat—that is, if the case has become hopeless. So, Gregory, sooner or later they will find out that the boat is here, and try to cut it adrift. You will go to the cabin-window which commands the boat's painter, and shoot down whoever tries to cut it."

Gregory nodded, took a gun and some cartridges, and walked to one of the cabin-windows, then to another, and changed again.

He had hardly reached the last and looked out when there was a shot, a yell, and a second shot.

The captain rushed to his officer's side.

"What is it?" he cried.

"Only just in time," said the mate, coolly reloading. "One of the scoundrels had swum round, was in the boat, and cutting her away."

"Did you—"

The captain paused and looked inquiringly in the mate's eyes.

"We're fighting for our lives and the lives of these ladies, Captain Strong," said Gregory. "Suppose we do our duty and ask no questions afterwards. The Malay did not cut the painter."

Captain Strong nodded and returned to where the men stood by the barricaded door, to answer the major's inquiring look with a few words as to matters being all right, and then they waited, with the ladies pale and anxious, in one of the cabins, and Mark standing ready to supply ammunition when it should be required.

They had not long to wait for an attack. The discovery that the man who had tried to get the boat had been shot was met with a loud burst of angry yells, and this was followed by a fresh attempt, as was shown to the defenders of the door by another shot from the mate.

There was another burst of yelling, and at intervals three more shots were fired by Mr Gregory.

"Why, he's getting all the fun, Strong!" said the major. "They might come this way; but the mischief is that we've left no holes to fire from. Never mind; if we had they would have been able to see in."

Mark about this time walked to where Mr Gregory was leaning against the bulkhead with the muzzle of his gun bearing upon the spot a man must reach to cut the painter.

"Want any more cartridges, Mr Gregory?" said Mark.

For answer the mate bent down, glanced along the barrel of his gun and fired.

Mark darted forward and caught sight of a hideously-distorted face and a pair of raised hands before they disappeared beneath the surface, and just at that moment he darted back, barely in time to avoid a spear which stuck quivering in the woodwork round the window.

"Not a very safe place. Squire Mark," said the mate, reloading without taking his eyes from the boat, and firing again as a dark head literally flashed into sight, one of the Malays having dived and so arranged his plunge that he should form a curve in the water and rise close to the boat's stern.

"I wish they would get tired of this," said Gregory, again reloading, and speaking through his teeth. "If they put no value on human life I do."

The ill success of the venture to cut the boat adrift seemed to have maddened the Malays, for after a burst of angry talking there was a loud yell, a pattering of naked feet on the deck, and the next minute a furious attack was being made upon the cabin entrance, blows were delivered with axes, and it soon became evident that a way would be made through.

"Ah! what are you going to do?" roared the major, as he saw a man about to fire. "Don't waste your shot, man. Stand back till you can see the whites of your enemy's eyes, and then let him have it."

There was a thrill running through the men, and click, click, of lock after lock.

"That's it," said the major, "cool as cucumbers. Bravo, lads! What soldiers I could make of all of you! Now, look here, I'll give the order to fire, but what you have to do is this: wait till these black murdering scoundrels make a hole in the defence, and then you fill it up with the mouth of your pieces, and look sharp, before they thrust through a spear."

The men uttered a low growl, and the captain now stood by the major, while Morgan after a smile at Mark seated himself upon the cabin table to watch for an attack from the sky-light, toward which he held a loaded revolver.

A sharp report from Mr Gregory's gun was followed by another yell, telling painfully enough that the Malays had been deceived in imagining that the whole of the little force would be defending the door, and that now was the time to cut the boat adrift.

The yell from the water was followed by a fierce one on deck, and the chopping and splintering of wood. The door was stoutly built, but those behind were very slight, and it was not long before the panels began to show gaps of splinters and jagged holes through which spears were thrust so suddenly that the men fell back, and the blows were redoubled.

"Ah! they are nasty weapons, my lads," said the major coolly. "Serve them this way."

As he spoke he watched his opportunity, waiting till a spear was darted in for some distance, when, catching it in his left hand, he pressed it aside, readied forward, and discharged his revolver right through the hole by which the spear had come.

The proof of the efficacy of this shot was shown by the major drawing in the spear and throwing it upon the deck, while his example was followed more or less by the men, who now sent shot after shot through the various holes made in the door.

"Don't waste your fire, lads; don't waste your fire," cried the major; and his words were not without effect, as the slow delivery of shots, and the yells of pain and rage which followed many of the discharges, told.

No more attempts were made to cut away the boat, and Mr Gregory's piece became silent; but it soon grew evident that a fresh attack was to be made upon them, for the crashing and shivering of glass was heard in the sky-lights, and directly after, heavy blows from an axe. This was soon followed by the appearance of an opening through which a spear-head gleamed as the weapon was darted down so adroitly that it passed through the fold of the boatswain's trousers, and pinned him to the table on one side of which he too leant.

The answer to this was a shot from Morgan's revolver, and another from the gun the boatswain held, after which he proceeded leisurely to wriggle out the spear and draw it away.

Then more blows were heard, and a fresh hole was made in the sky-light defence, but the spear thrust down more than met its match, and after a shot or two no more blows were delivered there.

By this time the Malays had grown less daring, and though a man or two rushed forward now and then to dart a spear at them, there was a cessation of the work of destroying with axes, and the sailors were able to keep command of the holes, and send a well-directed shot through from time to time.

But the encounter, badly as it had gone with the Malays, had had its effects among the defenders of the place. The major had an ugly gash in his left arm delivered by a knife-bladed spear. Billy Widgeon's ear was cut through, and he had a slight prick in his right arm, while one of the other men had a spear stab in the left leg.

The withdrawal of the Malays from the attack enabled the injured to go into hospital as the major termed it, and each wound was carefully bandaged by the major's wife or by Mrs Strong.

"They're about beaten, I should say," said the major, cheerily. "By the way, Strong, a little bleeding is very refreshing. I feel like a new man."

"So do I," said the captain grimly.

"Here, quick, look out!" cried Mark at that instant, for, wincing from seeing the dressing of his father's wound, he had unscrewed one of the little side-lights and was looking over the calm sunlit sea, when he caught sight of a prau gliding along from the *Petrel's* bows, and it was evident that she was coming to attack simultaneously from the stern.

"Hah! that's it, is it!" said the major. "Hitting back and front too! Confound that fellow! how badly he steers the boat!"

As he said these words he clapped his gun to his shoulder and fired.

The steersman fell, but it had no permanent effect, save to draw a little shower of spears at the window opening, one of which passed through and stuck quivering in the bulkhead. Then another man took the steerer's place, and the prau glided by evidently to take her station astern.

"We shall lose the boat, major," said the captain bitterly.

"Shall we!" replied the major. "Just take my place, sir, by the door. I'm going to use my little hunting rifle now alongside of Gregory; and if a man does reach that boat I'm going to know the reason why. I'm not much given to boasting, but I can shoot straight."

He had already proved it to some purpose, and without a word the captain took his place by the barricade, while the major went into his own cabin and returned with a little double rifle and a pouch of ammunition.

"I did not want to use this," he said; "but things are growing serious."

The prau had by this time been rowed to its station, and from the stir on deck it was now evident that the brass swivel-gun was being loaded and preparations made to send a volley of missiles tearing through the stern windows.

"That will be awkward, Gregory," said the major.

"Do a lot of damage, sir," said the mate coolly. "They are so low down in the water that they can't send a shot along our floor. The charge will go right up and through the deck."

"Well, at any rate I think I'll try and stop them."

"By all means," said the mate, and he watched keenly as the major knelt down, resting his rifle on the sill and taking aim, but waiting.

All at once there was a puff of smoke, a sharp crack, and at the same moment a deafening report from the prau, but the charge of missiles went hurtling and screaming up through the mizen rigging and away over the ship to sea.

The major's shot was more successful, for a man fell.

"He was a little too quick for me," said the major, reloading and waiting for another chance. "Nasty work this!" he added; "but I suppose it's necessary."

"Necessary, sir!" cried Gregory angrily; "think of those poor women in the cabin."

There was a sharp crack from the major's rifle, and another man fell.

"That's the left barrel!" said the major, reloading. "Yes, my dear sir, I am thinking about those poor women in the cabin. Ah, would you!"

He drew trigger again, and another man who had been about to fire the lelah sprang up and dropped the match.

There was a yell, and a fresh man picked up the piece of burning match from the deck, shouted, and giving the fire a wave in the air, he was in the act of bringing it down upon the touch-hole, when the major, who had not stirred to reload, drew trigger once again, the rifle cracked, and the Malay dropped upon his face.

There was a fierce yell at this, and in the midst of tremendous confusion on board, the prau continued her course, the sweeps being worked rapidly by the crew, who were evidently in frantic haste to get out of the deadly line of fire.

"Ah!" said the major, coolly reloading, "now I could pick off the steersman, or that chap with the red handkerchief; but it would do no real good. We've scared them off, and that's good work."

"Splendid, major. Why, that rifle is a little treasure."

"Well, yes," said the major, patting it; "but it was meant for tiger and leopard, Gregory, not to kill men."

"You may make yourself easy," said the first-mate quietly; "these are savage beasts more than men. It is life for life."

"Ah! that's comforting, Gregory, and I take it as kindly of you, for I'm not fond of this sort of work, though I say I am. Well, let's see how they are getting on yonder."

He went out of the cabin, leaving the first-mate to resume his watch over the boat, for during the time this episode of rifle practice was in progress another furious attack had been made upon the barricaded door. Spears had been thrust and darted through, blows struck through cracks and holes with krises and the deadly sword-like parang, and in spite of the fierce and slowly-sustained fire kept up, the defences were rapidly becoming more dilapidated, and several fresh wounds had been received.

But the determination of the men had not failed for a moment, while just at the worst time a change was made for the better by the fresh force put into the defence by Small and Mr Morgan.

The attack through the sky-lights had not been renewed, and, weary with sitting and watching through the films of blue smoke which filled the cabin their captain and the men so sorely pressed, these two suddenly dashed into the fray, each going to a hole and firing rapidly.

This checked the Malays for the time, but they came on again, and when the major joined in with a couple of shots from his little rifle the fight was still furiously raging.

Suddenly, however, just as the barriers were giving way, and every opening seemed to bristle with spears, there was a terrible shout, and the attack ceased.

"Failure of the rear movement, cease firing ordered from the front," said the major quietly. "Now we shall have time to repair damages."

"Ah, major," cried the captain, "if I could only be as cool as you!" and he wrung his hand.

"My dear Strong, you are a regular lion," replied the major. "You were getting hard pressed there."

"And you were as calm as if nothing were the matter."

"Way to win, my dear sir: way to win; but I say, between ourselves, things were looking ugly just then."

"I believe you saved us—you," said Morgan.

"Humph!" replied the major. "It's my belief, sir, that if those scoundrels had not let themselves be damped by the failure of the plan, and had kept on, we should have been all prisoners by now. Or—"

"I understand you," said the captain gravely. "Well, we must still hope."

Chapter Eighteen
How the Major gave his Advice

As the major and Captain Strong hurried into the ladies' cabin on the cessation of the fighting it was to find them all ready, even to Mary, with bandages and pieces of linen to staunch the blood and help the poor fellows who had been wounded in their service; while as soon as Mark found that his services were no longer required as distributor of ammunition, he got together refreshments, and without being told handed them round to the wearied and bleeding sailors.

The food and the kindly words of sympathy they received seemed to put heart into the men, who had been ready to give up as soon as the rage and excitement of the fighting was over, but now they strung themselves up and patted their bandages, as if proud of having received them in the ladies' defence; though as the men grew more cheery the captain grew more serious.

"We shall have hard work to get through this afternoon," he said to the major, who lit a cigar and smoked as coolly as if there were no pirates for a hundred miles.

"No, you will not," was the blunt reply.

"Why, the savage wretches are swarming upon the decks," said the captain.

"Yes; but this afternoon is already gone. We shall have darkness soon."

"Gone! Why, it is five bells!"

"Yes, sir; fighting takes time. I say, how the smoke has cleared away!"

"Yes; it is less choking now," said the captain thoughtfully; and he went slowly to where Gregory was waiting and watching still for an attack upon the boat.

The captain said nothing further for some few minutes, and then returned to Morgan, who was very silent, and evidently weak and in great pain.

Here he had a long discussion, and as Mark watched him wonderingly, trying the while to make out what steps his father would take next, the captain went slowly to where the major was talking calmly enough to Mrs O'Halloran and his child.

"Nonsense!" he was saying; "there is no such a fine bit of Latin anywhere as nil desperandum. You never know what course a battle may take. Old Nap thought he had won Waterloo; but he had not. Cheer up, my dears! Look how young Mark Strong takes it. Well, captain, he added, leaving the cabin and joining him, what news? Have you naval gentlemen hatched the conspiracy?"

"It is no conspiracy, major," said the captain quietly; "but we have been trying to arrive at the best course of proceeding."

"Well, captain, and brother in affliction, what's to be done?"

"I propose a bold attempt to clear the deck of these scoundrels, major, during the night. Once get them over the side, we could keep them out. Will you give me your advice as a brave soldier who understands these things better than I, and will you fight with me?"

"My dear Strong," said the major sharply, as he caught the captain's hand; "you ought to have been a soldier, sir."

"But you see I am a sailor," said the captain with a sad smile.

"There's the pity, sir. Now to business. Will I fight with you! Bedad, sir, I've proved that."

"You have, my dear major, like the bravest of men."

"No, no. Tut, tut! Like a soldier should, sir. But now about this plan of yours."

"Yes, major, yes."

"Well, sir, there must be about eighty or ninety of these tawny rascals, and we are all more or less damaged, and, counting our young friend Mark, eleven men and three hospital nurses. Now the nurses can't fight, and Mark must still be powder-monkey, so there we are ten men, and, as I said, all damaged, to fight eighty."

"Yes," said the captain, "the odds are very great; but I think we might do it."

"Humph!" said the major. "I don't. No, my dear Strong; it would be a failure. I should like it immensely. I've been in several fights, and I was never in one yet which stood at eight to one. Yes, I should like it immensely; but there are the women."

"Yes," said the captain sadly; "there are the women."

"You don't think me turning tail because I speak so plainly?" said the major.

"No;—how could I, major!"

"Well, I don't know, sir. The world is far more ready to think a man a coward than a hero. But set aside that, it would not do, my dear fellow. We are Englishmen and Irishmen, and can do a great deal; but when it comes to eight to one there isn't room for one to move."

"You are right," said the captain with a groan. "My poor ship! my poor wife and boy!"

"Get out with you! Why, what now!" cried the major, whose eyes were wet with tears as he grasped the captain's hands. "We're not beaten yet, my dear boy, and we're not going to be. Now I tell you what is our duty, sir."

"Yes?"

"To put into that boat all the food and ammunition we've got, and then all get in quietly but one; and he'd stop back to get the old ship well alight; and then bad luck to the scoundrels on board, much good may it do them!"

"My poor ship!"

"But you'd rather sink her or burn her than let these dogs grow fat on what they get?"

"Certainly I would," said the captain.

"Then to-night, as soon as it's dark, let's do it, me dear boy, and make for one of the islands."

"But we could hold out for long enough yet."

"No," said the major gravely; "we're beaten, me dear sor. The poor lads are getting more stiff and sore every minute. To-morrow morning they won't have a bit of fight in them; why, even your humble servant, sir, who adores a scrimmage, would rather lie on a sofa and smoke till his wounds are healed. Now isn't it all true?"

"Yes," said the captain; "you are quite right; but we'll hold out till to-morrow. Help may come."

"To be sure it may," said the major cheerily. "I'm ready to wait. I've only spoken my mind."

"I thank you, major," said Captain Strong. "You are quite right. I felt that my plans were next door to madness; but I was ready to do anything sooner than lose my ship."

Chapter Nineteen
How there was another Enemy to Fight

It was rapidly growing dark as Billy Widgeon went slowly up to Mark. He limped as he walked, and there was a bandage round one of his short legs.

"I've been having a look at that there monkey, Mr Mark, sir," said the little sailor. "He's just come out of his hole, looking scared because he thought the fellows was shouting at him. He came down over the stern and in at one of the windows, and he's been a-making no end of fuss over old Bruff's crocodilly leg, and he doesn't seem to understand it a bit. But I say, sir, what are we going to do next? Some of the chaps is rather bad."

"Poor fellows!" said Mark. "I suppose we shall have to fight again."

Billy made no answer, for another engagement seemed terrible enough to think of now in cold blood, and they were soon after joined by Small, who said nothing, but held out his hand to Mark, to give the lad's fingers a long silent pressure, which seemed to him to mean only one thing, and that was good-bye.

After a time the captain's voice was heard to summon the men, and Small was sent to relieve Gregory; but the mate declined to leave his post, and no attempt was made to enforce obedience.

Then half the men were placed at the barricade, and the weapons of the other half were placed by them, while these latter were drawn up by the saloon windows.

"What's we going to do?" whispered one of the men to Mark; but he could give no answer.

It was now dark, even darker than the previous night, but a slight breeze was beginning to rise in fitful gusts, and there was now and then the ripple of water against the stern.

"You've made up your mind then?" said the major.

"Yes," replied the captain firmly. "We have done our duty. Now humanity must be heard."

The captain then spoke a few words to Mr Gregory, and the question of how the boat was to be brought from where she was secured exactly under the cabin-window was discussed and settled by Mark volunteering to go down.

"You lower me into the water with a rope," he said, "and I'll soon swim to her and get in."

The captain hesitated for a few moments, and then the sheet-rope was once more brought into use, and with it fastened round his waist Mark climbed out, glanced up at the stern-rail to see if anyone was waiting ready with a spear to thrust him through, and directly after he was lowered into the water.

A few strokes took him to the boat, and after a good deal of trying he managed to scramble in. The unfastening was a matter of very few moments, and then with the painter in hand he worked right beneath the cabin-window, when Mr Gregory slid down and joined him.

For the next two hours slowly and silently ammunition and such food as they possessed in the shape of preserved meats and such like from the captain's store were lowered down and packed in the bottom of the boat and beneath the thwarts, and this was hardly done when a dull glow seemed to show up the window above their head.

"Climb up, Mark, and tell them to put out that light," whispered Mr Gregory.

Mark obeyed, not without some difficulty, and found that the saloon was in a state of excitement.

"I've been smelling it this last half 'our, sir," said Billy Widgeon, "but I thout it was some queer kind o' bacco as they Malay chaps smoked, so I didn't speak."

"Ah, there's no mistake about it, Captain Strong!" said the second-mate; "the ship is on fire, sir. They'll take alarm directly."

Almost as he spoke the Malays, who must have been asleep, did take the alarm, and in a minute the whole deck was in an uproar.

"We've no time to lose," said the captain, and he ran to the window and whispered down to Gregory what was wrong.

"Go down, Small," said the captain then, "and help take the ladies as we lower them. Every man keep to his arms."

"Ay, ay, sir."

"Is the ammunition down?"

"Yes, father," said Mark. "I stowed it myself in the locker."

Already the smoke was gathering in the cabin, and bright light shining in through the damaged barricade, but thanks to the example set there was no confusion after the first minute. The captain took his place by the window and gave his orders, and one by one the ladies, the wounded, the dog, and the monkey were lowered down, and then turn by turn the men followed.

It now became evident that there was no farther need to fear attack, for the Malays were rapidly quitting the burning ship amid yells and confusion, while the light increased, and fortunately made the spot where the boat lay beneath the stern seem by comparison more dark.

At last Mark followed the men, and was resting on the sill trying to recollect whether all the arms were in the boat, when he heard the captain say:

"Did you set her on fire?"

"My dear boy, no," cried the major.

"You proposed burning the ship."

"Just as I would if I were in command and about to evacuate a fort, my dear sir; but how could I do this? She caught fire somewhere amidships, I should say from their carelessness. Gun-wads have been smouldering about, perhaps."

"Perhaps so," said the captain thoughtfully; and Mark sat with one leg in and one leg out of the window gazing at his father as he stood there, his fine, manly face thrown up for a moment by the glow which shone through a hole in the door as a puff of wind set in through the open stern and wafted back the smoke which seemed to settle down directly.

"Well," said the major, speaking as coolly as if he were on parade, "shall I go first?"

"I was thinking, major. I can't do it. It seems like breaking my pledges, and acting dishonourably to the owners of the ship to leave her."

"My dear Strong," said the major, clapping him on the shoulder, "the more I know of you the more I regret that you took to the sea."

"My dear sir," said Captain Strong angrily, "is this a time for compliments?"

"It was meant sincerely," replied the major; "but let me point out to you that however painful this may be to you we must go now."

"Why?" said the captain. "The Malay scoundrels are escaping to their praus."

"Yes, there is no doubt of that."

"Then it is my duty to call back my men, and attack the flames."

"Now, my dear Strong, even if we had the whole crew instead of half a dozen men, all more or less wounded," said the major, "you know as well as I do that we could not master a fire like this. Look out of the window yonder, how the sea is lit up, and then through that hole; why, the mainmast and rigging must be all in a blaze!"

"Yes," said the captain, as if to himself, "from deck to truck, and the burning pitch falling in a fiery rain. But if we could master the flames, now the enemy are gone—"

"They would be waiting close at hand to come back and take possession, my dear sir. Come, Strong, you've done your duty to everyone; it is now time to save life."

"I cannot go," cried the captain fiercely. "I must have one try first."

He ran to the barricade, closely followed by the major, to see that the deck had become quite a furnace, the waves of fire running upward, and seeming to be borne here and there by the strong current of air which the heat produced, and which now swept through the saloon, clearing it of the smoke and rushing out of the jagged openings to fan the flames.

The captain stood gazing through for a few minutes without speaking, and then turned sadly away.

"It would be impossible," he said.

"Is anything wrong?" came in a whisper from the boat to Mark.

"No, no," he whispered back; "they are coming directly."

"Yes, impossible, my dear fellow," said the major quietly.

As he spoke there was a sudden flash and a roar; the barricade was driven in, and Mark felt as if something soft, but of enormous power, drove him from his hold where he sat, so that he fell headlong into the boat, his fall being broken by his coming down upon the men in the bows.

He was not hurt, and as he struggled up it was to see that there was comparative darkness and a huge cloud of smoke over them; but directly after, there was a rushing noise, and a glare of light seemed to blaze out, showing the smoke rising red-edged and lurid, while the effect of the explosion seemed to be that there was more food set free for the flames.

"Help me up," said Mark excitedly. "Let me go back. They must be killed."

"Nay, nay, my lad, it's all right," whispered the first-mate; "they're coming down."

It was a fact, for the major slid quickly down the cotton rope, and the captain could be seen leaning out ready to follow, as he did directly and took his place in the boat.

"Will you give orders, or shall I?" whispered Gregory, as Mark gazed to right and left, and then back over the stern, where his mother sat by Mary O'Halloran, and as he looked he could see that there was a black shadow of the ship stretching far away over the shining waters.

"Go on," said the captain; and, taking an oar to steer, the mate gave a short order, oars were dipped, and the heavily-laden gig moved slowly out from under the stern, the mate keeping her in the shadow as soon as she was turned.

In the act of turning Mark caught sight of one of the praus glistening as if gilded, and just a slighter glimpse of the second prau, while for a minute or two all sat in silent dread of their having been seen.

But there was no yell to announce their discovery, and directly after they were back in the shelter of the shadow, and moving steadily in the face of a soft breeze farther and farther from the praus.

Chapter Twenty
How they fell in with greater Peril

The peril was still great, and there was the risk that at any moment another inadvertent movement on the part of the boat, such as that made by Mr Gregory in his ignorance of the side on which the enemy lay, might result in discovery, for the sea glowed in the intense light shed by the burning vessel, and the faces of all in the gig stood out so plainly that it seemed to be only a question of moments before they were seen.

But the mate carefully manoeuvred his steering oar; the men pulled a slow, silent, and steady stroke; and fortunately for all, the Malays were so intent upon the fire that they did not alter the positions of their vessels.

For a very short time the boat was in the black shadow cast by the stern; then they were floating as it were on golden waters; and the same feeling animated every breast, though it remained an unspoken thought: This is all in vain; we must be seen and brought back.

"A little more room there; sit close; move steadily," said the first-mate hoarsely. "Now two more oars."

These were laid in the rowlocks silently, and with four men pulling in place of two the heavily-laden boat made more rapid progress, so that before long there was a space of several hundred yards between the fugitives and the flaming ship, and they could look at the two praus lying a short distance away without so much fear of being seen.

"Steady, my lads! pull!" said the mate, whose was the only face turned from the ship, and as he stood in the stern his shadow was cast upon the water.

"Were you hurt, father?" said Mark.

"No, my lad, not much," said the captain. "The explosion struck us both down. That was all."

Nothing more was said, for everyone was too much intent upon the sight before them, one which was grand in the extreme, and lit up the ocean far and wide. The main and fore-masts were blazing right to the very trucks, and as the fugitives watched the mizzen-mast caught, and they could see the flames leap from spar to spar, running along ropes with quite a rapid motion, while great burning drops seemed to keep falling toward the deck. By rapid degrees the burning ship now assumed the aspect of a pyramid of fire, sails, yards, cordage, and masts being all involved, while from the blazing cone a steady burst of great golden sparks rose toward a huge purple canopy, all folds and wreathing volumes edged with orange and gold, the cloud of smoke that floated lazily in the heated air.

By degrees the sparks became invisible, and the flames were merged, many tongues in one, as the distance was increased; while the praus, out of whose sight it was no longer necessary to keep, looked comparatively small, with their sides still glistening in the light.

"There is no occasion to keep silence now," said the captain quietly. "We are far out of hearing."

"What caused that explosion there?" said the mate, as he seated himself now, but continued to steer.

"We cannot tell for certain," said the captain.

"No," said the major; "but there seems to me to be no doubt that it was a powder-keg which the Malays had brought on board, I should say to blow open the cabin-door. And it did," he added grimly, "and I hope they liked it."

"What do you propose doing, captain?" said Mr Gregory at last, and the answer was eagerly listened for. "We are heavily-laden and ought to make land."

"Yes, but it must not be in the sight of the praus. It is early in the night yet, and we are evidently in a sharp current."

"Yes, a strong current," said the mate.

"Then row steadily till daybreak, and by then we shall be well out of sight, and can make for one of the islands to the south, or try and get in the route of the China ships."

"Right!" said the mate. "Give way, my lads; a slow easy stroke, and we'll all relieve you in turn."

This was done all through the rest of the night, but with great caution, for the gig was very low in the water; and while they rowed in turn those who were not at the oars sat gazing at the burning ship, and the wounded men sometimes slept.

But wounded or no, all took a turn at the oars, from the captain downward; and towards morning, when all were utterly exhausted, fair progress was still made in the boat as she was pulled by the two ladies, and Mary O'Halloran and Mark.

The night had not been without incidents, for when they were about a couple of miles from the ship the mainmast fell over the side with a rush of flame, and lay burning on the surface of the water; to be followed almost directly by the fore-mast; and the mizen alone remained standing like a pillar of light for about another hour before it fell in the opposite direction.

This altered the shape of the fire, but the ship blazed on, the size of the conflagration seeming less as the distance increased, but still flaming plainly on the horizon, till just at daybreak a low cloud seemed to come sweeping over the sea, borne on a sighing breeze, which faintly rippled the surface, and as this enveloped them the glow astern was blotted out and a soft rain began to fall.

As it grew lighter the rain became more heavy, and at last it came down in a perfect deluge, increasing so in violence that before long one of the men was set to work with the baler emptying the water out that collected under the thwarts.

It was a depressing time, for as the hours passed on, the rain never ceased for a moment, but kept on in a regular tropic deluge; while, in spite of food and stimulants, exhaustion and suffering from their wounds told more and more, till one by one the men gave up, and the boat at last drifted with the swift current into which they had been drawn.

A short consultation was held between the heads, and failing observations, it was decided that it would be better to make for the island off which the ship had been becalmed; but even that desperate resolve had now to be given up, for the strength of all seemed gone, and the current set in, as far as they could judge, the opposite direction.

"We can do nothing, major," said the captain at last; "nothing now but trust in God and hope for the best."

"Amen!" said the major quietly, and he calmly took his turn at the baling, which had now become the one task undertaken, so as to keep the boat clear of water.

Night came slowly as they drifted on, but it came at last—a densely dark night, with the rain still falling; and in spite of their being in the tropics, the cold and suffering, as they all sat in their saturated garments wishing for the cessation of the rain, was terrible; and how those hours next passed none seemed to know, for they were utterly stupefied with weariness and exhaustion.

Morning at last, and with the break of day the rain partially ceased, for its violence was not so great, but it kept falling; and now to add to their peril a gusty wind came from astern as the sun began to rise.

It was plain to all on board that if the surface became rough their boat must sink. For she was so heavily-laden that the space of side above the water was small indeed. Under the circumstances Captain Strong decided to raise the little lug-sail neatly rolled round its mast, and this latter being stepped, the sail was unfurled, and in a few minutes they were gliding rapidly on, shipping a little water from time to time, but no more than could be easily mastered and kept down.

Where to steer was not in their choice. All that could be done was to keep the gig afloat, and to this the captain and mate directed all their energies.

Food was distributed, and of water they felt no want, their saturated garments having quenched all thirst; but matters seemed to grow worse. Mr Morgan was delirious, and one of the men lay rambling on about some place in London where he meant to have called.

Morning, noon, evening, and the gig rushing on through the broken water with a thick misty rain all around and no chance of making out their whereabouts.

"Shall we be saved?" said Mrs Strong at last in a whisper as, utterly worn out, the captain came at last and sat down between his wife and son.

"Don't ask, my dear," he said calmly. "We have done, and are doing, all that men can do. The rest must be left."

Night came, a night that was even blacker than that which had passed, but the rain did not cease nor the sky clear. Everything a hundred yards away seemed to be so much solid darkness; but, on the other hand, the sea grew no rougher, and the wind sent the boat rapidly along.

It must have been about midnight that, as nearly everyone in the gig were plunged in a stupor-like sleep, the first-mate was steering, the boat gliding swiftly through the broken waves. The major sat on one side and Mark on the other talking from time to time in a low voice.

A calm feeling of despair had settled down among them, and when they did speak it was about some indifferent matter, all shrinking from anything concerning their approaching fate, when Mark, who was stooping to pat the poor wounded dog at his feet, where he lay curled in company with shivering Jack, suddenly laid his hand upon Mr Gregory's arm.

"What's that?" he said in a whisper.

"What? I heard nothing," said the major.

"Silence!" cried the mate sternly; and he listened intently to a low roaring noise.

"Breakers!" he said suddenly. "We are near land."

"Land?" cried Mark.

"Yes, my boy. Oh, if it were day!"

The mate changed the course of the boat directly so as to run off to the left, but at the end of five minutes he altered the course again.

"Breakers there too," he said. "We are between them."

"Well, then, quick!" said the major. "Go about and let's turn back."

"My dear Major O'Halloran," said the mate calmly, "if I attempt to go about, the boat will fill instantly and sink. Our only chance is in keeping on."

As he spoke he resumed the course they had been just taking, and now, rapidly increasing in power, the sound of the waves breaking on rocks could be heard to right and left.

"But you don't know where you are going," said the major.

"No, sir. But it is all I can do. Mark Strong, rouse your father; and, major, be prepared to swim right ahead if anything happens."

"What's the good?" said the major calmly. And then, "Shall I wake them, or let them meet it asleep? I'll wake them," he said; and he crept cautiously to arouse Mrs and Mary O'Halloran, as Mark was rousing his father, his mother waking too.

"Breakers?" said the captain. "Well, I have been expecting it for hours. Can you make anything out, Gregory!"

"No, captain. All's like pitch ahead."

The captain uttered a sigh, and as the rest were roused, and realised what was taking place, they received it all with a dull quiet resignation, as if death would be almost welcome now.

The moments passed, and right and left the breakers roared, seeming so near that they fancied they saw them, and then as they rode on all at once there was a roar of breaking water right ahead.

But it was impossible to change the boat's course, and sitting stern and with his teeth set, Mr Gregory bent at the tough ash oar, as the boat refused to swerve a little to the right, where he thought the roar of breakers was less loud.

Then, with a shock which seemed to electrify all on board, the keel struck upon a rock, there was a crushing grating sound, a roar of waters, a wave leaped in, deluging all afresh, and the gig rose high in the air, and then plunged down as if into the depths of the ocean never to rise again.

Chapter Twenty One
How Help came in Time of Need

The shock was so sudden that the half-awakened and helpless occupants of the boat made no effort to move, but clung to the thwarts of the boat, while the mast, with its heavy rain-saturated sail, snapped off short and fell over the side, dragging by its cords, as the boat rose again after its dive, gliding up a hillock of water, halted for a moment on the summit, and then glided down again.

This was repeated two or three times, and each with less violence, after which, to the surprise and joy of all, the little vessel rose and fell easily as the sea undulated, the officers knowing at once that they had struck upon a reef, which they had but just touched, and then had been carried over it into the calm water of a lagoon, where they rocked peacefully and safely, while only a short distance away the waves were thundering upon the coral rock, and fretting and raging as they roared, apparently wroth at not being able to reach their escaping prey.

"No water to signify," said the mate, as Billy Widgeon and Small baled hard till their dippers scraped the bottom without success.

The captain did not speak, but pressed his wife's hand, while for the first time Mrs O'Halloran displayed emotion by taking her half-numbed child to her breast, and sobbing aloud.

The major did not move, but laid one hand on Mark's knee and gave it a firm grip, sighing hard the while, and then there was silence for a time, as the gig rocked easily in the darkness, while the thunderous roar of the breakers grew less violent; and, instead of being deluged with spray as every billow curved over, there was a sensation as of shelter and warmth which pointed to the fact that the boat must have drifted behind rocks as into some channel; but the intense darkness rendered everything obscure.

"Cheer-ri-ly, mates," said a voice suddenly, as a slight splashing was heard. "We're not a-going to be drowned—dead this here time, for I've just touched bottom with the hitcher."

"Now, my lads," said the captain gravely, "our lives have been spared, thank Heaven! and we are to see the light of another day."

There was again silence, with the muffled roar of the breakers farther away than ever, and as the boat rocked away slowly with the same gentle motion, the wet, cold, and misery were forgotten by one after another, the darkness helping, the occupants of the little craft dropped off to sleep, one of the last being Mark.

Cramped, faint, and miserable, the lad woke at last with a start, to lie with his eyes open staring straight up at the blue sunlit sky, his mind for the time being a perfect blank. In fact it was some minutes before he realised that he was in the bottom of the boat, with his head resting upon Bruff's curly coat, and that Jack was huddled up close to him staring down into his face with an inquiring look, which, being interpreted, really meant, Where is the food?

Mark struggled up so painfully that he felt ready to lie down again; but he persevered and knelt in the bottom of the boat, to see as strange a sight as had ever before met his eyes. For, in spite of their cramped positions, every soul on board was sleeping heavily, the men in the bottom of the boat forward making pillows of each other, the tired ladies clinging together in the stern, and the officers amidships—the extreme stern with its limited space having been left to Mark, Bruff, and the monkey.

Haggard, pale, some with faces blackened with powder, others with their heads bound up with handkerchiefs and bandages which showed the necessity for their application, and all in the sleep which comes of utter exhaustion.

The ladies, with their hair dishevelled and their wet garments clinging to them, evoked most of the lad's pity, which was the next moment withdrawn for his father, who looked ghastly pale, and lay back with his head against the side of the boat, his hand resting upon that of Mr Morgan, whose face was buried in his chest as he leaned against a thwart.

The first-mate, too, crouched amidships in a very uneasy position, where he had tried to settle down with the major so as to leave more room. While the latter seemed the most placid of all, and lay back with half a cigar in his teeth—one which had evidently been cut in two, for there was no sign of the end having been lit.

Mark gazed round in a half-stupefied way for some minutes, hardly realising what it all meant, and it was only by scraps that he recalled the events since the fight in the cabin.

But by degrees all came back, even to the grazing of the reef and the gliding into calm water, and he looked to the right, to see about a mile away a long line of white foam, whose sound came in a low murmur, while between them and it lay blue water quite smooth and unruffled, save that it heaved softly, and far beyond the line of white foam there was the sunlit sea.

Sunlit, for, save to his left, there was not a cloud to be seen. The sky was of an intense blue, and the cloud that remained was peculiar-looking — fleecy and roseate, and hanging over the centre of a beautiful land whose shore was of pure white sand, rising right out of which and close to the water were the smooth straight columns of the cocoa-nut trees with their capitals of green.

He could see little but these beautiful vegetable productions, save farther along the shore, and beyond the belt of cocoa-nut trees a pile of rocks ran right down into the water; but from a glimpse here and there it was evident that there were tall trees and high ground beyond the palms.

Greatest boon of all to his eyes was the sun, which was not yet high, but whose warm beams provided him with an invigorating bath and seemed to send life and hope and strength into his cramped and chilled limbs.

He turned to look in another direction, and found that the boat was within a few yards of the pure white sands of a sort of spit or point which ran down into the lagoon, whose limpid waters were sheltered by the barrier reef; and as he wondered how it was that they had not drifted quite ashore he realised that the sail with its yard half sunken beneath the surface had caught in a piece of jagged coral rock, which rose from the bottom covered with its freight of animation, and to this they were anchored.

"Shall I wake them?" thought Mark as he looked round him at the sleeping people; but he did not stir, for the act seemed cruel. They were sleeping soundly and resting; the sun was rising higher and drying their wet garments; and at last, deciding that it would be wiser to let them wake of themselves, he turned his longing eyes to the soft white sand, which he felt must be warm, and it was all he could do to keep from lowering himself over the side and wading ashore, to lie down in it, to cover his limbs with it, and try once more to sleep.

The act would have aroused the sufferers about him, and he refrained, contenting himself with gazing down over the side at the coral rock three feet below the bottom of the boat, and seeing there among the miniature groves of wondrously tinted weeds shoals of silvery fish; translucent shrimps; curiously long snaky, scaly looking objects which wound in and out and undulated among the weeds, while every here and there played about some tiny chubby-looking fish like a fat young John Dory, but gorgeous in colour in the sunlit waters almost beyond description, so vivid were the bands of orange, purple, azure-blue, green, and gold.

Every here and there were curious shell-fish, some creeping like snails with their heavy houses upon their backs, others were oyster and mussel like, anchored and lying with their valvular shells half open; while a couple of yards away lay one monster about two feet long, a bivalve with ponderous shells, whose edges were waved in three folds, and a glance inside whose opening showed a lining of the most delicate pinky tint.

The warmth of the sun and the wonders of the coral-reef beneath his eyes made Mark forget his troubles for a time, but he was recalled to his position by his sensations of hunger, a whine from Bruff, and an inquiring chatter from the monkey, who changed his position and sat up on one of the thwarts looking very skinny and miserable, his face wrinkled and puckered, and the appealing inquiring look in his eyes growing more intense.

Mark gazed from one countenance to the other, all haggard and troubled, and he was beginning to long to awaken some one when the major stirred slightly, and drawing a long breath rolled the half cigar to and fro between his lips. Then without unclosing his eyes he grunted out:

"Bring me a light."

Miserable, wet, and hungry as he was, Mark could not restrain a smile.

"Bring me a light," growled the major again. "Do you—eh?" he ejaculated, opening his eyes and gazing round. "Oh! hah! I remember now. Huph! Oh my legs; they're as stiff as if they'd no joints! Why, Mark, my lad, good morning."

His words were uttered in a low voice, for he had glanced round and seen that everyone was asleep.

Mark reached over and extended his hand, which was warmly grasped, and this done, the major gave a glance round, grasping at once their position.

"Shame to wake them," he said, "but I want to stretch my legs. Ah, that's it! Give me your knife, lad."

Mark drew out his pocket-knife, and the major took hold of the sheet which reached to the submerged sail, and drew upon it so as to set the boat in motion. Then letting it go again he dexterously cut the sheet in two upon the edge of the boat before there was any check, and the gig floated slowly towards the shore.

"We shall be able to find that afterwards," he said in a whisper; and then he waited till the boat softly grounded upon the sands, so close to where they lay dry, that the major was able to step ashore, rocking the boat so slightly that no one stirred.

Mark made a sign, and Bruff limped up on to the thwart painfully, and made as if to leap ashore, but hesitated, lifted up his wounded paw, and whimpered.

The difficulty was solved by his master lifting his hind quarters over the side, the dog offering no resistance, and touching bottom he managed the rest himself, and splashed through the water to limp a few yards, and lie down and roll in the warm dry sand.

Jack needed no invitation or order, for, hopping to the side rather stiffly, he leaped over the intervening water on to the sand, and bounded to Bruff, chattering and revelling in the sunshine, while the dog ran on along the shore, and the two now began to gambol and roll.

Mark was the next to step ashore, and as he followed the major he limped, feeling as if every joint had been wrenched; but the pain wore off a little as he persevered, and following the major's example he stretched himself upon the sand.

"We're not much more than damp now, my lad," said the major; "and this will dry us and warm us too. I say, my boy, I thought we had come to the end of the book. Didn't you?"

"No," said Mark quietly. "I knew we were in great danger; but I felt that my father would save our lives."

"That's right," said the major. "Always have faith in your father, my lad. He's a fine fellow, and if you follow his example you will not go far wrong. Now, then, I begin to feel much better, and if I could light my cigar I should feel better still."

"Have you no matches, sir?"

"Yes, my lad, but if they are dry they may be wanted to cook something if there is anything here to cook, and I mustn't waste them on my luxuries. I wish I had awakened my Mary, but it's best to let her waken herself, and if I woke her I should have awakened them all."

"There's Mr Gregory opening his eyes, sir," said Mark eagerly; and he made a sign to the mate.

Mr Gregory stared hard at him for a few moments before any sign of comprehension came into his face. It did, however, at last, and he rose stiffly and stepped ashore.

"Good morning, indeed," he said; "it's more than good, for yesterday I thought it was good night for all of us. Why don't you light your cigar, major?"

"Don't tempt me, man, I'm going to practise chewing. Have this other half. Will you chew it?"

"No," said Mr Gregory, taking out a little silver matchbox; "I've plenty of lights, quite dry."

He struck one, and the two men lit their half cigars and sat in the sun smoking, while Mark watched them, the sun begetting a delicious sense of content and satisfaction, making him half-close his eyes as he listened to their conversation.

"Where are we, major! Can't exactly say. Small coral island somewhere near the track of ships to the east."

"It must be a good-sized coral island," said the major, "for there seems to be quite a mountain yonder."

"Can't be the mainland," said Gregory. "Yes, you're right. That is a hill of some height, and—why, there are clouds upon it and—why, they are only half-way up, and there are more on the top."

"Why, Gregory," cried the major, "it's a volcano!"

"No," said the mate; "there is no volcano anywhere near where we can be. You're right, sir, after all. Well, I'm puzzled; for that's a burning mountain certainly!"

Mark gazed with wondering eyes at the mountain, to see that the clouds which he had noticed when he first gazed shoreward were slowly dissolving away, leaving a line of mist apparently about a thousand feet above the sea; while above that the mountain was visible running up in a perfect cone to quite three thousand feet higher, where the point was hidden in a steaming cloud.

"You don't know where we are, then?"

"No, sir; perhaps the captain will know when he wakes. I've been out here again and again, and never seen that mountain. We can't, I am sure, be on the mainland, and it seems impossible that we can have been driven anywhere near Java. However, we are safe ashore, and, judging from the look of the trees and the sea, we shall not starve."

"I shall," said the major, puffing away at his bit of cigar. "If we don't soon have food I shall either kill and eat the monkey or Master Mark here! I must have something. By the way, don't throw your cigar-end down—save it. Tobacco may grow scarce."

The mate nodded; and just then Mark uttered an ejaculation, for he saw Mrs Strong move; her companions started into wakefulness at the same time; and the next moment, as they rose painfully the major and Mark helped them ashore, where they sank down in the warm sand.

The captain was roused by the motion of the boat; and he would have come ashore without awaking his men, but the boat was so lightened now that the men were roused. The least injured came ashore, and after an effort or two ran the gig up on the sands, with the two men who were worst lying in the bottom—Mr Morgan and one of the fore-mast men—these two being carefully lifted out and laid on the sand in the shade of the cocoa-nut trees, while something in the shape of breakfast was prepared.

At first everyone moved painfully, but every step in the light and warmth seemed comforting; and before long all were busy, the men finding shell-fish in the hollows and crevices of the coral rocks; others collected wood, while a fire was made. Billy Widgeon, after rubbing his legs and bathing his feet first in the sea and then in the warm sand, volunteered to climb a cocoa-nut tree and get down some fruit; the ladies went to a pool in the rocks to try and perform something in the way of a morning toilet; and the major turned chef and cooked the shell-fish, and opened some tins of preserved meat and biscuit; Mark being the successful discoverer of a spring as he went in search of Bruff, to find him drinking thereof.

Shortly afterwards, in earnest thankfulness, a hearty breakfast was eaten upon that lonely shore. But when cuts had been bathed and re-bandaged and evidences of the conflict removed, and a short inspection made to see if there was anything to fear from savages, the arms were examined and made ready, a watch was set; and in the shade of the cocoa-nut grove the greatest boon of the weary was sought and found—for by mid-day, when the sun was scorching in its power, all had gladly lain down to rest and find the sleep that would prepare them for the struggle for life in which they were to engage.

"So we are to be the first watch—eh, Mark?" said the major.

"Yes, sir," was the reply.

"Four hours. Shall we keep awake?"

Just then there was a low moan.

"Yes," said the major; "we shall not want to sleep with poor Morgan like that."

"Will he recover, sir?" whispered Mark as he knelt in the sand by the sick man's head, and raised some cocoa-nut leaves over his head as a screen.

"Please God!" said the major piously; and he followed Mark's example and screened the injured and now delirious fore-mast-man from the sunbeams, which streamed like silvery arrows through the great founts of verdant leaves.

Chapter Twenty Two
How the Watch heard a Noise

That was a weary watch, but, as the major said, they did not want to sleep, with the wounded men moaning and muttering in their uneasy rest. For there was so much to do, seeing to the shade and altering the positions of the leaves, so that while the sun was kept off, the soft breeze from the sea was allowed to cool the fevered brows of the patients.

Then there were flies which were disposed to be troublesome and had to be kept at a distance, Mark making a loose chowry, like a horse-tail, of long wiry grass, and this proving so effective that the major annexed it, and advised Mark to make another.

And so an hour passed away, after which Mark took a tin and fetched some of the cool spring-water which came trickling down from the interior, deeply shaded by the ferns, and so low among mossy stones that he had to climb into a narrow chasm to the clear basin-like pool.

With this he prepared to bathe Morgan's forehead; but as he bent over him the poor fellow's countenance wore so terrible an aspect, the skin being absolutely green, that the lad shrank away and signed to the major.

"Well, my lad, what is it?"

"Look!—his face! What does it mean?"

"Eh!—mean! What?"

"Don't you see? That horrible green!"

"Tchah! what are you talking about?" said the major, picking up a leaf and holding it over his head. "Now, then, what colour is my face?"

"Green," said Mark, smiling. "How stupid of me!"

"Well, we will not call it stupid, my lad; but with so many real difficulties we must not make imaginary ones. Why, Mark, this voyage is making a man of you—self-reliant, business-like, and strong. When we get over it—"

"Shall we get over it, sir?" said Mark sadly.

"Ah!" said the major, speaking in a low tone so as not to disturb the patients; "now, that's a chance for a sermon for you, my lad, only I can't preach. Look here, Mark, ten thousand things may happen to us, one of which is that we may all die here of starvation."

"Yes, sir."

"Well, then, that's ten thousand to one. Bah! Don't fidget now. We have just landed in a little paradise, after running terrible risks from spear and kris, explosion, fire, storm, and wreck. You ought to be thankful, and not growl."

"I am thankful, sir."

"Then show it, my lad. Take what comes, like a man; do the best you can for everybody, and leave the rest."

"I'll try, sir."

"Try! nonsense! I know you already, my lad, better than you know yourself. You'll do it naturally without trying."

They sat here in that golden glow of shelter for some time in silence, watching their patients and the glittering sea, broken every now and then by the splash of a fish.

"Do you think Mr Morgan will get better, sir?" whispered Mark at last.

"Certainly I do. Why shouldn't he? A strong healthy man with his wound waiting to heal as soon as he could have rest and proper sleep. What we have gone through was enough to give us all fever, so no wonder a wounded man is so bad. I expected that your father would give up."

"But he has not, sir."

"No; mind has kept him from breaking down. He has all the responsibility, you see. You must try and grow up just such a man, my lad."

There was again a silence, broken at last by the major.

"I want to go exploring here, Mark," he said. "I expect this will prove to be a very wonderful place."

"But I thought such an island as this would be full of beautiful birds."

"Perhaps it is, but the birds are all sitting under their sun-shades till the sun begins to go down. Why, Mark, we shall be in clover!"

"But about food, sir? What shall we do for food for such a party? The stores won't last long."

"Now, that's a boy all over," said the major, chuckling. "Food! My word, how a boy does love the larder! There, don't look so serious, Mark. I was just as bad, I can remember, at home, enjoying my own school-room breakfast, then getting a little more when my father had his; having a little lunch; then my dinner, followed by my tea; after which dessert, when they had theirs, in the dining-room; lastly, a bit of supper; and I finished off by taking biscuits or baking-pears to bed."

"Yes, sir," said Mark; "but that was in England."

"Well, never mind. We shall find something to eat here, I daresay. Enough to keep us. Why, Mark, I don't suppose we should have to put you in the pot for quite a year."

Mark laughed, and the major's eyes twinkled as he went on.

"What nonsense, my lad! we couldn't starve here. The sea teems with fish waiting to be caught. Look yonder."

Mark glanced in the required direction, and could see the smooth water in the lagoon dappled and blurring as a shoal of fish played upon the surface.

"But how are we to catch them, sir?"

"Hooks and lines; make nets; fish-traps. Why, Mark, if a savage can do these things, surely we can!"

"Do you think there are any animals here?" said Mark, glancing round.

"Sure to be of some kind. The place is evidently extensive. Pig, perhaps deer; plenty of birds; and we have guns and ammunition. Then there will be fruit."

"Do you think so, sir?"

"I'm sure of it. There are the cocoa-nuts to begin with. Fruit! yes, and vegetables too."

Mark smiled.

"Ah, you don't know! Knock that fly off Morgan's cheek. But I do, my lad. We sha'n't get any asparagus; but we can eat the palm-shoots; and as for cabbage, we sha'n't regret that as long as we can get at the hearts of the palms."

"Do you think there will be any snakes?" asked Mark.

"Sure to be."

"Poisonous?"

"Very likely. Perhaps some big ones. They'll do to eat if we are very hungry."

"Ugh!" ejaculated Mark, with a shudder.

"Well, I'm like the Yankee backwoodsman, Mark, my lad. He didn't 'hanker arter crows' after he had eaten them once. I don't 'hanker arter' snakes, but I'd sooner sit down to a section of boa-constrictor roasted in the ashes than starve."

"I don't think I would."

"Wait till you are starving, my lad."

"Should you say there are any big dangerous animals?" continued Mark, after a pause; "lions, or tigers, or leopards?"

"Certainly not; but there may be rhinoceros or elephant, if the island is big enough, or near the mainland, and—what the dickens is that?"

He jumped up as rapidly as Mark sprang to his feet, for just then there came, apparently not from very far off, so terrible a roar that the major ran to the nearest gun, examined the loading, and then stood with the weapon cocked.

Mark involuntarily caught his arm.

"Don't do that, boy," said the major in a low angry voice. "That is what a woman would do—try to find protection, and hinder the man. Get a weapon if it's only your knife."

Mark's pale face flushed, and he caught up a gun, to stand beside the major, as the terrific harsh yelling roar came again.

It was a sound horrible enough to startle the stoutest hearted, so weird and peculiar was it in its tones; while the silence which succeeded was even more terror inspiring, for it suggested that the wild beast which had uttered the cry might have caught sight of them, and be coming nearer.

The sound seemed to come from the rocky rapidly-rising ground beyond the narrow tree-fern shaded gorge where the spring had been found; but though they listened intently for a few moments, there was utter stillness till all at once there was a fresh sound, something between a sigh and a moan, such as an animal might utter if it had been struck down.

Mark's eyes swept the land beyond the cocoa-nut grove wildly; but he could see nothing save the rocks and flowering shrubs; then he glanced at the shaded sands where their friends were sleeping, but the sound had not awakened them.

"I can't make it out, Mark," said the major, as he keenly swept the place as far as the trees would allow. "Couldn't be fancy, could it?"

The answer came in a piteous burst of howls, followed by a hissing sound, and directly after Bruff appeared, tearing along on three legs, his last tucked out of sight, the rough shaggy hair which formed a ruff about his neck bristling; and close behind him, Jacko running as if for his life.

"No," said the major; "it couldn't be fancy. They heard it too."

Bruff ran up to Mark, and crouched at his feet shivering and whining; while Jacko kept running from one to the other, chattering in a low tone and staring wildly about as if in a terrible state of excitement.

"Can you hear anything coming, Mark?" said the major. "Down, dog! lie still!"

Mark listened intently; but there was not a sound to be heard but the distant boom of the breakers on the barrier reef, the beating of his heart, and the growling of the dog. Once only came a shrill chizzling chirping, evidently made by some kind of cricket, otherwise there was the stillness of a torrid day when the very vegetation begins to flag.

"I can't hear it, sir," he whispered.

"So it can't be coming," said the major, looking uneasy. "I'm puzzled, Mark. It was neither lion nor tiger, though something like the roar a lion can give; it was not like an elephant's trumpeting, nor the grunting of a rhinoceros; and it could not be a hippopotamus, for we are out of their range, and there is no big river—there can't be—here."

"Could it be some enormous serpent?" whispered Mark.

"I never heard a serpent do anything but hiss, my lad, though they say the anacondas make strange thunder in the North American forests."

"It might be a large crocodile."

"Yes, it might," said the major; "but if it was, the noise is something quite new to me."

"It is more likely to be some terrible beast here that we never heard of before, sir," faltered Mark. "Don't laugh at me, sir, I can't help feeling nervous."

"You'd be a wonder if you could," said the major. "I feel ten times as uncomfortable as I did at any time yesterday. We knew what we had to meet then, but this is something—"

Whoor–r–oor!

The sound came again with terrible violence, but though it was as horrible and awe-inspiring it was either farther away or the animal which uttered the cry had turned its head in another direction.

"It's beyond me, Mark, my lad," said the major, drawing a long breath; "but it can't see us here, whatever it is, and it is something strange to be roaring like that by day."

"I wonder it has not woke anyone up," whispered Mark.

"Worn out," replied the major, laconically; and then they stood peering out from among the trees, and watching intently for a long time without hearing a sound, till the cricket began to utter its chirruping note again.

This was taken up by another close by, and by another at a distance, and then quite a chorus followed, resembling the sounds made by the house-cricket of the English hearth, but more whirring and ear-piercing.

"It must have gone back into the jungle, Mark," said the major, "or else fallen asleep. Anyhow I'm not at all pleased to find we have such a neighbour."

"Do you think it is a dangerous beast?" whispered Mark.

"I can't say till I've seen it, but it sounds very much like it."

"I know what it is!" said Mark in a low excited voice.

"You do?"

"Yes. It is in that jungle, yonder."

"I don't know where it is, but it must be somewhere near. Well, what is it?"

"A wild man of the woods."

"What! an orang-outang?"

Mark nodded.

"Well, if it is, we shall have to tame him. My word, he must have a fine broad chest, Mark, and he has a wonderful voice for a song. There, I don't think we are in any danger for the present, and it must be nearly the end of our watch by the look of the sun. Here comes the captain."

Chapter Twenty Three
How Billy Widgeon was damped

Mark turned sharply, to see that his father was approaching, and his first words were concerning the time.

"It must be beyond your watch, major," he said. "Why didn't you wake me?"

"Well, the fact is, we've had a scare," said the major; and he related their experience.

"It's strange," said the captain; "but we are well armed. It may be, as Mark says, some kind of monkey. They can make atrocious noises. How are the sick men?"

"Sleeping beautifully," said the major. "And you?"

"Far better; that little sleep has worked wonders. I'll go and rouse up Small."

"No; let the poor fellow sleep," said the major. "I don't want to lie down. Do you, Mark?"

"No; I couldn't sleep with that noise so near," said Mark. "I should like to stay. But wouldn't it be best to get the boat launched again in case there is any very great danger?"

"It would not take long to launch that," said his father. "If we are not molested for the night we will begin exploring to-morrow. This evening we must try and rig up a shed for the women. To-morrow we shall be better able to think what we can do."

The captain looked at the two wounded men, who seemed to be sleeping now more easily, and then taking his gun he proposed to the major that they should make a little search round their resting-place to see what was the cause of the noise they had heard.

This meant leaving Mark alone, and he looked up so ruefully at the major, that, recollecting his own qualms, the latter objected to the plan.

"No, no, Strong," he said; "if there is any danger let it come to us, I don't see any use in going to meet it."

"As you will," said the captain quietly. "What we seem to want now is rest and strength. Oh, here is one of the men!"

Bruff and the monkey drew their attention to him by going toward the place where the men were sleeping, Bruff limping, but wagging his bushy tail, and the monkey cantering towards his old friend Billy with plenty of low chattering and sputtering noises.

This awoke Small, who rose and came out of the grove to walk slowly along the sands comparing notes about their injuries, which were fortunately very slight.

"What shall we do, captain?" said Small.

"Take the boat and see if you can recover the sail. You can go with them if you like, Mark."

Mark turned to go eagerly.

"Can you launch the boat?"

"Ay, ay, sir; it ain't far," was the reply; and the three went down to the spot where the gig lay, ran her down into the smooth water, and pushed out, Small thrusting an oar over the stern and giving it the necessary fish-tail motion known as paddling, while Mark and Billy Widgeon looked out for the submerged sail.

It was soon found and towed ashore, where, after the boat had been made fast to a piece of rock, the canvas was drawn over the dry burning sands, first on one side and then on the other, parting readily with its moisture, and being finally left in the hot glow.

The captain joined them directly after with the major.

"Did you hear it, father?" whispered Mark.

"No, my boy; all has been perfectly silent. Now, to see if we cannot make some kind of shelter."

It was by no means a difficult job, for Small and Billy Widgeon soon set the boat mast free from its lashings, which were utilised to fasten the slight spar horizontally between two thin cocoa-nut palms at about three feet from the ground, which was here, as for the most part about them, covered with soft dry drifted sand.

Over this it was proposed to hang the sail as soon as it was dry and peg out the sides, for which purpose Small and his companion took out their knives, and, attacking a low scrubby bush, soon had a sufficiency ready.

"Not much of a place, Mark," said the captain cheerfully; "but it will make a dry little tent for the ladies till we see what we can do."

The next thing was to overhaul the stores, which made so poor a show that the captain knit his brow, but cleared it directly, and helped to place all together in a little heap beneath the cocoa-nut trees in company with the ammunition, of which there was a fair supply, and the arms.

"I think these men should carry revolvers in their belts," said the captain, "in case of there being any danger."

"Decidedly," said the major in an emphatic way.

"Which I shouldn't say as there was, sir," said the boatswain, "unless some of these copper rascals come and land, for this here must be only a little island, as a climb up the mountain will show us when you like to go, sir."

"Never mind, Small, carry a loaded revolver. Better be prepared than be caught helpless. Besides, you might, perhaps, unexpectedly get a shot at a pig, and such a chance mustn't be lost."

Danger past, a sailor soon recovers his good-humour, and Billy Widgeon ducked down, doubling himself up in a silent laugh.

"Which is right, Billy, my lad," said the boatswain good-humouredly. "He thinks if we waits for pork till I brings down a pig with a six-shooter the crackling won't burn and the stuffing spoil."

He thrust the weapon through the waistband of his trousers, right at the back, so as to leave his hands free, and then looked up at the captain for orders.

"We shall have to set-to and get provisions somehow, Small," said the captain, "and begin in real earnest to-morrow, trying what we can do with the guns inland. Suppose you and Widgeon try to unlay one of the sail-ropes and make a fishing-line."

"And about hooks?" said the major.

"Ah! that has been a puzzle," said the captain, "that I have not solved as yet."

"I know," said Mark eagerly. "The ladies are sure to have some hair-pins."

"Which we can temper in the fire and hammer into shape," said the captain. "Think you could raise a barb at one end before we point it, major?"

"I think I can try," replied the major.

"And I could pynt 'em on the stones," said Billy eagerly.

"Then the fishing difficulty is over," said the captain. "Fish are sure to swarm off those rocks."

"I say, Billy," said Small, giving one ear a rub, "aren't there a couple o' fishing-lines in the locker of the gig?"

Billy gave one of his short legs a slap, turned sharply and ran down to the boat, where he lifted a triangular lid in the bows, and gave a cheer as he plunged in his hand.

"Three on 'em," he cried, "and good uns."

"Then we sha'n't starve yet, major. There are fish and water."

"And cocoa-nuts in plenty," cried Mark.

"If we can get at them," said the major.

"Why, Billy, couldn't you climb one o' them trees?" cried Small.

"I could—one of the small ones," said Mark.

"But the small ones don't seem to bear nuts," said the captain quietly.

"I dunno," said Billy, after a spell of thinking. "I'm a bit skeert about it."

"What, afraid?" growled Small.

"No, no, not afraid," said Billy; "skeert as I couldn't get up. You see there's no branches, not a sign o' one till you gets to the place where the nuts grows, and then the branches is all leaves."

"No," said the major, looking at Billy with his head on one side, "he is not a countryman of mine. That was an English bull, Mark."

"Why, o' course!" cried Billy, slapping his leg. "I've got it."

"Got what, m'lad?" said Small.

"The coky-nuts," said Billy, smiling. "'Tis his natur' to."

"Don't talk conundydrums, m'lad," said the boatswain. "If so be as you've got the coky-nuts, let's have 'em, for I'd like a go at one 'mazingly."

"Why, I aren't got the nuts, gentlemen," said Billy; "but, as I said afore, it is his natur' to."

"Whose, Billy?" said Mark.

"Why, the monkey's, sir. Here, Jack."

The monkey, who was performing a very kindly office for Bruff, as the dog lay stretched upon the sand, and making a slight repast off the insects, left off searching, and ambled in a sideways fashion to Billy.

"Look ye here, my hearty," said the latter, as the monkey leaped lightly in his arms, and holding him with one, the sailor picked up an old dried nut in its husky covering.

"These here's coky-nuts, as you knows very well; so let's pick out a good tree, and up you goes and gets some and throws 'em down."

Jack uttered a chattering noise, took hold of the light nut, turned it over, and let it fall.

"Toe be sure," said Billy, smiling with pride. "Then let 'em fall, and 'below!' and 'ware heads!' says you. Ain't he a monkey to be proud on, Master Mark?"

"Send him up then, Billy, and let's have some down."

"That I just will," said the little sailor; and toddling to one of the most heavily-laden of the trees near, where the nuts could be seen pendent beneath the plumose leaves which glistened in the evening sun, he placed the monkey against the smooth-stemmed tree.

"That's your sort," he cried; "up you goes, Jack, and shies down all the lot."

The monkey seemed to enjoy the task, and catching the smooth stem with its fore-paws he began to ascend quite readily, while those below watched him till he reached the crown of the graceful tree, fifty feet above their heads.

"Bravo, Jack!" said the major. "I claim the three first nuts for the ladies."

"And I the next for the wounded men," said Mark.

"And you shall have 'em, my lad," said Billy excitedly. "I say, Mr Mark, sir, aren't he a monkey to be proud on? He's cleverer than lots o' men."

Meanwhile Jack had climbed solemnly into the verdant nest above the nuts, and now looked down to where Bruff was staring wonderingly up at him, and uttered a low chattering, to which the dog responded with a bark.

"That's them, Jack. Chuck 'em down, old lad," cried Billy, smiling gleefully, as he rubbed his hands up and down his sides.

Jack changed his position, his tail giving a whisk or spin round, and looked down at Bruff, who now ran to the other side.

"Come, matey! Let's have 'em," said Billy. "Here, look sharp! Chuck down the whole lot."

Jack chattered again, and then as Bruff barked he barked in no very bad imitation, while he took hold of a leaf and gave it a shake.

"No, no; the nuts, stoopid, not them there leaves," cried Billy.

Jack shook another leaf and barked at the dog, who barked up at him, and reared up and scratched the tree.

"Here, you be off, and don't interrupt," cried Billy, throwing his cap at the dog. "Don't you see he's busy?"

Bruff caught the cap up in his teeth and trotted away with it, whereat Jack chattered and sputtered more loudly, and again shook one of the leaves, whilst the little party below looked on in an amused fashion.

"Why, Billy," said the boatswain at last, in the most stolid of tones, "don't seem to me as that there is a monkey to be proud on."

"Oh yes, he is, Mr Small, sir! He's a good un, and he'd ha' sent them there nuts a showering down if that there dorg hadn't begun his larks. Here, give me my cap."

"Never mind the cap, Billy," said Mark, laughing, "we want the nuts."

"So do I, Mr Mark, sir," said Billy, scratching his head, "and I'd give old Jack such a clout o' the head if I was up there."

"Ah! you'll have to teach him how, my man," said the major. "No nuts that way."

"He knows, begging your pardon, sir," said Billy. "You just wait a minute, sir, and you'll see."

"No," said the major, "it does not seem any use to wait. Come, Strong, let's see how our wives are getting on."

"Well, I do call that shabby," muttered Billy. "Just as I was a taking all this trouble. Here, you, sir, shy down one o' them nuts."

"Chick!" said Jack.

"Do you hear?"

"Chack!" said Jack.

"Now, look here," said Billy, stooping down and picking up a handful of sand; "if you don't chuck down some of them here nuts I'll shy this here at you and knock you off your perch."

"Chick, chick, chick! Chack, chack, chack! Chicker, chicker, chacker, chacker, chacker, chack!" sputtered the monkey, dancing up and down in the tree.

"Well, I am blamed!" cried Billy savagely, as he saw the captain and major strolling away and the boatswain and Mark laughing at him. "It's all his orbstinacy—that's what it is. I'll give him such a wunner when I gets hold of him. I'll make him say 'chack!'"

But there seemed to be no more chance of Billy getting hold of the monkey than of the nuts, and the more he scolded and abused the curious animal the more loudly it sputtered at him, and seemed to expostulate and scold by turns.

"There, it's of no good," said the boatswain; "give it up, my lad."

"Yes," said Billy sulkily, "I'm a-going to; but if I don't sarve him out for this my name aren't Widgeon."

"Come along, Mr Mark," said the boatswain, "Jack's going to roost up there to-night."

"Wish he may tumble out o' the tree, then, and break something," growled Billy, whose dignity was touched.

"He won't tumble," said the boatswain, "he knows better. Come along, Mr Mark."

"Want him down, Billy?"

"Course I does, and I'm sorry for him when he do come, for I'm a-going to warm his skin, that's what I'm a-going to do for him."

"Shall I get him down?"

"You can't," cried Billy sourly.

"Better than you can get cocoa-nuts," said Mark, laughing, for the perils were all forgotten, and the strange noise in the jungle might never have been. "Here, Bruff."

The dog trotted up with Billy's cap in his mouth, surrendered it dutifully; and then Mark caught up a piece of drift-wood—a branch swept ashore by the current—and raising it in a threatening way, Bruff uttered a low howl.

Whish went the stick through the air, and Bruff crouched at his feet, grovelling in the sand, and holding up his wounded and bandaged paw as he whined piteously, as if that injury were sufficient to exempt him from being beaten.

Mark bent over him, caught him by the loose skin of his neck, and struck the sand a heavy bang.

The dog whined softly as if beaten, and Jack began to dance about up in the cocoa-nut tree, snaking the leaves and chattering savagely.

Another blow on the sand, a howl, and a furious burst from the monkey, who spat and scolded more fiercely.

Another blow, and another, and another; and as Bruff whined, the monkey came scuffling down the smooth columnar trunk, and was evidently on his way to attack Mark, but Billy caught him before he could reach the ground, administered a smart cuff on the ear, and would have delivered another, but, quick as thought, Jack sprang from his grasp, spun round, leaped upon his back like lightning, bit him in the thick of the neck, and then bounded away towards the jungle, followed by the dog.

"Now I calls him a warmint," said Billy, rubbing his neck softly. "A warmint—that's what I calls him. Only let me get hold on him again; and if I don't make him warm, my name aren't Widgeon."

"You've got about the worst on it this time, my lad, and no mistake," said Small, laughing, while Mark stamped about and held his sides.

"Yes, I've got the worst on it," said Billy; "but I'll sarve him out—a warmint. My neck a-bleeding, Mr Small?"

"No, m'lad, only a bit red. He's give it a bit of a pinch; that's all."

"Yes, and I'll give him a bit of a pinch when I ketches him. I calls him a warmint—that's what I calls him."

Billy kept on repeating this as he followed Mark and the boatswain to where the two wounded men were lying, and just then one of the sailors came out of the grove to join them, his services being enlisted to help stretch the sail over the mast and peg it tightly down, for it was now pretty well dry, the result being that a fairly good shelter was provided for the ladies, who soon after came out to join the captain and major just as the sun was going down, and the short tropical twilight set in.

There was no desire for another meal, the weariness consequent upon the exertions and anxieties of the past still inviting rest; and after all had sat upon the sands for a while gazing at the phosphorescent sea, and the great stars which glowed out of the purple sky, a fresh watch was set, Mr Gregory being roused now from his heavy sleep.

"Shall I tell him about the noise we heard?" said the major.

"It would only be fair," the captain said; and the result was told.

"Well," he said, "Small's going to share my watch, and we'll have the guns. If whatever it is comes, I daresay we shall have a shot at it before it does us any mischief, and I suppose if you hear firing, gentlemen, you'll rouse up."

Half an hour later those two were keeping their lonely vigil, while the rest followed the example of the men who had not yet been awake, and sought in sleep and in simple trustfulness for the rest which was to give them strength for the labours of another day.

Chapter Twenty Four
How Mark Strong passed a bad night

The sand made a comfortable bed, and Mark had not lain down very close to one end of the little tent before he became aware that he had two companions in the shape of Bruff and Jacko, who just at dusk had come stealing back out of the jungle, and kept close to him and out of Billy Widgeon's reach.

Weary as he was, Mark found it a difficult task to go to sleep. Nothing could have been more comfortable than his bed, the soft dry sand fitting in to his shape so as to give rest to his tired muscles, and the pleasantly cool night breeze that floated through the leaves of the tall palms breathed upon his sun-scorched cheeks. Now and then there was the hum of mosquitoes, but they did not molest him; and as he lay listening to the distant boom of the surf and watched the great twinkling stars he now and then nearly lost consciousness, and the tall columns of the cocoa-nut trees took the shape to him of the supports of the old four-post bedstead at home.

Then he would start into wakefulness again and listen, fancying that he heard rustling sounds from the jungle inland, and as he raised his head he fully expected to hear the awful roar of the uncouth beast as it came down toward the grove.

But all was silent, and he was obliged to confess that it was fancy as he turned over, and with his back to the sea and its murmuring boom as in slow pulsation the billows curved over and broke, he now lay looking inland.

The cocoa-nut trees formed quite a narrow belt, so narrow that where he lay he could see between their trunks the starlit sky over the sea on the one side and the darker sky over the mountain a few miles away.

The stars shone very brightly here, too, and every now and then there was the nicker of lightning, generally so slight that it was but pale; but now and then there was a flash which seemed as if the sky opened and displayed the shapes of the clouds, and these were like mountains, or might be the mountains themselves as far as he could tell.

Still sleep would not come, and he turned again and again till he grew more hot and weary, and began to think at last how delightful it would be to go down to the edge of the sea, undress, and bathe in the cool sparkling water.

Very nice, but there were drawbacks. He did not know what strange creatures might be roaming about in search of prey, and he had often read that the lagoons about the tropic islands were infested with sharks.

Then he began to think over their future in this strange place, not with any feeling of dread, for there was a delightful novelty in the idea of exploring this unknown island; of building their own houses, making their own gardens, and fishing, hunting, and leading a life of adventure. All this seemed delightful, for he would not be alone. At times he thought of how pleasant it would have been if there were a companion of his own age; but on the whole the prospect was fascinating, and even the sensation of dread did not master the satisfaction.

There would be journeys into the interior; the burning mountain to ascend; strange birds, butterflies, and reptiles to discover, and perhaps mines of precious stones and gold. Plenty to see, plenty to find, especially wild fruits, such as were written of in the tropics. Everything with its spice of danger was tempting, till the recollection of that appalling roar came again, and with it a sensation of dampness about his forehead.

At last, just as Mark had decided that he would get up and go and join Mr Gregory and Small, to sit and talk to them, he dropped off fast asleep, and started into wakefulness again listening, for he fancied he had heard that appalling roar.

All still save the sigh of some sleeper, and once more he lay down hot, weary, and uncomfortable, for sleeping in his clothes seemed to be a horrible mistake. He had never before realised how many buttons he had about him; for, if he lay on one side, a brass button seemed to be thinking that it was a seal, and his ribs were wax. On the other side it was just as bad. If he turned over on his face, as if about to swim in the soft sand, the sensation was horrible from his throat downwards; while, if, in despair, he lay flat on his back, he felt as if a couple of holes were being bored into his waist, working their way on slowly till he told himself he could bear no more.

Just then Captain Strong came to the front of the bed, stepping on to his legs, walking right up him, and sitting down upon his chest, telling him he was a disobedient son for not going down into the hold of the ship to dig out the stowaway with the old blue earthenware shell that lay in the tea-caddy at home, a measure which, when filled three times, was considered sufficient for the pot. After that Mrs Strong came and looked at him reproachfully for feeling dissatisfied with his father's proceedings. She told him he had no business to consider the captain heavy, for he had often carried him when a little boy, while now it was his duty to carry his father.

The position seemed painful and tiresome to Mark, for the captain was so unreasonable; he kept on scolding him in a gruff voice for not getting up to dig out the stowaway, who by some singular arrangement was deep down in the hold below the packages of cargo, and at the same time standing at the foot of the bed with a handkerchief tied round his head, looking wistfully at him, as if appealing to him to come and use the caddy-spoon, and yet the captain would not get up.

It was a terrible trouble to Mark, for his reason told him that his father's conduct in sitting upon him was absurd and bad for his chest, and yet all the while he felt that his father must know best.

But then there was the little brittle caddy-spoon. He wanted to think it was correct; but his reason told him it was absurd to attempt to dig up a man with such a pitiful tool. If his father would only have got off his chest and reasoned with him he would not have cared; but here he was, a big heavy man, squatted just upon the top button of his waistcoat, his legs drawn up, his knees at his chin, and his face staring right into Mark's.

It was no wonder that the lad felt in a perspiration, and was ready to reproach his mother for not assisting him in what was minute by minute growing a more painful position; but Mrs Strong did not stir; the captain kept up in constant repetition his scolding apostrophe, and the stowaway looked more dismal than ever.

Mark tried to change his position a little so as to get ease, for the heels of the captain's boots were very hard, but to move was impossible, try how he would. He wanted to speak, but the words would not come; the oppression on his chest grew more terrible; and at last, unable to bear it any longer, he took hold of his father's thick, short, curly whiskers with both hands as he tried to thrust him away.

For response the captain uttered a low deep remonstrant growl, and Mark awoke, to find himself on his back holding Bruff's coat in his hands, and the dog protesting, for he found Mark's chest a comfortable place. Jack had agreed with him, and the pair were cuddled up together in a sort of knot which rolled off on to the sand as the lad threw himself upon his side.

Mark lay panting and hot for some time, and then once more oblivion came over him, this time with no painful nightmare full of absurdities, but a deep heavy dreamless sleep, from which he started up in horror with that appalling roar ringing in his ears and dying away in the distance.

This was no delusion, for Bruff was standing beside him whining and shivering with terror, the monkey was grovelling in the sand, and all around there were eager voices inquiring:

"What was that?"

Chapter Twenty Five
How the awful Roar was canvassed

No one could tell what, or whence came the noise, but the terror it inspired was sufficient to chase away sleep from all. Everyone had been awakened, and the captain had at once gone to the watch, followed by Mark, after he had been to the end of the little tent and tried to give some comfort by telling its occupants that the noise came from some wild beast in the jungle.

Mr Gregory and Small were on the alert. They had had a perfectly quiet watch till just then, as they were noticing the first signs of daybreak, when, increasing in volume and then dying away, there came this appalling roar.

"Just the same as we heard, eh, Mark?" said the major, coming up.

"Yes, just the same."

"Well, Gregory, what do you make it?" said the captain, who had rather doubted before.

"Don't know—some beast of the forest."

"You have heard nothing before?"

"Not a sound. Small thinks it must be a lion."

"Well, something of that kind, sir. I once heered a lion make such a row that he nearly blew off the roof of his cage! but it wasn't quite the same as this here, as is hollerer."

"Well," said the captain, "it can't be a lion; and as it does not seem disposed to molest us we must be—"

He stopped short, for there was a low moan from the same direction as that in which they had heard the cry.

"Is that something it has killed?" whispered Mark in an awe-stricken voice.

The captain did not answer; and as all listened for a repetition of the sounds the day began to dawn rapidly, the birds twittered and piped, and shrieked at the edge of the jungle, while flecks of orange and scarlet appeared high up in the sky.

Then a low murmur of admiration burst from the group as they saw a roseate cloud upon the top of the conical mountain begin to glow and burst into a dozen tints of purple and gold, shot with the most effulgent hues; and then slowly there was a glowing point to be seen just above the cloud, which circled it like a ring of gorgeously-coloured vapour; then slowly the light descended the mountain till from top to bottom it was aglow with purple and green and orange; and they turned sharply, to see that the sun was just rolling up over the smooth sea, spreading a pathway of light from the horizon to the isle.

So glorious was the scene, as the light wreaths of mist above the purple rolled away, that the terrible awakening from sleep was forgotten, and a spirit of thankfulness that they had been saved from the sea to land in such a paradise filled the breasts of all.

Beauty is beauty, but the loveliest scene is soon forgotten by a hungry man. Rest, freedom from peril, wounds and bruises amending, and the fact that the previous day's supply had been very short, combined to make everybody ravenous; and the captain, though without a ship, had his hands full.

He satisfied himself that Morgan and the sailor were better, the fever having abated, and then gave his orders shortly.

Two men were set to make a fire, two more to cut down a cocoa-nut tree that was of small size and yet bore several fruits.

The major and Widgeon started off along the shore with a biscuit-bag to collect shell-fish, and at the muddy exit of a tiny stream came upon quite a swarm of little crabs, who challenged them to fight—so Billy afterwards said—by snapping their claws at them and flourishing them above their heads as they retreated to their holes.

Mark and Small provided themselves with a bag of bivalves for bait and went off to the boat to fish.

Lastly, the captain and the ladies walked to the edge of the jungle in search of fruit, while the former shot a few birds.

The morning was delightful, and Mark and Small were soon afloat, to Billy Widgeon's intense disgust, for it had been his full intention to take Mark's place and form one of the fishing party.

Mark soon had a line ready, and after opening some of the shell-fish with his knife baited a couple of hooks and waited till the boatswain had piloted the boat to where there was an opening in the reef and the sea was setting into the lagoon.

"Now, lookye here, my lad," said Small; "when I was a boy I used to fish in the mill-dam at the back of our cottage, and I always found as there was most fish where the stream set in or came out. Now that's deep water, and I'll hold on to the bit of rock here while you chuck in; and if you don't get a bite we'll try somewheres else."

He laid in the oar, and taking the boat-hook had no difficulty in taking hold of the coral, which was only a couple of feet below, and Mark made his first cast right into the running current.

It was a good throw, and he stooped down and picked up the loose rings, to lay them out quite neatly and wind some of the superabundant line about the little frame, when there was a whiz over the side, the line darted out, there was a painful sensation of cutting, a jerk at the lad's arm as if it were about to be dragged out of the socket, and—that was all!

"Well, you hooked him," said Small grimly. "He must have been a big un."

"Big?—a monster!" cried Mark excitedly. "He must have broken the line."

"Haul in and bait again," said Small; and as the line was drawn in it was found that there was no breakage, but the soft metal hook had bent out nearly straight and torn from the fish's mouth.

"It hurt my hand horribly," said Mark as he bent the damaged hook back into position; "but it must have hurt the fish more."

"Sarve him right, my lad!—he was on his way to kill and eat some other fish. That's it. Chuck out again, and this time let him have it easy, and if he's a big one give him time."

The carefully-baited hooks were thrown out again, and before the bait had sunk a couple of feet it was once more seized.

"Sha'n't starve here, my lad!" said Small gleefully.

"Not if we can catch the fish," said Mark, whose fingers were burning with the friction of the line. "I say, Small, is it a crocodile?"

"G'long with you! Crocodile!—no; it's not a very big one."

"But see how it pulls!" cried Mark as the fish continued its rush and would have been off, line and all, some twenty fathoms, if it had not been that the cord was securely fastened to the winder, which was suddenly snatched from the bottom of the boat to fly with a rap against the lad's knuckles.

"Don't you let him go, Mr Mark, sir!" cried Small, who was as excited now as the lad. "Hold on! That's all our braxfusses."

"I'm going to hold on if I can," said Mark between his teeth; "but I shall let him run if he's going to pull me out of the boat."

As he spoke the fish was tugging furiously at the line, drawing the holder's arms out to their full stretch, and actually threatening to jerk him over the side of the boat. Now it rushed to right, now to left, and then made straight once more for the sea, and so full of strength that this time Mark set his teeth, feeling sure that line, hook, or his fingers must give way.

"You'll lose him. I know you will," cried Small, though how the fisherman was to prevent the catastrophe now that he was at the end of the line the boatswain did not say; and while finding fault, after the fashion of lookers-on, it never occurred to him that he might help the capture by letting the boat follow the fish.

Matters then had just as it were reached a climax, when, instead of the line breaking or Mark going over the side, the strong cord, which had been hissing here and there through the water, suddenly grew slack, and the tension was taken off Mark's muscles and mind to give place to a feeling of despair.

"Well, you are a fisherman, sir," growled Small, spitting a little tobacco juice into the water in disgust. "You've lost as fine a fish as was ever pulled out of the sea."

"How do you know?" said Mark, beginning to haul in the line slowly hand over hand. "You didn't see it."

"See it! Why, I see it pull. It was a fine un, and badly as we wants a bit o' fish too. There, haul in sharp and put on a fresh bait."

"It doesn't seem much use," said Mark bitterly. "My hands are quite sore."

"You'll be obliged to let me have a try. Skipper'll come down on me if we don't have something to show when we get back. Ah! there's a nice fish now," he continued, as a great fellow looking like a fifty-pound salmon sprang a full yard out of the water and fell back with a tremendous splash.

"Why, that's him," cried Mark, "and he's on still."

"Hooray! then: get him this time, my lad," cried Small; and it was evident now that, finding its course out to sea checked, the fish had suddenly turned and darted back, swimming toward the boat and causing the slackening of the line, but directly in the hauling it felt the hook it sprang right out of the water and made a fresh rush.

But this was not so powerful a run as the first, and as Mark held on, the fish repeated its manoeuvre and swam toward the boat.

This time Mark was able to haul in nearly half the line before the fish made another dart, but only to be checked, and rush to and fro, forming zigzags through the water, which it varied by a series of leaps clear out.

"You'll lose him, my lad, you'll lose him," grumbled Small at every bound; but the hook was fast in, and Mark instinctively gave line at every rush till the fish grew weary, and was drawn in closer to the boat after the wild dashes, and then, for the seventh or eighth time as it was hauled in, and Mark was prepared for a new dart, and in dread that this time the hook should straighten or break away, the panting creature suddenly turned up and floated upon its side.

"Well hauled," shouted Small. "You have done it this time, my lad."

"Not caught yet!" said Mark. "How are we to get it in the boat?"

"Oh, I'll show you about that," said the boatswain, loosening his hold of the rock, and, watching his opportunity, he gaffed the great fish cleverly with the boat-hook by drawing it into the prize's gills, and the next instant it lay splashing at the bottom of the boat.

"Well done us!" cried Small, as Mark stood gazing down at his prize, a magnificent fish of over forty pounds weight, with brilliant silvery scales double the size of those of a salmon, and all flashing in the morning sunshine.

"What is it?" said Mark.

"Well, I don't rightly know," said Small drily. "'Taint a sole."

"Why, of course not."

"Nor it arn't a salmon, you see, cause it's got all them stickles on its back. Some kind o' shark, I should say. Look at its teeth."

"And you've been to sea all your life, Small, and don't know a shark!" cried Mark. "Why, I know that isn't a shark, or anything of the kind."

"Yes, because you've had books to go at all your life, my boy, while I've been knocking about in ships. Man may learn to be a good sailor, but he don't learn much else aboard ship afore the mast."

"Never mind," said Mark; "the question for us to settle is—Is it good to eat?"

"Just you wait till we've cooked him over the fire," said Small, as he extracted the hook from the fierce jaws. "I'll answer that question then. 'Most anything's good to eat when you're half starved, my lad. I've knowed men eat their shoes. Going to have another try?"

"Yes, I should like to get some more," said Mark; and as soon as the captured fish was laid under the thwart he baited and threw out again.

This time he waited so long that he began to draw in the line, expecting to find the bait gone; but long before it reached the surface it was seized by another ravenous fish, and after a sharp fight this was also got into the boat, proving to be something similar to the other, but only about half the size.

"As I said before, I says it again," said Small oracularly, "we sha'n't starve here."

Mark thought of his words as he paddled ashore—Small cleaning the fish the while and throwing the offal overboard for ground-bait, as he said—when he helped carry the prizes up to the fire in triumph, for there he found that the major had returned, he and Widgeon having quite a load of shell-fish; the men had cut down the cocoa-nut tree, and the nuts were lying on the sand; while the captain and the ladies were back, the former with about a dozen small cockatoos, and the latter with handkerchiefs full of jungle fruit, a good deal of which promised to be valuable.

A large fire of drift-wood and old cocoa-nuts and their husks was burning, making a fierce blaze, before and partly over which the fish were soon roasting on wooden spits, the sailors being particularly handy in obeying orders for anything which they could provide by means of their knives.

The shell-fish soon followed, being ranged round the glowing embers to cook in their shells, and before long there was an odour rising that was little short of maddening to the hungry throng, several of whom directed envious glances at the birds which were hung up in the shade to be prepared for the next meal.

"Well, not so very badly," said the major about half an hour after the fish had been declared done. "I missed my cup of coffee and my dry toast, but I never ate fresher fish; and as to the scalloped gentlemen in their shells, captain, with one exception I never ate anything more delicious. Whether they were oysters, clams, cockles, or mussels, I'm sure I don't know, and what's more, I don't care. I say they were good."

"What was the exception?" said Mrs O'Halloran, smiling, for that lady seemed to bear everything with equanimity, and always proved herself a campaigner's wife.

"The exception, my dear," said the major, "was that spiral gentleman handed to me all hot by friend Mark, who took it sizzling out of the fire with a bit of bent stick held like tongs."

"But I meant that for Miss O'Halloran, sir," said Mark, flushing.

"Then, for what reason, sir, did you try to poison my daughter?" cried the major. "That fish, or mollusc as the naturalists would call it, was undoubtedly something of the whelk family; and if you can only find some of them large enough to cut up in slices, we shall have nothing to ear as to a supply of india-rubber shoe-soles. I've had some experience of contract beef in the army; but that is calves'-foot jelly compared to Mark's whelk."

"I thought it would be a delicacy, sir," said Mark, whose ears were particularly red as he saw Mary laughing.

"And I thought it was a trick," said the major; "so, after wriggling the monster out with my penknife and trying it fairly, I gave it to Mark's dog, and he has looked very unwell ever since."

The major's high spirits, and the calm matter-of-fact way in which his wife and daughter bore their privations, had an influence on the rest of the party, the captain looking less troubled, and Mr Gregory less serious. As for the sailors, they appeared to be quite enjoying themselves and treating the whole as a kind of picnic.

But there was plenty of work to be done, for as soon as the captain had seen to the two wounded men, who were able to talk now feebly, but without a trace of delirium, he began to make his plans, talking the matters over with the major and the mate; while the men, pending instructions, cut off all the cocoa-nut leaves to lay to dry, and gathered plenty of fuel for the cooking fire, whose place Small decided ought to be in a nook among some rocks, where it would be sheltered from the wind, and the rocks would grow heated and help the roasting or baking.

"It is gloriously fine now," the captain commenced by saying; "and one of the first things we ought to do is to provide a kind of hut or shed against the tremendous showers we are sure to have before long."

"My dear Strong," said the major, "I'm ready for anything, from shooting savages to cutting down trees."

"Then take your gun," said the captain, "and shoot a few savages, only keep yourself to the smaller inhabitants of the place, as we are not cannibals."

"Can I have Mark for my game-bearer?" said the major; and the lad darted a grateful look at him.

"I was going to propose that he should take a gun and go with you," said the captain. "He can catch a fish, and the sooner he can shoot us food the better. But be careful, my lad, and don't waste powder."

"I'll drill him," said the major; "and, by the way, would it not be as well to hoist something in the shape of colours on the top of the highest tree one of the men can mount?"

"I had planned that too," said the captain. "I hope our signals will soon be seen; but we must go on as if we expected to be in this place for years."

"That's good policy, my dear Strong," said the major; "so we'll leave you to your work, while we two idlers see what we can find inland. Now, Mark, guns and cartridges, and call your dog. His leg seems to be healing fast."

"Keep a sharp look-out," whispered the captain. "That noise must be made by some uncouth creature, so be on your guard."

"That's why I'm going to have the dog," replied the major; and, leaving the rest all busy over some preparation for the future comfort of the party, the ladies preparing to go fruit-seeking after attending to the wounded men's wants, while Mary collected some large pearl-shell oysters and the halves of the cocoa-nuts for cups and plates, the major and his young henchman set off.

Chapter Twenty Six
How Mark and the Major saw Signs

Bruff limped up eagerly, and sometimes put down his injured paw, which he had been dressing after nature's fashion by licking it well, and trotted by their side; but it was evident directly that another was to be of the party, for before they had gone fifty yards Jack bounded up and placed himself beside the dog.

The major hesitated for a moment.

"He won't do any harm," he said at last. "Let him come. I say, Mark, my lad, all that was very comic about the little fellow climbing the tree; but do you know, if you took pains I'm sure you might teach him to go up into the leafy crowns and screw the nuts round till they dropped."

"I was wondering whether it would be possible," said Mark eagerly.

"Quite. He is an intelligent little fellow. Try. Now, then, let's take our bearings," continued the major, and he pulled out a pocket-compass. "Don't let's be wearied out in finding our way back when we are tired."

"Which way are we going, sir?"

"That depends, my lad. It is not as we please, but as the jungle allows. You talk as if you were in a country full of roads."

"I forgot," said Mark, changing the position in which he carried his father's double gun.

"First lesson in using a gun," said the major: "either point the muzzle at the ground or up at the sky. It's considered bad manners, Mark, to shoot your companions."

"I—I beg your pardon, sir," faltered Mark. "It was very clumsy of me."

"Not a bit more clumsy than every young fellow is, when he first handles a gun. That's the way. I'm sure you don't want to have to carry me home without a head. Now, then, our easiest route would be to go along the sands at the edge of the cocoa-nut groves; but I propose we strike in beside the first stream or through the first valley we find. Come along."

They followed the beautiful shore line for about five hundred yards, and at a turn came suddenly upon a lovely little stream which offered far better facilities for obtaining drinking water than that from which it had been obtained, and as soon as he saw the spot, the major exclaimed that this was the place for their temporary home.

A cocoa-nut grove, a sandy cove, plenty of nipah-palms ready for making into thatch or wails for their hut, and an abundance of slight young palm-trees like scaffold poles exactly suitable for making their hut or shed.

"We must go back, Mark," said the major. "This is a find that will save them endless trouble."

It seemed a pity to return, as the sun was growing very hot; but they tramped back, and the captain followed when they again started, to decide with Gregory whether it would be a better site.

"Now," said the major, leaving them to their discussion, "you shall try and bring down the first eatable bird we see, and I'll look out for pig or deer."

"Are you going straight inland?" asked Mark.

"No, but just as the open ground beside this stream will let us. I want to get to the high ground and reach the slope of the volcano if we can."

It was not an easy task; for though the jungle was open here in comparison to what it was on either hand, every step of the way was impeded by creepers, awkward roots, patches of moss into which their feet sank, and by the rattan-canes that draped the trees and ran in and out and enlaced them together, as if nature were making rough attempts to turn the edge of the forest into a verdant piece of basket-work.

The heat was great and it was rather exhausting toil, but at every turn the beauties of the place were quite startling to Mark in their novelty. Over the clear sun-spangled stream drooped the loveliest of ferns, whose fronds were like the most delicate lace; while by way of contrast other ferns clung to the boles of trees, that were dark-green and forked like the horns of some huge stag; great masses and clusters, six or seven feet long, hung here and there pendent from the old stumps.

Flowers too were in abundance, but for the most part quaintly-shaped orchids of cream, and yellow, and brown, some among the moss, others clinging to the mossy bark of the trees. But the greatest curiosities of all were the pitcher-plants hanging here and there, some fully suspended, others so large that they partly rested on the moss, forming jungle cups capable of containing fully a pint of water, some of them even more.

The beauties of the scene increased, in spite of each one in which they paused seeming as if it could not be surpassed; for as they penetrated more deeply they not only came upon flowering trees about which tiny sun-birds, whose plumage was a blaze of burnished metallic splendour, whirred, and buzzed, and darted, or probed the blossoms with their beaks, but they found that the island, if island it should prove, was inhabited by endless numbers of gorgeous butterflies.

Great pearly-looking insects, whose wings gleamed with azure reflections, floated calmly down the glades, their wings fully eight inches across. Others were specked and splashed with scarlet, or barred with orange, or dashed with glistening green. Then, as if there was to be no end to the feast of beauty for their eyes, great quick-flying insects came darting among the sunny openings, butterflies with elongated, narrow, and pointed wings similar to those of the sphinx moths of our own land.

Mark could have sat down and watched the various gorgeously-coloured beauties for hours, but theirs was a business task, and he plodded on behind the major, both the monkey and the dog untiringly investigating everything they saw.

But there was no trace of large animal, no sound that suggested the neighbourhood of anything likely to be inimical, while the best test was the fearlessness with which their two companions kept by their sides.

"Ah!" ejaculated the major at last, as a low cooing noise fell upon their ears. "Now for something for dinner! You go first, Mark, and let them have both barrels sharply—one after the other."

"Let what have them?"

"The pigeons. Creep on yonder softly, and you will soon come upon them—a flock of pigeons feeding in one of the trees."

Mark went on as silently as he could, and the major kept back the two animals and waited a minute—five minutes, ten minutes—and then softly followed, to find the lad at the edge of a glade watching a flock of great lavender-hued and feather-crowned pigeons, as big as fowls, feeding in the most unconcerned manner.

The major did not hesitate for a moment, but fired at the spot where the birds were thickest, and again as they rose with whirring and flapping wings in a little flock.

Three went down at his first discharge, two at his second; and Mark started as if he too had been shot.

"You here, sir?" he said.

"Yes. Why didn't you shoot?"

"I forgot to," said Mark hesitatingly; "and I was admiring them."

"Yes, admirable, my young naturalist!" said the major. "But we are sent out here to find food for so many hungry people; and these are glorious eating."

"Yes; I forgot," said Mark, helping to collect the birds, which were tied by the legs and hung over the trunk of a tree, as the stream would act as their guide on their return.

Then going on, the little rapids and falls in the tiny river showed that they must be steadily rising, but at so slow a rate that it soon became evident that, unless the country opened out, they would not reach the mountain that day.

At the end of a couple of hours, though, when they paused to rest and began refreshing themselves with some fruit similar to a large nut, but whose interior contained a couple of kernels imbedded in custard, they found themselves quite upon a hill, with a valley dipping down below along which the streamlet came, and beyond these the mountain-slope rose, so that they had a good view of the cone, with the film of cloud still rising, but looking almost transparent in the bright sunrise.

"There ought to be pigs here," said the major; "but it does not seem as if we shall see any. But look yonder; there's another of those fruit-trees, with pigeons feeding beneath. Go and try now."

Mark hurried on, and threading his way among the trees took a long and careful aim before firing; and, as might be expected, missing. But as luck had it, the flock rose with a tremendous beating of wings and went right over the major's head, giving him an opportunity to get a couple of good shots, with the result that three more of the great pigeons came crashing down.

"I think I hit one," said Mark as he came panting back, to find that the major and Bruff between them had retrieved all three birds.

"Where is it, then?" said the major.

"The smoke got in my eyes, and I could not see whether one fell."

"Take the dog, then, and see if he can find it," said the major, smiling to himself. But after a good search the lad came back hot and disappointed.

"Better luck next time, my boy," said the major. "You are not the only one who did not hit his first bird. Shooting is not so easy as fishing in the sea."

The question now arose whether to go on further or to return. They had obtained eight good weighty birds, and the heat was great; but Mark was so anxious to try and make better use of his piece that the pigeons just shot were hung up similarly to the first, and they proceeded, to find hopeful signs of an abundance of fruit, some of which was familiar to the major from his having encountered it in different parts of the East, while other kinds looked promising enough for testing.

But though a sharp look-out was kept, no other opportunity for a shot presented itself.

The reason was plain enough—they were unable to get along without making a good deal of noise; and though the smaller birds of brilliant plumage paid little heed, the larger, such as might have been used for food, took flight before they got within shot, as they often knew by the flapping and beating of their wings.

They were slowly descending one beautiful slope after carefully taking in some landmarks so as to guide them on their return, when all at once Mark laid his hand upon the major's arm and pointed to an opening in the jungle about a hundred yards away.

"What is it?" said the major sharply. "Ah! that looks bad;" and he pressed Mark back under cover.

"Savages?" whispered the lad.

"I'm afraid so. It's a bad sign and a good sign."

Mark looked at him interrogatively.

"Bad sign if they are a fierce lot like the New Guinea men; good sign if they are peaceable fellows, for it shows that it is quite possible to live here."

The sight which had caught Mark's attention was a thin cloud of vapour rising slowly from among some low bushes, and it was evident that there was a fire and some cooking operation going on.

"Better part of valour is discretion," said the major softly. "Not going to run away, Mark—soldiers can't do that—but we must retire and take up fresh ground, my lad, for your father expressly pointed out to me that we were not cannibals, and that I was not to shoot the human savage. Keep out of sight. Perhaps we had better return."

They backed away softly, the dog following, and the major whispered:

"The mystery is explained, Mark. It must have been one of those interesting gentlemen who made that terrific row. His idea of a cooey, I suppose."

A low growl came from Bruff just then, and they stopped short, the silence being broken by the dick, dick of the major's gun.

They had on retiring gone a little higher up the slope so as to be more among the trees, and the result was that they found themselves at the top of a little ridge and at the edge of the denser growth, so that, as they paused, they could look down into another part where the trees gave place to low bushes and glorious ferns, the whole being a glade of surpassing loveliness, such a spot as might very well be chosen by a party of simple savages for their home.

The major pressed Mark down, and they cowered among the trees, for they were evidently going right in sight of a second encampment.

"Keep the dog quiet if you can, lad," whispered the major, peering among the trees. "Can't see their attap (see note 1) huts, but there are plenty of fruit-trees."

"Have they seen us?" whispered Mark.

"Impossible to say. You go along first between those trees bearing to the right. Stoop. I don't want you to get a notice to quit in the shape of a spear."

Mark obeyed, and went on as swiftly and as silently as he could, so as to reach the path they had made in coming, and to this end he had to quit the denser shade and pass through a clump of foliage plants and flowering bushes of the loveliest hues.

The way seemed easy, and the bushes were not so closely together, but the ferns were enormous, their fronds stretching out in all directions and having to be pressed aside.

"Never mind me," whispered the major, as Mark held an unusually large frond aside. "Bear down more to the right and strike the stream. We mustn't leave those pigeons."

Mark forced his way on, with the growth completely hiding him from his companion, while the heat seemed to be more and more oppressive. It was a dank stewing heat, very different to the scorching of the sun out in the more open parts, and both were longing to get to a spot where they could breathe more freely, when Mark, who was about six yards ahead, leaped down into a little hollow to save himself from a fall, his feet having given way as he trod upon the rotten roots of a large fern.

It was a matter of a few instants, for as the lad alighted he found that it was upon something soft and elastic, and at the same moment there was a disturbance among the undergrowth and a sharp angry hiss.

He bounded back with a faint cry of horror, turned, and taking rapid aim at the spot where he had leaped fired downward.

"Quick! load again," said the major.

"A great serpent," panted Mark, obeying with nervous fingers.

"Killed him?"

"Don't know, sir," said Mark, staring down among the ferns and arums which filled the hole.

"Must have killed him, for he does not move. Squat down. We don't want the savages to see us. They are sure to come."

"Let's run."

"What? The gauntlet? No, thank you, my boy. We are safer here. Hist!"

They crouched there listening for the sounds of the enemy's approach, but all remained silent. Mark could hear his heart beating with excitement, and he found himself wondering why it was that he, with a serpent on one side and savages on the other, was not more alarmed.

"Keep still," whispered the major; "we must hear them directly. What's that?"

"The dog," said Mark in the same low tone, for Bruff had softly crept to their side, looked up in their faces, and lain down.

"Why, hallo!" exclaimed the major, "this isn't natural."

"What?"

"This dog. There can't be any savages on the way; and, what is more, you can't have shot a serpent, or Bruff here would have been excited and routed him out. Did you see the serpent?"

"No, sir; I didn't see it exactly, but you heard it hiss."

"But, hang it all, Mark! You didn't shoot at a hiss, did you?"

"Well, no, sir. I was horribly startled, and shot down at the soft thing upon which I jumped."

"But if you are entrusted with a gun," said the major angrily, "you mustn't take fright and shoot at what you hear and feel, my lad."

"Did you see the savages, sir?" said Mark in self-defence.

"Well, no, but I saw the smoke of their fire; and here, Bruff, fetch him out, boy," he continued, breaking off his speech, and with cocked gun he parted the twigs and fronds cautiously as he stepped down into the hollow from which Mark had fled.

Hiss! hiss! hiss! came sharply from where the major stepped, and he in turn bounded back to Mark's side, falling over the dog, and having some difficulty in recovering himself.

"That's good! I like that," he cried, as, instead of helping him, Mark covered his escape by taking a step forward, and bringing his gun to bear on the spot whence the sounds came.

"Did—did you see it?" said Mark huskily.

"See it! No, my lad. Only that! Look!"

He pointed as he rose to a filmy vapour floating away and dissolving in the sunshine. "You did not see that before because you fired. Don't you see? It's steam."

"Steam!" said Mark.

"Yes. Look here. Give me your hand. I don't want to go through."

He caught Mark's hand and stepped cautiously down, keeping one foot on sure ground, as with the other he pressed and stamped upon a spot that was quite elastic. At every stamp there was a hiss—a sharp, angry hiss and a puff of vapour rose from among the leaves.

"There's your serpent," he said, laughing. "No wonder you did not hit it."

"Then that must be steam we saw over yonder, and not savages' fires."

"Right, my lad. A false alarm. We're in a volcanic land, and if we search about I daresay we shall find hot springs somewhere."

"It can't be very safe," said Mark thoughtfully, as he watched the little puffs of steam rise.

"Not if you jump on a soft place, for there would be no knowing where you went. But come along, I think we've done enough for one day, so let's find our pigeons and get back."

"Where's Jacko?" said Mark, looking round.

"Jack! Last time I saw him he was up a tree eating those sour berries just after I shot the last pigeon. He must have stayed back to feed."

They whistled and called, while, as if comprehending it all, the dog barked; but all was still, and in the hope of finding their hairy companion they now pressed steadily on, passing the tree laden still with a bright purple kind of berry, but there was no sign of Jack.

"He'll return to savage life, safe," said the major. "It is too much of a temptation to throw in his way. Why, Mark, if I were a monkey I think I should."

"I don't think he'd leave Bruff now," replied Mark. "They're such friends that they wouldn't part, and I'm sure my dog wouldn't go."

He glanced down at Bruff as he spoke, and the dog barked at him, and raised his injured paw.

"Well, we shall see," said the major, as they forced their way on. "There's where we stopped to listen for birds," he continued, "and there's the tree upon which I hung the pigeons."

"Where?" asked Mark.

"Yonder, straight before you. There, lad, fifty yards away."

"But I can't see any pigeons," said Mark.

"Not near enough. Let's get on, I'm growing hungry, and beginning to think of dinner, a cigar, a good rest, and a bathe in that delicious-looking sea. By the way, the clouds are gathering about the top of that mountain. I hope we shall have no storm to-night. Why, Mark, the pigeons are gone! I hung them upon that branch."

Mark turned from gazing at the clouds, which seemed to be forming about the cone away to his right, and was obliged to confess that the pigeons were gone.

"Savage, or some animal," said the major, peering cautiously round.

"Would it be a big bird—eagle or vulture?" said Mark. "I saw one fly over."

"Might be," replied the major. "I'm not naturalist enough to say; and if I was, I daren't, Mark, for what a bird will do in one country it will not in another."

Mark stared at him.

"Well, I mean this, Mark, my lad. At home, in England, the kingfishers sit on twigs over the streams, and dive into the water and catch fish. Here, in the East, numbers of them sit on twigs in the forest paths and catch beetles, so there's no knowing what a bird of prey would do in a place like this."

Just then they were close up to the tree, and Bruff set up a joyous barking, which was answered by the chattering of the monkey.

"Why, there's Jack!" cried Mark.

"The rascal, he has got down my pigeons!" cried the major.

Just then a puff of feathers flew up in the air, and the two travellers stepped forward and simultaneously burst into a roar of laughter.

For there, in amongst the undergrowth, sat Jack, his hairy coat, head, arms, and legs covered with feathers, which formed quite a nest about him, and as they came up he chattered away loudly, and went on tearing the lavender plumage out of one of the great pigeons which lay in his lap, and scattering the soft down far and wide.

"Why, he must have seen the birds plucked yesterday," said the major, wiping his eyes, so comical was the monkey's seriously intent aspect, as he kept glancing up at them sharply, and then chattering and peering down at the half-denuded pigeon, his little black fingers nimbly twisting out the feathers, and his whole aspect suggestive of his being a cook in a tremendous hurry.

"There, come along," continued the major; "pick up the birds, Mark."

Easier said than done. There were three, but two, half-picked, had to be hunted out from the heap of feathers, and Jack objected to part with the third, holding on to it tightly till he was pressed back with the stock of the gun, after which the miserable half-picked birds were tied together by the legs and hung over the barrel.

They had no difficulty in finding the rest of the morning's sport, and this done, the first being shouldered by the major, they walked as fast as the nature of the way would allow, back to the shore, unwillingly on Mark's part, for there was always some brilliant bird or insect flitting across their path and inviting inspection.

But this inclination to stay was always checked by the major, who kept on bringing his companion back to the commonplace by uttering the one word, "Dinner!" and this sufficed.

> Note 1. Attap, thatching made of the leaves of a palm—the nipah.

Chapter Twenty Seven
How Mark encountered a Savage

"We were beginning to think you long," said the captain as they reached the cocoa-nut grove, having found that though there were signs of palm leaves and young trees having been cut by the mouth of the stream this had not been selected as the site of the huts.

"We've been a long way," said the major. "Not empty-handed, you see."

"Splendid," cried the captain; "but you need not have stopped to pick them."

"Thereby hangs a tale," said the major, laughing. "How's Morgan?"

"Much better, and sitting up. There, you see, we've not been idle."

He pointed to a large low hut formed in the cocoa-nut grove by utilising six growing trees as corners and centre-posts, and binding to these thin horizontal poles, freshly cut down for eaves and ridge. Others formed gables, being fixed by the sailors with their customary deftness, thin rattans being used as binding cords. Then other poles had been bound together for the roof, and over these an abundant thatching of palm leaves had been laid and laced on with rattan till there was a water-tight roof, and in addition one end was furnished with palm-leaf walls.

"That will keep us dry if the rain comes," said the captain, after due praise had been awarded for the energy displayed. "But now, quick: have a wash, and we'll dine. Every one is hungry."

Mark's eyes twinkled as he saw the preparations. Palm leaves were spread in two places, but the food supply was the same for all; and if they were going to feed as well during their stay on the island, they felt that they would not have much cause to complain.

Food is so important a matter in our everyday life that, even without being sybarites, one may pause to give an account of the savage banquet prepared in the rock kitchen by the captain's and major's wives, aided by Mary O'Halloran, whilst the rest were busy hunting and building.

There was another fish secured by Small, similar to the one Mark had caught, about two dozen little roast cockatoos, and an ample supply of baked shell-fish. These delicacies were supplemented by plenty of cocoa-nut milk and wild fruit, some of which was delicious.

"I never had a better dinner in my life," said the major. "It has been so good that I never once remembered our heavy fat Goura pigeons, which I had reckoned upon having for a treat."

"I think we ought to compliment the cooks," said the captain. "Poor Morgan quite enjoyed his fish, and Brown says he didn't know cockatoos could taste so good."

"I think we've fallen into a kind of Eden," said Gregory pleasantly. "If we could find some tea-trees or coffee-bushes, and a wheat-field and windmill, we shouldn't want anything more."

"Ah!" said the captain gravely; "we should want a great deal more than those to make up for the loss of civilisation; but let's try and do our best under the circumstances."

"Why, we are doing it," said Mrs O'Halloran with a smile.

"True, madam; and I thank you for your brave, true womanly help, both for the wounded and for my men."

"Thank your wife too, captain," said Mrs O'Halloran gravely.

"She does not need it, madam," said Captain Strong. "It is her duty."

That night passed quite peacefully, the watch hearing nothing of the strange roar. The next day busy hands were at work making a second hut for the men, every one working his best so as to be prepared for the tropical showers, which have a habit of coming on nearly daily; but this day broke gloriously fine, and palm leaves were cut and carried, bamboos discovered and cut down for poles and rafters, and the men worked with such good heart that the second hut towards afternoon began to assume shape.

The ladies were as busy as ever, undertaking the nursing and cooking; but Morgan relieved them of half the former by getting up to seat himself under a shady tree and watch the progress made.

Mark and the major were told off for their former task of finding provisions; and, nothing loth, they started in good time, choosing another route—that is to say, they struck off to the east—going beyond the cooking place among the rocks, meaning to see if any of the great grey pigeons were to be found in that direction by some other pass into the interior.

Their walk was glorious; with the beautiful lagoon on one side, evidently crowded with fish, and the fringe of cocoa-nut trees on their left;

while from time to time, as the groves opened, they obtained glimpses of the volcanic cone.

Bruff and Jack took it as a matter of course that they were to belong to the foraging party, and trotted along over the sand, the one eagerly on the search for something that he might hunt, the other with his little restless eyes watching for fruit. But neither met with any reward.

Picking out the firm sand where the tide had gone down the hunters found good walking, and were able to leave the encampment several miles behind without feeling any fatigue, but the game-bags which they had this time slung over their shoulders, remained empty, and the guns seemed to increase in weight.

"I wish we could get right round and prove that this is an island," said the major; "but we must not attempt it to-day. Are these cocoa-nut palms never coming to an end?"

"Let's go through them, and try to reach the foot of the mountain," said Mark at last. "I want to get a supply of something to eat, but I should like to see the mountain close to."

"And go up it and peep in at the crater, eh?"

"Indeed I should, sir."

"Ah, well! we'll see about that; but work first, Mark. We must get a load of birds or a pig."

"Think there are pigs, sir?"

"Can't say. I haven't seen a sign of one yet. If it is a part of some great island we may find deer."

They tramped on, hoping to find a stream, but another two miles were traversed before they came upon a rushing rivulet, gurgling down from among piled-up masses of blackish vesicular rock, which the major at once dubbed scoria.

"Now for a good drink," he said. "I'm thirsty;" and they both lay down to drink from a pool of the loveliest nature, so clear was the water, so beautiful the ferns and other growth that overhung.

But at the first mouthful both rose, spitting it out, and ready to express their disgust.

"Why, it's bitter, and salt, and physicky as a mineral spring," said the major.

"And it's quite hot," said Mark. "Ugh! what stuff!"

It was disappointing, for they were both suffering from thirst; but it was evident that to penetrate the jungle from where they stood would be next to impossible, so craggy and rocky was the ground, while, as after struggling on for about a couple of hundred yards, they found the water grown already so hot that it was almost too much for their hands, they concluded that if they persevered they would find it boiling—an interesting fact for a student of the wonders of nature, but an unsatisfactory matter for a thirsty man.

"What a place for a botanist!" cried the major. "We could fill our bags with wonders; but a good patch of Indian corn would be the greatest discovery we could find now, for, Mark, my lad, we shall find that we want flour in some form."

"Is Indian corn likely to grow here?"

"If some kind friend who has visited this shore has been good enough to plant some—not without."

They stood gazing for a few minutes at the wondrously fertile growth of the plants whose roots found their way to the warm stream, and whose leaves received the steamy moisture, and then climbed slowly back.

"We must explore inland some day, Mark, and see if we can find a hot spring of good water fit to cook in. I must say I should not like my cabbage boiled in that."

"That's better," said Mark as they reached the sand once more, and stood panting.

"Yes; the other's 'pad for the poots,' as a Welsh friend of mine used to say. Now, then, forward to find fresh water and birds. We'll go another mile, and if we don't find a stream we must try for some fruit."

The dog trotted on a little ahead, and, to their great delight, they came to the end of the monotonous fringe of cocoa-nuts and found that quite a different class of vegetation came down close to the shore, which now grew more rocky, and it was not long before they were able to slake their thirst on the pleasant sub-acid fruit of a kind of passion-flower.

A few hundred yards further and Bruff began to trot, breaking into a canter of two legs after one, and suddenly turned into the jungle, to come back barking.

They soon reached the spot, to find that quite a fount of pure-looking water was welling up out of a rock basin, trickling over and losing itself in the sand, while upon a tree close at hand were at least a hundred tiny parrots not larger than sparrows, fluttering, piping, and whistling as they rifled the tree of its fruit.

"Too small for food unless we were starving," said the major. "We shall have to fill our bags with what answer here to cockles and mussels, Mark. We must not go home empty-handed."

"Shall I try the water first?" said Mark.

"No need," said the major, pointing to where, at a lesser pool, Bruff and Jack were slaking their thirst.

The example set by the two animals was followed, and deep draughts taken of the delicious water, which was as cool and sweet as the other spring had been nauseous and hot.

"Now, then; forward once more," said the major. "Just one more mile, and then back, though I believe we could get round, for we must have come so that the huts are quite to the south. Yes; we're travelling north-west now, and when we started we were going north-east."

"Hist! Look!" whispered Mark; and he pointed forward.

"Phew!" whistled the major. "Down, Bruff! To heel!"

The dog obeyed, and cocking their guns, and keeping as close to the trees as the rocky nature of the soil would allow, the two hunters approached the game Mark had pointed out.

Strange-looking birds they were, each as big as a small turkey, and, provided that they were not of the gull tribe, promising to be an admirable addition to the pot.

But though they advanced cautiously, neither the major nor Mark could get within shot, the birds taking alarm and scurrying over the sand rapidly.

They tried again, taking shelter, going through all the manoeuvres of a stalker; but their quarry was too wary, and went off at a tremendous rate, but only to stop when well out of reach and begin digging and scratching in the sand somewhat after the fashion of common fowls.

"It's of no use," said Mark at last, throwing himself down hot and exhausted after they had followed the tempting creatures for fully a mile.

"No use!" said the major. "What, give up! Do you know what Lord Lytton says in Richelieu?"

"No," said Mark wearily; and then to himself—"and I don't care."

"'In the bright lexicon of youth there is no such word as fail.'"

"But then Lord Lytton had not been out here hungry and thirsty, toiling after these sandy jack-o'-lanterns with a heavy gun," said Mark.

"Probably not," said the major. "But, never mind: we may get a shot yet. One more steady try, and then we'll go back."

"Oh, Major O'Halloran, what a man you are to walk!" said Mark, rising wearily.

"Yes, my lad," said the major smiling. "I belong to a marching regiment. Now, look here, Mark; I'm quite sure those birds would eat deliciously roasted, and that the ladies would each like a bit of the breast."

"Let's try, then, once more," said Mark; and they went on, with Bruff dutifully trotting behind waiting for the first shot and the fall of a bird.

But no; as they advanced the birds still went on, running well out of range and stopping again to scratch and feed.

There were about fifteen of them, and the more they kept ahead the more eager grew their stalkers, till after this had been going on for another half-hour Bruff could stand it no longer, but dashed off at full speed, barking furiously, with the result that instead of running off like the wind the birds stopped staring for a few seconds and then all took flight.

"That's done it!" cried the major angrily. "Hang that dog! No: look, Mark!"

"Yes, we may get a shot now," he cried; "they're all in those trees."

"Well, keep close in, and we'll have a try."

They had a couple of hundred yards to go to where Bruff stood barking furiously at the birds, which kept in the moderately high boughs staring stupidly down at him, and so intent upon the beast, so novel evidently to them, that the two hunters had a chance to get close up, and taking his time from the major, Mark fixed the quivering sight of his gun on one of the birds, and drew trigger just as the major fired twice.

As the smoke blew away there was a whirring of wings and three heavy thuds upon the ground.

Away went the birds, but only about fifty yards more, to settle again, Bruff keeping up with them, and again taking their attention by barking furiously.

The manoeuvres of approaching were again successfully gone through, and this time the major whispered:

"Loaded again?"

"Yes."

"Then fire both barrels this time. Try and get a right and left. Fire!"

Their pieces went off simultaneously the first time; then the major's second barrel rang out, and Mark's second directly afterwards, and by sheer luck—ill-luck for the birds—he brought down his first bird from the branch of the tree dead, and in his random flying shot winged one of the others so badly that it fell, and Bruff caught it before it had time to recover and race away.

"Hurrah!" shouted the major as the diminished flock now flew inland over the jungle. "Seven birds, Mark: a load. And you said you couldn't shoot! Why, it's glorious!"

"I'm sure it was accident, sir," said Mark with his cheeks burning.

"Then bless all such accidents say I, a hungry man!"

"Yah!" came faintly from a distance.

"What's that?" cried the major.

"Yah!" came again, or what sounded like it, for to their startled ears it was more like a savage yell.

"Load quickly," cried the major, setting the example. "Savages at last. Now, the birds and a quick retreat. Wonder how heavy they are; but save them I will if I have a stand to defend them, and send you back for help."

Mark caught up his heavy birds and ran back with the major to where the first they had shot lay, while from behind came another yell, and looking over his shoulder Mark saw that a spear-armed figure was coming rapidly in pursuit.

Chapter Twenty Eight
How Mark found something
that was not Game

They had not far to go, but in a hot sun, and with the double guns, ammunition, and the heavy birds, they were panting and in a profuse perspiration.

"Can't do impossibilities, Mark, my lad," cried the major. "We must either run for it without our game, or stop and fight for it."

"Oh!" cried Mark; "we can't leave the birds."

"But you can't fight," cried the major, who, as he spoke, began throwing the great birds behind a clump of rocks.

"But they have taken so much trouble to get," panted Mark.

"And I'm so hungry that I feel like a dog with a bone," snapped the major. "I won't give 'em up without a fight. Come in here, my boy, and I'll have a good try for it. We've plenty of ammunition, and perhaps a peppering with small-shot will scare the blackguards away."

Mark obeyed, and the next moment, with their birds, they were snugly ensconced in a little natural fortification, open to attack only on one side, the others being protected by the rocks and the dense jungle.

This movement took them out of sight of their pursuer, who was hidden now by the trees.

"Now, my boy, lay out some cartridges, and keep down out of sight. You reload, and keep on exchanging guns. I'm a soldier, and will do the fighting. I meant to run and leave our dinner, undignified as it may be; but hang me if I do at the sight of a half-naked savage with a spear."

"But there must be a whole tribe of them behind, sir," whispered Mark.

"Yes; that's the worst of it. But never mind, I'll pepper their skins, and perhaps that will stop them. But look here, my boy, if matters begin to look very ugly you are not to hesitate for a moment."

"Yah!"

A pause.

"Yoy-oy-oy-oy!"

This last in a different tone, but both yells were of a most savage, highly-pitched nature.

"Another of them," whispered the major; and then, as the sounds were repeated faintly a long way off, "There's the main body coming on. Mark, my lad, never mind me. I didn't know what I was saying before. Here, shake hands, and God bless you, boy! I don't suppose I shall hurt. Run for it at once, and I'll cover your retreat."

Mark sprang up, placed one foot on the rocks, shook hands with the major, and in his excitement and dread, as another yell rang out much nearer, gathered himself up to spring clear of the rough scoria that lay about, and then turned sharply round and leaped back in his place.

"What now?" cried the major sharply.

"Who's to reload if I go?" said Mark hoarsely; and he looked very white.

"I can, boy. Quick! there's no time to lose."

Mark hesitated for a few moments. On the one side seemed to be safety; on the other, perhaps death from a set of spear-armed savages. Then he ground his teeth, and stood fast.

"Well, why don't you go?"

"I won't be such a coward," cried Mark in a hoarse whisper.

"It is no cowardice to retreat," cried the major, "when your superior officer gives the word."

"You're not my superior officer," said Mark between his teeth. "What would my father say?"

"That you obeyed orders."

"He wouldn't," growled Mark. "He'd call me a contemptible cur. So I should be if I went. How could I face Mrs O'Halloran and Miss Mary again?"

The major seemed to choke a little, and he gave quite a gasp, whilst certainly his eyes were suffused with tears as he cocked his gun and turned upon Mark.

"I order you to go, sir," he said. "Run for it while there's time."

"I won't," cried Mark fiercely. "I'm going to stop and load the guns."

The major gave a long expiration, as if he had been retaining his breath, but said nothing, only laid his gun-barrel ready on the natural breastwork of rock before him, waved Mark a little way back into shelter, and then stood ready as the beat of feet on the sand was plainly heard, accompanied by a hoarse panting as of some one who had been running till quite breathless.

Then from just round behind some intervening branches which grew out broadly by the projecting rocks there came another hoarse yell.

"Yah!"

There was a pause, and from the distance an answering cry.

Then a terrible silence. The steps had ceased, but the hoarse panting continued, and for the moment Mark was in hopes that their concealment might prove effectual, and the savages pass on, and to aid this he bent down softly to make a threatening gesture at Jacko, and to hold Bruff's muzzle tightly closed as the pair lay on the birds, among whose feathers Jack's fingers were already busy.

The major had evidently caught the idea, and he too drew back, when once more came the terrible yell, and the keen point and half a dozen feet of the lance dropped into sight, while through the leaves which partially concealed him they could make out a portion of the figure of the savage.

The silence now was terrible, and Mark held his breath, hardly daring to breathe, in dread lest the major should fire, for he could have laid the man lifeless without raising the gun to his shoulder.

Then all at once, in the midst of the hot stillness of that tropic land, with the blue sea lying calm beyond, the sparkling creamy foam where the ocean pulsated on the coral-reef, there came a hideous screech and the swift beat of wings.

Startling enough, but only the cry of a passing parrot, and the sound had hardly died away when the point of the spear was slowly raised, and disappeared behind the trees.

Then once more came the loud yell.

"Yah!" and its repetition three times, now telling of the savages being scattered. And then—

"Oh, dear! oh, dear! Where can they be got to? I'm sure I saw 'em come by here."

"How—how—how—how!" burst out Bruff, and shaking his head free he leaped out, followed by Mark and the major, to confront their spear-armed enemy, about whom the dog was leaping and fawning.

"Why, Jimpny," cried Mark, "is this you?" as he caught the stowaway's hand.

"You scoundrel!" roared the major. "You frightened us, and—no, you didn't quite frighten us," he said, correcting himself, "but we thought you were a savage!"

"So I am, sir," whimpered the man. "Look at me."

He did look one after a fashion as he stood there, Malay spear in hand, his only garment being a pair of canvas trousers whose legs had been torn-off half-way above his knees. For he was torn and bleeding from the effects of thorns, his skin was deeply sunburned, and a fillet tied about his head, stained red with blood, kept back his tangled hair, while his eyes had a wild and scared look.

"Well, it was excusable to think you one," said the major.

"But how came you here?" cried Mark excitedly.

"I don't know, sir," whined the man, piteously. "I've been mad, I think. I believe I'm mad now; and I was just telling myself that it was another of the dreams I had while I was so bad from this chop on the head; and that I had only fancied I saw you two shooting, when old Bruff barked and came out."

"You've been wounded then?"

"Yes, sir, badly, and off my chump."

"But how?"

"One of those Malay chaps gave me a chop on the head with his sword, sir; and I fell down on the deck and crawled right forward down by the bowsprit and lay between some ropes and under an old sail, and then I got mixed."

"Mixed?" said the major.

"Yes, sir; I was so bad I didn't know which I dreamed and which was real, only it seemed that there was a lot of fighting and shooting and yelling."

"You didn't dream that," said Mark sadly.

"I'm glad of that, sir; but I suppose I dreamed that the Malay chaps made the sailors go over the side into one of the boats and row away."

"That must be quite true," said the major gravely.

"But I was very much off my head, sir, and so weak and thirsty. I know I didn't dream about the fire though, for the ship was afire."

"Yes," said Mark; "the poor *Petrel!*"

"It was very horrid, gentlemen; for as I lay there I couldn't speak nor move, only look up at the glare and blaze and sparks, and from where I lay, afraid to stir in case they should chuck me overboard, I saw those savage chaps go over the side and leave the ship; and then there was a blow-up, or else it was before—I don't know, for I was all in a muddle in my head and didn't know anything, only that it was getting hotter and hotter; and at last I was in a sort of dream, feeling as if I was going to be roasted."

"How horrible!" cried Mark.

"Yes, sir, it was horrid, for the masts ketched fire and burned right up, and the great pieces of wood kept falling on the deck, and ropes were all alight—and swinging about with the burning tar. I didn't dream all that, for I see the big mast blazing from top to bottom, and it fell over the side; and then the others went, and the spars was on fire, and the booms at the sides. And at last, as the fire came nearer and nearer, sir, I knew that if I lay there any longer I should be burned to death, and I thought I'd move."

"And very wisely," said the major.

"Yes, sir; but I couldn't," said the stowaway. "I wanted badly, and tried and tried, but I was much too weak. And that's what made it seem like a dream; for the more I tried to creep out from under the sail, the more I lay still, as if something held me back. And all the time there was a puddle of melted pitch bubbling and running slowly toward me. My face burned and my hands were scorched, the wood was crackling, and the pitch rising up in blisters. And if the smoke had come my way I couldn't have breathed; but it all went up with the flames and sparks. But the heat—oh, the heat!"

"And you couldn't crawl out?"

"No, sir; couldn't move—couldn't raise a hand; and I lay there till I couldn't bear it no longer, and tried to shriek out to the Malay chaps to come and put me out of my misery, for I wanted to die then; and I'd waited too long, for I couldn't even make a sound."

"And what happened next?" asked Mark, for the man had ceased speaking.

"Dunno, sir. One moment it was all fiery and scorching, the next I seemed to go to sleep like, and didn't feel any more pain till I woke."

"Till you woke?" said the major.

"Well, yes, sir. It was like waking up, to find it was all dark, and the wind blowing, and the rain coming down. Then the sea was roaring horribly; and after lying perished with cold there and helpless for a long time, I suppose I went to sleep again. Oh, dear me!"

The major and Mark exchanged glances, for the poor fellow put his hand to his head and stared about him for a few moments as if unconscious of their presence.

"But you got safe to land?" said Mark at last.

"Eh?"

"I say you escaped," said Mark.

"Did I, sir?"

"Yes, of course. You are here."

"Oh, yes—I'm here, sir! but I don't know hardly how it was."

"Can't you recollect?"

"Yes, I think I can, sir, only my head's so tight just now. I think this handkerchief I tied round when it bled does it, but I'm afraid to take it off."

"Wait a bit and we'll do that," said the major kindly.

"Will you, sir? Thank ye, sir."

"But how did you get ashore?" said Mark.

"In the ship, sir. I suppose the rain and the waves must have put out the fire, and what's left of her went bumping over rocks and knocking about, making my head ache horribly till I went to sleep again; and when I woke it was all bright and fine, and the half-burned ship close to the sands in shallow water, so as when the tide's down you can walk ashore."

"The ship here?"

"Yes; round there, sir," said the poor fellow wearily. "There's some half-burned biscuit in her, and I've been living on that and some kind of fruit I found in the woods when I could get ashore. I brought this thing for a walking-stick."

"Then the ship is ashore here?" cried the major joyfully.

"Yes, sir; but she's not good for anything but firewood," said the stowaway sadly.

"Ah! we shall see about that," said the major. "I'm glad you've escaped, my lad."

"And has everybody else, sir?" said the man.

"No, not everybody," said Mark; "but my father and the ladies and the officers are safe."

"Don't say as Billy Widgeon isn't saved, sir," cried the man piteously.

"No, because he is," replied Mark.

"That's a comfort," said the stowaway.

"Look here, my man," said the major, "how far is it to the ship?"

"I don't know, sir. I'd come a long way when I heard guns, and walked on till I saw you; and I thought I should have dropped when I lost sight of you again."

"Ah, you're very weak," said the major.

"'Taint only that, sir; for it's enough to frighten a man to death or send him mad to be all alone here in a place like this."

"Why, it's a very beautiful place, Jimpny."

"Yes, sir, to look at; but as soon as you go into the woods to find fruit there's things flies at you, and every now and then in the night there's a great bull roaring thing that makes a horrid noise."

"Indeed!" said the major, exchanging glances with Mark.

"Yes; something dreadful, sir."

"Ah, well! we needn't talk about that now," said the major. "We will not go on to the ship, but get back to camp—eh, Mark?"

"Yes, sir: the news will be glorious," cried Mark.

"And what are you going to do?" said the major drily. "Go back to the ship?"

"Go back to the ship, sir!" cried the stowaway wildly. "No, no, sir! Pray don't leave me alone! I can't bear it, sir—I can't indeed—it's too awful! Mr Mark, sir, don't let him leave me! Say a kind word for me! I'd sooner lie down and die at once!"

He flung himself upon his knees, the spear falling beside him on the sand, as he joined his hands together and the weak tears began to stream down his cheeks.

"Get up!" said the major roughly, "and act like a man. Don't be such a whimpering cur!"

"No, sir, please, sir, I won't, sir; but I'm very weak and ill, sir. Take me with you, please, sir, and I'll do anything you like, sir."

"Why, you ought to be ashamed of yourself," said the major sharply, "for thinking that two English gentlemen would be such brutes as to leave a sick and wounded man alone in a place like this. Eh, Mark?"

"Yes, sir," said the lad, flushing at being called an English gentleman. "But he is very weak and ill."

"That's it, sir—that's it," cried the man piteously. "You will take me, then?"

"Of course. Come along," said the major. "Confound that monkey!"

For, while they had been intent upon the man's account of his escape, Jack had been busy covering himself with feathers, as he plucked away at first one and then another of the birds.

"Ah! would you?" cried the major as Jack chattered fiercely upon the bird being taken from him, and then retreated behind Bruff.

"I'll carry those, sir," said Jimpny. "I'll take that too. Would you lend me a handkychy or a bit o' string, Mr Mark, sir, to tie their legs together, and then I can carry the lot over my shoulder, some before and some behind."

"Fore and aft," said Mark, taking a piece of fishing-line from his pocket.

"Yes, sir, that's it," said the man; "but I can't never recollect those sailors' words.

"That's your sort," he continued cheerfully, as the birds' legs were securely tied, and as he knelt on the sand he got them well over his shoulder, got up slowly by a great effort and essayed to start, then reeled, and recovered himself, reeled again, and fell headlong with his load.

He raised himself slowly to his knees, and looked pitifully from one to the other, and then at his load.

"I'm no good," he said in a whimpering tone. "I never was no good to nobody, and I never shall be."

"Bah! stuff!" cried the major. "Here, untie them, and tie two, two, and four together, Mark. I'll take four, and you a pair each."

"Let's make Bruff carry two," said Mark, as soon as the birds were freshly disposed, and hanging a pair pannier fashion over the dog's back, leaving thus a pair apiece, they started, after a vain attempt on the part of the stowaway to obtain permission to carry four.

Bruff protested at first, and seemed to consider it to be his duty to lie down and get rid of his load; then when it was replaced, with stern commands to him to carry it, he took upon himself to consider that it must be carried in his jaws, when Jack bounded to his side and began to pick out the feathers.

But after a little perseverance the teachable dog bore his load well enough, and the little party trudged back over the firm sand. They made a pause by the clear water for refreshment and then went on again, but only slowly, for the stowaway was very weak and the heat great, while it was piteous to see the brave effort he made to keep up with his load. This at last was plainly too much for him, and he was relieved, Mark and the major taking it in turns.

But even then it was all the poor fellow could do to keep on walking, and the journey back proving longer than they had imagined, it was night and quite a couple of miles away when Jimpny broke down.

"I don't mind, gentlemen," he said; "I shall be so near the camp that I sha'n't mind."

"Near the camp!" cried the major; "why, we are nearly an hour's walk away."

"Yes, sir; but that can't matter now. I know that there's someone in the place and that my trouble's over, so I can lie down here in the soft sand and go to sleep till morning, and then I shall be able to come on."

"Here, Mark," said the major decisively, "pick out a comfortable spot somewhere. Here, this will do—by this point. We'll settle down here. Leave the birds, my lad, and go on with the dog. Ask the captain to send three men to help us back into camp. I'll stay with Jimpny till they come."

"No, no, sir. I shouldn't like that," said the stowaway.

"Let me stay with him, sir," cried Mark; and after a great deal of arguing it was finally decided that Mark should stay, and selecting a hollow beneath some jutting masses of rock where the sand lay thick, the stowaway was helped to his natural couch, the birds were thrown down, and after another brief argument, in which Mark declared he should feel far more nervous in going alone along the shore than in stopping, the major started off on his journey in search of help.

Chapter Twenty Nine
How Jack did not appreciate a Storm

The night was intensely dark, not one star shining, and before many minutes had elapsed after the major's steps had died away the face of Mark's companion was invisible, and he could not help a sensation of awe invading his breast as he felt how absolutely alone they were, and this made him realise more fully the feelings of the stowaway, wounded and faint, and believing himself entirely alone in that desert place.

But the darkness seemed to trouble no one else, for after saying a few words about its being a shame and that he could never forget it, Jimpny fell off at once into a deep sleep, his hard breathing telling its own tale; while Bruff and Jacko obtained a delicious couch by scratching away some of the dry sand and making pillows of the birds.

More and more, as he listened to the breathings of his companion, Mark began to suffer from the horror of thick darkness. For to quote the familiar old term he could not see his hand before his face. Out by the edge of the lagoon, where a slight ripple was phosphorescent, it might have been possible, but there, beneath the shadow of the rocks, nothing could be seen.

All was wonderfully still, not so much as a whisper could be heard of night bird or animal astir. Once he thought he heard a querulous cry far out on the shallow sea-washed shore such as a wading bird might make, but it was not repeated, and at last he found himself listening, with his heart beginning to beat heavily, for the terrible roaring sound, and the more he tried not to think about it the more the thoughts would come, till at last he felt sure that he could hear something moving in the jungle. Then again all was still, and though he had been in momentary expectation of hearing the awe-inspiring roar, it did not come, and he grew a little more calm, telling himself that he had nothing to fear, and wondering why he could not lie down and rest there as peacefully as the animals by his side, who were sleeping happily enough and troubling themselves not in the least about darkness or danger.

All at once, after wondering how long it would be before the party came from camp, and making up his mind to be very watchful so that they should not pass him in the darkness, there was a vivid light, which showed the sand, the glistening sea, and the distant line of breakers quite plainly, followed at the distance of time of quite a minute by a low muttering roar which seemed to make the air quiver and the earth shake.

Then all was black again for a time, during which, with the sensation of drowsiness which had been slowly coming on completely driven away, Mark sat and watched for the next flash of lightning, and before long it came, displaying the shapes of the clouds which overhung the sea.

It was worth watching, for anything more grand could not be conceived. One moment everything was of a velvety blackness, then in an instant came the flash, the sky seemed to be opened to display the glories beyond of golden mountain, vivid blue sea, and lambent yellow plain. In the twinkling of an eye the sky closed again, and the darkness was more dense than before, while, as Mark sat thinking of the wonderful contrast between lying in his bed at home in North London and being there, once more came the deep, booming, heavy, metallic thunder.

Again a pause, with the three sleepers breathing regularly. Mark was weary, his legs and back ached, and there was a suggestion of a blister on one heel; but he felt no inclination now to sleep, and lay there upon his chest listening for the dull sound of footsteps on the sand in company with the murmur of voices.

Who would come? he asked himself. Mr Gregory and two men, or Small? He came to the conclusion that it would be Small, and at times he almost fancied that he heard the distant murmur of the boatswain's deep rough voice.

Then came another flash more vivid than ever. And this time it was as he turned in the direction where Jimpny lay sleeping. The result was that he saw the poor fellow's swarthy panic-stricken countenance, and the dog and the monkey snuggled up together as comfortably as they could make themselves; and they did not even start as a tremendous peal of thunder broke, seeming as if it would shake the rocks down above their heads.

Then all was pitchy blackness again, and the silence by contrast was awful.

Another flash, and while it was quivering in the air the thunder came with one sudden instantaneous crash as if some magazine of powder had been exploded, while after the first burst the peal rolled round and round and slowly died away, as if it were passing along vast metallic corridors to be emptied far away in space.

As Mark sat listening to the dying away of the thunder and watching for the next flash, comparing the noise with that which he heard from the jungle, and wondering why the one should be looked upon as a matter of course while the other caused the most acute horror, he became aware of a strange hissing sound, apparently at a great distance, but evidently coming on rapidly. The sound increased till, from a hiss it became a rush, then by rapid degrees a tremendous roar, and then, as if in an instant the hurricane was upon them, the rain came down in sheets, the sound swept by the rocks, and as the lightning flashed Mark became aware of the fact that the air looked thick and dense and as if filled by the spray from off the sea.

But the storm swept over from behind, so that though the water poured down from all round the rock beneath which they were sheltered none was driven in.

To sleep was out of the question had the watcher felt disposed, for he was bound to confess that it was impossible for help to come to him in the midst of such a terrific deluge. Meanwhile as the rain came down in a veritable water-spout, hissing angrily as if a myriad of serpents were in the air, the lightning flashed and the thunder roared so incessantly that it became almost a continual peal.

At the best of times, and in company, the storm would have been attended by feelings of awe; but now, comparatively speaking, alone in that solitude with the deafening din and the terrible weird glare of the lightning flashing through the rain, Mark could not help for the second time that day a strange feeling of dread come upon him with chilling force.

Just when the storm was at its worst there was a soft whining sound on his right, and as he sat up and listened in that direction a cold nose touched his hand, and Bruff thrust his head into his master's lap, uttering a low snuffling sound indicative of content.

Almost at the same moment, as the thunder paused for a moment, came a whimpering chattering from his left, and a little thin hand caught hold of him.

"Why, Jack, old fellow, frightened?" he said, as he passed his arm round the human-looking little animal.

"Chick, chack!" cried Jack, and accepting the invitation he huddled up close to Mark's breast, tucking his nose under his arm, and directly after the lad could feel that both the thin little arms were clinging to him tightly.

"No wonder I feel a bit afraid," he said to himself, "if they wake up and come to me for protection."

And with something of a warm glow at his heart as he felt himself occupying the position of protector, he sat there waiting for the storm to cease, the danger dying out of his mind, his head drooping down upon his chest, and at last Mark and his two strange bed-fellows were fast asleep, with the thunder roaring to them its deep-toned lullaby till it slowly died away.

Bruff was the first to wake and begin barking loudly, for Mark to start up in wonder, perfectly ignorant of where he was. It was as dark as ever, but the rain had ceased, the lightning merely flashed now and then, and there was a delicious sensation of cool freshness in the air which came most gratefully to the senses.

"Where am I?" thought Mark, "and what does this mean?" for he had been awakened by the dog's barking from one of those heavy dreamless sleeps where the mind refuses to open and take in facts as quickly as do the eyes.

The dog barked again more loudly than ever and now rushed from out of the shelving rocks.

"Mark, ahoy! Where are you, lad?"

"Here, father, here!" he shouted, but still wondering what it meant, till he heard the loud thud of approaching feet coming through the darkness, and once more there was a hail.

"Where away, lad?"

Mark ought to have answered, "Three points on your port-bow," but he was not well up in nautical terms in this, his first voyage, and so he simply cried out, "Here!"

The result was that in a few minutes the captain, Small, and Billy Widgeon came feeling their way into the hollow.

"Are you all right, my boy?"

"Yes, father."

"How dark it is! We were afraid we should miss you. Strike a light, Small, and let's see."

The boatswain struck a match, and while the thin splint burned there was time for the position of all to be observed, and Billy Widgeon immediately placed himself alongside of Jack.

"We started to come to your help directly the major came into camp," said the captain, "but we were driven to take shelter till the storm was over. I don't believe I was ever in such a downpour before."

"How long did you have to wait?" asked Mark, who felt guilty at having been to sleep.

"Six hours at least," said the captain. "It must be very nearly morning. How is Jimpny?"

"He has been fast asleep all the time."

"Well, then, we will not wake him," said the captain. "It is so intensely dark that we shall have difficulty in getting him home, and it can't be very long to-day."

It was longer than the captain thought, but he sat chatting about how busy they had been setting up the second hut and improving the first, besides making preparations for their home becoming permanent.

"The ship will supply us with endless useful things," he said, "even if much of the cargo is burned. This man has again proved himself a treasure, Mark, for it might have been a long time before we had explored far enough to enable us to find the hull."

"When shall you go to see it, father?" asked Mark.

"To-day, my boy. We'll get back to camp and have a good breakfast and then start. By the way, the major says you have got some capital birds."

"Eight, and they are bigger than fowls. Curious-looking things, with a sort of helmet on their heads."

"I think I know them," said the captain, "a sort of brush-turkey, I expect, the maleo birds I think they are called, and they are splendid eating. I don't think we shall starve, my lad."

"Day!" said Mark eagerly, pointing to a faint gleam away to his right.

"Yes; the first touch of dawn. I think we may prepare to go now. Get together the birds, my lads."

Widgeon and Small obeyed, finding them already tied, and slinging them over their shoulders.

"Now, Mark, wake up your companion," said the captain. "He ought to be able to walk after eight hours' rest."

Jimpny started into wakefulness at a touch, and on being spoken to answered, in a vacant wandering way, something about the fire and wanting his spear; but the day was rapidly coming round, and the faces of those in the shelter of the rocks growing visible.

"What's the matter?" said the stowaway suddenly. "Have they got off the bales and boxes.—No, I—I—is that you, Mr Mark?"

"Yes, all right, Jimpny. Had a good sleep?"

"Yes, I think so. I—I'm not quite awake. Yes, I recollect now."

"Can you walk a couple of miles or so, my lad?" said the captain.

"Yes, sir; yes, I can walk," said the stowaway; "but there are some birds here. Let me help carry the birds."

"No, no; they're all right, my lad," said Small. "You carry yourself. That's enough for you to do. Ready, sir."

"Come along, then," said the captain; and he led the way out into the delicious early morning with the light growing rapidly now and showing the trees laden with moisture, whose only effect upon the sand had been to beat it down into a firm path, so that they would have been able to go rapidly had it not been for the weakness of the stowaway.

"Better when I've had some breakfast," he said feebly. "Been a bit bad, sir. Soon get well, though, now."

He did not look as if he would, but there was plenty of the spirit of determination in him, and he plodded on till they came in sight of the grove where the huts had been set up, and there in the first beams of the morning sun the ladies could be seen anxiously on the look-out for the lost ones, while, to mingle matter-of-fact with sentiment, there, from among the rocks rose up in the glorious morning the thin blue smoke of the so-called kitchen fire, telling of what was to follow after the welcome—to wit, a good breakfast of fruit and freshly-caught fish, with other delicacies, perhaps, by way of a surprise.

Safely back, and the night's anxieties soon forgotten in the light of the sun, the storm having made everything seem bright, and by comparison peaceful and calm.

"Now, Mark," said the captain after the refreshing sensation consequent upon a good bathe and a hearty meal, "you will be too tired to go in search of the ship to-day."

To which Mark gave a most emphatic "No," and declared himself quite ready for the start.

Chapter Thirty
How Mark saw the Sea-Serpent

"He's about the most misfortnatest chap as ever was born, Jimpny is," said Billy Widgeon. "He do get it bad and no mistake, allus."

For the stowaway had been at once taken up to the hospital, as the shady spot under the cocoa-nut trees had to find him lying there looking already quite another man. Kindly hands had been busy with water and bandages; he was decently clothed, and the feverish haunted look had gone out of his eyes, as he lay chatting with the sailors under a capital shedding of palm leaves and bamboos, which had been rigged up just in time for the storm, and which, like the other huts, had proved fairly water-tight.

"Oh yes, Mr Mark, sir, I'm a-getting on splendid now," he said. "This is a deal better than being aboard."

It was an understood thing that the party should start at once so as to have a long day for the search for the ship, and they had just prepared to start well armed for defence and to obtain fresh supplies of birds when Mark got back to the men's hut. The captain was loth to leave the camp, but most eager to see the ship, so it was decided that the major should remain and Mr Gregory be the captain's companion, Billy Widgeon and another man being appointed to the party.

"Good luck to you!" said the major. "We'll defend the camp, and have a splendid dinner of roast turkey ready when you come back. By the way, Mark, show them how to shoot these maleo birds. You will not run after them again as we did."

"No; I shall know better now," he replied; and, after another glance round at the arms, they were just setting off when an idea struck the lad.

"I say, father," he exclaimed; "it's going to be a very hot day, and all along by the side of those trees and rocks you get hardly a breath of air."

"I suppose not," said the captain drily.

"And after a time the guns get very heavy to carry."

"Very," said the captain.

"And the maleo birds are regular lumps, if we shoot any."

"So I suppose, my boy. There, don't beat about the bush. We can find our way, of course. You are tired with yesterday's exertions, so why don't you frankly say that you would rather stay?"

"But I wouldn't rather stay, father. I only thought it would be much pleasanter to ride."

"Ah, to be sure!" said Mr Gregory grimly, and with a sarcastic smile. "Widgeon, run round the corner and call a couple of hansom cabs."

The men laughed and Mark flushed up.

"Couldn't we ride as well in a boat as in a hansom cab, Mr Gregory?" he said.

"Done!" cried Gregory, giving his leg a slap. "Here, captain, we had better take second grades. Of course: why not row round?"

"Why not, indeed?" said the captain smiling. "I daresay we can keep in the smooth lagoon all the way; and when we cannot, we can land and continue afoot. Did you notice the water, Mark?"

"Yes, father; it was exactly like this all the way, only, I think, the line of breakers comes in nearer."

"Here, launch the boat, my lads," cried the captain; and she was run down, the guns, ammunition, and provisions placed in the stern, and ten minutes later they were all riding easily over the blue waters of the smooth lagoon, the men bending to their oars, tiring their arms perhaps, but saving their legs, as the gig ran easily over the bright surface.

It was a glorious ride, and they had not gone twenty yards before there was a rush along the sands and then a plunge as Bruff came swimming after them; while Jack, chattering loudly, came cantering down toward the edge of the water, and then ran along the sands.

"We may as well take him in," said the captain; and giving orders for the men to cease pulling, they waited till Bruff came alongside, Billy Widgeon receiving orders to help him in at the bows, where he was allowed to have his customary shake and go off like a water firework as the drops flew in all directions, glittering in the sun.

"Now, men, give way again," said the captain.

The men obeyed rather unwillingly, and Jack, who was being left, ran along by the edge of the water shrieking and chattering to be taken with them, Bruff answering with a burst of barks.

"He'll soon go back," said Gregory.

Billy Widgeon looked appealingly at Mark.

"Let's have him with us, father; he'll be quiet enough."

"But I want to get on, my lad."

"Begging your pardon, sir," said Billy Widgeon respectfully; "me and my mate here's willing, and he won't weigh heavy in the boat."

"Run in and take him," said the captain shortly; when one man backed, the other pulled, the bows of the gig were run in to the sand; and Jack leaped on board, chattering in duet with the dog's excited fit of barking; after which, as they continued their way, Bruff seemed disposed for a gambol; but Jack was decidedly stand-offish, from the fact that he was comfortably dry, while the dog was most unpleasantly wet.

They soon settled down, however, and the journey continued, with the shore presenting a succession of lovely pictures which could be enjoyed from the boat far more than while trudging over the sand. Groves of cocoa-nut trees, and beyond them the dense green of the jungle, with, as they progressed, piled-up rocks, black, dark-brown, and glorious with parasitical and creeping growths.

Then every here and there, through some opening where the trees were a little lower, glimpses of the conical mountain appeared, always with the film of vapour hanging about its point, and inviting an ascent to see what wonders it had to show.

When weary of gazing at the shore there was a submarine forest to inspect beneath them where the sea-weed waved and the corals and other sea-growths stood up in the tiny valleys and gorges which the rock displayed. Sea-anemones waved their tentacles as they looked like tempting flowers which invited the tiny fish and crustaceans to inspect their beauties, and at the slightest touch of one of these waving petals fell paralysed, or were drawn into the all-absorbing mouth that took the place of the nectary in a flower.

Every stroke of the oars, too, sent the brilliant little fish scurrying away in shoals—fish that were gorgeous beyond description, and were to the water what the sun-birds were to the air.

All at once the men ceased rowing and allowed the boat to stop.

"What is it?" said the captain.

Billy Widgeon, who had been looking out seaward, pointed with his oar to something glistening on the top of the water, and then, giving a whispered hint to his companion, the latter gave one sturdy tug at his oar and then raised it and let the boat glide on, curving in a semicircle toward the object on the water.

"A sea-serpent!" whispered Mark.

"Yes, and a real one," said Gregory as they all watched the creature lying basking and evidently asleep in the hot sunshine.

Setting aside its shape, which always seems repellent, it was beautiful in the extreme, being marked with broad bands of orange upon a purple ground; and as it lay there on the blue water it seemed hard to believe that it could be dangerous.

"We're not on a collecting expedition," whispered the captain, taking up his gun; "but I should like to have that to show to people who say there are no serpents in the sea. What's that, Gregory—ten-feet long?"

"Twelve at least. Aim at his head."

He was too late, for the captain's piece was already at his shoulder, and as he drew trigger the charge struck the serpent about a third of its length from the head, making it heave up out of the water, while a convulsion ran through it, and then it lay motionless upon the surface.

"Dead!" cried Mark excitedly; and he made a dash to check Bruff, but too late, for the dog plunged over the side and swam towards the serpent.

"Stop him, Billy!" cried Mark; and the little sailor, who had laid in his oar and stood ready with the boat-hook, made a snatch at the dog's collar, but did not succeed in gaffing him, and Bruff swam on.

"It's dead, Mark," said the captain; and then, more quickly than it takes to describe it, Bruff made a snatch at the nearest portion of the snake—its tail—caught it in his teeth, and was in the act of turning to drag it after him back to the boat, when there was a rush in the water, the creature heaved itself up, and quick as lightning threw itself round the dog, and they saw its head raised and darted down at the dog's neck.

Instantaneously as it had constricted poor Bruff, it untwined itself as rapidly; and as in his wonder and alarm Bruff uttered a furious bark, he unloosed his hold upon the slimy creature's tail, before he could recover from his surprise and make a fresh attempt at seizure the serpent had dived and was gone.

"Did you see the snake strike him?" said the captain.

"Yes; and they are terribly poisonous."

"Said to be," said the captain, "but I never knew anyone bitten."

"I have," said the mate in a low voice, "two cases; and both people died."

"Call the dog on board," said the captain; and in obedience to his master's call the dog swam alongside and was hauled in, to stand barking with his paws resting on the bows after his regular shake.

They all looked hard at the dog, but his only concern seemed to be as to where the serpent had gone; and that was very evident, for as the water grew quiescent they could see it about eight feet below them swimming slowly with an undulating motion in and out among the weeds and corals, apparently none the worse for having been perforated with small-shot.

"Couldn't we get it?" said Mark, glancing at the boat-hook.

"No," said his father decisively; "and even if we could, I think we are better without its company. Go on."

The oars dipped again and the boat glided rapidly over the calm waters, while Mark spent his time between gazing at the beauties of the shore, with its many changes, rocky points, and nooks, and watching Bruff, who exhibited no signs of suffering from the venom of the serpent's bite.

It was a long pull for the men, and from time to time the captain and mate exchanged places to give them a rest; but it was far more easy for all than toiling over the heated sands, while, as far as they could judge, there seemed every probability of their being able to row on as far as they liked, the broad canal-shaped lagoon being continued right onward—the reef of coral only varying a little by coming nearer at times, and always acting as a barrier to break the heavy swell.

At last Mark caught sight of that for which he had long been watching, having made out the sheltering rocks where he had slept quite early in their journey. The sight for which he had attentively watched was a set of specks far off upon the yellow sands, and as soon as they came in sight he pointed them out to his father.

"Well, I see nothing," said the captain; "but wait a moment."

He took up his gun, opened the breech, and removed the cartridges, after which he held the double-barrel up to his eyes as if it were a binocular glass and looked long and attentively through it.

"Oh, yes, and I can make them out now," he said; "twenty or thirty of them scratching in the sand not far from the trees."

Mark had a look through the barrels, and then, with rather a sneer on his face, the first-mate had a look, but changed his expression as he did so.

"Well, you can certainly see them better," he said rather grudgingly.

"Better! yes," said the captain; "it's a simple plan for anyone out shooting, and worth knowing."

"But it can't magnify," said Mark.

"No," replied the captain; "but it shades the eyes and seems to increase the length of their sight as they peer through these long tubes."

"You'll try for a few of the birds, I suppose?" said the mate.

"By all means. Half a dozen such fellows as those will make a capital addition to our table—I mean sandy floor, Mark," he said, smiling.

The birds, as they neared them, seemed to take no heed till they attempted to land, and Mark could not help noticing the annoyance painted in the mate's face, as, eager to have a shot at the fine fat-looking fellows, he saw them move off in a rapid run.

"Row a little farther," said the captain.

This was done, and the boat was pulled a hundred yards and the same evolutions gone through on both sides.

"Why, I thought you said they were easy to shoot!" said the mate impatiently.

"So they are," said Mark, smiling with the confidence of his hard-bought experience, "if you know how."

"Show us then," said his father, handing him his gun. "We shall never get any this way, and I suppose if we land and try and stalk them they'll keep running out of shot."

"Yes," said Mark. "The major and I followed them for over a mile."

"Ah, well! let's see the wise man give us a lesson," said the mate grimly.

Mark took the gun, and after they had been rowed another hundred yards he bade the men pull in sharply right to the shore, taking his place previously in the bows alongside of Bruff.

The boat touched the sands and Mark leaped out, followed by Bruff, who charged the birds, barking furiously the while, with the same result as before; the birds ceased running, turned to gaze at their enemy, and then took flight to the trees.

"Now, Mr Gregory," shouted Mark, waiting till he came up, when they fired together and each got a bird.

Following the flock after these had been retrieved and carried to the boat they obtained another, Mark missing an easy shot. Soon after they both missed, and then the mate obtained two with his right and left barrels.

This was carried on for about half an hour, when with a bag of nine birds they stopped, the supply being considered ample to last three or four days.

Chapter Thirty One
How they entered Crater Bay

The birds were now stowed away in the bows and stern, the former lot being investigated with plucking views by Jack, who, however, was stopped by his master and forced to seat himself on one of the thwarts, where he sat eyeing the game and evidently longing to begin, while the boat was now once more propelled swiftly, and judging from the numbers of these curious birds they saw, it seemed that a supply for food was not likely to fail for some time to come.

They rowed steadily on for quite a couple of hours more, beyond where Mark and the major had their encounter with the supposed savage, but there was no sign of the ship.

"He didn't dream it, did he?" said the mate gruffly, as he stood up and scanned the line of coast in front.

"He could not," said the captain smiling. "His coming here was no dream."

"No; we did not bring him," assented the mate. "Let's see; we are going due west now. No doubt, I think, about this being an island."

"Not the least," said the captain. "Come on now and let's take the oars."

They changed places with the men, Mark also taking his turn, and pulled steadily for quite a couple of hours more, but still there was no sign of the ship; and at last, as they came abreast of a little stream flowing down from a gorge in a high and rocky part of the land to leap from rock to rock with a musical plashing before it came gurgling through the sand, they decided to land, go and find a shady spot, and there rest and partake of the provisions with which they were prepared.

The boat was run ashore, the grapnel placed on the sand, and as they leaped on to the level surface one by one they reeled and caught at the air to save themselves from falling, for the sand seemed to heave like the sea.

"Are we giddy from rowing in the sun?" said the captain excitedly.

"No; the earth moved. Hush!"

It was Mark who spoke, and they listened to a dull rumbling sound. Then there was a smart shock, a great cloud seemed to be puffed out of the mountain, whose top they could see plainly dominating the gorge, and then all was still.

"An earthquake!" said the captain. "Here, stand up, men, what are you doing?"

This was to Billy Widgeon and the other sailor, who, immediately upon feeling the tremulous wavy motion of the earth, had dropped into a sitting position, and from that lain flat down upon their backs.

"Is it safe to get up, sir?" said Billy pitifully.

"Safe!" said the mate. "Yes, for you. You wouldn't fall far."

"No, sir, not so werry far," said Billy apologetically; "but you see I ain't used to walking when the ground's a-heaving up like that there."

"My good fellow, who is?" cried the mate.

"Never felt anything like it before, sir. Hadn't we better go back?"

"Quick!" cried the captain; "run—for those rocks."

He led the way, and all ran, followed by Jack and the dog, and as they ran a rushing sound came behind them, nearer and nearer and louder and louder. Mark glanced over his shoulder and saw that a great white-topped wave was dashing in from seaward, turning the calm lagoon into a fierce scene of turmoil, and racing after them so rapidly that before they reached the rocks it was half-way up the sands. As they climbed up about twenty feet the wave struck the foot, sending the spray flying over their heads, and then retiring with a low hissing roar back to the lagoon, across it, plunging over the barrier reef, and as they watched they could see that the ocean was heaving and tossing in the brilliant sunshine, and then in the course of a few minutes all was peaceful once again.

"Oh, the boat!" cried Mark, for he had been intent upon the wave. The captain had, however, been watchful of the boat the whole time, and had seen it caught by the earthquake wave, swung round, and carried up over the sands to be thrown at last and left close to the pile of rocks to which they clung.

Fortunately it had been heaved up gently and allowed to fall easily upon the soft sands, so that when they descended to it and swung its stern round so as to place it in an easy position for running down, they found it to be perfectly uninjured, and that it had not shipped a drop of water.

All joined to run her down again toward the sea, but the captain concluded to wait till they were ready to start, in case another wave should run in and worse mischief befall them.

It was not a pleasant preparation for their meal, but the sea now calmed down, the water of the little stream came gushing perfectly clear, the sun shone brightly and not a cloud was visible; in short, but for their memories, it was impossible to tell that anything had befallen them. Still it required a little effort to sit down where only a short time before the earth had been trembling, and it was impossible to avoid a sensation of dread lest the trembling of the ground should only have been the precursor of a terrible earthquake when the island would open and swallow them up, and this idea was fostered by the behaviour of Bruff, who kept running here and there snuffing the sand and uttering every now and then an uneasy whine.

After the first few mouthfuls, however, their confidence began to return, and a hearty meal was eaten, and supplemented by some draughts of cool, sweet cocoa-nut milk obtained by Billy Widgeon, who contrived to climb a young newly-bearing tree.

After this the boat was run down to the lagoon, and they continued their journey refreshed and ready to send the little vessel rapidly through the water.

The land trended more and more now to the west, but in front of their course a long spit of rocks ran right out for a considerable distance, and after scanning the shore carefully the captain concluded that if the ship was anywhere it must be just beyond the point.

The state of the atmosphere made the distance deceptive, and the rocky spit proved to be far nearer than had been anticipated. And here as they drew close to see that the rock was of a blackish-brown it became evident that unless they cared to row completely out to sea and then back so as to double this point, where there would in all probability be a tremendous current, they must now land and continue the journey on foot.

The latter was decided upon and the gig run up on a beach whose sand was of some sparkling black mineral, the grains all being of a good size and tremendously heavy. The rocks towered above them and were extremely craggy, but of a columnar, basaltic nature, which formed plenty of steps for the climbers, who mounted some fifty feet and then were able to look down into a perfectly-formed semicircular bay, the spit on which they stood forming one side, a similar spit being on the other about a hundred and fifty yards away, while the whole wore the aspect of a volcanic crater, one side of which had been washed down by the sea, the black jagged rock and barren aspect being suggestive of this having been once the scene of an eruption.

As they stood on the rocks gazing down before them there was a slight quivering to be felt, and soon after a dull heavy explosion, which sounded as if it had taken place far below, while directly after a ball of vapour shot up out of the conical mountain, here about a couple of miles inland, right from the head of the bay.

It was a wild and desolate scene, for instead of the volcano being shut off in its lower parts by bands of vegetation, there rose from the water great swarthy walls of basaltic rock, all looking as if they had lately cooled down after being in a state of incandescence; while to add to the weird aspect of the place, so strange in the midst of so much verdure and lush growth, the waters of the little bay were of pitchy blackness, and hardly showed a ripple upon the jetty sand.

Desolation in its wildest form, but at that moment it seemed the framing of one of the most attractive pictures the travellers could find; for half hidden by rocks, but as it were just at their feet, lay the blackened hull of the ship, just as it had drifted ashore and been heaved up and tossed higher and dryer by the late earthquake wave.

No time was lost in climbing down to the black sands, while the burnt and torn-off remains of the shrouds which hung over the side of the hull rendered an ascent to the deck quite easy, the captain leading, Mark following, and the others rapidly joining them where they stood. But as it was, only Mark heard the low groan the captain uttered as he stood and gazed about him on the charred deck of his ship.

It was a pitiable spectacle indeed, for the planks were almost entirely black; three charred stumps showed where the great masts had been, and saving that the bowsprit was nearly intact the fire had made a clean sweep of the deck, even the greater portion of the bulwarks having been burned away.

Here and there the planks were so completely burned through that the greatest care was needed to avoid a fall below, but by picking their way they were able to go from end to end of the charred hull. As the burning masts had fallen they had carried with them over the sides the greater part of the standing and running rigging with every spar, while the shrouds and ropes that had been dragged across the deck were reduced to cinders which crumbled at a touch.

Everything pointed to the truth of the stowaway's story, for as they stood in the bows there was a portion of the deck almost untouched, and the remains of a stay-sail furled up and only burned through. There could be no doubt that the fire was blazing furiously, had burned all the boats, and was eating its way down toward the cargo and stores when the tropic downpour came and extinguished it before greater mischief was done; for though the vessel had become a complete hulk there was one fact perfectly evident, and that was that they had only to descend below to find in the hold and stores a perfect mint of useful treasure for people in their condition.

"Yes," said Gregory, as if someone had just spoken these words to him, "we can get enough out of her to live on for a couple of years, and stuff sufficient to set-to and build a little schooner or smack big enough to take us to Singapore."

"I was thinking precisely the same," said the captain eagerly, while Mark said nothing, for with the ship's stores and treasures to work upon it seemed as if they could make themselves very happy in such a glorious place. With a comfortable home, plenty of fruit and birds, and their friends about them, life on the island would be a very happy one, so it seemed to him, and he felt a kind of wonder that there should be a difference of opinion. But then there was the volcano and the earthquake!

They were now picking their way aft, and here the destruction was greater. In one place it was perfectly plain that the powder-keg must have stood, for coamings, bulwarks, skylights, everything had been swept clear off at the time the explosion occurred, while as they reached the saloon entry it was to find only its place, for here the fire had been raging furiously, the poop-deck and the cabins on either side of the saloon being burned completely away.

"Well," said the captain, after a long inspection, "we've found the poor old girl, Gregory, and she's past mending."

"Yes," said Gregory with a short sharp nod of the head.

"But she will be a treasure-house for us, and some of her cargo may be saved, so we must make her fast."

"Not much fear of her breaking away," said the mate; "she's well wedged in these sands, and it strikes me—yes, it is so, that big wave to-day gave her a lift up and drove her farther ashore. No tide would ever float her off."

"No," said the captain, "but all the same let's make sure. We could get a cable out to yon piece of rock and moor her safely."

"Yes," said the mate. "Now, my lads, bear a hand."

All joined in, from the captain to Mark, and in half an hour a cable was run out of one of the hawse-holes, dragged high up the sands, one end taken round a huge mass of rock, tied and lashed, and the other end well stopped in the ship.

"There," said the captain, "that's enough. Now for home. Shall we go back the same way?"

"Well, the worst that could happen would be that we should have to camp out," said Gregory; "and as I make it we've one knot to go this way to two the other."

"If it's an island."

"As I believe it is, sir. What do you say? We must explore it some time, and if this is the nearest way to fetch cargo we'd better find it."

"Unless we come and make our home here."

"No, sir. The ladies wouldn't like this black furnace hole of a place. Let them stop where they are."

"Perhaps you are right, Gregory; but now how to get back? Shall we row out right round the point?"

"No, sir. I'm thinking there's an opening about a couple of hundred yards out yonder, and if there's no water perhaps we can get the boat across."

"Come on, then."

The captain sighed as he gave one more glance round, and ended by picking up one of the charred handles of the wheel, which he put in his pocket before returning to the boat.

"There is plenty of powder and shot in the magazine," said the captain, thankfully; "and we can find no end of useful stuff if we break bulk."

"Ay, we shall manage, sir," said the mate. "Now, my lads, all together," and the boat was once more run out and rowed to the opening the mate had seen.

It proved enough for them to pass through with their oars laid in, and as soon as they were through the change from the brilliant blue water with the lovely coral and sea growth beneath to this jetty black bay was quite awe-inspiring.

"The water's clear," said Mark. "What makes it so black?"

"I should say," said the captain, gazing down over the side, "that it is of almost unfathomable depth."

"And was once a pit of fire," said the mate. "But let's try."

He took one of the fishing-lines, fitted a leaden weight to it, and lowered it over the side, when it went down and down till the end of the line was reached. Then another was tied on, and this went down, making together nearly 200 yards. There was yet another line, and this was fastened on, another fifty yards going down.

"There, you see," said the captain.

"Bottom!" cried the mate, as the weight ceased and the line slackened.

"Two hundred and fifty yards," said the captain: "a hundred and twenty-five fathoms."

"No," cried the mate excitedly, "it isn't bottom, it's a fish."

"Nonsense!"

"It is; I can feel him," cried the mate; and he hauled rapidly in, with a heavy fish playing about till, just as it reached the surface and displayed a hideous pair of jaws, it let go, and with a flounder disappeared.

"Glad he was not hooked," said the mate, as Mark shrank away. "What a brute!"

"Horrible!" exclaimed Mark, shivering, for the idea of being overboard in such a black bottomless hole sent a chill through him. But they were soon across, to find they could drag the boat over fifty yards of black sand and launch her again in blue water, where all around was bright and attractive; for though no large trees were growing near the shore, the land was covered with a glorious vegetation, and looked attractive right away to the slopes of the volcano, as soon as the crater bay, with its lowering black basalt, was left a quarter of a mile behind.

"Now," said the captain, "how are we steering?"

"Nearly due south," said the mate, glancing at a pocket-compass.

"Then you are right, Gregory, and this is the nearest way home."

"If it is an island, father," said Mark, smiling.

"And that it must be, Mark, my lad, and a very small one, as we shall see."

Chapter Thirty Two
How that Fish meant Mischief, and became Meat

Their way still led them along the peaceful waters which girt the island—for so they now felt that they might venture to call it—the strong barrier reef of coral keeping back the heaving swell of the ocean, which foamed and broke outside, leaving the lagoon perfectly calm, save here and there where they came across an opening in the reef through which a fleet might apparently have sailed into fairly deep anchorage, sheltered from the wildest storm and the roughest sea.

Here and there the reef was so far above water that vegetation had taken root, and young cocoa-nut trees were springing up to form the beginning of a grove, but for the most part there was the dead coral, the gleaming sand, and the pearly foam glistening in the sun.

No currents to stay them, no rough winds to check. Their journey might have been upon some peaceful lake, whose left-hand shore was one succession of cocoa-nut groves; and beyond that, rocky jungle, full of ridge and hollow, mound of verdure, and darksome glade and chasm, down which trickled streams of water, such as had risen in the heights which culminated in the smoking cone of the volcano, while here and there the streams gave marked traces of their sources by sending up faint clouds of steam.

Mark felt as he lay back in the stern and gazed at the glorious panorama that he could watch the various phases of beauty in the landscape for ever. But then he was not rowing, and the motion of the boat and the dipping of his hands in the water kept him comparatively cool.

Still, in spite of its beauty it was impossible to gaze shoreward without a feeling of awe. For there had been that trembling of the earth; there were here and there openings in the trees through which vast blackened roads of rock seemed to come down to the sea, zigzag tracks which it was plain enough were the cooled-down and hardened streams of lava which had made their way to the sea during some eruption of the calmly beautiful mountain which rose so peacefully toward the clouds, one of which seemed to have remained to act as its feathery crown.

Then, too, there was the remembrance of that terrible roar which they had heard in the jungle, and every now and then Mark's eyes searched the trees at the edge beyond the sands, and he longed with a sensation of shrinking to catch sight of the creature which had given them all so much alarm.

But search how he would, as the boat went steadily on, there was no sign of animal life ashore but the birds. Once or twice he fancied he could see something like a lizard run across the heated rocks, but he could not be sure. But of birds there seemed to be plenty. Flocks of doves, large lavender-plumed pigeons, white cockatoos, long-tailed lories, and parrots whose feathers bore all the colours of the rainbow; but shorewards that was all. In the lagoon it was very different.

"Sha'n't want for fish," said Gregory, as he dipped his oar—he and the captain now giving the men a rest.

As he spoke a shoal was making the water dance just ahead and completely changing its colour, for, as they fed upon the small fry with which the surface gleamed, the sea was dappled with rings, serried with ridges, and seemed as if it were a fluid of mingled gold and silver beneath which some volcanic action was going on, which made it boil and flush and ripple till the bows of the gig reached the shoal, and then instantaneously the surface became calm.

"Plenty of work for you, Mark," said the captain. "You will have to be head of our fishing department, and keep our little colony supplied."

"You must get Small to help you make a net," said Gregory, "and contrive some long lines."

They ceased rowing, for they were now opposite a spot where the jungle came close to the edge of the lagoon, being only separated by a smooth patch of sand. Here, too, were quite a flock of the maleo birds, scratching and searching for food, after the fashion of fowl; but as the boat stopped they took alarm, and seemed to skim over the sand, their feet striking the ground so rapidly as to become invisible.

"They can run," said the mate; "but we seem to have learned their secret. What's that?"

All listened, but there was no sound.

"I fancied I heard a low distant roaring noise," said the mate, dipping his oar again, "but I may have been mistaken."

The captain was in the act of dipping his own oar when Billy Widgeon, who was seated just in front of Mark, whose place was right astern, turned sharply and caught the lad's arm:

"Look, Mr Mark, sir, look!" he cried, pointing with his other hand, "there he goes!"

"Who?" cried Mark excitedly; "a savage?"

"Yes, sir," said Billy, grinning and holding Bruff, "savage enough. Nay, nay, my lad, you lie down. It wouldn't do you no good to go overboard now."

"A large one, too," said the captain, resting on his oar.

"Ay, he's a nasty customer," said the mate.

"What is?" cried Mark eagerly. "What is it you can all see?"

"Shark!" said the captain.

"Where? Where? I want to see a shark."

Mark's eyes were roving all about, but he saw nothing in any direction save a little dark triangular piece of something, with the forward side a little curved, and this was moving slowly through the water.

"There, my lad, there," said the captain; "can't you see his back fin?"

"Is that a shark?" said Mark, in a disappointed tone, as the black object, looking like the thick lateen sail of some tiny invisible boat, glided along the surface not fifty yards away, and making as if to cross their bows.

"Yes," said the captain, "that's the fin of a shark, ten-feet long I should say."

"And I a dozen," said the mate.

"Like to see him a little closer?" said the captain.

"Yes," cried Mark eagerly; and then he wished he had said "No," for the oars were, after a pull or two, laid inboard, while the captain took hold of the sharply-pointed hitcher, and held it balanced in his hand.

The impetus given to the boat was sufficient to drive it onward, so that it was evident that the back fin of the shark and the bows of the gig would arrive at the same point together, and Mark rose eagerly to see what would follow, when the captain made him a sign.

Mark sat down, and suddenly saw the shark's fin stop some three or four yards from the boat, change its position, and come end on towards where he was seated; and his eyes were fixed so firmly on this that he quite started, as he saw before it, and very close to where he sat, a dark-looking body, with a rounded snout and two pig-like eyes.

"Don't know what to make on us, Mr Mark, sir," said Billy Widgeon, grinning. "See his old shovel nose?"

"Yes," said Mark, "but I can't see his mouth. I thought they had great gaping mouths, full of sharp teeth."

"He keeps his rat-trap down underneath him, sir, so as not to frighten the fishes."

"Hand me that gun, Mark," said the mate.

Mark passed it along; and as he did so the shark glided round the stern, and came along the other side.

"You don't think he'll attack us, do you?" said the captain.

"There's no knowing what a jack-shark will do," said the mate, quietly cocking both barrels, and making the muzzle of the gun follow the movements of the great fish, whose elongated form was perfectly plain now in the clear water as he slowly glided on. The long unequally-lobed tail waved softly to and fro like a peculiarly-formed paddle, and the motion of the fish seemed to be peculiarly effortless as he went on right past the gig, and continued his course a dozen yards ahead.

"Off!" said the captain laconically; but as he spoke the shark turned, and the fin came toward them again, always at the same distance above the water, and again on their starboard side, by which it glided, went astern, and turned, to come back once more.

"Hadn't we two better pull, sir?" said Billy. "He means mischief, that he do."

"Think he'll attack?" said the captain again.

"I'm beginning to think he will," said Mr Gregory.

He had hardly spoken when the shark turned, and there was an eddying swirl in the water where his tail gave a vigorous stroke or two, and almost simultaneously a long glistening cruel-looking head rose out of the water.

The monkey uttered a shriek, and would have leaped overboard in his fright, but for Billy Widgeon's restraining hand, when the poor little animal took refuge beneath his legs, while Bruff set up a furious bark, his hair ruffling up about his neck, and his eyes glistening with anger.

But shriek or yell had no influence upon the hungry shark, which seemed to glide like a glistening curve or arch of shark right over the bows of the boat, striking her side in the descent as the fish passed into the sea again; but so heavy was the blow, and so great the creature's weight, that the gig was extremely near being capsized.

"Pass me the other gun, Mark," cried the captain. "Look out, Gregory, whatever you do. Another attack like that, and the brute will have us over, and—"

He left his sentence unfinished, while Mark passed the gun, and then resumed his grasp of the thwart upon which he was seated, holding on with both hands, while in the agony of dread he suffered the great drops of perspiration stood out upon his forehead, and ran together, and trickled down the sides of his nose, as his breath came thick and fast.

Some very heroic lads would, no doubt, have drawn a knife, or seized an oar, or done something else very brave in defence, but in those brief moments Mark was recalling stories he had read about sharks seizing struggling people as they were swimming, and that the water was stained with blood, and one way and another he was as thoroughly frightened as ever he had been in his life.

"Now, then!" said the captain, as the shark completed another circuit of the boat, and was about to repeat his evolution. "Both together at his head, and fire low as he rises."

It was a quick shot on the part of both, delivered just as the shark rose from the water again to leap at the boat, which probably represented to him an eatable fish swimming on the surface, while, as the two puffs of smoke darted from the guns and the loud reports rang out, the great fish fell short, but struck its nose against the side of the gig, and sank down in the water, the back fin disappearing, and coming up again fifty yards away.

"I think we'll be contented," said the captain, closing the breech of his piece, and passing it to Mark. "Let's make a masterly retreat, Gregory."

"Think he'll come back?"

"I should say no," replied the captain. "The brute has evidently had quite as much as he requires for the present."

"Will it kill him?" asked Mark.

"Can't say. I should think not. He must be badly wounded though, to sheer off like that."

"Look at that," shouted Billy Widgeon excitedly, as all of a sudden the shark was seen to leap clear out of the water, and fall back with a tremendous splash, not head first, so as to dive down, but on its flank, sending the water flying, while directly after the sea in that direction became tremendously agitated, sending waves toward them sufficiently big to make the boat rise and fall.

"He's in his flurry, Mr Mark, sir," said Billy Widgeon gleefully. "I can't abear sharks."

"Pull hard, Gregory," said the captain; "the sooner we are away from here the better."

He spoke in a low voice, and exchanged meaning glances with the mate, who at once bent to his oar.

"No, no: don't go," cried Mark. "I should like to see him when he's dead."

"I'm afraid there will be no shark to see," said the captain grimly, as the gig surged through the water.

"Why, there's his back fin, and there it is again and again," cried Mark. "How he keeps curving out of the water and dashing about! I say, father, row back and put him out of his misery."

"I daresay he is out of it by this time, my boy," said the captain, rowing hard.

"But there he is again, swimming round and beating the water."

"Why, Mark, can't you see that the water there is alive with sharks, and that they are devouring their wounded brother—fighting for the choice morsels, I dare say. This is a warning never to bathe except in some pool."

"What! do you think? Oh, I see now! How horrible!" said Mark.

"Horrible, eh?" grunted Gregory. "I wish they'd make a day of it, and eat one another all up. We could get on very well without sharks."

Mark said no more about putting their enemy out of his misery, but sat watching till, at the end of a few minutes, the surface of the lagoon grew calm; but until they had turned a low spit of sand, the black fins of at least a dozen sharks could be seen cruising round and round, and to and fro, in search of something more to satisfy their ravenous hunger.

"We are getting some experience of the dangers we shall have to encounter," said the captain, as the scene of their late conflict with the shark passed completely out of their sight, and they rowed on steadily. "That's your first shark, Mark, eh?"

"Yes," said Mark, thoughtfully, "I shall know what a shark is now."

"I think we'll give them a turn now, Gregory," said the captain. "No, no, one at a time," he cried angrily, as the men sprang up together. "We must not capsize the boat here. Now you, my man," he continued, sitting fast, as the sailor stepped across and took the mate's place before Mr Gregory rose. "Now you, Widgeon."

Billy crept very softly into the captain's place, and the latter seated himself on the thwart in front of Mark, to be joined directly by Gregory.

"There," cried Mark, as the oars dipped, "I heard it. There."

"What?" said his father.

"That roaring which Mr Gregory heard."

"It was the creaking and groaning of the oars in the tholes."

"No, no, father. It was that deep savage roar heard ever so far off."

They ceased rowing again and again, but the sound was heard no more, and the captain began to talk rather anxiously to Mr Gregory as the sun grew low in the west, and it became evident that they had a long way yet to row.

"Tired, Mark?" cried the captain.

"No, father," he replied, laughing; "but if you'll say hungry, I'll tell you: Yes, very."

"Ah, well, I keep hoping that every headland we pass may bring us in sight of the camp! It cannot be very far now."

"But suppose it isn't an island," said Mark; "we might be rowing right away."

"Come, come," cried the captain cheerily; "you the son of a navigator, and talking like this. Now, then, which way did we row when we started?"

"North-east," said Mark.

"And then?"

"North."

"Yes, go on."

"Then I think we went north-west."

"Well, and after that?"

"West, father."

"Then as we ran from the shark we went south, didn't we?"

"I don't know," said Mark. "I was too intent on the way in which they were tearing him to pieces."

"Well, you might have said you were too frightened to notice," said the captain, smiling. "You need not have been ashamed. But come now, which way are we going now?"

"Away from the sun," replied Mark, who felt no inclination to show that he had felt too much alarmed to take any notice of the direction they rowed. "I suppose we must be going east."

"Well, then, if you started by going east, and kept on rowing till you are going east again, I think you may conclude that you have gone nearly round a piece of land, and that the said piece is an island. It might not be, for we may be going right into some gulf; but this place looks as much like an island as is possible, and I don't think it can be anything else."

"Island," said Gregory, gruffly, "volcanic, and the coral has risen up round it, and kept it from being washed away."

"But could an island like this have been washed away?" said Mark.

"To be sure it could, my boy," said the captain. "From what I have seen a great deal of it is loose scoria. You saw plenty of big stones lying about?"

"Yes," replied Mark, "but they were huge stones. Some of them must weigh half a ton."

Mark knew that half a ton meant ten hundredweight; but his comparison was a shot at a venture, for he had no idea how big, or rather how small, a rock is which weighs half a ton.

"I don't think the sea would make much of a rock weighing half a ton, Mark," said the captain, smiling. "Why, in one of our great storms it would move that almost as easily as if it were a pebble. Mr Gregory is quite right. Volcanic islands have before now been formed, and been in eruption for a long time, and then been slowly swept away by the action of the sea."

"How long to sundown, sir?" said Mr Gregory.

"Half an hour," said the captain, after a glance at the slowly descending orb.

"And then it will be dark directly. What do you say, sir, give it up, land and set up camp, or keep on?"

"Keep on, Gregory," said the captain, quietly. "There is a headland away yonder. Once we get round that we may see home. Tired, my lads?"

"Tidy, sir," said Billy Widgeon. "But if it's all the same to you, we'd rather keep on as long as we can."

"Why, Billy?" asked Mark.

"Well, sir, since you put it like that," said the little sailor, smiling sheepishly, "it is that."

"Is what, Billy?"

"Why, what you mean, sir. You meant wittles. That's what you was a-thinking about. You see if we goes ashore we shall have to pick they fowls, and make a fire, and wait till they're cooked afore we can eat 'em, and to men as hungry as we, sir, that's a deal wuss than rowing a few miles; eh, mate?"

This was to the man at the oar forward. The response was an affirmatory grunt.

"There, Gregory," said the captain, "what do you say now?"

"Keep on," replied Gregory, shortly. "Widgeon is right."

The island never seemed more beautiful to them than now as the sun went down lower and lower till, like a great fiery globe, it nearly touched the sea: for rock, jungle, and the central mountainous clump, with the conical volcano dominating all, was seen through a glorious golden haze, while the sea was first purple and gold, and then orange, changing slowly into crimson.

The sun disappeared just as they rounded the point for which they had been making; but still there was no sign of the camp. Nothing but the purple lagoon stretching on and on, with the creamy line of surf on one side, the fringe of cocoa-nut trees right down to the sand on the other.

"A good clear row at all events," said the captain. "Here, Gregory, let's take the oars and pull till we can't see."

The mate changed places with the sailor in front, the captain took Billy Widgeon's oar, and the boat began to travel more rapidly, but still there was no sign of the camp. The stars came out, the water seemed to turn black, and in a very short time all was darkness; but there was no difficulty in keeping on, for the light-coloured sands on the one side acted as a guide, and the roar of the breakers on the reef kept them away on the other.

There was something very awe-inspiring though in the journey in the dark; and in spite of himself Mark could not help feeling that it was rather uncanny to be riding over the black water with what seemed to be golden serpents rushing away in undulating fashion on either side. Then, too, there was a curious quivering glow, something like an aurora, playing about the top of the mountain on their left; while all at once, plainly heard now by all, there came the distant roar of the creature which had so far remained undiscovered.

"We must be getting near home now," said the captain quietly, "for that sound comes always from the north-west of the camp."

He spoke calmly enough, but Mark detected a peculiarity in his voice which he had noted before when his father was anxious, and this finally gave place to words.

"I hope the women have not been alarmed by that sound, Gregory," he said at last.

"I hope so too," said the mate quietly. "It may be a timid creature after all. I believe it's one of those great orang-outangs. I've never heard one, but I've read that they can roar terribly."

"I hope it's nothing worse," said the captain in a low tone.

"Keep on, of course?" whispered Gregory.

"I think so, as long as we can see. We must have nearly circumnavigated the island, and it will have been a splendid day's work to have discovered the ship and done that too."

"I've got two hours' more row in me," said Gregory quietly. "By that time the men will have another hour in them, and at the worst we could manage another hour afterwards. Before then we must have reached camp."

"Ah, what's that?" cried the captain as the boat struck something.

"Bock," cried Gregory. "No, too soft."

"Row! row!" said Mark. "It was a monstrous fish—a shark."

"You could not see it?" cried the captain hoarsely, as he bent to his oar, Gregory following his example, so that the boat surged through the water.

"I saw something dark amongst these golden eel things, and they all seemed to rush away like lightning."

There was a dead silence in the boat for the next quarter of an hour, during which the rowers pulled with all their might. No one spoke for fear of giving vent to his thoughts—thoughts suggested by the adventure early in the day; but every one sat there fully expecting to see the savage-looking head of some shark thrust from the water and come over into the boat.

The suffering was for a time intense, but no further shock was felt, and as the minutes glided away their hopes rose that if this last were an enemy they were rapidly leaving it behind.

All at once Mark half rose from his place.

"Is that the light over the mountain?" he exclaimed.

"Nay," cried Billy, "that's a fire. You can see it gleam on the water."

"Hurrah!" cried Gregory, "then that means home, and they are keeping it up as a guide."

Another quarter of an hour's rowing proved this, for a big fire was blazing upon the sand, and before long they were able to make out moving figures and the fire being replenished, the leaping up of the flames and the ruddy smoke ascending high in the air.

"Now, then, give a hail," said the captain, "to let them know we're safe. They'll think we are coming from the other direction."

Billy Widgeon uttered a loud "Ahoy!" and then putting two fingers in his mouth, brought forth an ear-piercing whistle.

A distant "Ahoy!" came back, and a whistle so like Billy Widgeon's that it might have been its echo, while directly after there was a flash and then a report.

"A signal from the major," said the captain. "There, Mark, a chance for you. Fire in the air."

Mark caught up the gun, held the butt on the thwart, and drew trigger, when the flash and report cut the air and echoed from the wood.

Another ten minutes' hard pull and the boat touched the sands close to the fire, where all were gathered in eager expectancy of the lost voyagers, who had, to meet the complaints about dread and anxiety, the news of their discoveries.

"But you have not been much alarmed, I hope?" said the captain, drawing his wife's hand through his arm.

"But we have, captain," cried the major; "for Morgan and I have been in momentary expectation of an attack from that terrible wild beast."

"But there, you are tired and starving," said Mrs Strong. "We have food waiting. Sit down and rest, and we'll tell you all the while."

Chapter Thirty Three
How the Circumnavigators rested and heard News

"This here's just what I like, mates," said Billy Widgeon, as he sat on the sand in the full light of the blazing fire with his fellow-sailor opposite to him, and a large piece of palm-leaf for a table-cloth. Jack was on his right munching fruit, and Bruff on his left, sitting up, patiently attentive, waiting for bones from the hissing, hot maleo bird that had been kept for the sailors' dinner.

Small and the other men were close by smoking, and Jimpny, with his head neatly and cleanly bandaged, was lying upon his chest, resting his elbows on the sand and his chin in his hands, kicking up his heels as he stared at Billy Widgeon and listened to his adventures.

Billy was hungry, and so was his mate, and when Billy carved he prepared so to do by opening his jack-knife and whetting it on his boot, after which he seized the bird, which was double the size of a large fowl, by one leg.

"Now, shipmet," he said to his companion, "lay holt o' t'other understanding with both hands, and when I say haul! you put your back into it."

The sailor took hold of the leg, Billy held on by the other, and placed the blade of the knife between two of the fingers of the left hand while he made believe to spit in his right. Then seizing the knife firmly, he plunged the point right into the breast of the fat, juicy bird, a gush of gravy came oozing out, and he began to cut so as to divide the food into two equal portions.

"My hye! he is a joosty one," cried Billy. "It's worth waiting till now to get a treat like this, mates. Can't you smell him? Anyone going to jyne in?"

"No," said Small; "we've all had plenty, my hearty. So go on, and tell us all about what you've done to-day."

"All right!" cried Billy. "Now, then, messmet, she's nearly through. Now haul, my son. Hauly, hi, ho!"

Billy's fellow-traveller hauled at the bird's leg; but that bird was rather overdone. Mrs Strong, aided by Mary O'Halloran as cook and kitchen-maid, had done their best in the rock kitchen with a fire of cocoa-nut shells and barks; but some piled-up pieces of coral and basalt, though they are great helps, do not form a patent prize kitchener; and though the result was very tempting to hungry men, there was a want of perfection in the browning of that bird. In fact here and there it was a bit burned, notably in its right leg—the one Billy's companion held—and that leg was so horribly charred that when the man hauled it snapped off like a burned stick, and the bird, by the recoil and drag, came right into Billy's lap.

"What are you up to now?" cried the latter. "Well, you are a chap, playing your larks when we're so hungry! Don't you want none?"

As he spoke, he worked his knife to and fro, and ended by making a division of the bird that could hardly be called a fair one.

"Look at that," he said. "You've got first pick, as I'm carver; and though I feels a deal o' respect for you, matey, I don't think as how as you'd pick out the smallest bit, and hang me if I would, so here goes for another try."

Billy made another cut at the bird, hewing off a good slice of the plump breast, which he laid on to the smaller side, giving it a flap with his blade to make it stick, and then passed it over.

"There," he said, "that's fair; so here goes to begin. Hullo, matey, won't you bite?" he continued to the dog. "There, then, you can amoose yourself with them till your betters is done."

He hacked off the bird's head and neck; and after slicing off a portion of the meat, added the drumstick to Bruff's share. He then began eating voraciously, giving his messmates a version of their "adventers," as he called them, since the morning.

Billy would have made a splendid writer of fiction—a most exciting narrator, for he forgot nothing, and he added thereto in a wonderful manner. He threw in, with his mouth full, touches of description that made his companion stare, and his eloquence about the blackened hull of the vessel was wonderful.

"Talk about charkle fires," he cried; "why, if my old mother was here she'd nail the lot and save it, to use up the fruit off some of these here trees and make jam."

"Why, you can't make jam out of a burnt ship," said the stowaway.

"Who ever said you could, Davy Jimpny?" cried Billy. "But you wants charkle to make it with, don't yer?"

"Yes, if you can't get coke," said the stowaway sadly.

"Well, I aren't seen no gasworks on those here shores nowheres, and so you can't get no coke, can you?"

"Course not."

"Well, then, charkle it is. The whole deck's charkle, and so's the bulwarks, and the chunk end o' the bowsprit?"

"And the masts, Billy?" said Small.

"Dessay they are, but they're floated away. The whole ship's a reg'lar cellar."

Billy then got on about the length of time they stopped, about the wonderful nature of the crater bay, and the depth of the water.

"Why, when you was rowing acrost it you could feel as it must go right through to the other side, it was so deep. No water couldn't be so black as that was without being hundreds o' knots deep."

"I say, Billy, ain't you getting hundreds o' knots into your yarn?" said Small.

"Not I, bosun. It's all fact; you ask my mate here if it aren't. I suppose you don't want to know about that there shark?" he continued, as he picked a bone in a very ungentlemanly manner, taking his hands to it, and once leaving it stuck across his mouth like a horse's bit, while he altered his position.

"Oh yes, we do! Let's hear about the shark," cried all present.

"Well," said Billy, "there aren't much to tell, only that as we was going along I says to the skipper, I says, 'There's a whacking great shark along yonder.'

"'Ay, Billy,' he says, 'that's a thumper, and no mistake.'

"There he was, going round and round us with his back fin above water, just like a steam launch, and before you knew where you was he puts his head out o' water, gives a squint at us to see which was the best looking to swaller—"

"And he chose you, Billy, because you've got such short legs as wouldn't kick about much when you was down."

"Wrong, Mr Small, sir," said Billy, handing the remains of his half of the bird to the dog and cleaning his knife by sticking it in and out of the sand; "wrong, sir. I think he meant Jack here; but the monkey squeals out and hops under my legs in no time, and Mr Jack-shark alters his mind and goes for Muster Gregory, shoots out o' the water, he does, and he was aboard of us afore we knowed where we was."

"Get out!" said Small.

"It's a fact, Mr Small, sir; ask my mate if it aren't. He didn't stop aboard cause he come crostwise over the bows; but there he was aboard for a moment afore he slips off, and when he comes round to try it again the skipper and Mr Greg lets him have it out o' their guns, and scared him off; and, bless your 'arts, I have seen a few rum games in the sea, but the way his mates chawed him up arterwards beat everything. Why, the lagoon, as they calls it, was chock full o' sharks—millions of 'em."

"Were there now, Billy?" said Small, smiling.

"Well, of course I can't say to a few, for we was a good ways off; but what I do say is that it seemed the sharkiest spot I ever see; and, if they'd only have stood still, you might have walked on their backs for miles."

"Give Billy Widgeon a cocoa-nut to stop his talk," said the boatswain; "and there's a bit o' 'bacco for you, Billy, to clear your memory, my lad."

"Oh, my memory's clear enough, Mr Small, sir," said Billy, who was eating something all the time; "but thanky all the same. And now, how have you got on?"

"Oh," said the boatswain, "we've had a bit of a scare!"

But a narration of this was being given where the other occupants of the boat were partaking of their evening meal.

"Did the creature seem to come any nearer?" said the captain as the little group sat beneath the edge of the cocoa-nut grove, satisfying themselves with the reflected light of the men's fire, which had been lit as a beacon to attract them home.

"I think yes, decidedly," said Morgan, who was rapidly getting better.

"So did I at first," said the major; "but I have been in Africa as well as India, and have heard lions roar. When one of these gentlemen is doing a bit of nightingale he roars in one direction, then in another, now with his head up, and now with it down; and when you add to it that he roars loud and roars soft, he seems to be quite a ventriloquist, and you are puzzled."

"But I think the animal came nearer, my dear," said Mrs O'Halloran.

"I think so, too," said Mrs Strong.

"I'm sure it did, papa," cried Mary.

"Then I'm not," said her father. "It is impossible to tell how near a cry from a jungle may be."

"Well," said the captain, "it is not pleasant to know that such a savage creature is close to our camp. Something must be done."

"Seems a pity to pull up stakes and move," said the major.

"Pity!" said the captain. "Suppose we do move to the far side, we shall still be within reach. We are fixed here, and it seems to me to be the best spot we can find, and the farthest from the volcano. I'm afraid it must be a case of war. Either our friend must be driven away or killed. What do you say, major, to an expedition in search of him?"

"I'm willing," said the major.

"But the risk?" said Mrs Strong.

"More risk in waiting to be attacked than in attacking," said the captain. "I feel that we must put this danger beyond doubt, or we shall have everyone in the camp suffering from nervousness."

"If you would wait a few days I could be of some use," said Morgan.

"Then we will wait a few days," said the captain sharply. "It will give you something to anticipate and help you to get well."

"I am well now," replied Morgan. "I only want strength."

The report of all was the same, that over and over again the creature had been heard to roar savagely, and to be at times very close at hand.

Still all this did not interfere with Mark's appetite. On the whole, though sorry that his mother and the O'Hallorans should have been alarmed, he was rather pleased to find that he had been right in his belief that from time to time he could hear the roaring. Maleo bird roasted—the repast being made off those that were first shot—was excellent; so was the acid fruit squeezed over it—fruit picked by Mrs O'Halloran while the others cooked. Then there was a kind of oyster which was delicious roasted in its shells. And one way and another Mark felt that he had never before partaken of so appetising a repast, especially as he sat sipping cocoa-nut milk when it was done.

Everyone was in good spirits, for the captain promised tea and chocolate from the stores that were untouched by fire, and plenty of flour and biscuit—treasures, which would make their stay on the island far more bearable, without counting upon the many other things which the ship would supply.

At last they separated to their couches of leaves and sand, after an arrangement being made for an early start next day to explore the island by a party well armed and ready to do battle with any enemy that might present itself.

Mark's, sleeping-place was next to the major's now, the hospital being closed, for the stowaway wanted to be along with his mates; and the other wounded sailor sturdily declared that he was quite well now, and walked very nimbly to the men's hut.

Mark recollected lying down, and then all was perfectly blank till he began dreaming in the morning that his father told him that he was not to go with the expedition; but just then the savage beast in the jungle roared and repeated its cry in a way which suggested that he was to come, for the creature particularly wanted him.

This woke him; but all was perfectly still, and he could not tell whether the sound had rung upon his ears or not.

It was daylight though, and, rising, he went out, to find that Small and Mr Morgan were taking the morning watch, while Billy Widgeon was lighting a fire in the rock kitchen.

He was very sleepy still, and his couch coaxed; but he mastered the sluggishness, fetched his piece of calico which did duty for a towel, and after a careful inspection of the water, in company with Mr Morgan, he had a good bathe, and came back to shore feeling as if filled with new life, and ready for the expedition of the coming adventurous day.

Chapter Thirty Four
How Billy Widgeon went somewhere

The preparations were soon made, and directly after breakfast, in spite of Mr Morgan's desire to be of the company, the little band of half the occupants of the isle gathered for the start. Mr Gregory was obliged to remain and take charge of the camp, leaving the captain free to be the head, with the major for his lieutenant, Small, Billy Widgeon, and two other men.

Mark was to be left behind, but a piteous appeal reversed the edict, and, armed with a gun, he took his place with the expedition folk ready for the start.

They took a bag or two for fruit and game, a small amount of luncheon for each, and their arms and ammunition. Thus equipped and with the good wishes of those they left behind, the party set off for the creek where the nipah-palms grew, and up the path followed by Mark and the major before, but with the intention of turning off where the steam issued from the earth, as everyone seemed to select the jungle between that and the mountain-slope as being the spot from whence the roaring sounds were heard.

Backed by the knowledge already gained, there was not much difficulty in reaching the scene of the fright with the supposed serpent; and here they paused to try the ground, which sent out puffs of steam with a loud hiss directly it was pierced.

Billy Widgeon shook his head at it and looked at Small, who frowned, took off his cap, and scratched his head, as if he did not approve of the place as one for a walk.

Just then there was a capital opportunity for a shot at the great pigeons; but shooting was forbidden until their return, the object being to trace the strange creature if possible and see what it was like.

"It can't be a crocodile," said the major, "for there is no river up this way except this bit of a stream; great snake I can't believe it is; what is it, then?"

"The only way is to examine every bit of soft ground for traces of footprints," said the captain. "Nearly every beast has its times for going to drink; so we ought to get some inkling of what it is like at the various springs."

They were not long in coming to one in a hollow beneath a great pile of moss-grown rock down whose sides trickled the water to form at last a good-sized pool of the most limpid kind; but the mossy boggy earth around was untrodden, the water clear, and no trace to be seen of a single footprint other than their own.

The water was delicious on that hot day in the steamy jungle, and the band was refreshed—Mark having hard work to refrain from chasing some gorgeous butterfly of green and gold, or with wings painted in pearl-blue, steel, and burnished silver. At other times some lovely kingfisher, with elongated tail, settled almost within reach. Then it would be a green barbet, with bristle-armed beak and bright blue and scarlet feathers to make it gay. Or again, one of the cuckoo trogons, sitting on some twig, like a ball of feathers of bronze, golden green, and salmon rose.

But this was not a collecting trip. Earnest investigation was the order of the day; and after carefully taking their bearings the captain pressed on, with their way always on the ascent and growing wilder and more rocky.

This had its advantages as well as its disadvantages; for though the path was from time to time one continuous climb, they were not compelled to force their way through tangled growth, with trees bound together by canes and creepers, as if nature were roughly weaving a stockade.

Another stream was passed rising out of a boggy patch of ground, and here footprints were plentiful, but they were only those of birds that had been down to drink.

Onward again, and to ascend a steep precipitous slope right before them they had to descend into a dank, dark, gloomy-looking gorge, whose vegetation was scarce, and yet the place seemed to grow hotter as they went down.

A peculiar whistling sound came now from before them, and they stopped to listen, with the day evidently growing hotter, for down in the gorge there was not a breath of air; while as they listened the whistling grew louder and was accompanied by another in a different key, the two producing a curious dissonant sound for a few minutes, increasing rapidly, and then ceased, to be followed by absolute silence, and then a dull sound followed as if something had burst.

"Steam—a hot spring, I should say," exclaimed the captain, going cautiously forward, parting the low growth as he went.

His progress became slower, and at the end of a minute he stopped and stepped cautiously back.

"Not safe," he said; "my feet were sinking in. We must go farther round."

He led the way, and they forced their way through the sickly-looking bushes till they came all at once upon a glistening patch of whitish-looking mud some thirty or forty yards round, and above which the atmosphere seemed to be quivering, if it were not so much clear steam rising in the air.

Here they found the cause of the noise, for as they approached there was a tiny jet of steam issuing from one side near the dense growth of a peculiar grass, and when this had been whistling for about a minute, another jet burst out on the other side, whistling in the different key, while in the middle of the mud-pool there was a quivering and rifting of the surface, followed by the formation of a huge bubble, which kept on rising up larger and larger till it was a big globe of quite two feet high, when it suddenly burst with a peculiar sound, as if someone had said the word *Beff*! in a low whisper.

This occurred several times before they went on, having vainly searched the borders of the mud-pool for footmarks; and at the end of another few hundred yards loud hissing and shrieking noises led them to another pool, but, far from being so quiescent as that which they had left behind, this was all in commotion. The hot shining mud was bubbling furiously, rising in mud bladders, which were incessantly rising and dancing all over the surface, while one in the middle, larger than the rest, rose and burst with a loud puff.

Very little steam was visible, and though here too the edge of the pool was examined, there was not even the footprint of a bird.

Still ascending, and with traces of the volcanic action growing more frequent as they progressed, the mud springs were left behind, and an opening reached so beautiful, that all stopped to rest in the shade of a wild durian tree, whose fruit were about the size of small cricket balls, and chancing the fall of the woody spinous husk, all sat down to admire the beauty of the mountain rising before them, and to partake of some of the fallen fruit.

They would not have been touched if the major had not pounced upon them, and declared that they were a delicacy; but as soon as he opened one with his knife, and handed it to Mark, that gentleman's nose curled, in company with his lip, and he threw the fruit down.

"Pah! it's a bad one," he exclaimed.

"Bad! you young ignoramus!" cried the major, taking up the fallen fruit, and beginning to pick out its seeds and custardy interior with his knife. "You have no taste."

"But it smells so horrible!" cried Mark.

"Bah! Don't think about the smell. Taste it."

He opened another, and handed it to Mark, who, seeing that his father was eating one, proceeded cautiously to taste the evil-smelling object, and found in it so peculiarly grateful a flavour that he tried it again and again, and before he knew what he was about he had finished it.

"Try another, Mark," said the major. "I learned to eat these at Singapore, where they cultivate them, and they are twice as big, often three times."

Mark took another, and sniffed at it, to find when he had done that Billy Widgeon had been looking on with an air of the most profound contempt.

"Haven't you had one, Billy?" said Mark eagerly.

"Haven't I had one, Mr Mark, sir! No, I haven't; and how people of eddication can go and eat such things as them is more'n I can make out."

"You try one," said Mark. "They're lovely."

"Too lovely for me, Mr Mark, sir. I'm going to have a chew of tobacco!"

Mark was so highly pleased with his experiment that he turned to Small, who was seated staring straight before him and listening.

"Try one of these, Mr Small," he said.

Small took the fruit, smelt it, and then jerked it away.

"Don't you try to play larks on them as is older than yourself, young gentleman," he said so sourly that Mark walked away discomfited, and the boatswain went on listening till the sound he had heard increased in violence, and he found that everyone was on the *qui vive*.

"It comes from over the other side of that rocky patch of hill," said the major, pointing. "It's a waterfall, and we did not hear it before on account of the wind."

But if it was a waterfall, and that it sounded to be, it ceased flowing as rapidly and suddenly as it had begun, for once more all was still in that direction, and they sat resting and gazing with mingled feelings of awe and delight at the glorious landscape of black and brown rock and wondrous ferny growth rising before them from beyond a little valley at their feet right up to the summit of the mountain, about whose top the little cloud of smoke or vapour still hung.

It was a never-to-be-forgotten scene of beauty that no one cared to leave, but the captain soon gave the word, for he was desirous of finding some sign of the strange creature that had caused so much alarm.

They had climbed far above the spot whence the sounds seemed to come, but all felt that probably the beast would come down from the mountain and make that his home; and in this belief the party once more started, directing their course so as to go down and round the rocky eminence in face of where they stood, and then begin to climb the mountain where it steadily rose in one long slope to the summit.

The major was leading as they went down, and he had no sooner reached a spot whence he could see beyond the long mass of rock than he waved his hand for the party to come on.

Mark was the first to reach him, and as he did so it was to see a tall column of water as big as a man's body rush down a hole, which seemed to have been formed in the centre of a pale stony-looking basin.

"Look, my lad, look!" cried the major.

There was no occasion for him to speak, for Mark was already gazing with a feeling of shrinking awe at another of these stony basins, in which a quantity of clear hot water was boiling up and steaming. It rose from a hole in the middle, quite four feet in diameter, and simmered and bubbled and danced, and then suddenly disappeared down the hole with a hideous gurgling, rushing sound, followed by horrible rumblings and gurgitations in what seemed to be an enormous pipe of stone.

Once more it rushed to the surface, and then disappeared again, leaving the opening clear of water, so that the major went to the stony bottom of the basin, or saucer, to try whether it was slippery; and finding it firm, he walked on to where he could gaze down the well-like hole.

He did not stop many moments, but stepped back.

"Horrid!" he said. "Right down into blackness. Come and look."

Mark hesitated for a moment, and then took the hand his father extended, and they walked down the slope of the basin to where the opening gaped.

As they reached it there was a puff of hot vapour sent up, followed by hollow roaring sounds, mingled with the gurgling of water. Then there was such a furious hissing rush that they started back, and had just stepped clear of the basin when a fount of boiling water rushed up with terrific violence, maintaining the shape of the tube through which it had risen to the height of a hundred feet in the air, and keeping to that height for a minute or two, looking like a solid pillar of water. Then the force which had ejected it seemed to be spent, and the huge fountain descended slowly lower and lower, with several other elevations, and finally descended below the surface with a hideous rushing turmoil, and was gone.

They were about to advance and look down again, but there was a roar, and the water rushed to the surface just high enough to fill the basin, and for a portion to run gurgling over where the rim, which seemed to be formed of a curious deposit, was broken away, and trickle down toward the valley.

"I say, aren't it hot?" said Billy Widgeon, who had thrust in his hands before the water ran back. "Why, you might cook in it. I say, bo'sun, look ye here; why if it aren't just like the stuff as my old mother used to scrape out of the tea-kettle at home."

Small stooped and broke off a scrap of the deposit, and examined it, holding it out afterwards to Mark.

"Yes," said the major, who examined it in turn, after Mark had taken it to him, "the man is quite right. It is a limy deposit from the boiling water, similar to what is found in kettles and boilers. Shows that the water is very hard, eh, captain?"

"Yes, I suppose that's it," replied Captain Strong. "But all this is very interesting for travellers, and does not concern us. We've come to find out our noisy friend, so let's get on. Some day, when we've nothing to do, we may come here on a pleasure trip. To-day we must work."

"Stop a few minutes longer, father," said Mark, as the men went to another of the geysers a little lower down, one which had just thrown a column of water up some forty feet, and then subsided—a column not a third of the size of that which they had just seen.

"Very well," said the captain. "Want to see it spout again?"

"I should like to, once," said Mark; and then, moved by that energetic spirit which is always inciting boys to do something, he ran to the other side of the basin, where a good-sized piece of rock lay half incrusted with the stony deposit of the hot spring. It weighed about three-quarters of a hundredweight, but of so rounded a shape that it could be easily moved, and Mark rolled it over and over into the basin of the geyser while his father was pointing out something to the major across the little valley, and just as the stone was close to the rock-like opening the captain turned.

"I wouldn't do that, Mark," he said, as he realised his son's intention; but his warning came too late, for the final impetus had been given, and the stone disappeared in the hole.

Mark looked up apologetically as his father and the major came closer, and were listening to hear what would be the result, and expecting to note a tremendous hollow-sounding splash from far below.

What seemed to be a long time elapsed before there was any sign, and then with a roar up came the volley of water again so instantaneously that they had only just time to flee to the other side of the basin to avoid a drenching, possibly a scalding, while to the surprise of all there was a dull thud. The water descended with its furious hissing and gurgling, rose again to the top, and then, judging from the sounds, came up less and less distances in its vast stony pipe, and then all was silent once more, and they were gazing at the piece of rock Mark had thrown down, now lying in the basin about three feet from the well-like central hole.

"That's the way to make it spurt," said the major, laughing. "The hot water-works don't approve of stones, Master Mark."

The men were delighted with the hot springs, and after the fashion of sailors were pretty ready at giving them names according to their peculiarities. One was "The Grumbler;" another "The Bear-pit." A whistling hissing spring became "The Squealer." One that gurgled horribly, "The Bubbly Jock;" whilst others were, "The Lion's Den," from the roaring sound; "The Trumpet Major;" and the noisiest of all, from which a curious clattering metallic sound came up, "The Bull in the China-shop."

All at once the investigating party were aroused by a tremendous burst of laughter, which came from behind a clump of bushes where the men had gathered to watch the action of one of the smaller geysers.

The captain led the way toward the spot, for the noise was very boisterous, and as they approached it was to see the men rush away in the height of enjoyment, laughing again, for the spout of hot water, which seemed less steamy and hot, played up again and descended, while as it ran back with a low bellowing roar, the men followed quickly, evidently to watch its descent down the stony tube, just as so many boys might at play.

But there was no play here, for the comedy of running away to avoid a wetting with the hot water, and rushing back to look down, turned into tragedy. Short-legged Billy Widgeon, in his eagerness to be first, tried to take long strides like leaps, and bounded with a hop, skip, and a jump right into the wet basin, when the men set up a wild cry as, to the horror of all, they saw the little sailor's feet glide from under him, his hands thrown up wildly to clutch at something to save himself, and then he seemed to glide down the narrow well-like hole and was gone.

Chapter Thirty Five
How the Sulphur Cavern was found

For a few seconds every one stood still as if petrified by the horror of the scene. Then with a hoarse cry the captain dashed to the opening, slipped, and would also have gone down, had he not made a leap and thrown himself headlong across to the other side.

Mark stopped short, with a horrified expression on his face, for in those brief moments he suffered all the agony of having seen his father disappear, but almost before the captain had regained his legs the men uttered a warning shout, for there was the gurgling roaring below, a vibration in the earth, and the hot fountain played again to the height of twenty or thirty feet, descended almost as rapidly, and those on one side of the basin, as the water descended, saw the captain on the other side holding Billy Widgeon by the jacket, dragging him from the very edge of the hole to some half a dozen yards away.

The next minute all were gathered round where the little sailor lay apparently lifeless.

"Is he dead?" whispered Mark, catching at his father's arm.

"Not he," cried Small, stooping down and shaking the prostrate man. "Billy, old chap; here, wake up, I say! How goes it?"

Billy Widgeon opened his eyes, stared, choked, spat out some water, looked round, and shook his head to get rid of some more.

"Eh?" he said at last.

"How are you, my man?" said the captain.

Billy Widgeon stared at him, then looked all round, rubbed his eyes with his knuckles, stared again, rose, and trotted slowly to the basin, into which he stepped cautiously, and before he could be stopped peered down the hole.

He came away directly thereafter shaking his head.

"It's a rum un," he said, rubbing one ear, and slowly taking off and wringing his jacket to get rid of the water.

"You're not hurt, then?" said the captain, anxiously.

"Hurt, sir? No, I don't know as I'm hurt, sir, but I'm precious wet."

"How far did you go down?" cried Mark.

"How far did I go down?" said Billy, sulkily. "Miles!"

"Was it very hot, my man?" said the major.

"Hot! Well, if tumbling down a well like that there, and then being shot up again like a pellet out of a pop-gun aren't getting it hot, I should like to know what is?"

"I mean was the water very hot?" said the major, as the men, now that there was no danger, began to grin.

"'Bout as hot as I likes it, sir; just tidy," replied Billy.

"But what did it feel like?" said Mark; "I mean falling down there."

"Oh, there warn't no time to feel, Mr Mark, sir. I went down so quickly."

"Well, what did it seem like?" said Mark.

"Don't know, sir. I was in such a hurry," said Billy.

There was a laugh at this, in which Billy joined.

"You can't give us any description, then?" said the captain smiling.

"No, sir. I only found out one thing—I didn't seem to be wanted down there, being in the way, as you may say, and likely to stop the pipes. And now, Mr Small, sir, I'd take it kindly if you'd come in the wood there with me and lend a hand while I wring all the wet I can out o' my things, as'll make 'em dry more handy."

The boatswain nodded, and the pair went in among the trees, leaving the others discussing the narrow escapes and sending a stone or two down, and then a great dead dry stump of a tree-fern, all of which were shot up again, the stones after an interval, the fern stump, which was as long as Billy Widgeon and thicker round, coming up again directly.

"Why, major," said the captain at last, "if you had told me all this some day after dinner back in England, I'm afraid I shouldn't have believed you."

"I'm sure I should not have believed you," said the major laughing. "It sounds like a sea-serpent story, and I don't think I shall ever venture to tell it unless I can produce the man."

At that moment Billy came back out of the jungle, looking very ill-tempered, and his first act as the fount played again, was to go close to the edge of the basin and try the temperature of the water.

"Just tidy," he said, as they descended from the level shelf where the geysers were clustered, and along by the little gurgling rocky stream which carried off their overflowings before reaching the slope of the mountain, and beginning to climb with fresh and unexpected wonders on every hand.

It was nervous work, for as they climbed the earth trembled beneath their feet; low, muttering, thunderous sounds could be heard, while here and there from crevices puffs of sulphurous, throat-stinging vapour escaped.

Then a bubbling hot spring was reached, not a geyser like those on the shelf across the long valley, but a little gurgling fount of the most beautifully pure water, but so heated that it was impossible to thrust a hand therein.

"Are we going much higher, Mr Mark?" said Billy Widgeon at last. "Feels to me as if we should go through before we knowed where we was."

"Going to the top, I suppose," said Mark, smiling at the man's face, though he could not help feeling some slight trepidation as strange volcanic suggestions of what was beneath them in the mountain kept manifesting themselves at every step.

"Oh, all right!" said Billy in a tone of resignation; "but I do purtest, if I am to die, agin being biled."

The climb up the mountain side was continued for some time, fresh wonders being disclosed at every step. The jungle grew less thick, with the result that flowers were more plentiful, and if not more abundant the birds and gloriously-painted insects were easier to see. Hot springs were plentiful, and formed basins surrounded by the deposit from the water, a petrifaction of the most delicate tints, while the water was of the most exquisite blue.

A little higher, and in a narrow ravine among the rocks a perfect chasm, into which they descended till the sides almost shut out the light of day, so closely did they approach above their heads, Mark, who was in advance, made a find of a deposit of a delicate greenish yellow.

"Why, here's sulphur!" he exclaimed, picking up a beautifully crystallised lump, while the rock above was incrusted with angular pieces of extreme beauty.

"Yes, sulphur," said the captain; "and I don't think we'll go any farther here. It may be risky."

"I'll just see how soon this cleft ends," said the major, approaching what seemed to be the termination of the gorge—quite a jagged rift, cut or split in the side of the mountain.

The major went on cautiously, for, as he proceeded, it grew darker, the rift rapidly becoming a cavern.

"It runs right into the mountain!" he cried, and his voice echoed strangely. "Here, Mark, my lad, if you want to see some specimens of sulphur, there are some worth picking here."

There was something so weirdly attractive in the cavern that Mark followed, and in setting his feet down cautiously on the rocky floor his eyes soon became accustomed to the gloom, and he found that the rock joined about a dozen feet above their head, and was glittering as if composed of pale golden crystals of the most wonderful form.

Before him, at the distance of a dozen feet, he could dimly make out the figure of the major, while behind stood the group formed by their companions, looking like so many silhouettes in black against the pale light sent down the chasm from above.

"Mind what you're doing," said the captain. "Don't go in too far."

"All right!" cried the major; "there's good bottom. It's a lovely sulphur cave. Coming in?"

"No," said the captain, sitting down; "I'll wait for you. Make haste, and then we'll go back another way."

"Can you see the sides, Mark?" said the major.

"Yes, sir. Lovely!" replied the lad. "I should like to take a basketful. I'll break a piece or two off."

"Wait a bit," said the major; "there is a lovely piece here. What's that?"

Mark listened, as he stood close to the major, where the cavern went right in like a narrow triangle with curved sides.

A low hissing noise saluted their ears, apparently coming from a great distance off.

"Snakes!" whispered Mark.

"Steam!" said the major. "Why, Mark, this passage must lead right into the centre of the mountain. There, listen again! You can hear a dull rumbling sound."

"Yes, I can hear it," said Mark in an awe-stricken whisper.

"I dare say if we went on we should see some strange sights."

"Without lights?" said the captain, who had approached them silently.

"Perhaps we should get subterranean fire to show us the interior of the mountain. What do you say?—shall we explore a little further? One does not get a chance like this every day."

"I'm willing to come another time with lights, but it would be madness to go on in the dark. How do you know how soon you might step into some terrible chasm?"

"Without the slightest chance of being shot out again, like Billy Widgeon!" said the major. "You are quite right; it would be a terribly risky proceeding."

They listened, and this time there came a low boom and a roar as if there had been an explosion somewhere in the mountain, and the roar was the reverberation of the noise as it ran through endless passages and rocky ways echoing out to the light of day.

"No, it does not sound tempting," said the major. "I don't want to go far. But I must get a specimen or two of this sulphur for the ladies to see."

He walked on cautiously.

"Mind!" said the captain.

"Oh, yes, I'll take care," came back out of the darkness. "I can see my way yet, and the sulphur is wonderful. These will do."

A tapping noise followed from about fifty feet away; then the fall of a piece or two of stone, followed by a low hissing sound.

"Hear the steam escaping, Mark?" said the captain. "Ah, that's a good bit, as far as I can see. Come, major."

There was no answer.

"O'Halloran!" cried the captain, and his voice went echoing away into the distance, the name being partly repeated far in, as if whispered, mockingly by some strange denizen of the cavern.

"Major O'Halloran!" shouted Mark excitedly. "What's that?"

"What, my lad?" cried the captain.

"That curious choking sour smell. Ah!"

"Back, boy, for your life!" cried the captain, snatching at his son's arm and half dragging him towards where the cave was open to the sky. "Are you all right?"

"Yes, yes, father," panted Mark, who was coughing violently. "Is—is—Oh, father! the major."

The captain had taken a handkerchief from his pocket and loosely doubled it, and this he tied over his mouth and nostrils.

"Hold my gun, Mark," he whispered; and then hoarsely, as if to himself, "I can't leave him like that, come what may."

He paused for a moment to breathe hard and thoroughly inflate his lungs, and then, regardless of the risk of falling, he ran rapidly in, while Mark stood horror-stricken listening to his retiring footsteps.

His next act saved the lives of the two men.

"Small!—Widgeon!" he cried. "Here, quick!"

The two men ran to his side, ready to help.

"My father has gone in to help the major. As soon—as he comes—near enough—go and help."

The men stood listening; and then, as they heard the coming steps, made a dart in, but returned.

"You can't breathe. It chokes you," cried Billy Widgeon.

"Take a long mouthful, my lad, and hold your breath," growled the boatswain. "Ha, he's down! Come on!"

Chapter Thirty Six
How Mark and Billy Widgeon went wrong

Mark did as the others did; inflated his lungs and rushed into the darkness, till they nearly fell over the captain; and then how it was done the lad hardly knew, but the two insensible men were dragged out to where there was pure air to breathe, and the rescuers sank down beside them, panting and exhausted. "Too late!" groaned Mark.

"Not we, my lad," growled Small. "I know. It's bad gas."

"It's the sulphur," cried Mark piteously.

"Well, aren't that bad gas? I know. They're just the same as if they was drowned, and we've got to pump their chesties full of wind till they begins to breathe as they ought to."

Small's ideas were doubtless quite correct, and fortunately but little effort was needed to bring the sufferers to their senses, for the fresh air soon recovered them, and they sat up looking wild and confused.

With the help of an arm to each they were soon able to walk back to the open mountain side, and after a rest declared themselves ready to proceed.

"I think we'll go back away north of the hot springs," the captain said.

"Certainly," exclaimed the major with quite a sound of contrition in his voice.

"The jungle is dense, but I think with a little managing we can find our way."

"Well, yes, perhaps so," said the major. "It's down hill, and half our way will be fairly open."

"If it proves too dense we can but turn to the right and go back as we came," said the captain. "There, Mark, you need not look so anxious. There is nothing worse the matter than a bad headache. How are you, major?"

"Horrible!" he said. "I have a bad headache, and a bad mental pain, for being so absurdly obstinate and running all that risk for the sake of a few crystals of sulphur."

"Which, after all, you had to leave behind."

"Not all," said the major; "I had put a couple of lumps in my pocket when that overpowering vapour struck me down. My impression is—yes, of course, I remember clearly now—that where I broke the crystals away I must have opened a hole for the escape of the vapour."

"I heard the hissing noise," said Mark eagerly.

"Strong," said the major, "I know you will forgive me; but, believe me, it will be a long time before I forgive myself. I can't say much to you about thanks," he whispered in a hoarse voice; "but I shall never forget this."

"Nonsense, man, nonsense!" cried the captain warmly. "You would have done the same for me."

No more was said, for there was plenty to do to keep together, and the various sights and sounds as they bore away to the east of the hot springs set the whole party well upon the *qui vive*.

For on every side there were traces of volcanic action. Now they had to climb over or round some mass of lava that looked comparatively new as seen beside fragments that were moss-grown and fringed with orchids and ferns. In one place on the steep descent all would be one tangled growth of creepers, while a little farther on the ground would be sharply inclined and as bare and burned as if fire had lately issued from the earth. Every now and then they came, too, upon soft patches of mud firm enough to walk over and like india-rubber beneath their feet; but it was nervous work, and they crossed with care, feeling, as they did, a curious vibration going on beneath their feet.

Then came an exceedingly rugged descent of quite a precipitous nature, but lovely in the extreme, so clothed was it with tropic verdure, though this was more beautiful to the eye than to the feet, for it often concealed treacherous crevices between blocks of scoria, and ugly cracks and rifts, some of which were dangerous, while others were awful from their depth and the low, hissing, murmuring sounds which came from their inmost recesses.

At last the descent became so precipitous that they were brought to a stand-still and all progress seemed to be at an end, till, searching about, Mark and Billy Widgeon came upon a broad gash in the mountain side at the bottom of which there seemed to be a long slope of the smooth, hard-surfaced mud apparently running downward toward the spot they sought.

The captain declared the descent practicable with care, and Mark took the lead, going down with plenty of agility, and closely followed by the little sailor.

At the end of a quarter of an hour they were all on the stony brink of what seemed to be a mud-stream which at some time had flowed down from out of a huge yawning chasm high up above their heads, and perfectly inaccessible from where they stood. According to all appearances, this mud in a thin state must have come down in a perfect cataract till it filled up the space beneath the chasm, which resembled a huge basin, as level as so much water, and when this had become full the stream had begun to form, and down this mud-stream they proposed to go, though how far it extended and would help them on their way experience alone could show.

They stood just at the edge of the pool to find that a walk upon its surface would be dangerous in the extreme, for though the top was elastic a stick was easily driven through, with the result that a jet of steam rushed out with a noise like that of a railway whistle, but the surface of the stream on being tested proved firmer, and they began to descend.

Again the same sense of insecurity was felt, the india-rubber-like film giving way easily and springing up again, while the old muttering and murmuring noises thrilled beneath their feet.

But so long as it would hold it proved to be a capital road, for while there was a wall of dense verdure on either side, not so much as a scrap of moss had taken root on the surface of the smooth slope, which wound in and out with the ravine, acting in fact as a stream of water does which runs down some mountain scar, save that here there was no progress. The mud had once been hot and fluid, and doubtless was still so, to some extent, below; but, after filling up every inequality, it kept to one regular level, forming what Mark at once dubbed Gutta-percha Lane.

It was now long past mid-day, and as they walked steadily on, growing more confident as the toughness of the bituminous mud, for such it proved to be, proved itself worthy of the trust it was called upon to bear, the question arose where the stream would end.

As far as the captain could make out, in spite of its zigzagging and abrupt curves, the course of the stream was decidedly towards the camp, but as they descended lower one thing was very plain, and that was that they were getting into thicker jungle, which grew taller and darker with every hundred feet of descent.

"How do you account for it?" Captain Strong said at last to the major, as they now found themselves walking down a winding road some fifteen to twenty feet wide, and with dense walls of verdure rising fully two hundred feet in height.

"I think there must have been a stream here, and at some time there has been an eruption and the mud has flowed down it and filled it up."

"If there had been a stream," the captain said, "we should have seen some sign of its outlet near the camp."

"Then you have a theory of your own?"

"Yes," said the captain; "it seems to me that first of all this was merely a jagged ravine, running from the mountain's shoulder right down to the sea."

"That's what I thought. With a stream at the bottom."

"No stream," said the captain. "Nothing but vegetation. Down this a stream of red-hot lava must have flowed and burned the vegetation clean away, leaving a place for the mud to come down and harden as you have it now. It may have been a year after the eruption—twenty, fifty, or a hundred years, but there it is."

"If you are right, we should see traces of the burning on the trees," said the major.

"That does not follow. These trees may have sprung up since, right to the very edge of the stream, but no farther."

"Then under this mud or bitumen there ought to be lava according to your ideas. How shall we prove it?"

"If I am right," said the captain, "we shall find that this stream ends all at once, just as the lava hardened when the flow ceased, for there was no stream of volcanic matter right down to the shore."

"And there is no stream of mud any further," said Mark laughing; "for there's the end."

Mark was quite right, for about a couple of hundred yards below them the mighty walls of verdure suddenly came together and blocked out further progress, while, when they reached the spot, it was to find that the bituminous mud spread out here into a pool, further progress being, as it were, stopped by a dam of blackish rock which resembled so much solidified sponge, so full was it of air-holes and bubble-like cells.

"I am no geologist," said the major, "so I give in to you, Strong. You must be right."

"I think I am," said the captain, quietly examining the rocky dam and the surface of the mud. "Yes, I should say that here is the explanation of this curious stream."

"Then all I can say is," said the major wiping his forehead, "that I wish the eruption had been a little bigger, and the lava stream had ended on the sands exactly one hundred yards from camp."

"And the mud had flowed over it and made our road?" said Mark laughing.

"That goes without saying," cried the major. "Now, then, I propose a halt and food."

There was plenty of shade close at hand, but unfortunately no water. Still, a good rest and a hearty meal proved most grateful, and as soon as it was done the major lit a cigar, the captain, Small, and two of the men seemed to be dozing, and Mark and Billy Widgeon looked at them and then at each other.

"Going to do a bit o' hammock work, Mr Mark, sir?" said Billy.

"I'm not sleepy."

"More am I, sir. Let's see if we can't get some fruit."

"All right!" cried Mark, jumping up.

"Don't go far, my boy," said the captain; and Mark started, for he had thought his father was asleep, while on looking at him he still lay back in the same position with his eyes closed.

"No, father, I won't go far," he said.

"Keep within range of a shout—well within range, for it's very easy to get lost in one of these jungles, and we shall be too tired to hunt for you now."

"I won't go far," said Mark; and he and Billy Widgeon began to walk slowly back along the stream, looking to left and right for a way between the trees into the jungle.

"You thought the skipper was asleep?" said Billy in a whisper. "Never ketches him asleep, as we all knows. It's always t'other. So soon as one o' us as ought to be awake goes off, he finds us out, and no mistake."

Mark did not answer, and Billy went on:

"It's my belief that when the skipper shuts his eyes he sets his ears to work to see and hear too. Ah, here we are! Here's a place where we can go in. I say, Mr Mark, did you eat any o' that cold treacle pooden?"

"No? Bill, I did not."

"Good job, too, sir. It was cooked in one o' they hot springs, and I'm blest if it didn't taste like brimstone and treacle. Lor', how thirsty I am! Wish I could find one o' them wooden-box fruit."

"What? cocoa-nuts?"

"No, sir: durings. They are good after all. Give's your hand, my lad." He bent down from a mass of basalt, which seemed to be the end of a rugged wall which penetrated the trees, and along which it was possible to climb more easily than to force a way through the dense growth which wove the trees together.

"I can manage, Billy," said Mark. "Go on."

Billy turned, and, apparently as active as if he had just started, he climbed on, parting the bushes that grew out of the interstices and holding them aside for Mark to clear them, and then on and on, without the sign of a fruit-tree or berry-bearing bush. The sun beat down through the overshadowing boughs, but the two had risen so high that the forest monarchs had become as it were dwarfed, and it was evident that they would soon be above them and able to look down on their tops.

"Why, Billy," exclaimed Mark, "if we go on, we shall soon be able to see the sea, and the best way down to the camp."

"Sure we shall, Mr Mark, sir," said the little sailor, descending a sudden slope and helping Mark to follow, after which they wound in and out for about a quarter of an hour, thoroughly eager in their quest for a way to simplify the descent of the rest of the party.

All at once the captain's final words came to memory, and Mark exclaimed:

"Here; we mustn't go any farther, Billy. We'll turn back now."

"All right! Mr Mark, sir, we'll soon do that; and then we can all come on this way together. We can show 'em now, eh?"

"Yes," said Mark; "but let's see, which way did we come? Along there, wasn't it?"

"'Long there, Mr Mark, sir? No, not it. Why, we come this way, down by these rocks."

"No, that couldn't be right, Billy, because the sun was on our left when we turned round, and you helped me down that rock."

"Was it, sir? Then it must be down here."

Billy led the way and Mark followed; but at the end of a few minutes he called a halt.

"No, no; this can't be right," he cried, as he gazed about a wilderness of huge rocks and trees, where bushes sprang up on every hand.

"Well, do you know, Mr Mark, sir, that's just what I was a-thinking," said Billy. "I've been a-puzzling my head over that there block o' stone as is standing atop o' that tother one, and couldn't recollect seeing of 'em afore."

"No; it must be this way," said Mark uneasily. "How stupid, to be sure! We must find our way back."

"Why, of course, Mr Mark, sir; and we will; but it aren't us as is stupid, it's these here rocks and trees as is all alike, just as if they was brothers and sisters, or peas in a pod."

"Don't talk so," said Mark angrily, as he realised more fully their position; and a sense of confusion made him petulant. "Let's act and find our way. Now, then, which way does the mud-stream lie?"

Billy scratched his head, stared about, and then said softly:

"Well, sir, I'll be blest if I know."

And Mark thoroughly realised the fact that they were lost.

Chapter Thirty Seven
How Mark sought the Clue

Were you ever lost? Most probably not; and hence you will hardly be able to realise the strange sensation of loneliness, helplessness, and despair which comes over the spirit as the traveller finds that he missed his way and is probably beyond the reach of help in some wilderness, where he knows that he may go on tramping wearily until he lies down and dies.

Mark Strong's case was not so bad, but he felt it painfully for many reasons. Among others there was the knowledge that he had utterly forgotten the injunction given to him to take care and not go too far; while another was the dread that though they had been nominally searching all day for the strange beast that had caused so much alarm, and seen nothing, now that he and his companion were helpless they might possibly stumble upon its cave.

"Oh, Billy, what have we been doing?" he cried impatiently.

"Well, Mr Mark, sir, I don't know as we've been doing o' hanything pertickler."

"But we've lost our way."

"Well, yes, sir, I s'pose we've lost that there; but it don't much matter—do it?"

"Matter!—of course!" cried Mark angrily; and, as if born by nature to lead, he at once took the command and gave his orders. "Now, you climb to the top of that rock and see if you can make out the course we ought to take; and I'll climb that one yonder."

"All right, Mr Mark, sir!" cried the little sailor, starting off.

"And mind, we come back to this spot directly."

"Right, sir! we will."

"Then, off!"

Mark slowly and painfully scaled the side of a steep sloped ravine, and when he reached the top, with the perspiration running down his cheeks, he looked round, to see trees, rocks, and the beautiful cone of the volcano.

That was something; and he reasoned that if he turned his back to the mountain and walked straight down and onward, though he would not be able to join his party he would reach the shore.

But no sooner had he arrived at this comforting assurance that he would have nothing to fear from starvation than all his hopes were dashed to the ground, as he realised the fact that, as soon as he descended from the giddy height at which he stood, he would lose sight of the mountain and have no guide; while to go straight on among the mighty moss-covered rocks, which were pitched helter-skelter all over the place, was as impossible as to go through the jungle without a gang of men with bill-hooks to hack a way among the dense undergrowth.

Right, left, and before him he could see nothing that would suggest his having passed along there; and with his heart sinking he slowly climbed down part of the way, then reached a mossy stone which gave way beneath his feet and fell, while he followed, slipping down twenty feet, rolling another twenty; dropping sometimes into a thorny tangle of brambles, and dragging himself out, tattered, bleeding, and terribly out of temper, to walk slowly back to the spot from whence he and Billy Widgeon had started.

"How thirsty I am!" he said to himself; and then he listened.

All was horribly silent, and he called in a startled way, to be answered by a faint "Ahoy!"

"This way, Billy!"

There was again silence as Mark threw himself wearily on a mass of ferns; but after a time the rustling of boughs and breaking of twigs could be heard, and at last from apparently a long way off came Billy's voice again:

"Mr Mark, ahoy!"

"Ahoy! This way!"

Another pause, with the rustling of leaves and twigs continued, and Billy's voice again:

"Ahoy, my lad! Where are you?"

"Here!"

There was a low muttering as if Billy were talking to himself, and then another shout.

"Here!" cried Mark again wearily.

"Oh, there you are—are you?" cried the little sailor, struggling at last to his side. "I thought I was never going to get back. More you tries to find your way, more you loses it. I never see such a mess in my life! Why don't they keep a gardener?"

Wretched as he was, hot, weary, and smarting and stinging from scratches and pricks, Mark could not help laughing at the little sailor's irritable manner.

"Ah, you may laugh, my lad, a-lying all so comfortable there! but if you'd had such a slip as I did off a rock, and came down sitting on a thorn as big as a marlin'-spike, you wouldn't show your white teeth like that!"

"But I did, Billy," cried Mark, going off into a wild roar of laughter; "and I'm horribly pricked and torn. But never mind that. Did you find the way back to them?"

"Find your way back to 'em?—no. I never see such a muddle as the place is in. Every bit's like every other bit; and when you mark down one tree, meaning to come back to it, and do come back to it, why it's another tree just like the one you thought it was. I say, Mr Mark, sir, this place aren't 'chanted—is it?"

"Enchanted!—no. Why?"

"I d'know, only it's very queer like and puzzling. I can't make it out a bit."

"Why, how do you mean?"

"Mean as you can't seem to box the compass like, and don't know which way to steer, sir. I feels as if I should give it up."

"Give it up! What nonsense! Let's rest a few minutes and start again."

"Oh, I don't mind resting, sir; but I don't want to have to sleep out here. Why, we've got nothing to eat, and no lights, and—no, I sha'n't sit down, Mr Mark, sir. I don't want to disobey orders, but seems to me as we'd better get back to what you called Gutta-percha Road."

"Now, look here, Billy, how can you be so stupid?" cried Mark pettishly. "You know I want to get back; but which way are we to go?"

"Tell you what, sir, let's cooey," cried Billy, giving his leg a slap. "That's the proper thing to do when you're out in the woods."

"Well, cooey, then," said Mark. "Go on."

"No, sir; you'd better do it," said Billy modestly. "I aren't practysed it much."

"Never mind; go on."

"I'd a deal rather you would, Mr Mark, sir."

"But I can't. I never did such a thing in my life."

"Well, if it comes to that, sir, more didn't I."

"And you said you hadn't practised much."

"Well, sir, I haven't," said Billy coolly.

"Billy, you're a sham," said Mark angrily.

"All right, sir! I don't mind."

"You get one into a muddle like this, and then are no use at all."

"No, sir. That's about it," said Billy coolly, and all the time as serious as a judge. "I wish we'd got Jack here!"

"What's the good of him?—to send up the trees after cocoa-nuts?"

"Now, now, now, Mr Mark, sir, don't be hard on a fellow! I did think as he'd send some down; and I believe now as he wouldn't because I give him a cuff o' the head that morning for sucking the end o' my hankychy."

"Here, come along, and let's keep together."

"All right, sir!"

"Let's get up to the top of that rock first. I think that's where we came down."

"Nay, nay, Mr Mark, sir. I'm sure as that wasn't the way. It was up that one."

"I'm certain it was not, Billy. It was this. Come along."

"All right, Mr Mark, sir! If you says that's right, it's quite enough for me. I'll go anywheres you likes to lead; and I can't say fairer than that—can I?"

"No, Billy," said Mark; "so come along."

He led the way, and they climbed by the help of the bushes and aerial roots of the trees right to the top of the rugged bank of rock he had marked down in his mind's eye as being the way; and as soon as they were there they stopped and listened.

"Perhaps they're looking for us," he said.

"Shouldn't wonder, Mr Mark, sir."

But though they listened there was no shout, no distant sound to suggest that a search was being made.

"You talk about Jack," said Mark; "I wish we had got poor old Bruff here! He would find the way home."

"But you see, Mr Mark, sir, it aren't no use to wish. Lawk a me! sir, the number o' things I've wished for in my life—'bacco, knives, a silver watch, silk hankychies, lots o' things, but I never got 'em."

"Never mind them now. Let's shout."

"With a will, then, sir, and put your back into it. One, two, three, and ahoy!"

The peculiar duet rang out over the trees—a loud and piercing cry—and as it died away, Billy caught at Mark's arm, and gripped it tightly; his eyes staring wildly, with the pupils dilating, as from some little distance off on one side there came a mocking "Ha—ha—ha!" and from the other direction a peculiar hoarse barking croak, which can best be expressed by the word "Wauck!"

"Let's get away from here, Mr Mark, sir," whispered Billy. "I don't like this."

"Get away?"

"Yes, sir; they're a-making fun of us."

"Who are?"

"Oh, I don't know who they are, sir, but it's something. Let's get away, sir, fast as we can."

"Which way?"

"I d'know, sir, anyways as aren't near them."

"Why, it was a couple of birds of some kind."

"What! them snorky bill birds?" said Billy, alluding to the hornbills.

"Yes, I expect it was one of them, or a kingfisher."

"Birds!" said Billy in tones of disgust. "I never heerd no bird laugh at you when you was in trouble. I'm thinking as there's things in this here place as it wouldn't be nice to meet."

"I daresay there are, Billy; but these were birds."

"Birds! Hark at him! Would a bird shout to you to walk?"

"It didn't. It was a sort of croak."

"If we stops here I shall feel as if I'm going to croak, Mr Mark, sir. Why, them things made me feel cold all down my back."

"Nonsense! Come, shout again!"

Billy shook his head.

"Shout, I tell you. We don't want to stop here all night."

"No, Mr Mark, sir; don't, please don't. It's like showing 'em exactly where we are."

"Well, that's what we want to do."

"No, sir, I don't mean them. I mean *them*."

"What! the birds?"

"Them warn't birds, Mr Mark, sir," said Billy in a solemn whisper. "Don't you believe it."

"What were they, then?"

"Things as lives in woods, and never shows theirselves till people lies down and dies, and then they eats 'em."

"What do you mean? Vultures?"

"No, no; not them. I know what a wultur is. These is different things to them. Let's get away, sir, do."

"What do you mean, then?" persisted Mark. "Do you think there are goblins in the wood?"

"Something o' that sort, sir, but don't speak out loud. They might hear, and not like it."

"But goblins out here wouldn't understand English," said Mark laughing; but all the same it was rather a forced laugh, for the little sailor's evident dread was infectious.

"I wouldn't laugh if I was you, Mr Mark, sir. Come along."

"Shout," cried Mark, ashamed of the shadow of cowardice which had begun to envelop him, and he gave forth a loud "Ahoy!"

Ha—ha—ha!

Wauck!

The same two responses, but decidedly closer; and as Billy gripped the lad's arm again they heard from out of the darkest part of the jungle close by a peculiar chuckling, as if some one were thoroughly enjoying their predicament.

"Did yer hear that?" whispered Billy, whose sun-tanned visage was now quite pallid and mottled with muddy grey.

"Yes, I heard it, of course," said Mark, fighting hard with his growing alarm, "Ahoy!"

Ha—ha—ha!

Wauck!

And then the same peculiar low chuckle.

"Mr Mark, sir, this is hard on a man," whispered Billy. "I want to run away, sir, but—"

"Ugh! You coward!"

"No, sir, I aren't a coward. If I was I should run, but I can't run and leave you alone, and that's why it's so hard."

"I tell you it's the birds, Billy. Let's shout together."

"That aren't no birds, sir. It's things as it's best not to talk about. Now, look ye here, Mr Mark, sir: I'll run away with you, and fight for you, or do anything you like, sir, or I stands by you till I drops, so don't say I'm a coward."

"You are, to be afraid of birds. Ahoy!"

Ha—ha—ha!

Wauck!

Chuckle—chuckle—chuckle! A regular gurgle in a hoarse throat.

"I won't stand it. You come on," cried Billy, seizing Mark by the hand. "This way."

Mark did not resist, and the little sailor hurried him along as fast as the nature of the ground would allow; and with the full intention of going right towards where they had left the others, at the end of the bitumen river, he went right in the opposite direction, and farther and farther into the wildest recesses of the jungle.

Chapter Thirty Eight
How Mark and Billy found a strange Bed

For a good half-hour they toiled on through cane-woven thickets, in and out of wildernesses of huge tree-trunks, many of which had great flat buttresses all round, which were difficult to climb over or round, while other trees seemed to be growing with their roots all above ground, green, snaky, twisted and involved roots, that necessitated sheer climbing before they could get by. Now and then they came to an opening where the trees had been burned down by volcanic fires, and here all was light and beauty in the evening sunshine. Again rocky crevices ran through the forest, giving them terribly hard work to get over, perhaps to come at once upon some boiling spring, whose water, where it trickled away and cooled, was of a filthy bitter taste that was most objectionable. Then again there were blistering pools of mud ever rising in a high ebullition, and bursting with strange sounds.

But all these were similar to those they had before encountered, and the hiss of steam, when they stepped upon some soft spot, ceased to alarm them with dread of serpents, but merely made them avoid such spots in favour of firmer ground.

Such signs of the volcanic nature of the isle were constant, and no matter which way they dragged their weary steps it was to find tokens of the active or quiescent workings of the subterranean fires.

At last, just as they were ready to drop, and the sun was rapidly disappearing, as the ruddy sky in the west plainly showed, they staggered out of a more than usually painful part of the jungle into a rugged stony opening, with the rock rising nearly sheer for hundreds of feet, and to the intense delight of both, the ruddy light of the sky was reflected from a rock pool, which glowed as if it were brimming with molten orange gold.

"Water!" gasped Billy. "Come on."

"Be careful!" panted Mark; "it may be bitter or hot."

As he spoke the little sailor threw himself down, and plunged his fist within, scooped out a little, tasted it, and then uttered a shout of joy.

"Drink, my lad," he said hoarsely, and Mark followed his example, placing his lips to the surface as he lay flat down and took in long refreshing draughts of cool sweet water that seemed the most delicious thing he had ever tasted.

"Talk about grog!" cried Billy, as he raised his face to take breath, and then he drank again; "I never had grog as come up to this," he continued. "Ah!"

Satisfied at length, they sat there at the edge of the pool looking up at the rocky scarp before them, part of which glowed in the sunlight reflected from the sky, while the rest down by where they sat was bathed in purply shadows which were rising fast.

"Seems to me, my lad, as we must look out for a night's lodging. What says you?"

"Yes, Billy, we must get some shelter for the night. But let's try one more shout."

The little sailor protested, but Mark raised his voice as loudly as he could in a stentorian "Ahoy!" and as if the occupants of the forest had kept close upon their heels there came the same sneering laugh, and the hoarse croaking cry from among the trees.

"There! see what you've done!" groaned Billy. "Who's to go to sleep anywhere near here if they're arter us?"

"Nonsense!" cried Mark. "They'll go to roost directly, and we sha'n't hear them again."

"Roost! Nay, lad, that sort o' thing never roosts. Let's get on."

"Get on! why, it will be dark directly, and we shall be falling down some precipice, or getting into one of those horrible bogs. We must get some shelter where we can."

There seemed to be no difficulty about that, for a few feet up the face of the rock, and where it could easily be reached, there was a depression which looked as if two huge blocks of stone had fallen together, one leaning against the other, and as, after a great deal of persuasion, Billy Widgeon climbed up to it with his companion, they found this really to be the case, save that instead of its being two blocks of stone it was two beds of strata lying together, in such a position that they formed a cavern some ten-feet high and as many wide, and with a peculiarly ribbed and cracked floor.

It was rapidly growing too dark to see of what this floor was composed, the gloom being quite deep as soon as they were inside. Neither could they explore the interior, though it seemed to form a passage going in for some distance; but a careful searching of the floor and the neighbourhood of the entrance failed to show them the slightest trace of animal occupation.

"But it's very risky work, Mr Mark, sir, coming and settling down in a rat's hole of a place like this."

"My dear Billy, if you can show me a better place, one where we shall be in shelter from the rain and the heavy dew, I shall be glad to go to it. I don't like sleeping on stone floors."

"Well, for the matter o' that, I daresay I can get enough o' them big leaves, nice dry uns, to make you a bed, Mr Mark, sir, and I will. But hadn't we better try somewheres else?"

"There will not be time, man," cried Mark angrily.

"All right, Mr Mark, sir! but don't you blame me if anything happens."

"No. Come along, and let's be thankful for finding such a shelter. We may as well get as many leaves as we can."

They found time to collect three loads of large dry palm leaves, and as they carried the last armful into the rocky hole, the night was quite closed in, and the crescent moon shone over the trees and silvered their tops faintly, while a soft wind whispered among them and reached the nostrils of the occupants of the cave, bearing with it the peculiar salt strange odour of the sea.

"Say," said Billy, as they sat upon their heaps of palm leaves gazing out of the mouth of their resting-place, "think of our being 'bliged to stop in a hole like this when you can smell the sea."

"Not a bad place," said Mark; "and I wouldn't mind if I could feel sure that my father and mother were not in trouble about me."

"My father and mother wouldn't trouble about me," said Billy, "even if they know'd. But do you really think it was birds as made those noises, Mr Mark, sir?"

"I feel sure it was."

"I wish we was birds just now. How we could fly right over the wood and get back to the camp! Wonder what's for supper?"

"Birds," said Mark, stretching himself in a comfortable position upon the palm leaves, and gazing at the great stars in the purple sky.

"Ah, yes," said Billy, "birds! and they'll be roasting at the fire now, and spittering and sputtering, and smelling as nice as roast birds can smell. I wish we was in camp."

He sighed and stretched himself on the leaves, grunting a little as he felt the hard rock through.

"Aren't you very hungry, Mr Mark, sir?"

"No; I feel too fidgety about my father looking for us to want any food."

"Ah, it's a bad thing to—Yah!—hah—hah—hah!"

Billy finished his sentence with a tremendous yawn, and then rustled the leaves as he tucked some more of them beneath him.

"Roast birds," he muttered; "and then there'll be some o' them big oyster things all cooked up in their shells!"

Mark did not answer, for though in his mind's eye he saw the camp fire, he did not see the cooking, but the cooks, and thought of how anxious his mother would be.

"I should have said they was mussels," said Billy, in a low voice.

"What, Billy?"

"Them shell-fish, sir, more like oysterses than—I mean more like muss—muzzles—oysters—muzzles—muzzles!"

Mark raised himself upon his arm and looked at his companion, who was dimly-seen in the starlight.

"Why, Billy, what's the matter?" he said. "Sleeping uneasy?"

"Easy it is, sir. Eh? Sleep. No, Mr Mark, sir. What say?—sleep, sir. No; wide-awake as you are, sir."

"That's right," said Mark, gazing out once more at the softly glowing stars. The crescent moon had gone down in a bed of clouds, and all around the darkness seemed to grow deeper and softer, till it was as if it could be touched, and everything was wonderfully still, save when there came from the distance a sharp whistling that might have been from a bird, but was more probably escaping steam.

Now and then Mark could see strange lights glowing, and then feel a tremulous motion such as would be felt at home when a vehicle was passing the house, and as if this might be thunder, it was generally after he had noticed a flashing light playing over the trees, sometimes bright enough to reveal their shapes, but as a rule so faint as to be hardly seen.

He thought about his father going back wearied out with a long search. Then he wondered whether he had gone back, and at last the idea struck him as strange that the party had not fired a gun at intervals to attract their attention.

He had just arrived at this point, and was considering whether a light he saw was a luminous fungus, when a strange noise saluted his ear, a sound that for the moment he supposed to have come from the forest. Then it seemed to be in the cave, and he was about to spring up, when he realised that the noise was made by Billy Widgeon, who was too tired to let his nervous and superstitious dread trouble him any more, and was now sleeping as heavily as if he were in his bunk on board the *Petrel*.

Mark felt a curious sensation of irritation against a man who could go off to sleep so calmly at a time like this, but the man's words came to mind about his father and mother, and at last Mark was fain to say to himself, "If the poor fellow can sleep why shouldn't he?"

For his own part he had quite come to the determination that he would get what rest he could as he lay awake watching, for he knew that, anxious as he was, it would be impossible to sleep. Besides, he wanted to listen for the possibility of a signal being made. A gun fired would, he knew, be heard an enormous distance, and it would give him an idea of the direction in which the camp lay.

All this while Billy Widgeon lay snoring loudly, but by degrees, as Mark watched the stars that seemed to float over the jungle, the heavy breathing became less heavy, and by slow degrees softer and softer till it quite died away, and all was perfectly still to Mark Strong as he lay watching there.

But it was only in imagination that he watched, for nature had played a trick upon the lad, and in spite of his determination to keep awake, in spite of his anxiety, had poured her drowsy medicine upon his eyes.

For Mark had fallen into as deep a sleep as his companion.

Chapter Thirty Nine
How the roaring Spot was found

Ha, ha, ha! Ha, ha, ha!

Wauck! Wauck! Wauck!

There was a loud rustling of palm leaves, and Mark Strong and Billy Widgeon sprang to their feet and stared at one another as the warm glow that precedes sunrise penetrated the cave and lit up their faces.

"What was that?"

"I don't know. Did somebody call?"

"I—I thought I heered them things again," said Billy in a whisper. "Why, Mr Mark, sir, you've been asleep!"

"I'm afraid I have. Have you?"

"Dunno, sir. Well, I suppose I have. I feel like it. But I didn't mean to, sir."

"Neither did I mean to," said Mark. "I wonder I did go. How chilly it is!"

"Yes, sir, like one feels in the early watches. Why, it's quite to-morrow morning!"

"Or this morning, Billy."

"Yes, sir, that's what I mean. Now, then, what's the first thing, Mr Mark, sir? What do you say to finding a coky-nut tree? I'll swarm up and get the nuts."

"Let's start at once, and try to get to camp. That will be better than cocoa-nuts. Now, then, the sun is rising on our right; then it seems to me if we keep it there, upon our right, and walk as straight as we can, we shall hit the shore somewhere near our camp."

"Then you won't look for the Gutty Perchy Road, sir?"

"No, no; they would not have stayed there. We will try and get through the jungle—we must get through it, Billy, so come along."

"Shall I go first, sir?" said the little sailor.

"No, I'll go first. I wish we had lights to look a little further into this hole. Why, Billy, the floor's lava!"

"Yes, sir, I thought it was."

"You thought it was what?" cried Mark, staring.

"What you said, sir."

"Never mind, come along," said Mark; and he went to the edge of the cave and stood looking out like a pigeon in one of the holes of a dove-cot preparing to take flight.

"See anything, sir?"

"Trees, rocks, sky; nothing more," said Mark; "but the sea must be straight before us, and it cannot be many miles away."

He turned and began to climb down backwards, and reached the level at the bottom of the steep scarp, when, looking up, he could not help smiling at the great care Billy displayed in descending, for he lowered his short legs over the edge as he held on and began feeling about in a most absurdly comical manner for the nearest projection which he could touch.

He was in this position, about fifteen feet above the spot where Mark waited, when, with a noise that was almost deafening, the frightful roar which had startled the whole party burst out from just inside the cave where they had slept.

The sound was so awful in its intensity that Mark shuddered as he stood there almost petrified, while at the first burst poor Billy Widgeon loosed his hold and dropped down shrunken up together as if he were trying to emulate the manner of a hedgehog, and as he fell, he just touched the ground, sprang up, and began to run.

"Mr Mark, sir, run—run, my lad, run!"

To his credit, be it said, that he stopped short and waited for Mark to come up, terrified as he was, and then sent him on first, while he covered him from behind.

Neither spoke for some time, but, regardless of direction, ran where they could, but oftener walked, or even crept, through the dense forest, always with the sensation that the huge beast that had uttered that frightful roar was crashing through the trees on their track.

By degrees though they recovered their confidence somewhat, gradually realising that there was no sound behind them, and at last they paused panting and exhausted to wipe the perspiration from their brows, and listen.

"Hear it coming, Mr Mark, sir?"

"No," said Mark after a few moments, "I can hear nothing."

"Jim-a-ny!" panted Billy, "think of us a-going to sleep in his hole. Oh, Mr Mark, sir, what an awful beast! I thought he'd ha' had me. I was that scared I couldn't let go for a moment."

"Did you hurt yourself much?"

"Hurt myself! I should think I did. I must have half my bones broken. But what a roar!"

"What was it like?"

"Like, sir! Oh, I can't tell you what it was like."

"What! didn't you see it?"

"Don't you talk so loud, my lad, or we shall have him arter us."

"No, I won't, Billy; but did you see it?"

"'Cause, if we gets it arter us, it's all over."

"Yes, yes, I know that; but I want to know what sort of a beast it was. Did you see it?"

"Did you hear it roar, Mr Mark, sir?" said Billy, still fencing with the question.

"Of course I did. What was it like?"

"Well, you see, I didn't, as I may say, exactly see it, Master Mark, sir, so I wouldn't venture to say what it was like."

"But you saw something?"

"Well, I won't deceive you, Mr Mark, sir; I didn't see nothing."

"I wish you had, Billy. But what an escape! The thing must have been asleep when we went there last night, and did not wake till we came away. But we've found out its hole."

"Yes," said Billy, dolefully, as he rubbed one leg; "we've found out its hole, Mr Mark, sir, only, as you may say where is it?"

"Why, we could find our way back there, surely?"

"I don't believe nobody could find their way. I can't, sir. You're always going where you don't want, and turning up somewhere else. I feel like the needle in the bottle of hay, sir, and give it up."

Mark stood listening, but all was still.

"Shall we go back and try if we can see it?" he whispered.

"Go back! Now, my dear lad, don't. Don't think about that. Ugh! after such an escape! Come along."

"Wait a moment. Where's the sun? It should be on our right."

"Well, it's on our left, now," said Billy.

"Then we've been going farther away from the sea. Well, we can't go back."

"Go back, my dear lad! no! let's go this way, and make on till we come to somewhere. Anything, so as to get right away from that horrible beast."

In spite of his proposal to go back and try and get a glimpse of their enemy, Mark felt more disposed to hurry away; and for the next two hours they climbed and struggled on, half aware, and yet not willing to alter their course, that they were going farther from help.

Mark said so at last.

"But we don't want help so much now, sir, as miles of distance. Let's get away, right away, Mr Mark, and when we feels we're safe then we'll talk about going for camp."

Mark said no more, but trudged on, and struggled through the trees, with the ground growing higher and higher, till at last they came upon a sight which made Billy Widgeon try to throw up his cap; but he only struck it against a bough, and then made a dash forward in the direction of something which quite for the moment overmastered all his feelings of dread.

"Food!" he shouted; and Mark saw that he was making for a tall cocoa-nut tree; but before he had gone many steps the report of a gun rang out on the morning air, and this brought both to a stand-still.

"Ahoy!" they shouted as nearly as they could together, and a faintly-heard shout answered their call.

"Hurrah!" shouted Mark, and he hailed again and went in the direction of the response, closely followed by Billy, who cast longing eyes on the cocoa-nuts.

The rest was but a matter of time, and was achieved by keeping up the calls and answers. Sometimes they found they were going wrong, but this was soon rectified, and in half an hour Mark's eyes were gladdened by the sight of his father's face, as he forced his way out of a cane-brake.

"Oh, father," the lad exclaimed, "I am so sorry!"

"Oh, Mark, my boy, I am so glad!" cried the captain, catching him by the shoulders, and then pressing him tightly to his breast.

"You young dog! Here, Strong, give me leave to thrash him, and I'm yours truly for ever. Why, Mark, my dear boy, what a stew you put us in! There, if you'll go and look where I lay down to sleep for half an hour you'll find some tears on the leaves."

"I'm so sorry, Major O'Halloran."

"Bedad, and it don't matter, for we've found you again. Ugh! you ugly young ruffian! to go frightening your father into fits."

"It was an accident, sir."

"That's what your father said. He would have it that you had gone down a hole to see what made the mountain burn, and couldn't get out."

"If you wouldn't mind, Mr Mark, sir, I'd like to shake hands," said Small, "afore I punch Billy Widgeon's head."

"It wasn't his fault, Small," cried Mark, shaking hands heartily with the boatswain before turning to the captain.

"Was my mother very much frightened, father?"

"I hope not, my lad."

"Hope not! What! haven't you been back to camp?"

"Not likely, my boy. We found you did not come back so we went off from the mud-stream path to the right and searched for you till we could not see, and have fired off half our ammunition for signals."

"But we went off to the left, father," said Mark.

"And so we got farther and farther apart, so no wonder we did not find you."

"Did you shout?"

"Shout!" cried the major, who sounded very Irish that morning. "Why, can't you hear, boy, how dumb we are with yelling after you!"

"Never mind, you are found, so now for camp. They must be very anxious. But you are none the worse?"

"No, father, not a bit; only hungry."

"But did you hear that roar soon after daybreak?"

"Hear it! Yes," cried Mark; "it came out of the cave in which we slept;" and he related their experience.

The captain looked at the major without speaking.

"Oh, I'm ready," said the latter with a look of determination. "Let's have the rest of what we have to eat, and then set the matter at rest."

"We will," said Captain Strong, "and then we shall have a better right to face those in camp. I don't like for our visit to be purposeless."

Billy Widgeon's eyes glistened as they found a level place to sit down and make a fairly hearty meal, supplemented by some fruit picked by the men during the laborious search, which had only ceased on the previous night when they were quite exhausted.

As they made their sylvan breakfast the question was discussed as to the possibility of finding the cave again. Mark felt that he could not but express his willingness to try, and soon after, with guns loaded ready, they rose and set off in quest of the monster that threatened to make their life a penance.

Chapter Forty
How the Roar proved to be—a Roar

The task proved more simple than Mark had anticipated, and he went on, step by step, learning how it was that the Indians tracked their prey. Every now and then he was at fault, but on these occasions some other eye detected the trampled ferns, a broken twig, or a cane dragged out of place, and the result was that in a couple of hours the opening was reached where the rocky scarp rose up high toward the mountain, and the mouth of the cave yawned open before them.

Here there was a pause. What to do next?

"It's awkward," said the major, "supposing our friend's at home. I don't want to go first, and I'm sure I don't want you to go, Strong."

"Shall we send Billy Widgeon in first, sir?" said Small. "He's a little un, and knows his way. Here, Billy, where are you?"

An inarticulate noise above their heads made them turn, to find that Billy had rapidly climbed a tree.

"Well, of all the cowards! Here, you come down," cried Small.

He pointed his gun at the little sailor, and vowed so heartily that he would fire at his legs if he did not descend, that Billy swung himself reluctantly on to a thin elastic branch, and let himself swing lower till he could touch the ground.

"I think the best way will be to get a fire, and as soon as the brands are well alight one of the men must go underneath and throw them in, while we stand ready with our guns."

The plan was carried out; and eager now to show that he was not so great a coward as the boatswain had suggested, Billy volunteered to throw in the burning wood.

All was ready. The captain, major, Mark, and Small, with loaded pieces, and the latter with instructions to fire calmly and with good aim, and Billy with the burning wood, which was of a resinous nature, and burned fiercely.

"Now, my lad," said the captain after a glance round, and finally fixing his eyes on the mouth of the cavern, which looked black and grim, "when I say 'Ready!' get well under the cave mouth, climb up a little way, and hurl in the burning wood as far as you can."

"But suppose he comes out, sir?"

"If he does, you will be out of sight, and the beast will come right at us."

"You won't shoot me, gentlemen?"

"No, man, of course not."

"Nor you, Mr Small," pleaded Billy.

"Lookye here, Billy Widgeon," growled the boatswain, "if you don't do your dooty like a man, and chuck them there blazing sticks right into the back o' that there hole, I'm blest if I don't."

Billy Widgeon said never a word, but got his wood well ablaze, while the captain and major stood right in front of the cave, with Small and Mark on their right and left.

"Now, be careful," said the captain; and then Billy Widgeon crept cautiously under the mouth of the cave, and then began to climb, with the smoke rising from the fire, till he was so high that he could hold on with one hand and throw with the other.

"Ready!" cried the captain.

Whizz went the burning brands, so well aimed that they went right into the cave, and an unexpected result was produced. One of these went right in, and the other fell upon the bed of palm leaves which Mark had occupied. This began to blaze, the other caught, and in a few minutes the interior was full of flame and smoke, the former roaring, and the latter eddying out and up the face of the rock.

"Not at home," said the major, as they all stood breathlessly waiting for the outburst of the furious monster, which Mark painted mentally as something between a lion and a bear, but elephantine in size.

"Think not?"

"No wild beast would stand that without making a run for it."

Hardly had the major spoken when there was a deafening roar, accompanied by a rushing sound; Billy Widgeon dropped down, and rolled over, to lie among some ferns, crouched together like a ball; Small ran to the nearest tree, and peered round it, taking aim, while the other two men followed Small's example. The captain, major, and Mark stood firm, but the latter had so hard a fight with self that he would have had but little for any furious beast that had charged. For all the time nature kept on saying, "Run for your life!" while education whispered, "Face the danger like a man!"

Education won, and Mark stared as he saw his father uncock his piece and throw it over his shoulder, while the major began to laugh.

"Well, Mark, there's your wild beast," he said merrily, and he pointed up at the mountain.

"I—I don't understand."

"Steam, boy, gas, or something of that kind. Didn't you see the smoke and flame come out with a puff?"

"Yes, I saw that; but don't you think it is a wild beast?"

"No beast could roar like that, my lad," said the captain. "Don't you see that this is one of the ways into the mountain, and every now and then it blows off so much steam, or heated air. It must come from a tremendous distance through rocky passages, and the sudden blast makes this roar."

At that moment Billy Widgeon raised his head and looked up at them curiously.

"Aren't you going to shoot, gen'lemen?"

"Not this time," said the captain. "There, jump up, and let's get back. We shall be able to live here in peace while we get our boat built. I'm glad we've solved the problem."

"Well, I'm glad," said the major, "but it's a shabby end to the affair. I should have liked to get the monster's head and skin for my room."

"It's a rum un," said Billy Widgeon, climbing up and staring in at the hole. "That's what it is, Mr Mark, sir; it's a rum un."

"What's that?" cried Mark suddenly. "Here! hi! Bruff! Bruff! Bruff!"

He whistled loudly, and there was a joyous barking heard in the distance, and soon after the dog came bounding up from the more open ground at the end of the rocky scarp.

"That must be our way, then," said the captain. "Here, Mark, do you think he could lead us home?"

"I don't know, father—let's try," cried Mark, and after the dog had given every one a friendly recognition, and received his due meed of pats and caresses, he was sent on in front, going forward quite as a matter of course; but before they reached the end of the rock-encumbered opening, there was a roar of laughter from the men, as Billy Widgeon struck an attitude, smiling all over his face, resting his hands upon his short knees, and shaking his head.

"A pritty creetur! Look at that now, Mr Mark, sir!"

All joined in the roar of laughter as the "pritty creetur," to wit, Jack, came ambling along, and hopping from rock to rock, having followed the dog; and as soon as he reached Billy, leaping upon his back, and clinging tightly to his neck, chattering loudly the while.

"Forward!" cried the captain; and, following the dog, the little party went on, to find that they had a couple of hours' hard struggle through the tangled jungle, at the end of which time a familiar whistling sound was heard, one of the mud-pools reached, and from that point, over known ground, their course was comparatively easy to the camp, where the anxiety of the ladies ceased, though they owned that, knowing how difficult travelling was, they were not very much alarmed.

Judging, however, from the face of his mother, Mark rather doubted this, while, though as a soldier's wife she would not show it, Mrs O'Halloran had evidently passed a bitter night, and when Mark went up to Mary O'Halloran to shake hands, that young lady told him it was horribly cruel, that he ought to be ashamed of himself, and that she would never shake hands with him again.

Chapter Forty One
How there was no Peace on the beautiful Isle

Three months glided happily away, during which time there was no renewal of the earthquake, the lightning ceased to play about the cone of the beautiful mountain, and the roar from the lion's mouth, as Mark and Mary christened it, grew gradually less and less audible till it finally died away.

It was a busy time, and seemed to pass like magic in that wonderful clime of sunshine, verdure, and brightly winged bird and insect. There were occasional showers, such as fall with terrible violence in the tropics, but the mornings after were so delicious that the rains were welcomed.

There was shooting, and fishing, and fruit gathering, climbing for cocoa-nuts, work in abundance, which seemed almost like play; but the main task was the journey round to the ship to bring stores, of which there were ample, and to commence building a small sailing vessel, which would easily convey them all to Singapore.

But this part of the daily work was the only one which was distasteful to the men.

"You see, Mr Mark, sir, it's like this here," said Billy. "Me and my monkey's as happy here as the day's long, and so's my mates; for now, as Mr Morgan and Stowaway Jimpny and t'other chap's strong as horses again, what we says is this here, what call is there for us to want to get back to London town?"

"Ah, what, indeed, Billy!" said Mark.

"To smoke and fog and blacks, and black-beadles, and blackguards, and colds and coughs, and no sun never shining. Let's stop here, I says."

"To be sure, Billy!"

"I'm glad you think so, sir. Jack does, and so does old Bruff; and as for David Jimpny, 'Let me live and die here,' he says, 'for I didn't know as there was such places in the world.' But Mr Small says 'No,' he says, 'We've got to make that there boat,' he says, and he's a nigger-driving all day long. Blow the boat! I wish as it had never been begun, and the gig was burned."

But the making of the boat progressed, and at the end of six months from their landing she was finished, fitted with stores, and lay in Crater Bay ready for the projected voyage.

This readiness was welcome and unwelcome, for though the idea of getting back to civilisation was gladdening for some reasons, and the captain longed to give an account to the owners of the *Petrel* of his misfortune, and to get a vessel and men from Singapore to try and save all possible of her lading, there was something painful in the idea of giving up their deliciously calm and peaceful life.

"I shall never get such shooting again," said the major. "But duty, duty. 'Tention!"

"It has been a pleasant life," said Morgan thoughtfully. "I don't think I could have recovered from that wound any where else so soon."

"Yes, it's pleasant," said Mr Gregory, "but one can't study oneself. I've got a wife at home, who must think me dead."

"And I have someone waiting who is to be my wife," said Morgan, "and she must think me dead."

The men could not hear these words, or several of them could have spoken similarly; and somehow, in spite of the beauty of the place and the abundance, with the sun shining constantly, England mentally seen from a distance began to appear more and more attractive, and the time was coming when the place would be wearisome.

One day, while they were still halting before making a start, the captain wishing to make a few more additions to their vessel and then take her on a trial trip before venturing with all on board so far, the signal for starting came in a very unexpected manner.

David Jimpny, who had grown to be one of the strongest and healthiest looking of the men there, proved still to be one of the most useless as far as helping in matters nautical. But in anything relating to trips inland he was invaluable. There was so much of the vagabond spirit in him that he liked nothing better than being sent off inland to collect palm tops or shoots for cooking like vegetables. These he would get and bring into camp, and, what was more, try experiments on other promising things. He would come back hot and scratched, but generally with an eager look in his eyes as he had to announce the discovery of some fruit-tree of which there was an abundance, but almost invariably hidden in the depths of the jungle.

Off these trees he would bring in a splendid supply of fruit of strange look, but often delicious quality, and nothing delighted Mark more than a journey to one or other of these sylvan stores.

Upon this special day Mark had to take charge of the camp, for a rule was made never to leave the ladies entirely alone. The island, as far as they could make out, was uninhabited, the strange noises heard occasionally being invariably attributed to the volcano; but there was the possibility of danger coming from without, and it was considered advisable that someone should always stay to be on the watch.

Mark had been wandering listlessly about for some time wishing he could fish, or shoot, or collect insects—though he might easily have done the latter, for an abundance of beautiful butterflies came from the forest to settle wherever the skins of fruit were thrown. But he wanted to be free, and it was tiresome, he thought, to be so useless and do nothing better than to idle about the camp and watch the cooking—a tantalising matter when you could not eat.

It was getting toward afternoon when Bruff, who was with him, lying on the sand with his eyes shut and shaking his ears to keep out the flies, suddenly sprang up and uttered a low growl.

"What is it, old boy?" cried Mark.

Another growl, and a short snapping bark, which was answered by a chattering noise, told that the monkey was coming, and he appeared soon after followed by the stowaway.

Something was evidently wrong, for the man was waving his hand wildly, and beckoning to him to come.

Mark ran to meet him, to see, as he drew nearer, that Jimpny's face and hands were bleeding and his shirt hanging in strips from his shoulders, while his staring eyes and open mouth showed him to be suffering from excess of terror.

"Why, David, what's the matter?" cried Mark as he ran up to him, the stowaway sinking down upon the sand unable to answer, and his breath coming and going with a hoarse roaring noise that was terrible.

"Can't you speak?" cried Mark. "What is the matter?"

The stowaway uttered a few words hoarsely, but nothing was comprehensible but "quick!" and "run." He pointed seaward, though in the direction opposite to that which the party had taken that morning on their way round to Crater Bay, a journey which familiarity had made appear now comparatively short.

Mark looked in the direction in which he pointed, and could see the blue water of the lagoon, with to his left the long line of creamy surf and to his right the fringe of cocoa-nut trees just beyond the sand.

Jimpny pointed again, and on once more looking searchingly Mark made out a flock of the beautiful long-tailed parroquets which haunted the island groves, but nothing more.

"Have you seen anything—has anyone touched you? Oh, I say, David, do speak! What is the matter?"

The stowaway made signs again and pointed, striving once more to rise, but sinking back from utter exhaustion.

"Point, then, if you can't speak," cried Mark. "If the ladies see you like this they will be frightened to death."

The man pointed again toward where a long low point ran out into the lagoon, fringed with luxuriant growth, but nothing more was visible.

"There, I thought as much!" cried Mark as he saw his mother coming up, followed by Mrs O'Halloran, and Mary with them, the latter running on in advance.

"What's the matter, Mark?" she cried as she came up—and then, "Oh, Mr Jimpny, how you have got scratched!"

"There's nothing the matter, I think," said Mark laughing, for the stowaway's face was comical with terror. "I think David has seen another noise, or found a steam snake, like I did."

"No, no," panted the stowaway. "Boats! pirates! coming!"

"What! where?" cried Mark excitedly, as he looked in the direction pointed out; and as he did so Bruff set up the hair about his neck, and uttered a fierce and prolonged bark.

For there, just coming into sight beyond the point, was one of the long, low, peculiar-looking boats which the Malays call praus, boats which have been famous for ages as the means by which the fierce tribesmen made their way from place to place, killing and destroying ship and town wherever plunder was to be had.

"Down, Bruff! quiet, sir!" cried Mark. "Quick, every one! In amongst the trees!"

Mrs Strong and the major's wife had hardly comprehended what was wrong before they were hurried in among the trees, Jimpny following, limping and still breathing hoarsely.

"I was up—up the side of the mountain," he panted, "when I—I saw them coming. There's three boats."

"Three!" cried Mark, peering out from among the trees; and as he looked it was to see one prau clear of the point, and another coming slowly out into view.

"Do you think they saw us?" said Mary in a frightened whisper.

"No; not they," said Mark. "They could not, unless they had telescopes and were watching; but ah! they'll see that. Come along, quick!"

He led the way, taking upon himself the guidance of the little party in his charge, and together they hurried on through the trees to where the huts were erected among the trunks of the cocoa grove.

"They could not see these places unless they landed," said Mark, looking sharply about him, "and there is no boat nor anything that would take their attention, only that."

"Only what, my boy?" said Mrs Strong eagerly.

"That," said Mark—"the fire. Jimpny, hold Bruff and don't let him come after me. Lie down, sir. Let no one else show outside the trees."

"What are you going to do, Mark?" cried Mary.

"Put out the fire," he said quickly. "It will betray where we are."

He did not hesitate, but going down upon hands and knees crept down the sand toward where, in the midst of the coral rocks, the fire was burning in what they had called the kitchen.

Fortunately it was clear and glowing, the smoke having given way to clear flame, but there was still a faint thread rising, and unless the Malays took it for steam from one of the hot springs they might land there to see, and if they did, though nothing was visible from a distance, the trampled sand and litter of the camp, as well as the tracks left by the keel of the boat, would show plainly enough that there were inhabitants in the isle.

Those within shelter watched intently as Mark got over the intervening space and disappeared behind the rocks, where, using his hands as shovels, he rapidly threw on quantities of sand till the fire was completely smothered out, and the birds roasting for their dinners destroyed.

This task accomplished, Mark crept back, satisfied that if seen by the Malays he would be taken for some animal, and as soon as he reached the shelter of the trees, rising upright and gazing between the trunks out to sea.

The stowaway was right; there were three praus now visible, and Bruff was growling angrily, as if he recognised enemies in every long low boat.

"What are you going to do?" said Mrs Strong. "Keep in hiding and let them pass?"

"No," said Mark. "I must get round to Crater Bay and warn them there."

"Yes," said Mrs Strong, "that is right."

"How unfortunate that every one should have gone and left us this morning!" said the major's wife.

Mark hesitated for a moment as if making his plans.

"I can't leave you all and go," he said at last. "You must come with me. It will be a long hot walk; but you must come."

"I'm afraid the pirates have been round there, Mr Mark," said the stowaway hoarsely.

"No, no," cried Mrs Strong.

"Which, begging your pardon, ma'am, they seemed to come from that way as if they'd been round there."

"You've no business to say that," cried Mark excitedly. "It is only guesswork, mother—Mrs O'Halloran. Come along, and keep well in among the trees. Bruff, to heel, sir! You, Jimpny, lead the monkey."

"Yes, Mr Mark, sir; but hadn't I better get a gun?"

"Yes, of course," cried Mark eagerly, and together they ran into the officers' quarters, to come forth again, armed to the teeth, to where the ladies were waiting on the sand.

"Where is Mrs O'Halloran?" cried Mark, for she had disappeared.

"She ran into the hut," said his mother.

As the captain's wife spoke Mrs O'Halloran reappeared, laden with a bag and a couple of bottles.

"You must help me carry all this," she said. "We may be obliged to take to the jungle, and this will keep us from starving."

Mark saw the wisdom of the proceeding, and the load was shared as they went on through the loose sand, the lad's heart sinking at the thought of Jimpny's words, and he wondered what would be the result if it should prove to be true that the pirates had landed and attacked the party in Crater Bay.

He kept his thoughts to himself as he pressed on through the loose sand, giving an occasional glance through the trees to see what course the Malays were pursuing, and seeing clearly that their vessels were coming steadily along, evidently with a pleasant wind, while among the trees there was not a breath of air, and as they tramped on through the loose sand he could see that his companions were beginning to suffer.

There was nothing to be done, however, but to keep on and try to get round to Crater Bay. The stowaway began once about it being impossible that day, and Mark felt that it would be a tremendous task; but even if they did not, there was the prospect of their getting on past several of the points and well out of the sight of the Malays, so that if they only got far enough to encounter the boat returning to camp they could warn the occupants and then take to the woods.

Mark explained all this to comfort his companions as they tramped wearily on, and he had been successful in his efforts, giving comfort to his own mind as well, when it was swept away at a stroke, for Jimpny crept close up to him and laid his hand upon his arm.

"I say, Mr Mark, sir," he said in a whisper, "do you expect to meet them all as they comes back?"

"Yes."

"But Billy Widgeon told me this morning when they started as they was coming back t'other way."

Chapter Forty Two
How they struggled to Crater Bay

The stowaway's news fell like a thunderbolt, and Mark felt a curious chilling sensation come over him, as he tried to keep it from his mother and Mrs O'Halloran. But the latter was quick at seeing there was something wrong, and she stopped and asked what it was, and wrung it unwillingly from the lad.

"That's bad," she said quietly. "What do you propose doing?"

Mark stared at her in surprise to see how calmly she took the announcement of what might mean destruction, certainly a temporary separation from their friends.

"One of us must go back," said Mark, "and try to meet them that way. I will go."

"No," said Mrs O'Halloran; "the force is so small it cannot be divided. They may not be coming back that way; and if they do, we must hope and pray that they will be keeping a sharp look-out."

"But they may come right back to the camp and find the Malays in possession."

"If they are in possession," said Mrs O'Halloran, "it would be impossible for you to get along by them to give our party warning."

"Do you think I could get round at the back through the jungle?" said Mark, addressing Jimpny.

"No," said the latter. "I've tried it lots of times. You couldn't get a quarter of a mile through the woods in a day. There's no getting in till you come to the little river."

"And that is past the camp," said Mark sadly. "Ah!"

The ladies clung together, for at that moment they realised a sensation as if some monstrous roller were running slowly along beneath the sands and the roots of the trees. The ground heaved like a wave of the sea, the cocoa-nut trees rocked and bent their heads together just as the ears of corn do when a breeze sweeps over a field, and then all was still once more, save that a low muttering sound as of thunder ran along over their heads, leaving them all giddy, and feeling as if the qualms of sea-sickness were coming on.

They were to a certain extent familiar with such phenomena, and the minute it was over the dread it caused was swallowed up by that which was pursuing them, for a glance through the tree-trunks showed that the Malays were still coming on.

Mark hesitated for a moment or two, and then feeling that Mrs O'Halloran's prompt soldierly advice was for the best, he accepted it, and led the way.

Their march grew more toilsome as they kept on, the sand appearing to become looser and drifted up in waves among the cocoa-nut palms, while the presence of these was alone sufficient to keep them at work threading their way in and out till the peculiar growth came to an end; and they were stayed by the thick jungle.

Their only way of progression now was by the sands, where the walking would be easy in the extreme by comparison, for wherever the tide rose and retired the sand was either level and firm or slightly rippled by the sinking wave.

But to go along here was to place themselves in full view of the praus, and Mark felt that they would certainly be seen.

There was nothing to be done then but risk it or wait till night, while to hide till then might mean destruction to the party round at Crater Bay.

"Yes," said the major's wife, "we must risk it;" and Mark stepped boldly out, gazing anxiously back at the three praus.

They had no means of telling whether they were seen or no; all they could make out was that the praus were coming steadily along, sometimes sailing, at others, when the wind dropped, being urged forward with long oars.

The heat grew more painful as the fugitives kept steadily on, unable to select the best road on account of the necessity for keeping close in to the trees: but at last, worn out and exhausted, after leaving the sheltering rocks where Mark had rested during the storm, far behind, they came in sight of one of the points or angles of the island, where the land trended round to the north-west, and once past this the way would be out of sight of the praus.

With this to inspire them they all exerted themselves to the utmost, and reaching the rocks that ran out seaward they struggled by them, for the dog to lie down panting, and the monkey to display his distress by hurrying to a tree and eagerly picking some of its harsh sour fruit.

It was an example to be followed, though the party did not dare to rest, but gladly partook of some of the food Mrs O'Halloran's foresight had provided, and this and the firm sand they were now enabled to choose for their road, joined to the knowledge that they were screened from the enemies' view, gave strength to their efforts as they ate and walked on.

At the end of a mile they reached water—clear, cold, bubbling water—refreshed by which they pressed on quite cheerfully till they had passed another of the points of land and found double shelter from their enemies' gaze.

By this time a strange alteration had taken place in the weather. The sun, which had been shining brilliantly, now gradually changed in appearance till it grew copper-coloured; then its light came through a thick haze, which gradually darkened, and they were screened from the burning rays by a black cloud, which grew more and more dense, and seemed to float only a few hundred yards above their heads.

"A bad storm coming," said Mark, "but it may not break till we get to the bay."

Judging from appearances, however, it was likely to pour out its waters upon them at any moment; while, to add to their excitement, from over the jungle there were deep thunderous noises as if the storm were raging right in the interior.

The journey seemed interminable, but in spite of the thunder and coming darkness they toiled on, keeping a sharp look-out over the lagoon lest those they sought should have been in the gloom.

By degrees, though, the obscurity grew less, and seemed to be slowly floating in the direction of the praus. Once there was the wave-like motion of the earth again, making them catch at each other to keep themselves from falling, and then the sun appeared, growing momentarily more bright as it passed out from behind the dense black cloud which was gathered about the mountain, rolling along its flanks as they came to an opening in the jungle, and then appearing to circle slowly round and round.

The hours crept by as they toiled on exerting themselves to the utmost, for one of the dreads that oppressed them, now that they were out of sight of the praus, was that they would not get to Crater Bay before their friends started to go round the other way, though, saving on their own account, there was a certain hopefulness about their position, since the last they had seen of the praus showed them that they were coming their way, and therefore they might not see the gig and its occupants after all.

There was no fear of the captain passing the fugitives now, for as evening approached the lagoon was perfectly clear and the sky of a dazzling blue, but there seemed to be no end to the weary tramp over the hot sands, and at last Mary looked so exhausted that they were obliged to take shelter under a tree at the edge of the jungle.

"How much farther is it, Mark?" said Mrs Strong.

"About six miles," he replied. "Look here, Jimpny, we must wait here now. You go on and warn my father, and they'll come back with the boat."

"I shall be better soon," said Mary; but there was such a look of exhaustion in her eyes that Mark knew she would not be able to proceed, and he signed to the man to go on.

The stowaway looked at him blankly, and he repeated his orders.

"Yes, I see," said the man, staring stupidly, as if he were in a dream; and starting off, he went on a dozen yards, and then reeled, threw up his arms, and fell heavily.

Mark was at his side in an instant to find that the poor fellow was perfectly insensible, his face blackened with the heat, and his breath coming heavily and in gasps.

"Over exertion," said Mrs O'Halloran as she hurried up. "The poor fellow was done up before we started."

"Will—will he die?" faltered Mark.

"No, no," said the major's wife, "I've often seen men fall out of the ranks exhausted like this by hot marches in India."

"But what is to be done?"

"Help me," said Mrs O'Halloran. "That's it, get your arm well under his, close to the shoulder. Now together."

Mark followed her instructions, and together they dragged the poor fellow over the sand, in spite of their exhaustion, right up under the trees, and then let him sink down in the shade.

"Now, Mark, you go on and get help," said Mrs O'Halloran.

"And the Malays?" he said.

"They will not see us hidden here among the trees. They will pass us if they come. Make use of your landmarks, so as to find us, and Heaven give you good fortune, my dear boy!"

"No, no," cried Mark. "I cannot leave you all like this."

"It is to help us," said his mother. "Mrs O'Halloran is right. You see we can get no farther."

Mark saw that his duty lay in fetching help, and after a sharp look-out in the direction from which danger was expected, and another at the salient points of the shore, so as to guide him to the point where the ladies and the sick man were hidden, he forgot his own fatigue in the excitement, and leaving arms, ammunition, and everything weighty, he started off alone.

It seemed as if he would never reach that ridge of black rocks which formed the eastern curve of Crater Bay, and even when it came in sight there was a nightmare-like feeling upon him that he was no nearer.

Then, too, his despairing thoughts would keep getting the mastery, and asking him what he was going to do when he reached the bay and found that there was nothing visible but the charred hull of the ship, and that his friends were gone.

At last, though, he could feel that he was nearing the black ridge; the sand began to change from its yellow and white coral look, and became dashed with black. Then it grew blacker, and at last the grains were all jetty in colour, and there was the great black pile of basaltic rock, with its columns and steps rising higher and higher, and the question ever present:

Were his father and the rest all behind there busy over the little smack they had built lying now in the safe anchorage of the bay?

He could bear it no longer, and drawing a long breath, he started to run, though it was only a feeble trot, till the rocks rose up steeply, and he was compelled to climb slowly and painfully with many a slip, but always urged by the sensation that if he did not use every effort he would be too late.

He had climbed that ridge dozens of times. He knew the easiest way; but now its difficulties were terrible, and in his heated exhausted condition he could hardly drag himself up over the last steep block. The nightmare-like sensation grew more painful, and he felt that he must give way, but that dread of being too late spurred him on till he was on the very summit, where he sank down with a groan of despair, for there, hundreds of yards from where he lay, right on the other side of the western arm of the black crater, was the boat with a white sail spread, skimming along so rapidly that in another few moments it was hidden from his longing eyes.

He raised himself upon his hands, his eyes staring wildly, his lips parting to give utterance to a hoarse cry, but so feeble, that it was like the querulous wail of a sea-gull, and as his cry was lost in the immensity around, the boat glided onward and was gone, leaving him with his spirit as dark as the waters at his feet where they filled up the crater that lay between him and the help he had come to seek.

Chapter Forty Three
How Hope revived like a Sunshine Gleam

"What shall I do? what shall I do?" groaned Mark, as he stared at the black ridge which ran down to the sea on the other side of the bay.

Then he looked down at the carefully-moored little vessel that lay near the old charred and well-stripped hull, and lastly with a sigh at the cloud-draped mountain high up to his left, beyond the head of the little black-beached bay.

Wearied out, parched with thirst, and with his throat seeming to be half-closed up, he tried to give another hail, and then, knowing that his feeble voice would not travel across the bay, he descended slowly from step to step, from rift to rift. Sometimes he missed his footing, and slipped or rolled down; sometimes he lay for a few moments too much exhausted to attempt to rise, till the thought of those who were awaiting his return came back to him reproachfully, and struggling to his feet once more he continued his descent, gazing anxiously now before him in search of the praus, but the calm horizon, illumined by the setting sun, showed no sign of enemy, and he continued his descent and reached the sands.

"I must get back to them before it's dark," he said to himself; and this thought spurred him on to new efforts.

"What a coward I am," he said aloud, "to be damped at such a trouble as this! They will take care that the Malays don't touch them, and we can get round to them in the morning."

Some insane idea of getting on board the little vessel that lay in Crater Bay came into his mind for the moment, but with only David Jimpny for helpmate he felt that such an attempt would be useless, and gave it up.

He walked as fast as he could, but the pace was slow, and his feet felt heavy in the deep sand, which was once more growing white, and as he trudged on, wondering how soon he could get back to where his friends were waiting, and whether he would be able to make out the spot in the dark, the thought occurred to him that he would be able to guide his steps easily enough by means of the luminous rim of the sea, and make his presence known by uttering a low call from time to time, when his heart gave a tremendous bound, and he stopped as if petrified.

"Mark! Ahoy!"

There it was again, and turning, trembling in every limb, it was to see Morgan on the top ridge of the black rocks between him and the bay, distinctly seen against the sky-line, while directly after another figure appeared—that of his father.

He took off and waved his cap, for he could not speak, and then, suffocating with emotion, overcome by exhaustion, he reeled and sank half insensible upon the sands, but only to struggle up once more, and try to retrace his steps toward the black rocks.

He was in a kind of dream for the next few minutes—a dream in which sea, rocks, sand, and trees were slowly gliding round him. Then he was aroused by a pair of strong arms catching him by the shoulders, and a familiar voice crying:

"Why, Mark, my lad, what's all this?"

He could not speak, only stare, and as he looked in the second-mate's face another voice rang in his ears:

"He is overcome with walking in the heat. Hail the lads, Morgan, and we'll have him carried to the boat. Why, Mark, my boy, how foolish of you to come—and on such a day! Here, drink."

The captain held a flask of cool fresh water to his lips, and as he drank with avidity the reviving liquid seemed to give clearness to his brain, and the troubles there came back to mind.

"Let me help you toward the bay, my boy," said the captain. "There, your trouble's over now. We'll give you a ride back."

"No, no! Stop here. Listen, father," panted the lad; and then in agitated tones he told of their position, and of those who were waiting for succour among the trees.

The captain started and looked at his son half doubtingly, and as if he believed that this was some hallucination; but just then he raised his eye, and there, faintly seen in the evening haze, was the long low form of a prau just coming out from the projecting land.

"Hah!" he ejaculated, "we have left it too long. Morgan, go and take command, and send here the major, Small, and two men. We must help them to the bay. No; they are wearied out now, and there is a sick man. Let the major and you get the boat round as quickly as you can. Follow us along the shore—but you are too tired, Mark."

"No, father; I'm better now. I felt so miserable at seeing you go—that's what made me seem ill."

"Luckily Small caught sight of you as we were rounding the corner there, and we put back directly. But you are not strong enough to go. Turn back with Morgan and come on in the boat."

"I must go with you, father," said Mark desperately, "or you cannot find the place where they are hidden."

"True," said the captain. "There, lean on me. Quick as you can, Morgan."

The mate hurried back to where two or three more figures were visible now on the fast darkening ridge, while the black and purple clouds about the mountain peak seemed to grow richer in colour and to tremble as if there was a hidden light within.

But father and son gave but a glance at this, so anxious were they to reach the spot where the ladies were awaiting help.

The forms of two praus were now visible for a few moments and then they faded out, and the darkness came down as if poured out of the heavens upon the sands—a thick transparent darkness through which the stars seemed to peer and light up the sea on their left.

They had gone quite half-way before the regular rhythmical beat of oars, and the splash and rattle of water beneath the gig's bows were heard. Soon after the boat was abreast of them, the waves showing up luminously as the oars dipped.

"Now, Mark, go aboard," said the captain. "You can halt when you think we are abreast of the place, and give me a hail."

"No; you want me here," replied Mark. "I'm not so tired now."

The captain was so anxious that he did not press him; and after a word or two to the occupants of the boat, from which the major had sprung to join them, they went on.

The walk seemed as if it would never end; but at last Mark pointed to a couple of particularly tall palm-trees.

"It was about a hundred yards beyond these, father," said Mark; and as his voice was heard a sound or two came off the water, when a low angry bark was heard, and then a dull rushing sound of feet.

"Bruff! Bruff!—where are they, Bruff?"

The dog uttered a joyous whine as he seemed to leap upon them from out of the transparent darkness, and five minutes later the ladies' anxieties were temporarily at an end.

"There is nothing to mind," the captain said as he helped them down to the boat. "The Malays will no doubt pass us by. I expect that by morning they will be many miles away. Still it is a bit of a scare."

Neither Mark nor Mrs Strong made any reply; but the stowaway, who was pretty well recovered from his exhaustion, whispered to Billy Widgeon that he hoped it might be so; and then silence fell upon the boat as they rowed slowly back toward the crater, where it was the captain's intention to get the ladies on board the little vessel. But this proved to be no easy task in the darkness, and at last it was decided to make the sands their couch for the night, and then see what the day would bring forth.

Mark was so utterly wearied out, that after partaking of his share of the refreshments left, he lay for a few minutes gazing at the reflections of the flickering light from the mountain cast upon the sea, and then dropped fast asleep, but only to be awakened by a sound like thunder reverberating overhead. It died away and all was silence and darkness again; and then all seemed to be nothingness as he fell into a dreamless sleep, hardly even conscious of whether a watch was kept.

Mark was awakened by a hand being laid upon his mouth and a voice whispering in his ear the one word, "Hush!"

It was dark still and the stars were shining, while every now and then there was a flash as of lightning followed by an intense blackness in which the pained eyes seemed to repeat the form of the flash.

"What is the matter?" whispered Mark.

"Don't speak, but get up and follow. The others have gone on. Above all things keep that dog from barking."

"The Malays have come!" thought Mark on the instant, and as he rose he looked round; but there was nothing to be seen, and he was wondering where the danger lay as he followed his father over the black sand towards where the boat was always dragged over the low point beyond the rocks, where he had just time to catch Bruff's head and press his hands round his pointed muzzle; for from about a couple of hundred yards away there came the low muttering of voices, followed by a yawn, and by Bruff with a low muttering growl.

Chapter Forty Four
How Matters got to the Worst

It took Mark some minutes to get rid of the confused, half-stupefied sensation that remains after a very deep sleep when the sleeper is suddenly awakened; but as his head cleared he found himself threading his way among the rocks behind his father and crossing the lower part of the arm which separated Crater Bay from the lagoon. Once the highest part was cleared and they were descending toward the black waters the captain caught his son's arm.

"You may speak now in a whisper," he said. "The rocks are between us and the Malays."

"Have they come then, father?"

"Yes; Morgan heard them come stealing along the lagoon in the darkest part of the night, and they are lying less than a quarter of a mile away."

"Do they know we are here?"

"I hope not, my boy; but when daylight comes they are sure to come over into the bay, and—"

He stopped short, for a vivid light flashed out, and for a moment Mark could see the black bay, the wreck, the little cutter-like vessel lying by her, and a group of people down below them at the water's edge.

"Lightning?" said Mark.

"No; it is from the mountain."

As he spoke there was a dull vibration and a low rumbling sound, as if some heavy body had passed heavily beneath their feet.

"What are we going to do?" asked Mark eagerly.

"Escape if we can," said the captain. "We cannot take the ladies inland. The jungle about here is impassable."

"Then you are going to steal away?"

"Yes, my lad, if we can get aboard. We ought to have got the boat across last night, Mark, instead of leaving it till now."

"Are they going to get it across the point now?"

"Yes," replied the captain; and at that moment they were joined by Gregory, Morgan, Small, and the major.

"Ready?" said the captain.

"Yes," replied Gregory. "Come along, my lads."

Three men came up and stood waiting for orders, and the major joined the captain.

"You understand," said the captain, "there must not be a sound. If there is, we are lost."

"I understand," said Gregory gruffly.

"Have you got everything out?"

"Everything. She's light enough now."

"Come, major, then," said the captain. "You must be guard, Mark. Go with the major, and help to take care of the ladies. No, stop. Perhaps you can help me pick out the best route for the boat, but mind only one person has to speak, and that is I. Get rid of that dog."

Mark hesitated for a moment, and then laying hold of Bruff's ears, the dog followed him eagerly to where the ladies stood together shivering with anxiety in the darkness.

"Keep Bruff with you, mother," he whispered; and then, after a stern order to the dog to lie down, he hurried back over the black sand, and found the little party threading its way among the rocks and over the ridge to reach the spot where the gig lay drawn out of the water of the lagoon.

They all halted for a few moments as Mark joined them, and just then a vivid glare of light shone out, showing them plainly the hulls of three long low boats lying out in the lagoon, whose waters quivered, and looked for the moment as if of molten steel.

Then all was pitchy darkness, and through it came the sound of voices.

"They have seen us," said Morgan excitedly.

"No," said Captain Strong, "we were in the shadow. Now, then, three on each side. I'll lead. Slowly does it. Mark, my boy, go to the stern; you may keep it from touching the rock. Every pound of help will be worth something now."

Mark eagerly went as directed, and the next minute, with three strong men on either side, the gig was lifted up, and borne softly forward almost without a sound, the party listening intently to the loud jabbering going on aboard the praus.

The task was fairly easy at first, for it was for some distance over the nearly level sand that the gig was carried, but soon rocks began to crop up in their path, and in spite of the care exercised the keel of the boat suddenly grated loudly upon a projecting piece of stone; an effort was made to slew her round slightly to avoid it, and this caused Mr Gregory to catch his foot on another block of stone, and nearly fall.

The captain uttered a loud "Hist!" and all stood fast, with beating hearts, for a loud voice spoke in Malay, and the jabbering on board the boats ceased, as if all were listening to try and make out what the unusual noise was ashore.

Just at this moment there was another vivid flash from the mountain, and the praus could be plainly seen, while now the little party by the boat realised how thoroughly they were in the shadow of the black rocks.

"If there is a blaze like that when we are on the top of the ridge," whispered the captain, "we shall be seen."

Not another word was spoken, and for quite a quarter of an hour there was an ominous silence as they all waited for the talking to begin again on board the vessels.

But there was not a sound, and it was evident that the crews were listening, when suddenly Morgan laid his hand upon the captain's arm, and pointed in the direction of the lagoon about half-way between them and the praus.

Every one grasped the meaning, and a chill of dread ran through Mark, in whose mind's eye wavy krisses were flashed and razor-edged spears darted, for there, plainly enough, as shown by the flashing and undulating of the luminous creatures of the water, which they knew so well, two men were swimming ashore, to see what was the cause of the noise.

"It means fighting," said the captain.

"Why not leave the boat, father, and get aboard the cutter at once?"

"How?" said the captain coldly. "Wade through water five hundred feet deep?"

Mark felt as if he could have bitten off his tongue, and then his heart seemed to stand still, for there suddenly arose a shriek from the lagoon—a shriek that was terrible in its agonising intensity; there was the sound of splashing, and the water became ablaze with a beautiful lambent phosphorescent light, while there was an outburst of yelling and shouting on board the praus, accompanied by tremendous splashing, as if the water was being beaten with the oars.

"Quick! All together!" said the captain hoarsely. "Now, forward!"

The men were so paralysed with horror as they each for himself pictured the fearful scene of two Malay sailors swimming ashore, and being attacked by the sharks, that for a few moments no one stirred. Then with the hubbub and splashing increasing, and the water being, as it were, churned up into liquid fire, the sides of the boat were seized, and it was borne over and among the rocks to the very ridge, and then, with a feeling of relief that it is impossible to describe, down lower and lower, with the sounds dying out; while Mark, who was last, felt that if the horror had been continued much longer, it would have been greater than he could have borne, and he must have stopped his ears and run.

"I don't think they can hear us now," said the captain. "Hah!"

There was a tremendous flash, accompanied by a deafening roar from the mountain, and the whole of the bay, with its overhanging blackened rocks, were for a few moments illumined by the quivering light, so that everything was as distinct as if it were noon.

Then all was pitchy blackness again, and the thunderous roar died slowly away, as the thunder mutters into silence in a storm.

"That was a narrow escape from being seen," said the captain, cheerily. "Two minutes sooner, and we should have been in full view. All together, the ground is getting clearer now."

"If we might only give one good hooray, Mr Mark, sir," said a familiar voice, "it would seem to do us good;" and the lad realised that it was Billy Widgeon who had been working all along close to his elbow.

Mark felt with the man, for in his own breast there was an intense desire to cry out or shout, or give some vent to the pent-up excitement. But there was plenty to take up their attention, for the captain, now that the ridge was between them and their enemies, hastened their steps, in spite of the blackness, so that, after a few slips, and a narrow escape of breaking in the bows of the boat through a sudden fall upon an awkwardly-placed rock, she was safely run down to the edge of the crater, and the oars, mast, and sail replaced.

The next proceeding was to get the ladies on board the little cutter, which lay some twenty fathoms from the sands, and in darkness and silence they were handed into the gig, and were half-way to the little vessel, when, without warning, a vivid light flashed out from the mountain, and the oars ceased to dip.

But this was no lightning-like flash, but a continuous glow, which lit up jungle, rock, and the black waters of the bay, while every eye was turned in the direction of the ridge in expectation of seeing the praus plainly standing out in the glare.

Fortunately, the ridge was sufficiently high to conceal the occupants of the boat, and in place of the light proving their betrayal, it aided the embarkation, the boat going on at the end of the next few minutes, and all climbing safely on board. Then the gig was secured by a rope astern, and there was nothing now to be done but wait till daylight, and then trust to being able to escape by running southward along the lagoon before the praus could get round the northern arm of the little bay.

"Look at that," cried Billy Widgeon suddenly, as the light flashed out as quickly as it had appeared, the glowing scene changing instantaneously to the most intense darkness, while now a peculiar odour began to pervade the air, a suffocating hot puff coming from the land, charged with sulphurous vapours.

Everything was ready for a start, but there was one thing needful, light, for the risk was too great to attempt to get round the southern point in the darkness. It was dangerous with the gig, but they had learned the positions of the rocks by heart, and could come round now with ease. With a boat drawing so much water, however, as the cutter, it was different, and the course necessary so intricate, that, tremendously in their favour as a start would now be, the captain dared not run the risk.

"It's death to stay," said Gregory, as they stood in a group waiting for day.

"It's death to go," said the captain gloomily. "One touch on a sharp rock, and we shall fill, or be fast."

"Well, Strong," said the major, "I don't like to interfere in your navigating matters, but in this case, as a soldier, I say if we are to die, let's die like Englishmen trying our best."

"We are trying our best, Major O'Halloran," said the captain coldly.

"Yes, my dear fellow; but for Heaven's sake let's start."

"What should you do, Mark?" said the captain, laying his hand on his son's shoulder.

Mark was silent for a moment or two, and then said huskily:

"I don't like going against your opinion, father, but I should start now."

"In the darkness?"

"Yes. It seems to be our only chance."

The captain made no verbal reply, but took out his knife, and stepping to where the rope passed out from the stern, mooring them to a crag of rock that seemed to rise from unfathomable depths, he divided the strands, and the rope fell with a splash in the water. Then, going to the bows, where the other rope ran to one of the timbers of the *Petrel*, he cut that, and there was another splash.

Then giving his orders, a couple of the men passed sweeps over the side with the greatest of care, and the head of the cutter began to turn, and she was moving slowly toward the mouth of the bay when once more the intense darkness was cut as by a knife, and the little vessel seemed to be destined to have a light as clear almost as day for making her way round into the lagoon, where she could catch the wind and escape.

Chapter Forty Five
How Nature seemed a Foe

The distance was not great, and as Captain Strong gazed before him, knowing, as he did, the perils to be encountered, he hesitated, and was disposed to stay. But the first step had been taken, and, giving his orders in a whisper, he went to the helm, while Gregory and Morgan prepared to hoist the sail, and the men bent steadily to their long oars.

The light increased, and there seemed to be nothing to prevent the little vessel from passing safely round the southern point, for the water looked smoothness itself; but none knew better than the captain the rocks that were in his path, while away to his right over the northern arm of the bay lay three praus teeming with bloodthirsty savage men who would be ready to rush in pursuit the moment they were seen.

It was a painful dilemma for the captain, who had, however, been longing to make his present venture, but shrank therefrom as too risky till opinions other than his own urged his attempt. But there was his position. If he kept to the darkness, wreck seemed certain; if to the light, he must be seen.

And now the light was most vivid, but still he kept on, the little cutter gliding slowly on over water that seemed to be golden, while Mark held his breath as he watched the northern point till by slow degrees first one and then another and then the third of the praus came full into view with their rough rigging and cordage distinctly seen in the glowing light.

Other eyes than Mark's watched the praus, and it was a matter of surprise to all that the cutter went on and on to the second passage through the rocks off the south point, round which, if they were fortunate, she would be able to pass—the first passage being only safe for the gig—while the praus, if they started in pursuit, would have to sail out quite half a mile before they could round their point, and as great a distance back, which would give the fugitives a good start along the lagoon.

No one spoke as the cutter glided slowly on, the sweeps dipping regularly and almost without a sound. For fully five minutes this continued, but to all on board, as they crouched down for the shelter of the low bulwark, it seemed more like five hours. There they were in full sight of the praus, but not a sound reached them, and in a whisper the captain said to Mark, who was at his side:

"They must be all asleep. Oh for a little wind!"

But there was not a breath of air nor even a hot blast from the mountain, and in spite of the agonising desire to escape they could only creep slowly over the golden water in a terribly sluggish motion, though two men toiled hard now at each sweep.

Suddenly, and with a spontaneity which showed how suddenly they had been perceived, a tremendous yell arose from the occupants of the praus.

"Now, Strong," cried the major, as a thrill of horror ran through the occupants of the little cutter, "war is declared."

"Be ready with that sail," said the captain; but his words were not needed, for his two officers were standing with the ropes in their hands, and at a word the mainsail would have been hoisted.

The yelling continued and the thrill increased, for from moment to moment the escaping party expected to hear the sharp ring of the brass guns of the Malays and to have their tin bullets whizzing overhead.

It was a curious position, for the yelling of the Malays was as that of so many wild beasts unable to reach their prey, the long low spit of rocky sand lying between them and the bay, and near as they were now, they could only attack by rowing or sailing right out to where the current ran swiftly and tumultuously about the point, rounding it, and then making straight for the bay.

"They are going to fire," said the captain quietly as he stood at the tiller; "everyone but the men at the sweeps lie down or keep below."

"Which order does not apply to me, Mark," said the major coolly. "I'm an officer. Lie down, sir! Do you want to be shot?"

"Certainly not, sir," replied Mark, who, in spite of his dread and excitement, could not help feeling amused at the major's satisfied air, and the way in which he seemed to play with his gun.

Bang! A sharp ringing report from a lelah as the praus began to move, and the charge of tin bullets came screaming overhead as the report echoed from the rocks that surrounded the bay.

"Bad shot at close quarters," said the major; "and they are moving off. Can't you whistle for the wind and let's show them our heels!"

"The wind will come as soon as we get out beyond the shelter of the point," said the captain. "Pull, my lads."

The men tugged at the long sweeps, but the cutter was so substantial and heavily-built that she moved very slowly through the water, beside which, it was extremely nervous work to keep on pulling while at intervals of a few minutes there came a shot from one or other of the receding praus. Still they progressed, and if once they could get over a few hundred yards there was a prospect of their clearing the rocks off the south point and getting well along the lagoon.

Shot after shot, some whistling by the mast, some striking the water, and others going before or behind, but not one touched the cutter, and as the three praus rowed out and grew more distant the practice became more wild.

"Ah!" said the major, "being shot at is very exciting; but I don't think I like it after all. How are you setting on, Mark?"

"I'm all right, sir."

"Well, ladies, we shall not have breakfast till two hours after sunrise," said the major, as he bent over the entrance to the rough cabin where they were sheltered, "so I should advise a short nap."

A sad smile was the only reply to the major's cheery remark, and he nodded and then sighed as he turned to the captain.

"Cease firing, eh?" he said as there was a cessation. "They must be near the end of the point. Now, Strong."

"In another ten minutes they will be round it, and—what's that, Gregory? Did we touch on a rock?"

"No," said the mate. "It's deep water here."

There was another shock as if the cutter had gone upon a rock; but she went slowly on.

"Earthquake," said the major. "The mountain seems uneasy."

Almost as he spoke there was another shock communicated through the water, which suddenly boiled up and eddied about them, making the cutter rock to and fro and then roll heavily.

"Pull, my lads!" said the captain; and the men tugged furiously as their commander looked anxiously out toward the north point, round which the praus were faintly seen in the glow from the mountain, and then gazing round him at the black rocks of the little bay and its uneasy waters.

"No fear of their pulling," thought Mark, "if they feel as I do in this black hole!"

In fact the men were thoroughly sharing the horror of the lad, and sparing no efforts to get out of the water-filled ancient crater into the smooth lagoon.

For the black water that always lay so smooth and calm was now rapidly changing its character, and there was no doubt that a tremendous amount of volcanic action was going on beneath their feet. The surface heaved and eddied; waves rose in unexpected places; huge bubbles rushed to the top from the terrible depths below and burst with a loud puff. And all the time the cutter swayed and seemed to be receiving a succession of blows below water-mark, always suggesting rocks about her keel.

But still with the indomitable energy of Englishmen the long oars were used, and the little vessel moved forward till they were so near the point that in another ten minutes the captain felt that they would have the wind and be able to sail steadily along between the rocks where he had mapped out and sounded his course.

It was an awful piece of navigation, but he had no fear if they could only catch the wind.

Still there was that hundred yards to clear; and now, favoured by the currents that played round the north point, it was evident that at least one of the praus had cleared it and was coming down upon them straight for the bay. There was the loud rhythmical yelling of the men shouting together, and the slow beat of the sweeps as they rowed vigorously; while the two long oars of the cutter, only intended to help her out of harbour in a calm, hardly gave her headway.

The glare from the mountain increased so that every object was plainly seen; and Mark could not help gazing at the wondrous aspect of the mountain, the top of which emitted a light of dazzling brilliancy, while a thin streak of red seemed to be stealing in a zigzag fashion from one side.

Then there was a tremendous burst as if of thunder; a rushing, hissing noise, as if a shower of stones had been hurled into the sky; and then all was darkness for a few moments.

"Blown out!" said the major laconically as if he were speaking of a candle; but the words had hardly left his lips before with a frightful explosion the mountain blazed forth again, with the glare far more intense, and showing the prau they had dimly-seen before coming on fast.

"The eruption does not seem to scare them," said the captain.

"Well, it does me," said the major. "It's a kind of warfare I don't understand." Then in a whisper which Mark heard: "Shall we get round the point, or must we fight for it?"

"Unless we catch the wind," replied the captain, "they will be down upon us first; and then—"

"We must fight for it," said the major coolly. "Well, fortunately we are well prepared. Look here, Strong, you keep on with your navigation as long as you like, while I have the fighting tools ready. The moment retreat is useless, say the word and we'll show fight."

Captain Strong gave his hand a grip, and then stood gazing straight before him perfectly unmoved.

The position was one that would have blanched the cheek of the bravest man. For there in front was the prau coming rapidly on, full of bloodthirsty pirates, who had ceased firing as they saw their prey within their grasp; while behind was the volcano, whose eruption was minute by minute growing more terrible, and around them the luridly lit-up waters of the old crater in which they were, boiling up, hissing, and emitting great puffs of steam, where, as the cutter rocked and plunged, it seemed to be only a matter of moments before she would be engulfed—sucked down, as it were, into the awful depths below!

Gregory and Morgan stood ready to hoist the sail, but there was not a breath of air where the cutter lay. It was one awful calm, with the glow from the volcano seeming to scorch their cheeks, though high overhead there was a rushing sound as of a mighty wind setting toward the burning mountain, which now began to hurl volleys of red-hot stones through the dense cloud which hung above the top, and reflected the light far and wide upon the sea.

"Hopeless!" said the captain suddenly. "Arm, major, and let's fight it out like men! Stop!" he cried; "the boat—the shore!"

"Bah!" ejaculated the major angrily. "Are we fishes, captain, that you want to send us out of the frying-pan into the fire?"

He pointed to the shore as he spoke, and the captain grasped the horror of the scene. It would, he knew, be madness to land, for there were signs of fire now in place after place among the rocks; while before they could have crowded into the gig and tried to row to sea the Malays would have been upon them—shut in as they were in the bay, which was literally a trap.

Just then, too, the water began to heave and toss, huge geyser-like fountains shot up and fell back with a fearful hissing sound, and, as the light gig was tossed on high, the madness of attempting to crowd into her was manifest to all.

The arms were passed round, and every man's eyes glistened in the ruddy glare as with a furious yelling the prau came on, the water looking like golden foam on either side, and the glint of spears flashing out from her crowded bamboo deck.

"Don't fire till you can make sure of your man!" said the major sternly; and a low murmur arose from the little group behind the cutter's bulwarks, which told in its fierce intensity that if stubborn determination could save the helpless women crouching below they had nought to fear.

The prau was not fifty yards away now, and seemed to be glowing as if red-hot in the glare shed by the golden cloud above the mountain. The sight of their prey so close at hand set the Malays yelling more fiercely than ever, and at a shout the sweeps ceased beating the water, and every man seized his arms, when there was a peculiar hissing sound heard; the cutter heeled over, then righted, and, to the wonder and horror of all on board, she began to turn round slowly as upon an axis, as if preparatory to being sucked down into a frightful whirlpool. In one short minute she had turned twice, and then, as if caught in some mighty current, began to glide rapidly round the bay at first toward the burning mountain, and then outward to sea.

For the moment the horror and strangeness of their position made all on board forget their enemies, among whom a terrible silence had fallen, but as the captain glanced in the direction of the praus he saw that the distance between them had increased, and that, caught in the same wondrous current, the enemy's vessel was being carried rapidly out to sea.

The force of the current increased till they seemed to be rolling along the surface of some cataract, and in a few minutes, as everyone clung to bulwark or stay, the distance they had striven so hard to compass was passed again and again, for the sea was shrinking from the isle and they were being carried out on the retiring wave.

They were now opposite the rocks that they had striven to pass, while the prau, lighter in construction, was a hundred yards away. The hissing, rushing sound of the retiring water was terrible, and in blank despair in face of this awful convulsion of nature all gazed wildly before them, when all at once there was a sharp shock, the cutter heeled over a little, and this time there could be no mistake, she had struck upon the rocks of the north point or arm of Crater Bay, and the sea was retiring from them and leaving them fast.

Chapter Forty Six
How Safety was won

The captain recovered himself, but he was helpless in such an emergency, and no words passed. There was nothing to be done but wait.

"Are we in great danger, father?" whispered Mark, taking his hand.

"Yes, my boy, in great danger," replied the captain in a solemn whisper. "I can do no more."

"What is the great danger?" said the major quietly. "That," said the captain, pointing seaward. "The water retires like this, only to come back in force. There: it is coming back."

They needed no telling, for the awful roar of the earthquake wave announced its coming, and with it as they remained fixed and helpless upon the rock they could see the prau, after being sucked out, as it were, for nearly a quarter of a mile, being carried back at terrific speed. There was a fascination in the scene of the others' peril that took away from their own, though, had they paused to think, it must have been to realise that the cutter would be lifted up by the coming wave and dashed upon the black perpendicular rocks at the head of the bay.

But for the moment no one thought, for every faculty appeared to be concentrated upon the fate of that long low prau crowded with men, and now glistening in the volcanic light, as it seemed to be riding rapidly among so much golden foam. The roar of the wave was terrific as the waters surged, and for the moment it seemed to them that the prau would be hurled right upon the rocks where the cutter lay careened over, but with her bows to the coming wave that glistened luridly like a long wall of ruddy water crowned with foam.

"Hold fast by the bulwark, boy," whispered the captain as he passed his arm round Mark. "Cling all tightly for your lives."

Suddenly a low hoarse cry was uttered by all on board, for as the prau was borne toward them it must have caught upon the summit of some rock hidden by the wave, and that check was sufficient. As that cry arose the prau turned right over and disappeared completely from view, while at that moment there was another of the tremendous explosions from the mountain, succeeded by instantaneous darkness. The cutter was lifted up as the wave struck her, and then after a bound and a quiver she seemed to plunge down—down as if into hideous depths; while half suffocated by the broken water, drenched, shivering, and feeling as if his arms had been wrenched from their sockets, Mark Strong still clung to the bulwark, thinking of those below, and asking himself in his blank horror whether this was the end.

He was conscious of a crash as of the vast wave striking the curved wall of rocks at the head of the bay; of the noise of many waters; of the cutter plunging and whirling round and then seeming to ride easily in the midst of subsiding waves; and then of hearing a low hoarse sigh close to his ear.

"Father," he cried, "are you there?"

"Yes, my boy," came out of the darkness close at hand. "Thank God we are so far safe!"

Then, as if rousing himself to a sense of his position, he called aloud:

"Major O'Halloran!"

"Yes."

"Gregory!"

"Yes."

"Morgan!"

All answered to their names out of the pitchy blackness. The men, too, were safe, and upon crawling cautiously to the hatchway which closed in the cabin, Mrs Strong's voice replied, saying that all was well, only that they were in an agony of dread.

It was a dread likely to continue for they were perfectly helpless, and all that the captain could make out was that the cutter had been uninjured by striking upon the rock, and that she was now floating upon an even keel, but in what direction it was impossible to say.

People often talk of "dark as pitch," "black as ink," and the like; but if ever there was an exemplification of this darkness it was now, for a cloud of the most intense blackness shut them in, and the occupants of the cutter could only communicate by word of mouth or touch.

"Surely this will lift soon!" said the major at last; and his voice sounded shut in and strange. "If that light would only shine out again!"

"To show us to our enemies, major," said Gregory in a low voice.

"I don't think any light would show us to them, Gregory," said the captain solemnly.

"No," said the major, "we have no more to fear from them."

A dead silence succeeded for a few minutes as all realised how completely the slight prau had been engulfed while in such a chaos of waters no swimmer could possibly have been saved with a level sandy shore before him, far less among the black rocks of that walled-in bay.

Hours passed away, hours of dread, for from time to time the hull of the cutter seemed to be struck from below, vibrating through every timber as earthquake shock after shock was felt. Fearful booming sounds were heard from the island telling them where it lay, and again and again there were thunderous crashes, as if the whole of the vast globe were being crumpled up, and the end of all things was at hand.

But in spite of all this, as from being quiescent the sea heaved, and the cutter was tossed here and there like a cork in some torrent, not a gleam of light came to her occupants, neither the glow of the eruption nor the rays from the sun. It must have been day for many hours, but all around was a breathless calm, and the dense black cloud grew thicker, and they could feel that the deck of the cutter was thick with a soft powdery ash.

The anxiety of all was so great, the care induced by their position so terrible, that no attempt was made to obtain food or water till quite twenty-four hours must have passed, and then, utterly worn out with the awful explosions, as of a cannonade going on, one by one all fell asleep, save the captain and Mark, who sat there in the darkness talking in whispers, and listening to the distant sounds.

"We are drifting slowly in some current, Mark," said the captain at last.

"How do you know, father?"

"The reports are more distant. If we could but have light once more."

It was a weary time before the captain's desire was granted, and the first harbingers of that coming light were forty-eight hours after the first embarkation in the cutter. They came in the shape of a pleasant cool breeze which it was delicious to breathe, and by slow degrees there was first a faint light, then a glow as if the glare of the burning mountains were shining through, and then a joyful shout of thankfulness arose from officers and crew, for the light was from the rising sun, and they could see blue dancing water, and then, with one bound, they were in broad day, with a great black curtain riding slowly away from them across the sea.

Away south of the sun there was a huge black mountain of vapour quite twenty miles away, and evidently covering the island, while the cutter was drifting slowly farther and farther away in the light current in which she had been caught.

As for those on board, after they had each in his own way, and then collectively at the captain's wish, returned thanks for their preservation, the first thing to be done was to remove the blackening ashes from their faces, while Jimpny swept pretty well half a ton of the curious volcanic dust from the cutter's decks.

"What now?" said the major. "Back to the island to see what damage has been done?"

"No," said the captain; "we have a stout little well-tried vessel beneath our feet, and the next land I hope to tread is that at Singapore."

There was no further difficulty in this project, for the wind was favourable, and the dark cloud that overhung the island soon sank below the horizon, though during the following night a distant sound, as of cannonading, told that the explosion was still going on.

Captain Strong's navigation during the next few days was a good deal by guesswork, and consisted in making all the headway he could westward. At the end of the fifth day, however, a large steamer was made out going east, and in answer to their signals she hove to; and upon going on board the captain for the first time learned their position. This proved to be about midway between Sumatra and Borneo, and the island lay to the south-east as far as could be judged, though the officers of the great steamer could not give it a name.

Nothing could exceed the kindness of the captain and officers, and at their special request the major, and his wife and daughter, continued their voyage in the steamer, which was bound for Canton, from which place, if the steamer did not touch at it, the major would have no difficulty in reaching his original destination.

It was rather a painful parting, the major gripping the hands of Captain Strong and Mark very firmly as he said "good-bye;" while Mrs O'Halloran and Mary displayed for the first time the womanly weakness that their education as soldier's wife and daughter taught them to hide.

"Good-bye, my brave boy!" the major's wife cried. "Someday I hope we shall come back to England, and then we can go over our island troubles all again."

She kissed him very tenderly as she finished speaking; and then came Mark's parting from Mary—a true frank boy and girl parting, in the hope that some day they might meet again.

An hour later Mark was standing alone on the deck of the cutter, fancying he could still hear the O'Hallorans' words as he watched the hull of the steamer growing more distant, and her dense smoke trailing behind for miles.

"Life is made up of meetings and partings, Mark, my lad," said the captain. "That has been a pleasant friendship, and some day we shall meet again."

Mark sighed, and went to sit by his mother and watch the sunlit sea, for the cutter seemed to have grown dull and empty, and the gambols of Bruff, and the pranks of Jack fell as flat as the cheery words of Billy Widgeon and the stowaway.

Chapter Forty Seven
How they sought Mother Carey's Chicken, and she was gone

Singapore was reached in due time, and after communicating with the owners of his vessel, Captain Strong chartered a large schooner, engaged some additional hands, and sailed once more, this time for the purpose of reaching the *Petrel*—"Mother Carey's Chicken," as the men would call her—and getting out the portion of her cargo that remained uninjured.

There was some talk of Mrs Strong and Mark going back to England, but Mark was so pressing to be allowed to accompany the expedition that the captain gave way, and they sailed together.

"I may find the cargo so damaged as to be worthless," the captain said; "but if it is, I shall make expeditions to the best of the deposits, and come back laden with sulphur."

It was a pleasant voyage, one not troubled by calms, so that they had but little fear of being overhauled by the Malay praus. The captain had worked out his course very carefully, calculating with minuteness exactly where the island must lie, and in due time a look-out was kept for the conical point of the mountain, which Mark was sailor enough to know would be the first to catch the eye.

"No, my lad," said the mate, in answer to a question from Mark, "and I don't suppose we shall see it to-night. You come and keep the morning watch with me, and look out for the point when the sun touches it first. That's the time to see an island."

Mark kept the watch with the mate, but they did not see the island, and the captain changed their course.

"It must be somewhere here," he said; and he had a consultation with the two mates, who both agreed that they were near the spot, though no point was visible.

The change of course produced no good effect, and after sailing here and there for several days the captain decided to make for the island where they had landed to have the day's shooting.

This was reached with the greatest of exactness, and then, after examining the spot where the little engagement had taken place, a fresh start was made, and the vessel's course laid in a direction which they all felt must go over the same ground as the boat had drifted, and the ship had been carried after the fire, and she had gone ashore.

"Breakers ahead!"

"Ah! I thought we should manage it this time," said the captain eagerly, as, followed by Mark, he hurried on deck the next morning in the grey light, and there before them was a long curving reef of coral bending round to north-west and south-west, and inclosing smooth water apparently in a ring.

"Why, Gregory!" exclaimed the captain.

"Yes, sir; that's it!" said the mate.

"Nonsense!" cried Mark, laughing at what seemed to him a joke. "Where's the mountain?"

Where indeed!

With very little difficulty the opening in the reef was found, and a boat lowered and rowed into the lagoon, where the lead was lowered several times but no bottom found.

Returning to the ship sail was made again, and they went round to the north-west so as to prove that this was the reef by finding the opening which led into Crater Bay.

Sure enough the opening was found, and the boat once more lowered to investigate and find that the coral-reef still spread out like a barrier, but the coral insects were dead, and as they investigated farther it was to find that there was not a single shell-fish of any kind living in the shoal water, nor any trace of life, but on the highest part of the bleached white coral there were a few blocks of blackish-grey vesicular or cindery-looking stone.

"Gone?" said Mark, as he sat in the boat, "you think it's gone?" and he looked down with a feeling of awe.

"Yes," said the captain; "gone as rapidly as no doubt it once rose from the sea."

"But where was Crater Bay?"

"Here where you are seated," said the captain. "Shall we try the depth?"

"No," said Mark with a slight shiver; "it seems too awful. But do you really feel sure, father, that our wonderfully beautiful island has sunk down here?"

"I have no doubt of it, my boy," replied the captain. "The eruption was awful, and the island was literally blown up, and its fragments sank beneath the waves. What do you say, Gregory?"

"That's it," said the mate.

"And all those lovely palms and ferns, Mark," said Morgan, laying his hand upon Mark's arm.

"And I used to feel as if I should like to live there always," said Mark with a sigh. "Let's get back to the ship."

The captain gave another glance round, sweeping the surface of the lagoon inclosed by the irregular ring of coral, and then gave orders for their return to the ship.

While the men rowed back Mark tried to picture the scene as it last met his eyes; but turned from the contemplation with a shudder; and it was with a sigh of relief that he once more felt the firm planks of the deck beneath his feet.

"And you mean to tell me," said Billy Widgeon, as he stroked and patted his monkey's head one evening during the homeward voyage—"you mean to tell me, Mr Small, as that there island sank outer sight and is all gone?"

"That's it, Billy," replied the boatswain.

"But it'll come up again, won't it?" said the stowaway.

"That's more than anybody can tell, my lad," said Small. "All I know is as she's gone, and we're going back home. And a good job too."

Mark Strong heard these words; and as he sat on the deck that night, beneath the clustering stars, with Bruff's head in his lap, he too began to think it was a good job they were going home, for his perilous voyaging was drawing to a close, and that solitary sunlit island that shone like a green jewel out of the purple sea was beginning to seem to him as if it had never been.

"Thinking, Mark, my lad?" said a voice at his elbow.

"Yes, father," said the lad, starting.

"What about?"

"The Island, and Mother Carey's Chicken."